THE DEMON'S DELIGHT

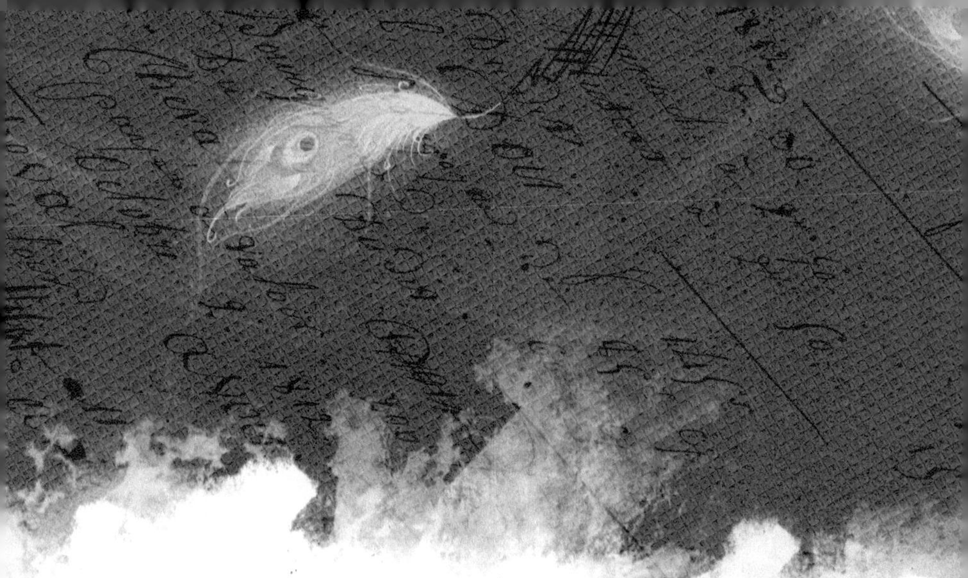

THE DEMON'S DELIGHT

THE DEMON PRINCES
BOOK THREE

L. ALEXANDER

For anyone who can't help but fall for a man like Gojo or Rengokou:
May you find your own slightly unhinged golden retriever
and live happily ever after. <3

EXILE ISLE
N
RAVENGLEN
REVALIA
CONCLAVE
EMANKOR V
STOLAS MANOR
GRANITE HILLS
CELESTARA SEA
THE GATES

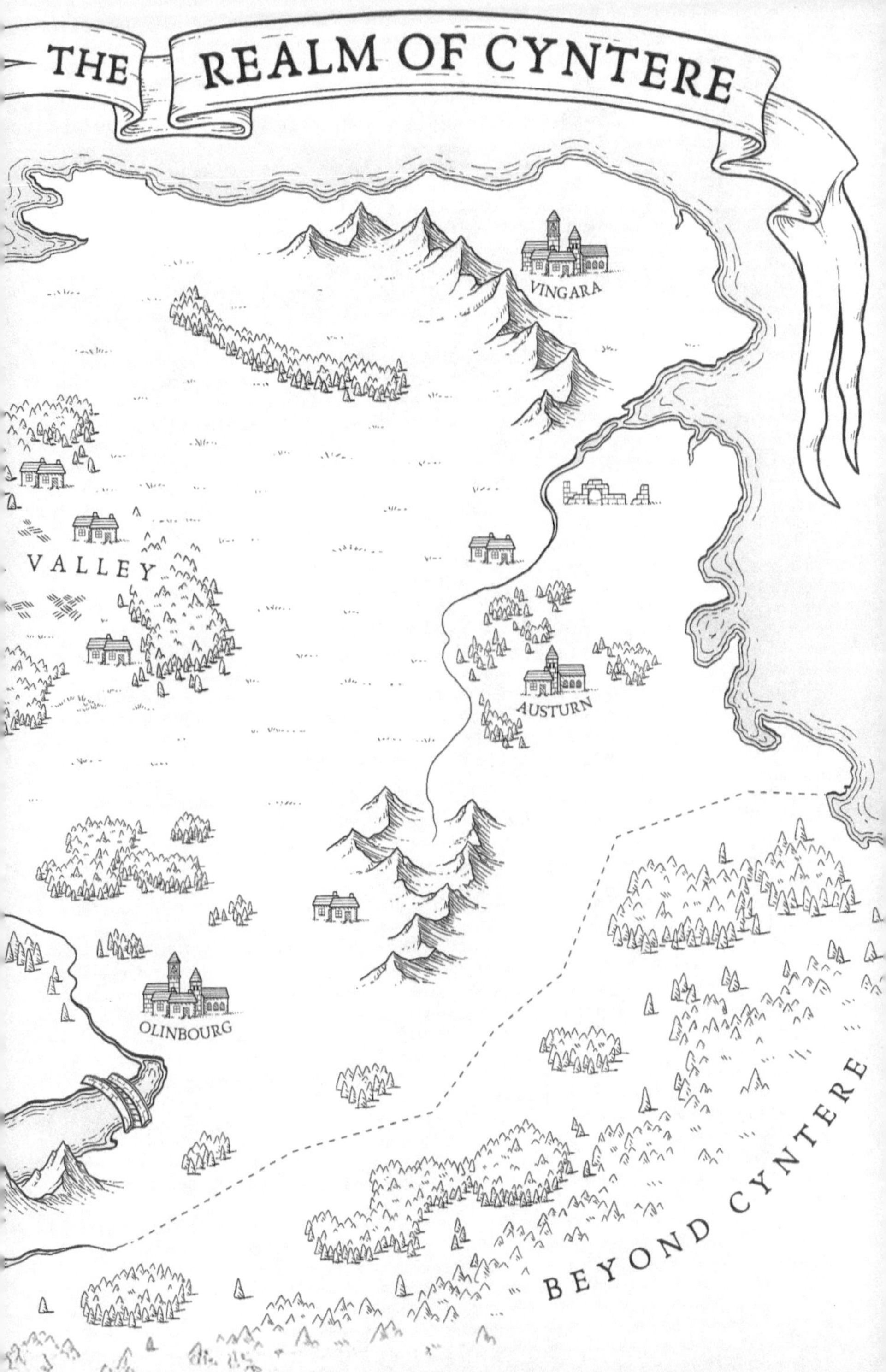

THE REALM OF CYNTERE
VINGARA
VALLEY
AUSTURN
OLINBOURG
BEYOND CYNTERE

The day

I MET YOU

I began to

forget a life

WITHOUT YOU.

— Jamie Cadima

AUTHOR'S NOTE

This is not a dark romance, but there are some potentially triggering themes that come up throughout the book. You can find a list of tropes and content warnings below as well as on my website.

Please reach out to me directly for specifics if needed, I'm more than happy to give details, page numbers—whatever helps you best decide if your wellbeing and this story are compatible.

Tropes: fated mates, a journey back home, gargoyles and demons, pseudo-medieval European setting, affection through caretaking, only one bed / bath, magical power discovery, golden retriever x black cat dynamic, found family, 'I like you just as you are'

Content: explicit violence, gore & death, kidnapping, mention of injuries, abuse and forced medical experimentation, explicit sexual content, reference to Christian-based mythos for angels / demons / gargoyles

Prologue
HAILON

I THRASHED AGAINST THE cloth being pulled over my head, the rope that bound my hands burning into my wrists.

Dr. Lang *tsked* at my behavior, his patronizing tone doing the opposite of calming me down.

"Now, Jane, be smart. It's just the veil. Would you rather Ignus came to retrieve you?" Ignus was the man who owned this house, my primary captor, and he was far less kind in his treatment of me. "There are people here to see you. We wouldn't want to disappoint them, now would we?"

I didn't give a single damn if they were disappointed. And my name wasn't fucking Jane.

I yelled as much against the leather strap he'd stuffed in my mouth, protesting every step, as Dr. Lang and another man hauled me from my room. The chains around my ankles clanked heavily as they guided me down the stairs.

Once we arrived in the den, they sat me in a stiff wooden chair with no cushion, covering my shabby nightdress, bindings, and bruised limbs with an itchy robe. The rope around my hands was undone, but fingers brutally gripped my wrists and guided them to the table in front of me. I couldn't see much of anything out of the heavy veil, nor was it easy to breathe through.

"Now, be a good girl, Jane. These people have paid for proper healing. Don't disappoint them. Or us." Dr. Lang patted my shoulder and stepped to the side. The other man stayed, one heavy palm on my shoulder.

This was his favorite job, the one he always volunteered for. He liked to hold me down. There were two men near the doors on this side of the room, two stationed on the other, and one more across the room near the fireplace. He always struck me as the most dangerous, though he was present infrequently and said the least. He was some kind of councilman and acted as though he were above any rules.

Seventeen weeks I'd been held in this terrible house, routinely forced to use my healing gift. Sometimes, I was brought so many people to heal I was depleted to the point I couldn't move.

This motley band of men seemed convinced they could replicate my gift, if only they could figure out the origin of it. Unfortunately for me, finding the origin required experimentation. And experimentation was easiest when I was weakened to the point of immobility, though that was never a requirement for these men to take the samples they wanted from me.

"We're ready," Dr. Lang confirmed, and one of the men near the doors tapped a coded pattern on the wood.

I could smell Ignus before he got past the threshold of the room. I stiffened in response to the sour odor. "Mr. Holleran is first," he said, leading in an older man with an audible wheeze.

"Alright then." Dr. Lang took a seat at the table to my left, the older man to the right. "If you please, Jane." He guided my hand to the man's chest, wordlessly ordering me to use my magic.

After I healed the old man, I was brought a little boy with a broken wrist. I had several questions about the cause of such a thing but was forced to keep them to myself. After that, a woman with a stomach ailment, a man with a limp. On and on they went, until I was swaying in the chair. The only thing keeping me upright was the silent man's hand, which had never once strayed from its place on my shoulder.

I fought the nausea that rose up, wishing for a drink of water to quench my raging thirst. But none would be forthcoming until they decided it was time—my needs were irrelevant here. I was just their tool. Rage simmered under my skin, my eyes seeking out any kind of weapon nearby since my hands had been left unbound. Unfortunately, the empty table was the only thing within my reach.

Dr. Lang went to speak with the man by the fire, leaning over conspiratorially instead of speaking normally. Ignus was loudly pouring drinks in celebration of another profitable day, my bodyguard was all but snoring on his feet, and the men by the door were playing cards.

I wanted to scream. A piece of me worried that if I started, I might never stop.

Dr. Lang and the councilman stood, gesturing around the room as they continued to speak in whispered tones. I drew my hands down into my lap, hoping that nobody noticed they remained unbound.

The councilman pulled a small book from his pocket and flipped to a page near the back. Dr. Lang looked at it thoughtfully, then nodded, gesturing for my bodyguard to join them. My body listed as he removed his hand from my shoulder, my balance thrown off.

Ignus came over and roughly removed the veil and robe, adding a chill to my list of bodily complaints.

"Hands," he ordered, and my heart sank as I raised my arms in front of my body.

I scolded myself for not having done something more while I'd had them free, though I knew if I had, the consequences might have been more than I could reasonably manage given my weakened state.

Ignus pushed me back down into the chair and ordered me to stay put.

I was fading in and out of consciousness when Dr. Lang stepped into my vision.

"Ready to go, Jane?" He and the silent bodyguard yanked me to my feet.

I stumbled my way across the den, dizzier now that I was vertical.

"Watch it!" the councilman grumbled as my lack of coordination forced my bodyguard to bump into him.

I raised my hands in apology, and he turned away, disgusted. My bodyguard clutched me tighter, and Dr. Lang spent a moment accepting partial blame and apologizing himself. I kept my eyes down and found myself looking at the little book, half hanging out of the councilman's pocket.

My pulse beat like a hummingbird's wings as I made the decision to take the risk. I leaned heavily to the side, hand stretched out. The leather felt smooth as I snatched it up between the tips of my first three fingers on either hand just as I was tugged out of the room. I sucked in a breath, praying I wouldn't drop it as I wiggled it between my palms.

Dr. Lang walked ahead of me on the stairs, the bodyguard at my back. I clutched the spell book as tightly as I could between my hands, braving a quick glance to be sure it wasn't visible.

Once I was seated on the bed, Dr. Lang sent the bodyguard down for my evening meal as he rearranged my bindings. When he knelt to swap out my leg irons, I stuffed the little book under the neckline of my shift. He glanced up, and I covered the motion by putting my hair behind my ears. His eyes glided over me, but didn't linger. I could barely make myself breathe until he turned away.

I gratefully accepted the skin of water he offered as he slid the tiny table close enough for me to eat from.

"You did well today, Jane," he praised, though his words were meaningless. "I feel we're getting rather close to a breakthrough."

I said nothing, heart in my throat, pulse thrumming so fast I could taste blood.

He removed the ropes from my wrists and crossed the room, squinting at me again before leaving, closing the door behind himself.

I sank into myself, tears prickling behind my eyes. I'd just stolen the councilman's spell book. If they figured out it was me, there would be no amount of apologizing that could get me out of a punishment I probably wouldn't survive.

But it was a chance to escape, and I had to take it.

CHAPTER 1
HAILON

THERE WAS A demon in the middle of my room.

He was tall and solidly built, but also quite beautiful, which surprised me.

I'd been expecting unconventional features at the very least, perhaps eyes with vertical pupils and hooves. But this demon could pass for human. Well, perhaps he could if he disguised the prehensile tail that was thumping along the floor in a manner that reminded me of a big cat.

"Hello," I demanded, pulling the shabby coverlet up higher against my chest, nudging the little spell book I'd liberated from my captor under my leg. It had taken me a handful of days and many tries, but the instructions inside it had worked. "Can you understand me?"

His head tipped to the side, russet-colored waves spilling over his shoulder as it tilted. "Yes. I can understand you just fine." A smile spread across his mouth, revealing two extra pointed teeth on either side of his canines as his gaze caressed my face thoroughly. So much for passing as human. He patted his hands over his body, as if checking that all his parts were intact. "I've never been summoned directly out of Hell like this before. It's quite an odd feeling. Why have you summoned me? *How* did you summon me?"

I tucked my knees under my body and straightened up, trying to increase my size. He still towered over me, but doing so made me feel a little less overpowered. I'd been desperate enough to try summoning a demon for help, but now I found myself completely unprepared to manage the consequences of it having worked.

At my lack of response, he made a thoughtful noise and stepped closer to where I had drawn my hasty summoning circle in carefully pilfered fireplace ashes on the floorboards. The demon smiled again as he leaned down, head nearly inverted. The tips of his hair brushed along the floor, his hands precariously linked behind his back as he examined the writing, all but folded in half.

"Ah! This rendering is quite good. You've used an old sigil of mine, but one of mine all the same." His head tilted to the side. "If I might make a little critique? This line here? And this? Those are unnecessary, but a nice artistic flourish." He erased a few things with long, tan fingers. The black lacquer on his nails shined in the light though it was chipped in several places. I focused on that detail as he scooped up the few meager drops of blood I'd used to seal the circle with his finger. "Other than that, it's all excellently drawn." His tongue flicked out, and he licked the blood from his fingertip. Then he stood up straight, that smile that somehow seemed charming despite what he'd just done focused fully on me. I flinched when he stuck out a hand. "I'm Seir." He frowned as he processed my reaction but didn't move.

To be polite, as I didn't want to offend a demon, I shook his hand. His palm was warm, calloused in the way hands that frequently wielded a sword often got. The slight contact with his skin made my pulse pound, a faint feeling of electricity passing between us.

"I told you mine, now will you tell me yours?" he suggested, eyebrows raised. "I promise I won't do anything inappropriate with your name." His voice dropped to nearly a whisper, and he winked. "I'm not fae." Then his smile returned, wider than before, like he knew a secret.

"Derne," I offered.

His head tilted to the side, and he gave a brief nod. "Pleasure to meet you, Derne."

My aunt Sal had taught me what she knew about things like demons, angels, and fae, but her knowledge was limited. I did know that giving my name, for example, should be avoided if possible for my protection—but not at the cost of a lie. This much was true for anyone asking, though, humans included. Giving my family name was skirting the actual intent of Seir's question, but still a valid answer.

He stared at me again, that odd grin on his mouth while I tried to find words with my heart thumping wildly behind my ribs. "So, Derne. Why have you summoned me?"

"I need your help."

"I see. How can I be of service?"

A door slammed downstairs. I jerked, wincing as my chains rattled against the iron bed frame.

The demon cocked his head and squatted down low to the floor. With nimble fingers, he lifted the corner of the sheet to find the place my leg irons attached to the bedposts.

He frowned, studying my unusual confinement. "Why oh why is a little thing like you chained to the bed?" A spark came to his eye, and he smiled broadly, all but leaping to his feet. "Are you dangerous?" His excitement was palpable. Suddenly his face fell. "Or is someone else the danger?"

My adrenaline surged as footsteps echoed up the stairs. "Unchain me, please? I shouldn't be here. They took me, and my aunt is—"

"You sleeping, girl?" Ignus's voice rumbled from the other side of the door.

The demon frowned and reached for the chain. "Who is that?"

"My captor. Hurry. Please, I have to leave this house. I need to get back to my aunt." Frantic, I tried to help him by pulling the slack tight, my feet dangling off the bed. The little spell book I'd lifted from the councilman's pocket fell to the floor, landing flat, open to the instructions I'd followed to draw the summoning circle.

The demon glanced at it as he tried to break the chains by sheer force of will. "I don't want to hurt you," he apologized, trying to pry the leg shackles apart by pushing his fingers between the iron and my ankle, then attempting to break one of the chain links with leverage from a dagger he pulled from a sheath at his back.

"I don't care if you do, please just get me out." I was already plenty bruised and battered, a few more injuries wouldn't make a bit of difference.

The steps approached the door. The demon stood, smoothly pocketing the spell book as he straightened up. He took up a defensive stance in front of me, a dagger gripped loosely out in front of his body. As I kicked my feet out, the stretched chain caught the leg of my small side table. I watched in horror as the table tilted, and the flask that my captor loved to leave just at the edge of my reach tipped. It hit the floor, spilling water across the circle. The demon hastily grabbed it up, but it was too late. The ash marks disappeared along with my hope of escaping.

"No. Wait!" A look of distress crossed the demon's face. "Where are we?"

"Olinbourg."

"I'll—" He reached out a hand as he vanished. One moment he was there, standing in front of me, and the next he was gone.

Disappointment crushed through me. For a moment, I'd actually believed I could get out of this house, away from this cruel situation. Then I'd acted in clumsy haste and ruined everything.

I swallowed a sob as I tossed my thin blanket to the floor and scrubbed with it. I hated to abuse my only covering by getting it wet, not to mention having to soak up my wasted ration of water, but there could be no evidence of what I'd done. I was almost certainly already facing punishment for making so much noise.

I'd barely gotten back onto the bed when my door slammed open, the knob coming to rest in a groove carved deeply into the plaster of the wall.

Ignus, a teamster at the grain milling warehouse by trade and a bully by nature, loomed large in the frame. His undershirt was stained, his body rank as usual with sweat and cheap booze.

He assessed me in bed, eyes traveling the rest of the room, a deep scowl on his face. "You talking to yourself, Jane?"

There was no safe answer with him, so I just pressed my lips together and shook my head.

He let out a crass belch that made my empty stomach turn. "You know what day it is." As if I could forget. As if I hadn't been measuring the weeks by research days for the past few months.

I carefully stood, lifting one foot at a time so he could replace one set of leg irons for another. Begrudgingly, I also allowed him to force the crude leather strap into my mouth. It was an improvement over the previous muzzles, at least. A length of rope pulled my wrists together at my back. When I'd first arrived, I'd tried using the ropes and chains as a weapon against him. I was no longer strong enough for that.

Ignus reached out a hand and clapped it painfully to my shoulder, leading me from the room. Every cell in my body cried out for a weapon. Intervention. Anything. I glanced longingly at the faint ash smear on the floor.

I whimpered, barely a breath of complaint, but my captor took this as a personal affront. He laughed and tightened his grip on my bony shoulder.

"You know whining won't help you."

Ignus led me down to the dark, wood-paneled den he did his after-hours business out of. The air on the main floor always smelled like old cigar smoke and felt heavy, like even the room couldn't process the horrors it saw.

My job was simple most of the time. Cure someone's aunt or granny of her joint pains. Take away the cough a merchant couldn't shake. Fix the ailments of anyone who could afford to pay Ignus to abuse my gift. I was an annoying but mandatory accessory to the process.

But research days ... they were different. I hated research days with twice the venom as regular ones.

The men gathered in the den were there to study me instead of watching as I healed people who had paid for the privilege of such a gift. I was more certain than ever that I wasn't even human to them, except the parts of me that were obviously female.

They'd all looked, too. Most of them for too long, too often.

The first and only time one of the men had actually touched me in a way I didn't care for, I'd bitten off the tip of his finger. I'd been soundly punished for my reaction, then fitted for the muzzle. But they were all much more careful about where they put their hands after that.

Ignus shoved me through the doorway of the den where four of the usual six other men were already waiting. "Go on."

I hesitated. In addition to the two missing men, the room was not arranged like it normally was. Instead of being in the middle of the room, the big table was pushed into the corner, all the chairs stacked on top of it. A simple wooden stool was the only seat, placed in front of the fireplace atop a patchwork of heavy cloths. I glanced at Ignus, eyebrows drawn together in question.

"Sit," he insisted, roughly shoving me again.

I complied, heart racing. Scanning the room over and over, I looked for anything I could use as a weapon.

This was not how things typically went. Usually, I was put at one of the chairs around the table or even on the table itself. I had learned to grit my teeth through their normal poking and prodding, the occasional bloodletting, and things like leeches, skin scrapings, dental examinations, nail and hair clippings. Anything they could think to study was taken from me.

My meager midday meal of broth and old bread turned in my gut. *This* looked like I was being prepared for sacrifice.

Ignus and the other men came closer, two heavy hands resting on my shoulders, pushing me into the hard seat, others holding my ankles still against the legs of the stool.

"You sure we shouldn't wait for—"

"We're fine," Ignus growled.

"But the ..." He gestured vaguely to the floor. "I'm not sure it's quite right, though. We don't have the book, so I was going off memory and—" Ignus slugged his friend in the jaw, drawing a glare and his silence.

"I said we're fine. We don't need to be babysat by those two haughty pricks. They think they get special privileges because of their money and connections, but they don't. I've done all the legwork here. The circle is fine. We can do this on our own. Now shut it."

"I do apologize, Jane," Dr. Lang said, a pensive frown on his face. Bile rose in my throat as he turned around, a tiny precision blade in his hand. I thrashed against the hands holding me, screamed into the leather strap as he moved closer. "This might hurt."

CHAPTER 2
SEIR

"—FIND YOU!" I shouted uselessly, hands reaching for a woman that was already gone. The familiar dark walls of my apartment in Hell surrounded me once more, the bright taste of her blood still on my tongue.

It had been a long time since I'd brushed up on summoning, but I did know that breaking the circle would temporarily send a demon back to wherever they'd come from, while leaving the contract open. According to the codex, unless I wanted to be punished, possibly demoted and perhaps even tossed into the wastes, the contract had to be fulfilled. I was obligated to return to where my summoner was, and to remain by her side until she banished me properly.

And that's exactly what I intended to do. She'd clearly been in trouble. The threat of repercussions for not seeing it through was the least of my concerns—she needed help. Immediately.

Besides, I had several questions, not the least of which had to do with how she'd happened to be in possession of a book that had specific instructions on how to summon demons and why she was chained to a bed.

I muttered the name of the place she'd given me, searching my memories for what it felt like and envisioning her face so I could get back there as quickly as possible. I spun, gathering up my other daggers, belt, and sword. One never knew what they'd need, even during a short time on Earth. After a moment's thought, I snatched up my money pouch and cloak. With another cursory glance around, I used my sifting ability to take me from my apartment to the set of rooms that housed Hell's system of portals and gates.

On my way, I stopped at the duty desk. Meg, a petite red shadow demon was behind it.

"Something exciting happening?" she asked, seeing my hurry.

"I was summoned!" Despite the situation, I was pleased to finally experience such a thing.

"I'll make a note for your unit leader. You're under Keplar, right? Think you'll be gone long?"

"I'm not sure. It's my first time. The situation seems straightforward, but there have already been complications."

"Understood. Broken circles are pretty common, people tend to get nervous. You're a long-timer to never have been summoned before, congratulations." She smiled as she stamped the document and slid it into a tray. The parchment dissolved into ash after a moment. I knew by the time I was done talking to Meg, the note would have already made it to Keplar's desk. Hell's magical communications systems had been rapidly evolving, and the new advances had unfortunately left my traveling powers less and less valuable. "Good luck. Be sure to check in once a shift cycle."

I had no idea if my unit leader would be upset by my absence, but there wasn't much of anything going on at the moment. I'd much rather be experiencing something new up on Earth than stuck sitting around waiting for a task. He'd never been very motivated to argue the rules with a Prince of Hell, though, so I wasn't too concerned. Besides, he mentioned often how he appreciated my presence on the team as I never caused a fuss, always followed directives, and took more of the assignments to undesirable locations than anyone else.

"Got it."

I sifted, arriving at the hall of doors nearly instantly, and chose the portal I thought would put me closest to the town the woman had mentioned. After a quick check that I had everything I needed, I walked through without hesitation, enjoying the way it made my body feel like it was turning inside out and back again before releasing me into the cool darkness of a forest. Being summoned had been more of a sensation of being disassembled altogether. I wasn't sure yet if I liked it or not.

Time passed differently between the planes of Hell and Earth, and the mere minutes I was gone had stretched longer this side of the gates. Focusing on my memory of her face, and the look of the room she'd called me into, I tried to sift directly, but my magic wasn't able to connect with only her face as a guide. Undeterred, I started to jog. I made my way through the trees toward a sleepy town that lay in a flat, meadowy area surrounded by forest.

Finding the building I'd been in proved less challenging than I worried it might. As I scanned the buildings around the main city plaza from the edge of the trees, I recognized the shape and latticing of the window in her room. Without stopping and blood primed to fight, I barged through the front door and raced up the stairs, throwing open the first door at the top of the landing.

The room was empty now, the chains the woman had been wearing on her legs open and lying on the floor in the same place she'd drawn the circle with my sigil. There was only one smudge of ashes remaining on the floorboards, though I could still smell the water that had spilled.

I turned and listened, the sound of a muffled scream making the hair on the back of my neck stand at attention. I followed the noise back down the narrow stairs to the main hall. The lower floor was far more odiferous than her room; the scent of old tobacco and burned onions stung my nose as I rushed through the first doorway I came to.

A man cursed, stepping forward with a small medical blade between his fingers. Behind him, on a low stool, sat the woman. Her brow was damp with sweat, her dark hair wild and tangled as four grown men held her down. She was slouched over to one side, and her hands were bound behind her back.

Rage filled me as I met her eye. She was in pain. There was no reason for her to be held down by so many men. Five to one was an incredibly unbalanced ratio. Even if she was dangerous, this was a disproportionate response to say the least.

I could also feel the faint pulse of magic nearby, though I couldn't see the source. Based on the awkward cloths covering the floor, I guessed there was a circle somewhere underneath.

"Is that him?" one of the men asked, glancing from me to his companions. "Did it work? Why did he come in through the door, aren't they supposed to appear from within the circle?"

The man with the tiny knife approached me, taking in my tail and horns with his eyebrows raised in curiosity. "Hello, demon. What's your name?"

I frowned at him, not wanting to give it, but knowing there wasn't much he could do with it anyway. "I'm Seir." I looked past him to the woman again, then stepped to the side so I could see what was happening behind her back. She was too close to the fire, to start. She was dripping sweat, and her skin was turning an intense shade of pink. One of her wrists had been sliced, and blood dripped down her bound hands into a small puddle on the floor.

There was no explanation for the situation that would have satisfied me. Whether she was my summoner or just a woman

I happened to stumble across, my response would have been the same.

This was *wrong*. I needed to help her.

I met her gaze again, fascinated by the colors of her eyes. Both were divided nearly in half, though neither perfectly down the center. The left was a deep brown on one side and a light jade on the other, the right bright blue and opaque yellow.

"Release her."

One of the larger men chuckled. "She's irrelevant. We summoned you, demon. You're under our charge now."

Amusement flooded in on top of the anger. My blood roiled under my skin, ready for the fight I knew was coming. "You didn't summon me."

"Of course we did! If we hadn't, you wouldn't be here." This man was seated on the floor, holding her ankle so hard against the edge of the stool it was blanched white. He seemed to realize as the words came out that perhaps that wasn't true and frowned.

I kicked at the edges of the cloths, turning them up. As I expected, there was a roughly drawn summoning gate on the floorboards, several very important lines blurred or missing altogether. Whatever they were trying to bring across wouldn't hear their request no matter how much of her blood was spilled.

Her eyes met mine again, a spark of hope in them. She was tired, I could see that much, but she shifted her weight as though she were ready to battle, if only she could get out from under her captors. I respected her grit.

The surly larger man seemed offended that I wasn't bowing to him immediately. "We drew the circle, we spoke the words, we made the sacrifice. You *will* do our bidding!"

I laughed then, long and loud. How foolish these humans were.

"You didn't draw a *good* circle. It isn't even complete, and your sigil is smudged. I can't think of a single demon who would respond to such disrespect. Never minding all that, *she's* the one bleeding for it, not you." I walked around, meeting each of their eyes. I loved the way their arrogance slowly faded the longer I held eye contact. "*She* summoned me. I accepted the offering made of *her* blood. I'm *hers* to command." I leaned forward, intentionally antagonizing him. "To be abundantly clear, I. Belong. To. *Her.*" I pointed my finger and the tip of my tail toward the woman. Something warm rattled under my ribs as I said the words.

"I didn't do all this work for nothing," the largest of them growled, advancing on me. "Damned witch is just the offering. The preparations were ours!"

I stepped into his path, dagger drawn before he fully registered what had happened. My tail wound around his throat, tight enough to make him wheeze. "Untie her hands. Now," I ordered, all levity gone from my tone.

The glass dome on the lamp nearby rattled as my command echoed through the room, and to my regret, the fire briefly surged in intensity. The man on the floor rushed to comply, but one of the others stopped him. I loved nothing more than to play this kind of game, but these men had tested my patience already.

I looked to her again, limbs trembling under the weight of her bodyguard's pressure. "You asked me for help, yes?" She nodded. "Do you wish to be left here, with these men?" She shook her head fervently, giving a muffled answer over the horrible leather strap. "Shall I kill them all for performing such terrible acts?" Her eyes widened, pupils dilating. I smiled, seeing a reflection of myself in her. "As their offense has been against you, would you like to help?" All sound vanished from the room; all attention directed to her. She nodded slowly. Excitement bubbled through me, and my smile stretched wide.

"Let's be reasonable about this," the man with the tiny blade said. "We're men of science is all, searching for answers a new way! There's no need for violence."

"I disagree. And did you not start with violence yourselves? Against her?"

He tried to protest, but I was done being patient. I dispatched the burly man I was holding, dragging my dagger across his throat then hurling him to the floor. Before anyone could so much as blink, I'd pulled my sword free of its sheath.

The science man rushed me, getting in a good swipe with his tiny blade. My forearm had a nice gash in it, the cut burning as it started to bleed. I tilted my head, making eye contact with him before I ran him through. He fell to the floor, choking on his own blood, face frozen in a mask of shock.

"In case it was unclear, I wasn't asking. Free her hands. And get that disgusting contraption out of her mouth."

"Yes sir, of course." The man on the floor scrambled to do so, then cowered in the corner with his two remaining friends. As she rubbed feeling back into her fingers, I pulled a small handkerchief from my pocket and folded it diagonally. I tied it tightly around her wrist, stanching the remaining slow flow of blood.

"What about you?" She gestured to the cut on my arm, which was freely dripping.

"It's nothing."

"Here." Her hand was warm as she covered the injury, and her eyes slipped closed for several seconds. When she opened them, the bleeding had stopped, and the wound looked well sealed.

"Thank you." I marveled at what she'd done, and it only made my rage deepen. A person with such a gift should not be treated so callously.

Her eyes landed on the dead men, then she stood and turned toward the three shifting restlessly in the corner.

"We never meant any harm, Jane," one of them offered, hands up in surrender. He was missing the tip of one of his fingers. I got the odd notion she was responsible for that somehow.

"My name is *not fucking Jane*," she hissed. "It never was. I've told you that a hundred times, you prick. And you can all go straight to Hell."

My blood rose, responding to her anger. "Yes," I agreed, bouncing a bit on my toes. "They are welcome there. I know several of my kind who will be more than happy to think up new and exciting punishments for them." I didn't move except to prepare to block their escape, should they attempt to run.

The woman snatched the dagger right out of my hand and made short, painful work of the men. Even in her weakened state, her aim was true as she plunged the blade through their necks, into their chests, and across their bellies, severing arteries, spilling organs. Impressed didn't quite convey how I felt as she very efficiently allowed the light to dim from their eyes, their efforts to fight back useless.

It was glorious to watch, as were the sounds of their screams.

Her breath came short and labored when it was done, her face spattered with gore as she handed me back my blade. I marveled at her, stunned even at myself for not having reacted when she'd taken it in the first place. Nobody touched my blades but me. Until her.

She was by far the most stunning creature I'd ever laid eyes on.

I reached out and touched her face, my fingers cupping her jaw as I brushed some of the spatter from her cheek with my thumb. She startled but relaxed when she realized what I was doing, her fascinating eyes staring directly into mine.

She nodded, watching me in a detached kind of way as I wiped my blade on the tunic of the nearest body.

"What do we do now?" she asked, arms limp at her sides.

"We leave," I said simply, unable to stop smiling at her. My heart felt strange in my chest, too big, too ... active. I tried to recall if I'd ever seen a human—man or woman—behave as she had. "Is there anything of value to you here?"

She started to shake her head but changed her mind mid motion. Without a word, she wiped her hands across her shift to clean them and went around the room collecting money and jewelry from the bodies. She also retrieved a medium-sized lockbox from a compartment hidden behind some liquor bottles on a shelf. Her hand hovered for a moment, then she snatched up one of the bottles, too, taking a deep drink before slamming it to the floor. It shattered, splashing potent grain alcohol across the room.

While she worked, I pulled one of the logs from the fireplace and tossed it directly onto the messy huddled bodies of the three men. Then another onto the cloth, and another between the other two. She stepped carefully toward the doorway as the flames caught, vanishing down the hall like a specter. I continued until the fireplace was all but empty and the room was filling with sour smoke. When I got to the entryway, she was just returning from what I guessed was the kitchen with a worn shoulder pack in her arms.

I reached for it, and after a moment's hesitation she surrendered it. Intending to sift us across town, I curled my arm around her shoulders. "Allow me." I reached for the place in my mind my power resided but found it empty.

"That's odd." I didn't want to alarm her, but I'd never not been able to find my magic, especially not twice in one day. Panic raced through me as I searched again and found the same void where it usually resided.

She pulled open the front door and walked without hesitation.

Perplexed by what was happening with my abilities, I followed her, jogging to catch up as she rounded the corner of the building. I was glad for the empty street and no onlookers considering the state of us, not to mention the flames becoming a warm glow through the main floor windows. Her feet were bare, and she staggered several times before going to her knees.

"Thank you for helping me get out of there, I'll be okay from here. I just need to ..." Her words slurred, and she blinked heavily, sitting back on her heels as her whole body trembled. She looked equally angry and confused by her weakness; the burst of energy she'd gotten from the adrenaline rush now fully depleted.

I rearranged the packs. "I'm going to pick you up, okay?" She scowled at me but reluctantly allowed me to put her arms around my neck so I could scoop her up. Her grip loosened almost immediately as she slumped over, unconscious. For extra security, I wrapped my tail around her waist and tightened my arms around her thin frame.

Then I released my wings and ... stumbled.

Horrified that my body had failed me, I tried again. And again. Each time, my bat-like wings deployed, but I simply could not rise from the ground.

I stared down at the woman in my arms and started walking, all the questions I had about her compounding as I carried us into the dense forest.

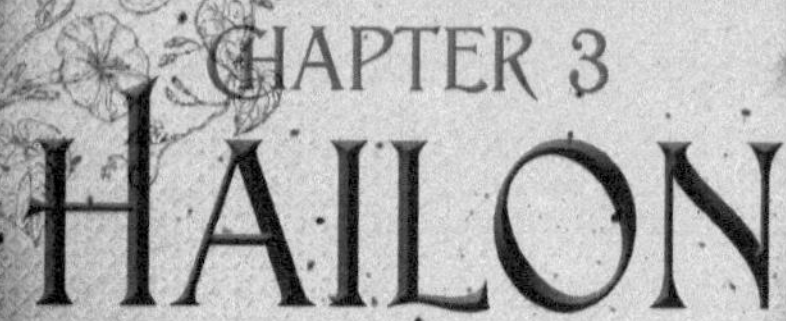

CHAPTER 3
HAILON

THE SKIN ON the back of my neck and shoulders prickled and ached, like it was pulled too tight. Everything felt dense, like I was breathing through a cloud. I was stuck somewhere between asleep and awake, the warmth around me soft and comforting. Unfortunately, now that I was even partially conscious, my body was letting me know it had complaints.

Many, many complaints.

My hand slid along the covers and paused, finding fabric far more luxurious than anything I'd been allowed to use since being taken from the forest near my home.

Forcing my heavy eyes to open, I grunted as my muscles protested me attempting to sit up. I was in some kind of cabin, a fire burning away in the hearth and a pile of assorted supplies set off to one corner of the single room.

"Oh good, you're up! Are you hungry?" the demon asked from the small table near the fire. The words were somewhat muffled, as his mouth was full. "It's nothing special, but it's tasty enough. I found salt and spices in the kitchen." He offered the half-decimated leg of fowl he'd taken a bite from in demonstration.

There was no point in pretending I wasn't starving. My stomach made a loud rumble as I stared at him, trying to make some kind of order out of my jumbled thoughts. I felt shaky and wrung out but also like I'd gotten the best sleep I'd had in weeks.

"Yes, thanks."

Seir got up from his chair, squatting to collect another plate and food from near the flames as I maneuvered myself out of the bed. I regretting having to part with the soft mattress. I stared as the demon's tail twitched on the floor behind him, an odd appendage that somehow seemed both natural and foreign at the same time.

Even the soles of my feet were sore as I made my way stiffly across the wooden planks of the floor toward the small bathroom. Between the way I'd been pinned to the stool and the unusually strenuous activity of taking down my captor's friends, I was a mess of bruises and aches. I could only imagine the picture I made: bloody, dirty, rangy at best thanks to the living conditions of that house.

After washing the grime from my face and fingers, I joined the demon at the table. He smiled encouragingly at me.

The plate was mounded with pieces of some kind of fowl that had been roasted, root vegetables, and what looked like wilted dandelion greens. It was a decadent feast compared to what I'd been fed for the last few months.

"Thank you," I muttered as I chewed the first buttery bite of meat.

Looking up, I found him watching me with amusement. His skin was a rich bronze spattered with even darker freckles, like he spent all his days out in the sun. His watchful eyes were a bright gold with a greenish ring in the center, and his head of messy russet waves added a gentle complement to the mix. The curled dark-brown horns I'd seen atop his head were gone now.

This demon looked young and seemed kind despite how sharp his smile was. The three-pointed fangs on each side of his mouth were one of the only menacing things about his appearance. However, I'd seen enough at the house in Olinbourg to know he shouldn't be underestimated.

"You're welcome, Derne. Feeling alright now? You were asleep for several hours."

I nodded as I chewed, the warm food settling pleasantly heavy in my empty stomach. "Better." I was very annoyed that I'd passed out; I should have been stronger than that. But finding myself in this place was far preferable to where I'd been kept for the last several months.

He continued to eat while watching me. "We should probably talk about what happened back there. And what happens from here," he suggested, silently offering me more food from his own plate after I finished what was on mine, and then more still from the pot over the fire as I devoured everything I could get my hands on.

I emptied the water from the heavy glass near my plate twice as I made my way through, my thirst intense. Wide eyed, he regarded me with wonder as I finally sat back in the rough chair. "More?" he asked, poised to stand.

From what I could tell, there was no more. And I was feeling the first pangs of embarrassment for having devoured everything in sight, including the remains of *his* plate.

"There's plenty more fowl nearby. Wouldn't take but a moment to catch another."

Awed, I stared. "No. No need for all that. I'm finished, thanks." I put my mouth into the bend of my elbow, trying to disguise the noise that crept out.

He smiled wide, teeth sharp, but the gesture friendly. "You flatter me. I'm glad you enjoyed it." Without another word, he cleared the table, tossing the bones and other scraps into the flames. He crossed to the small kitchen area and set to washing the plates.

A demon had just fed me dinner and was now cleaning the dishes, after helping me escape Ignus. It was all so normal and yet incredibly strange. And I still had no idea why or how he'd come back in the first place.

"Why did you come back? How did you know where to find me?"

"Once summoned, it is the demon's duty to remain by his summoner's side until their need for the demon's assistance is fulfilled." He recited the words like they came out of some kind of handbook. "The circle was broken is all, so I went back where I started, but you told me where we were. That was enough to find my way back."

"What if you hadn't?"

"Come back?" He frowned.

"Yes, would something have happened to you?"

He hesitated but gave a shallow nod. "Demotion and punishment are among the consequences."

"I see." I swallowed. Of course he didn't want to face such things simply because I happened to spill some water.

I could see the earnestness in his eyes, the way his hand twitched like it wanted to reach for mine. "You said you needed help. I could see that you did. I couldn't *not* come back."

"Thank you," I said, hoping he could hear how grateful I was over my exhaustion. "So, if what happened before wasn't a banishment, what is?"

"You need a complete circle and to speak the right words, much the same way you summoned me in the first place."

"I see." I glanced around, and he seemed to understand my intent.

"I'd rather not go back just yet, if it's all the same to you. Your initial request included something about getting back to your aunt? But if you insist, I'm sure some charcoal or ashes would work fine." He seemed ... sad.

He'd been helpful. Kind. There was probably no harm in letting him stay a bit longer.

"Where are we?"

"A way-house in the woods outside of Olinbourg. Nobody's been here in months if I had to guess. We'll be safe enough until I figure out why my wings don't work." The powerful muscles in his forearms rolled as he dried his hands on a towel.

"Who keeps a cabin like this but doesn't live in it?" I frowned, genuinely perplexed.

The demon shrugged. "There are many organizations that could have this kind of safe house set up. As long as we're not greedy, they won't mind us using it."

I nodded, rolling my shoulders to relieve the tension that had crept in.

"Why were you chained to the bed? Aside from you being dangerous, I mean. I saw that part for myself." He was smiling again, a gleam in his eye.

"Someone kidnapped me while I was in the forest gathering plants one day. I was sold to Ignus. I was his prisoner." The thought of home made my heart ache.

The demon's jaw tightened, the mirth fading instantly from his eyes. "Which man was he? The big one?" he guessed.

"Yes." I chose my words carefully, inclined to trust this man but wary because he was still both a demon and a stranger, no matter what had happened at the house. To his credit, he'd come back to help me and had done so without asking for any kind of payment or trade.

"For what purpose was he keeping you?" His rage was barely concealed, and I understood all too well what logical leap he had made. Thankfully, it was not correct.

"I have a healing ability."

"Mmm. Yes, you used it on me. Thank you for that." He crossed his arms, head tilted to the side. "And that was all? The way of men leaves me concerned their motives were not so simple." This was the colder version of him that had ordered them to release me. His eyes flashed red over the gold, and I suppressed a shiver.

"They were not kind, but they did not take advantage of me in that way."

The hardness in his expression was replaced by relief once he decided I was being truthful. "Where are your people?"

"The north mountains. Ravenglen."

"That's a long journey without sifting, portals, or wings." He glanced at the pile of supplies, rubbing thoughtfully at his chin with his thumb and forefinger. "You'll need to recover some before we attempt to make such a trip."

"I'm fine," I argued, face flushing hot in frustration. Feeling weak was my least favorite thing in the world, and I'd been stuck that way for months. "And while I genuinely appreciate what you've done for me thus far, there doesn't need to be a 'we,'" I said, still unsure if I could trust him. Besides that, my pride was wounded. I'd been humbled beyond recognition by my recent captivity. "I'm capable of making my own way home. Surely there's a horse or some other means of transportation to be found nearby."

"You need plenty more food and rest," he argued gently. "And I really wouldn't mind accompanying you. I might not be able to fly right now, but I could carry you." He grinned. "And I'd be happy to, for the record. It will take us a little bit longer that way, but at least you wouldn't have to spend your money on a horse."

I frowned, noting he was being serious. "That's completely unnecessary. I can walk just fine." I studied his face, finding a mix of emotions that confused me. "You really want to come with me? Why?"

He nodded enthusiastically. "I'm a traveling demon, it's what I do. And I've never been summoned before, so I'd really like to do a good job of it."

"I see." I wasn't sure I actually did, but there was nothing normal about this situation and I was truly exhausted.

He saw me hesitating and held up his hands. "You could always banish me when you no longer want my company, or if you decide I've served my purpose." His eyes rounded, hopeful.

I wasn't weak by any means, but I wasn't daft either. A woman traveling alone was a target for plenty of terrible things. He was clearly a good fighter and seemed kind enough.

"Is there a contract I need to sign in blood or something? Promise my firstborn, all that?"

"Not unless you want there to be." He looked confused by my suggestions. "The summoner contract doesn't require that. You called, I responded. The few drops of blood you left as an offering were more than adequate. Unless, of course, you'd rather have a paper contract?"

I shook my head. "No, that's not necessary."

"Good!" He clapped his hands together, positively beaming. "Do you have any conditions?"

"I want to leave as soon as possible."

"Of course. But we should probably get your strength up. Spending another day here before moving on will help. It's possible there will be more places like this between here and there, and other options besides, if you start to feel run-down." He considered something as I agonized in silence, trying to find an argument against his suggestions that made sense.

I knew my body needed rest and nourishment, and I didn't altogether hate the idea of being able to get that in this cozy place.

"Do you have gold or silver?" he asked. I was prepared to be defensive, but his question held no accusation. It was entirely logistical curiosity. "I saw you relieving the dead men of their valuables, but not exactly what you managed to take."

"Yes, I have some coin and some jewelry." I had a vague notion of what I'd grabbed, but I hadn't been taking inventory.

"Good. That's useful. Weapons?"

"Yes."

"Mmm."

After tossing the rag down, he came to stand in front of me, one hand outstretched. He'd walked the distance between us with it out so I wouldn't be surprised. Off guard, I took it. I couldn't help but notice that he even moved like a cat, all sinuous muscles and quiet power. The tail was just an added feature that lent to the overall feline impression. It was … disconcerting.

"The bath is probably cooling by now. Not the biggest tub, but I was able to heat plenty of water before you woke. This last pot should do it." I blinked at him as he pulled me to my feet, confused both by the abrupt subject change and the idea that this handsome demon had not only prepared my meal and cleaned up after, but had also manually heated water while I slept so I could take a bath. I simply couldn't get my brain to keep up with this information.

He reached for the massive pot held up by a rod inside the fireplace with bare hands. Without straining in the slightest, he lifted the rod out and carried it into the bathroom. I would have struggled to take even a single step without sagging under the weight. Numbly, I followed behind, a wave of emotion washing over me as the hot water poured into the tub, steam rising from the surface.

A warm bath was another luxury I'd been missing since the night I was taken.

I was disgusted to realize I was still dressed in my worn shift, complete with the bloodstains I'd accumulated before we left Ignus's house. "I don't have anything else to wear."

One side of his mouth lifted, and he stepped back, gesturing toward a small stool. "The clothing selection was limited, but I think what I laid out will fit you."

I narrowed my eyes and crossed my arms over my chest, hiding as much of myself as I could. He smiled wider, holding his hands up as if in surrender.

"There were only three choices. I picked the one I thought would work best, but you're welcome to try the others if you'd like." He gestured to the small countertop. "I found a bit of ointment in the cabinet. It should help any lingering aches and the scorch on your neck and shoulders. I can help apply it ...?"

"I can manage by myself." The earnest expression he wore made me feel bad for my short response, but I didn't really want anyone's hands on me. I'd had enough of that over the last number of weeks. "Thanks anyway."

He shrugged, the smirk on his face indicating while he might be a little bit disappointed, he didn't regret having made the offer one bit. It was mildly infuriating how it was endearing instead of obnoxious.

Seir left the room while I stood there staring, closing the door behind himself.

I looked around, trying to make sense of my current situation.

As I stripped off my destroyed shift and slid into the blissfully hot water, I mentally listed the positives of this new set of circumstances. I nearly cried as I started washing the layers of dirt, grime, and blood from my skin with the cake of fragranced soap.

Ignus was dead. I was with a demon who had helped me escape and wanted to make the journey to Ravenglen with me. There was a soft bed, hot water and soap, clean clothes, and ample food.

I was going *home*.

My body melted into the tub, allowing tears of relief to come as I scrubbed myself clean.

CHAPTER 4
SEIR

I ABSENTLY LISTENED TO the gentle splashes from the other side of the bathroom door as I reorganized our supplies.

It seemed ridiculous, but I was borderline giddy at the thought of getting to make a journey on foot. I'd never had to and had been thankful for my gift far more than not, but actually getting to see a realm as a slow traveler had always held a very specific kind of awe for me.

Never mind that I'd be at the side of such an intriguing woman. Derne was an odd name, but there was little about her that seemed ordinary. I wanted nothing more than to see her at full power facing down an enemy, because if how she performed at her weakest was any indication, she was nothing short of a goddess.

Nobody touched my blades without my permission, not even my brothers, but she'd snatched my favorite dagger from my hand and used it with such deadly precision it had made my blood sing. Part of me had hoped she'd say no when I asked if she possessed any weapons, so I had a reason to lend her one of mine. Such a thought was pure madness, but it held on with intensity.

I shifted around on my knees, trying to calm the sudden pulse between my thighs. She was hardly the first woman I'd come into contact with in recent months, but my body seemed convinced it had to prove that she might be the only one I'd *ever* really wanted.

Absently, I scrubbed the heel of my palm against the dull, hot ache in my chest that had cropped up at some point after I arrived earth-side. A possible side effect of being summoned and banished again I guessed, as portals never had that effect. Perhaps the food was to blame.

I wanted to see what she had brought but didn't want to overstep, so I left her bag alone. I'd scavenged enough from the cabin that we had food for a couple of days' hard travel if necessary, but I could also hunt and had some money besides. There was one good change of clothing for me, and hopefully we could find something better suited for her at the next town. We were both identifiable enough in appearance that we'd have to be somewhat careful, but if Rylan and Vassago could do it, surely I could as well. That meant being mindful of my tail and not showing my sense of humor quite as enthusiastically as I normally would, but I could manage.

I was moving around the table and chairs so I could make up a place for myself to sleep in front of the hearth when the bathroom door clicked open. Glancing up, I caught her wide-eyed expression as she emerged, the filthy old shift in her fingers and her wet hair soaking through the oversize linen tunic I'd found for her.

Which she was wearing as a nightgown. With nothing else.

I inhaled, the mild floral scent of the soap filling my lungs.

"That was more needed than you know, thank you." Her eyes dipped to the floor, then to the fire. "Can I ...?"

I was frozen, unsure exactly what she was asking me. Without waiting for a response, she stepped in front of the fireplace and tossed the tattered garment into the flames, one long leg close enough for me to touch.

The split in the side of the shirt revealed a swath of marked skin. There were bruises and cuts all up and down the strong thigh, and deep red and purple marks splashed across the ankle. Her knee was skinned from how she'd fallen earlier. My fingers twitched, but I kept them at my side, my teeth clenched together at the sight. Anger surged through me, the desire to kill those men all over again rising up. The kind of behavior she'd endured at their hands was completely unacceptable.

"Sorry," she apologized. "The pants fit okay, but they aren't very comfortable. I figured if we were just going to sleep …" Foolishly, I could only stare back, grappling between rage and attraction, which made her turn a fascinating shade of pink from her chest up. "The bathwater is cold and filthy, but I didn't want to drain it after you went to all that effort."

I cleared my throat and made myself look away from her. "I'll take care of it. Is there anything in your bag I should include in my count?"

She stared at me, eyes blank as she considered, then gave a short nod. She sank to her knees and dipped her hands into the pack she'd filled at the terrible house. No fewer than three small knives got piled off to the side, including one with a flat end designed to be held between her fingers when she made a fist. The last was a particularly wicked-looking dagger with a blade made from obsidian and finely crafted grip. Pride flared that she'd thought to grab such things in her hurry, followed by excitement to see her use them.

Several tins of food came out next, then an assortment of silver and gold items. She separated the silver utensils from a set of candlesticks, counting the spoons under her breath and frowning as though she would be held accountable for the number. Next was a thin leather belt with an unusual gold buckle that looked far too expensive to belong to any of the men I'd encountered.

The wooden lockbox from the study came out as well. She set it and its key to the side as she sorted through the handfuls of coins and jewelry she'd taken off the men's bodies.

"Damn," she swore, finally turning to the box. There was a solid click when she turned the key in the lock, and the lid creaked on its hinges as she opened it. She riffled through the paperwork inside. Reviewing it would surely be a worthwhile endeavor at some point, but she was in no state of mind for that. "I thought there would be more." There was some paper money mixed in with what looked like receipts of some kind, but not much.

Her hand closed around a carved wooden horse with gold-tipped ears and hooves. She squeezed her eyes closed and clutched the carving to her chest.

"Money isn't a problem," I assured her, though my ability to find it like I normally did was in question if I couldn't access my magic. Regardless, between what I already had when I arrived and what she'd taken, there was coin enough for now and there were items that could be traded.

She handed me a selection of the coins and put the rest back in the box along with the jewelry and weapons. The little horse remained in her hand.

"Here. This is yours too." I pulled the little spell book I'd taken from her floor out of my pocket and put it in the box. She stared at me.

"You don't want to keep it?"

I shrugged. "I flipped through it while you were sleeping, but there's nothing in there that I didn't already know. Whomever it belongs to has some very eclectic knowledge."

"Such as?" She picked it up and thumbed through it, brow furrowed. "I read through it several times, but most things I couldn't make heads or tails of."

"That is where you learned how to draw a circle, yes?" She nodded. "Well, that's a good example. The sigil collection is incomplete, and many are drawn wrong. The one for me was close enough it worked, but most would not."

"Oh."

"We can go through it more thoroughly if you like. When you feel up to it."

"Okay." She seemed skeptical of my offer but put the book in the box.

After packing her bag back up, she crossed to the bed and climbed under the sheet, a fierce yawn making her jaw crack as she leaned her back against the headboard. "I shouldn't still be tired."

I chuffed, stuffing my spare change of clothing into the bag of supplies and tying it off. "When was the last time you got any kind of decent rest?" She only blinked. "That's what I thought, Derne."

"Hailon."

Her chin was propped up on her knees, which she'd pulled to her chest. "What?"

"Derne is my family name. If we're going to be traveling together, you can call me Hailon."

Something fizzed behind my breastbone with the gift of trust she'd just bestowed upon me. I could understand completely why she'd given me the alternate before, and, having spent quite a lot of time with the fae, I knew what trust she was extending by allowing me to know her actual given name.

"I stand by my statement that you require ample feeding and rest, *Hailon*." The letters tasted sweet on my tongue. "Both can be found here."

Her mouth twitched, the closest I'd gotten to a smile. "Noted, *Seir*." I laughed aloud, the sound of my name from her mouth providing a ridiculous thrill. "Do you have a surname?"

"I have not adopted one. They are not common or required in Hell." I thought of my brothers, how after being on Earth so long, one had adopted his old name as his surname and another had chosen one in a language he was fond of. Perhaps I'd borrow one of theirs.

"I see." She glanced around. "Where will you sleep?"

I spread my arms. "Right here by the fire."

"But there's not even a rug there, only floor. No blanket, no cushion." A deep frown pulled her pretty features into harsh lines.

"I've had far worse," I assured her. And I had. Rocks and dirt, the fiery pits … several places came to mind. In comparison, a cozy fire and worn wooden planks were downright comfortable. Having seen her previous living quarters, I knew she could relate on some level and did not begrudge her the comfort the single bed afforded one bit.

"That's silly. Here." She climbed off the mattress, pulling one of the pillows and some bedding with her. "There's plenty." I moved aside and let her maneuver the blankets into a comfortable pallet. She looked it over critically, her hands on her hips, her face relaxing once she was satisfied.

"Much appreciated, kind lady."

She flushed that pink color again but said nothing as she returned to the bed. A deep sigh followed the rustling of her getting situated under the quilt once more. I made a round of the cabin, stopping in the bathroom to wash up quickly and drain the dirty water from the tub. I made sure the lamps were extinguished and the fire banked before curling up in the little nest she'd made for me.

Soft floral notes from the soap she'd used lingered in the fabric, along with the tang of old blood from before she'd cleaned up. I buried my nose and inhaled, enjoying the contrast.

Her voice was barely above a whisper and heavy with sleep as she said, "It took twenty-three days for them to bring me here. We went through at least three dense forests, and the road went up like we were climbing mountains twice. Once we went so high my ears popped on and off for most of the day. The air smelled of salt water for nearly a week before we got to Olinbourg.

"They gathered wagons and supplies the whole time. We started with one wagon and three men. There were six wagons and twenty-eight men by the time we arrived, but I don't think anybody but the three in my wagon knew I was there. They were very careful to keep me hidden and gagged."

"It's very canny of you to have kept track of things like that." My heart thumped behind my ribs, strangely heavy. She had impressed me several times already. I would never underestimate her intelligence or ability if this is how she managed through extreme circumstances. I rubbed the heel of my palm against my shirt, frowning as I pulled in another deep breath of lavender and iron.

"They kept my eyes covered, so I'm not sure if my timekeeping was right. They only allowed me out of the wagon after dark, but it always seemed long enough it felt like a day had passed between." She frowned. "Do you think it will take that long to get back?"

Her shadow danced behind her on the wall. "I don't know. Collecting such an amount of people and goods along the way is certainly time consuming in itself, but people doing nefarious things often take routes that double back or go inefficient ways to lose anyone who might be following." I ground my teeth together. Evil was certainly not exclusive to humans, but they had developed some of the most creative ways of expressing their darker nature I'd ever seen. Which, as a resident of Hell, was saying something. "I've never made that journey without some kind of portal or sifting. Never been to Ravenglen proper at all, that I can remember."

Her head bobbed gently, her voice thoughtful and quiet. "We should leave as soon as possible."

I smiled. I liked her spirit, though I worried her body wasn't quite ready for the trek. "We will. Rest yourself, Hailon."

"Good night, Seir."

The crackle of flames and her soft breathing lulled me into a doze and perhaps the first truly peaceful sleep I'd had in ages.

CHAPTER 5
HAILON

Nᴏᴛ ᴡᴀᴋɪɴɢ ᴜᴘ until after midday definitely diminished my credibility for arguing that I was well enough to get on the road.

When I rolled over on the plush pillow into a face full of sunshine, I immediately went into a panic. Heart racing, I sat up and had my eyes fixed in the direction my bedroom door should have been in before I realized what was happening. But there was no Ignus tromping up the stairs to retrieve me, no punishment to anticipate for sleeping in.

Instead of my dull room at the house, I was greeted by the soft sound of a big water pot steaming over the fire, the rounded log walls of the cabin, and the rhythmic thud of an axe hitting a stump somewhere outside. It was downright cozy. It would be far too easy to fall into a fantasy about having something like this every single day of a regular, boring life. Unfortunately for me, I'd never had one of those, and it was unlikely I'd get one in the future.

I let out a deep sigh when I moved my feet to get out of bed and heard no chains clanking, felt no bite of metal around my ankles.

My body was still sore and stiff, but my muscles warmed up quickly as I moved around the cabin. I made use of the bathroom, then reapplied the ointment Seir had found to as many of my bruises and scrapes as I could. To really do a thorough job, I would need help and probably a whole second tub, so I had to make some judicious choices. My neck and shoulders were still scratchy, but the burn was easing nicely after using the thick balm. The wound on my wrist thankfully hadn't been as deep as I'd thought and had scabbed over.

The demon had left me more food on the little table as well, which I happily sat down to enjoy. I probably should have been wary about it, but finally having ample food after weeks of being hungry left me far less suspicious than I should have been. His intentions seemed the very opposite of malicious toward me, besides. In fact, it was a wonder I felt inclined to fight so hard against his company when I tallied up how considerate and helpful he'd already been. I decided it was mostly that I'd always been the caretaker and didn't really know how to let someone else do that job for me.

As I was wiping up my plate with the last few bites of bread, he came through the door, arms stacked high with firewood.

"Oh good, I was starting to worry you might be dead," he teased, his tail efficiently removing the topmost pieces and setting them in the fire. It was fascinating to watch.

"Not yet," I replied, sitting back in my chair. "You didn't check on me?"

As he transferred the wood—now with his tail and hands—to the metal holder next to the hearth, he glanced over at me with a grin. He'd braided thin sections of hair on either side of his face and joined them behind his head with a strip of leather, showcasing his high cheekbones and the freckles sprinkled over them. His shirt was unbuttoned partway, and he had the sleeves rolled up past his elbows, giving me a good look at the greenish runes tattooed across his chest just below his collarbones and down his breastbone.

"Of course I did," he said, straightening up, dusting his hands together. "You were breathing just fine. And see? I was right. You needed the rest."

I rose to wash my plate, face burning with embarrassment. I'd been staring again. I was sure of it. And he'd seen me doing it. But there was no way to stop myself; he was ridiculously pretty.

"Point taken. But tomorrow, please wake me. I really would like to get on the road." My chest squeezed tight, worry that I had already been gone too long pressing in. My cursed gift had been part of me as long as I could remember and was needed by those closest to me for the same reasons I was taken and exploited for it. I had to get back to Sal.

Seir retrieved the pot of hot water and walked with it into the bathroom, filling the tub again. For himself, I presumed, since I'd done nothing more strenuous than sleep and he'd been busy with laborious things like chopping wood and foraging for food.

"No promises, but I think tomorrow is probably reasonable." He carried the pot outside, filled it with water from the pump and rehung it over the flames. The stray drops on the outside of the massive iron kettle hissed and popped as they burned away. "I know you just ate, but are you up to preparing supper while I bathe? Better chance of getting an early start if we're not tying up all the loose ends too late into evening."

"I'm not much of a cook," I admitted.

"Nothing complicated required, I was going to use up as many of the odds and ends as I could in a stew so they aren't wasted. A little chopping, some water, and let it sit on the heat." He smiled. "I do love food this side of the gates. Much more variety."

I nodded, thoughts scrambled by his statement, not to mention his half-dressed close proximity. I kept forgetting he was a creature of Hell until reminded. That was concerning, honestly, especially considering I'd just been marveling at the utility of his *tail*.

Seir showed me the small pile of oddly sized root vegetables and a freshly cleaned fowl he'd brought in while I was sleeping. He smelled like pine resin and sulfur as he leaned over me to pull down a heavy cooking pot from the shelf.

"Knife," he said, standing basically over the top of me as he pulled open a drawer.

I reached inside and picked up the well-used blade, weighing it in my hand. Seir's eyes flashed, somehow red in what had to be a trick of the light. "I'm sure you know how to handle yourself with that, so I'll go get cleaned up."

I stood in the tiny kitchen for far longer than I wanted to admit, staring after him with my heart thudding behind my ribs and his smirk burned into my thoughts.

TRUE TO HIS word, Seir had us both up and ready to go before sunrise the next morning.

"How have you got everything packed up already?" I asked, coming out of the bathroom to find him serving up some porridge with berries for breakfast, our bags waiting by the door, and the cabin restored to a perfectly tidy condition.

My stew had come out better than I'd expected the previous evening, and between us, we'd eaten the whole pot. I was pretty sure the amount of food I was taking in was ridiculous, but Seir mostly seemed amused by it, continually asking if I needed more. Climbing into that warm, comfortable bed with a full stomach had been one of the loveliest experiences of my life. I remained torn between my need to get back to Aunt Sal and the desire to stay in this little cabin and have more time to enjoy such indulgences.

"I don't sleep much," Seir answered quietly, almost as though he didn't want to disturb the peace of the morning quite yet.

As I sat to eat, he washed and dried the pot, spread out all the fire embers to cool and walked through the cabin as though looking for something.

"Are you going to eat?"

Satisfied with what he found, he huffed out a shy breath and smiled, sitting down in the chair opposite mine.

It was quiet for several minutes as we ate, the hot grains cereal never having been one of my favorite things but certainly something that would be good for a long day of traveling.

He shifted, brows drawn together in a pensive frown. "This morning, I went back to the portal I used when I first arrived. It wouldn't activate, which is disappointing, but in line with what's been happening with my other abilities." He stared off blankly for a moment, then shook his head. "No matter. It didn't work, but I did happen to find a map in the cabinet." He reached into his pocket, producing a little rolled piece of parchment. "Hopefully it's a decent rendering." The small map was perhaps the size of Seir's palm; we both had to lean close to make things out as he smoothed it flat on the table.

"This route will take us through or near Revalia." He grinned broadly as he traced a path that crossed a river and went wide, toward the western coast of Cyntere. "I have people there. But this"—he traced a route that ran from town to town, across the expanse of the realm, all the way to Ravenglen—"is probably the way they brought you."

I looked at the little triangles indicating mountains, *t*'s for forests, and illustrations of serpentine waterways. "What are these?" The markings looked like the letter *x* but with an odd flourish at the top. Some were grouped together in a way that made them look like skulls.

"I believe those indicate ruins."

I stiffened. "We should avoid that area."

"Why?"

"Do your kind not avoid haunted places?" I asked.

He snorted. "Demons have no rivalry with ghosts." He saw I was unmoved by this declaration and dropped his haughty grin. "But perhaps it's different here?"

"It is believed that a long-dead king haunts the remains of his castle there. The problem is the ruins are so decayed often travelers don't realize they've stumbled into them until it's too late. If the tales are to be believed, he doesn't take kindly to trespassing, even hundreds of years past his reign and death."

"Go on." Seir's eyes grew wide, and he struggled to contain his smile the more I told him.

"People who venture there often go missing or end up mysteriously dead. There are some rumors about those who survived but then suffered a lifetime of bad luck. Every child knows the stories, mostly to discourage them from wandering too far from home but also as a warning."

Instead of being put off by mysterious and gruesome deaths, unexplained bad luck, curses, and much more, Seir had grown positively starry-eyed with excitement.

"How thrilling! I'd love to meet such a wonderfully vengeful spirit." After that, he was suspiciously quiet, eyes narrowed in thought as he looked over the map. One of his palms made small circles against his chest, right over his heart.

Seir's expression went blank again, and he was suddenly impatient with his breakfast, inhaling large bites one after another.

"Are you alright?" I asked, watching with horrified fascination.

He paused, bowl held up near his mouth, spoon suspended mid-motion. "Fine. Why?" he mumbled.

"You seem to be in a hurry. Should I be worried?"

"Ah." He set his bowl down very gently, something like chagrin crossing his face. "Just anxious, I guess. I've never been on a journey like this before."

The admission took me by surprise. "No? I thought you said you were a traveling demon?"

He shook his head and licked the last bits from his dish with his tongue. I found it difficult to swallow for reasons I didn't want to think too hard about as I watched him efficiently clean his bowl.

"I'm used to portals, or jumping. Sifting. At the very least having functional wings. Walking long distance will be a novel experience for me."

I wasn't sure what to think about that. "We don't have to walk the whole way, do we?" I asked, calculating the kind of time that might add to the days I'd spent in the wagon, not to mention how taxing it would be to do so.

He shrugged and rose, collecting our dishes and taking them into the kitchen to wash. "I don't know. But I promise to get you home as quickly as I can."

"Thank you," I said, glad he couldn't see my face. If he did, he might see that I meant for more than the breakfast or the dishes. For more than offering to travel with me, even after I basically told him I didn't need his help. Twice. Especially for helping me escape Ignus. Not that I was ashamed over what I'd done, but he might see how thankful I was to him for allowing me to get revenge on those men for all the torment they put me through. He might see too much, and he'd already seen more than most, despite our very short time together.

The list of things I could owe him for—even just a "thanks"— was far longer than I liked, especially for someone I basically just met. I hated owing anyone anything.

And while I'd already protested needing his company, I wasn't completely ungrateful to have him willing to travel with me. Making my way all the way to Ravenglen on my own was a daunting task.

I could do it, but it would be easier with someone else there. Especially someone as quick to take care of things as this demon was.

"Shall we?" He reached out to help me up once he'd shouldered his own pack, and a flush ran through me from head to toe at the contact. "I suspect if we get going, we'll be able to make it to that little settlement near the river by nightfall tomorrow. Eddington, I think the map had it marked. Perhaps we'll be able to find a horse there."

"Ignus sometimes traveled to Eddington," I agreed. "I recognize the name. He was never gone more than a few days."

"He did business there?" Seir asked as he led me back down the street the way we'd come, my eyes warily watching for any familiar faces.

"Yes. He bartered grain for making liquor. I'm sure he peddled my healing services, too, given the number of strangers that came through the house just for that."

Seir's expression went stony again, and he grunted. His fingers flexed against my skin, his hand warm and still. After a beat, he turned and walked out the cabin door. I followed him, silently thanking the cabin for its hospitality, wishing things were different and I could just stay there in the nice bed for as long as I wanted.

As I walked out into the brisk morning air, I realized again that summoning Seir had changed everything about my life, and I was only beginning to see what all that might mean.

CHAPTER 6
SEIR

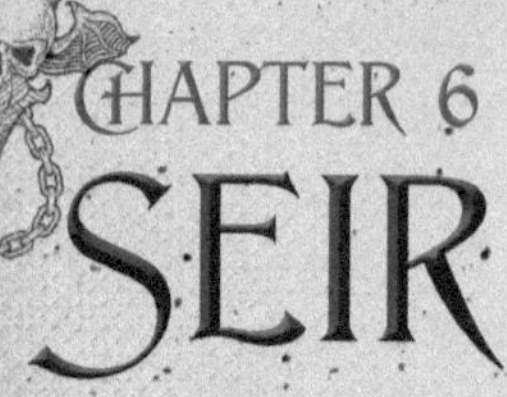

As we walked away from Olinbourg toward Eddington, the morning sun warmed our backs. Steam rose from the tall grass as the heat thawed the soil. We'd missed the sunrise thanks to some heavy fog, but it was shaping up to be a lovely day with a cool breeze. The change in foliage from the woods around Olinbourg to more grassy open areas as we traveled the well-worn road was nothing short of wondrous. I always missed the vibrancy of color that places outside of Hell had, and seeing all the wonderful things morning had to offer was an excellent reminder of just how dull the underworld could be.

Unfortunately, this section of the road was mostly barren aside from some distant groupings of pine trees and an occasional passing wagon, none of which were going the same direction as us and all seemed to have horses that couldn't give us a wide enough berth. My polite greetings to the drivers had been met with frustrated glares as they tried their best to control their beasts, though one did begrudgingly tip his hat to Hailon when she raised her hand in a wave.

I'd managed to start several short conversations with the interesting woman walking beside me, but she seemed focused purely on putting one foot in front of the next, even after I finally managed to get her to pass over her pack for me to carry.

"What is your home like?" I asked.

"Not much different from Olinbourg, I suppose. Colder, though. Ravenglen is right next to the northern mountains, and there's snow on the peaks there all year." I waited several beats for her to elaborate further, but she did not.

She glanced over, found me staring and asked, "Is it true that Hell is dark nearly all the time?"

I nodded. "Yes. It's not true dark, though. There's a brightness to the false sky like daylight, but it's always some shade of gray instead of blue like here."

"Are you always stuck there?" she asked, kicking at a pebble on the road.

"I wouldn't say stuck. I travel to other realms often, though my job is in Hell." My apartment, too, such as it was. It was a consistent place to return in order to rest, but I held no true attachment to it.

"I would miss the sunshine. I *have* missed the sunshine. I didn't get to go outside at all while I was at that house. I sometimes got to open the window though. Not enough to climb out, but enough to get some fresh air and a breeze. I missed the whole summer." Hailon turned around and bathed her face in the light, walking backwards with her eyes closed for several paces. A small smile ticked at her lips, and as I grinned in response to the pleasant sight, I found my heartburn flaring. Whatever the cause was, I was rather irritated by the gnawing sensation.

"Every realm is lovely in its own way. Hell is home, has been for a very, very long time. I don't mind it. But I do love visiting other places, and I do find I miss many things about this world when I am elsewhere."

"Every realm?" she asked, fidgeting with her tunic. "You've been beyond Cyntere?"

I chuckled. "Yes, many times. The world is very big, and there are doorways to places not shown on any map if you know where to find them."

She digested this quietly. To my dismay, the conversation never picked back up. Hailon had gone pensive and introspective, and I worried something I'd said was the cause of her withdrawal.

It wasn't until we stopped for a rest at midday that part of the reason my companion had grown so quiet was revealed.

Hailon stripped off the boots we'd found for her in the way-house the minute we were seated on some fallen trees in the shade of a stand of pines. She dug through her pack, bringing out the healing ointment and an extra pair of socks. I heard her mumble several colorful curses under her breath.

"What's wrong?" I asked, startled by her sudden intake of breath.

"Blisters," she said simply. "The boots are a little big."

My heart thumped rapidly behind my ribs, panic settling into my chest at the thought that she'd been quietly suffering the whole day.

I apologized, digging out some food to keep my hands occupied while she applied the salve to her heels and toes. She put her socks back on, hesitated, then layered on the last pair for good measure.

"It's alright. This should help."

I handed her one of the water skins and she took it eagerly, downing several gulps. I frowned harder. "You do not need to be thirsty or endure physical discomfort. Just say if you need something, Hailon. I could always carry you—"

"You will *not* be carrying me," she said firmly, shaking her head for emphasis.

"Then you must speak more freely about your needs. I've spent most of my time around demons and fae, I'm clearly not good at reading humans just yet. I just thought you weren't interested in talking, but if you were in pain ..." I couldn't piece together the words I needed to express my concern. Her eyes drifted to my tail, which was twitching irritably behind me in the grass. "I need to know. You must *tell* me. Okay?"

"I'll do my best to let you know if I need something going forward," she said before tearing into an apple with a noticeably aggressive bite. It was such a silly thing, and probably meant to deter me, expressing her displeasure as she was, but I adored her fire.

"Thank you. That's all I ask." I couldn't restrain my good mood as we ate, her eyes anywhere but on me and mine nowhere but on her.

With a rueful sigh, she pulled the boots back on once she'd tossed aside the apple core. "Bastard," she muttered. I couldn't help grinning. For all I knew, she was referring to me, though I assumed she meant the blisters.

"Your healing ability doesn't heal *your* body?" I asked as I shifted around the contents of the packs so they were more evenly distributed. "You healed my arm, and you mentioned that ability was being sold by your captor. The injuries from the day we met, the blisters. Your gift won't take care of them?"

Hailon shook her head, dusting her hands on her thighs as she stood. "No. It has only ever worked on others."

"That's quite unfair."

Her mouth twitched and she chuffed a harsh laugh. "Tell me about it."

"Are your bruises and cuts alright? Perhaps we should find somewhere to camp—"

"I'm fine."

"But you had several injuries, if I let my excitement about traveling cloud my judgment about your readiness, we should—"

"Seir?" She put her hand on my arm, right over where she'd healed my cut. The simple touch quelled the building storm of anxiety inside me, very effectively shutting me up.

"Yes?"

"I'm fine. Really. We should go."

"Are you sure?"

"Yes. Please. I'd like to make it to the village before nightfall tomorrow. If we stop moving now, it will only take us longer."

"Okay. Yes. We'll go." I gathered our things and followed behind her as she walked back through the tall grass toward the road.

THE AFTERNOON WAS almost stifling, with no hint of a breeze and unseasonably warm weather. When I was sure it was just the two of us on the road, I let my wings out and raised them as high as they would go. The angle of the sun was such that my face was still partially exposed, but at least Hailon had some shade. I was even graced with a small smile for my effort.

We were both worn out by the time the sun started to slip toward the horizon, providing relief from the heat and the sign we needed to find a suitable place for making camp.

"This will have to do," I sighed, the small grove of trees similar to where we'd stopped midday offering the only semblance of shelter on the flat, grassy plain.

"There's a creek at least."

"Small favors and all that," I muttered, collecting medium sized stones to make a fire ring.

"I'm going to go get some water." Hailon took the largest pot and went off toward the little stream.

She'd been stoic since our lunch stop, but the limp she'd picked up had only gotten worse as the day dragged on. I knew the blisters were bothering her, but still, she said nothing. She was proving both tough and stubborn, which together were an especially formidable pair of traits.

By the time she got back with the water, I'd gathered enough wood to cook our meal and keep us comfortable overnight. It took a few moments, but I managed to get a fire started with the little kit of flint and steel. One day, I would make it back to that cabin and replenish everything we'd taken so the next travelers to pass through could be as well supplied as we were.

"What are we going to do about shelter?" she asked, glancing around. "This feels rather exposed."

"It's not optimal, but we don't have much choice. It'll be alright, I don't sleep much." Hailon nodded, forehead wrinkled despite my claim. "I'm going to see if I can find something fresh to add to our dried meat for a stew."

"Do you know how to recognize dangerous plants?" she asked.

I nodded but hesitated. "I know about the poisonous mushrooms with red caps, and the vining plants with three leaves that will make you blister and itch." She frowned at my enthusiastic response. "Are there many dangerous plants somewhere like this?" I gestured vaguely to the sparse, grassy plain.

The corner of Hailon's mouth twitched. "Yes. There are many, many things that are toxic in places like this. Plants, animals. Even water." She waved me over, walking in the direction of the creek. "Come on. I saw what I think is cress and some kind of berry while I was filling the pot. Maybe we'll get lucky and find some edible roots."

"I always forget that Earth is like this. Humans are challenged at every turn just to keep themselves alive!"

She turned and glanced at me over her shoulder, judgment and concern pulling her eyebrows together. "You sound positively thrilled about that."

"Oh, I am! I love it here, there are endless adventures to be had, and the variety of life is fascinating. It's the same in the fae realm, but they're far less mortal than humans."

"Should I be worried?"

"Of course not. I'm no threat to you, Hailon. Besides, you're *also* dangerous, after all, have you forgotten? Should it come down to a battle between us, it would be a narrow margin that determined a winner." I gave her an exaggerated wink, pulse pounding in my veins. It would have been convenient to blame the hazards of Earth-dwelling for the exhilaration I was feeling, but there was more to it than that. Her, in particular. And the idea of sparring with her ... well. I forced myself to inhale slowly several times and considered a quick swim in the undoubtedly icy stream.

My comical wink and commentary amused her, and the short laugh she gave only thrilled me further.

"I don't know much at all about the fae, so I can't speak to that. Is it not like this in Hell?"

I considered as we pushed through the tall grass, the blades making a soft swishing noise as we flattened it with every step. "I suppose for some it is. But most of the inhabitants are either already dead or demons, so it's different." I frowned. Was it, though? I battled legions of lesser demons often. They were mindless hordes, bent on nothing but destruction. What kind depended on who their master was. I knew my brothers were helping the stone kin face down similar infestations here on the surface. "There are no unknown dangers in Hell, only consequences. Everyone is aware of evils lurking, and if they decide to take a chance ..." I grinned and spread my arms wide, indicating that was the choice they were free to make.

Hailon had turned to look at me and stood quite still with her mouth open slightly. "I see."

I felt a rush of heat prickle along my neck. There seemed to be equal measures of thoughtfulness and judgment in her gaze, but she continued on her mission to find us some edibles.

"Wait, are you saying there are some live residents of Hell who aren't demons?"

"Ah, you were paying attention. Yes, there are. They are very few, but there are some … interesting contracts that currently exist between demons and mortals allowing them to live and work in Hell. Part of the time, at least."

Hailon only made a thoughtful noise at this information as she came to the edge of the water.

The creek itself was perhaps as wide as I was tall, the rocky bottom perfectly visible. There were sadly no fish, at least not ones large enough to see. Hailon stripped off the boots and her double-layered socks, grimacing as she peeled them down her heels. Had I not been carefully watching her face, I wouldn't have even noticed the flinch she made. After rolling up the legs of her trousers, she stepped into the frigid water, wading carefully into the center. It only came up to her shins, but the current was powerful enough she had to rebalance on the pebbles below her feet more than once.

"The little greens with oval leaves and white flowers? That's cress." She pointed to a plant on the far bank as she continued to cross. "There might be some farther down on your side too. It likes to grow in the little places the water has carved out. See?" Her fingers traced the little cove the plant had nestled in.

"Yes." I nodded happily, then plodded slowly along the muddy edge of the water as I looked for the plant. I yelled out proudly when I found some, startling the birds and bugs into momentary silence. Hailon's nod of approval, complete with the hint of a proud smile, made my whole body warm.

Before long, we had plenty of fresh greens and even a few handfuls of slightly tart berries between us.

"I'd like to stand here a bit longer, if that's okay?"

I took the food from her outstretched hands. "Aren't your feet chilled by now?"

Her head bobbed. "A little, but it feels nice on my heels." She trailed off, as though embarrassed to admit such a thing.

Frustration bloomed, but I didn't want to add to her discomfort. "I'll go start cooking then. Call me when you're finished, and I'll come get you."

She huffed. "No need, I'll walk."

"Your feet will be wet, and it will be worse tomorrow if you have damp socks or boots to wear. I'll carry you back when you're done."

"Seir, I don't need you to—"

"If you walk through the grass, you will cut your feet, Hailon. It's sharp, like little blades. Then you would have injured, dirty, blistered, wet feet. *I will carry you.*" My heart was pounding as the overwhelming need to help her, to protect her, for her to allow me to do something so simple for her throbbed through my bones. The seriousness of my tone had her mouth dropping open, then shutting again into a tight line.

"Fine. But I think this is entirely unnecessary, for the record."

"Noted." Surprised at her giving in, but grateful, I left before she could change her mind.

I HAD SOME OF the dried meat in the pot simmering away with a handful of the small root vegetables I'd found near the cabin by the time her voice rang out.

"Seir?"

I jumped to my feet. "Coming!"

She was squatted down by the edge of the creek when I approached, a large frog cradled between her hands.

"What's that you've got? An addition to our meal?"

She shook her head. "No, he's not for eating. He was hurt." The fat little creature hopped out of her palm and back into the shallows, promptly snatching up several bugs. Hailon rinsed her hands in the water and stood, a relaxed tilt to her full mouth.

"My mistake. Kind of you to fix him up." My heartburn kicked up something powerful as she met my eye. The odd color variations of her irises packed a powerful punch in the late afternoon glow. The heel of my hand reflexively scrubbed at my chest to ease the ache as I tried to remember how to breathe. She was truly something else, and I wanted to understand better why she affected me so strongly. Perhaps it had something to do with her magic.

"I bought him a little time before he becomes something's dinner, anyway." Her eyes scanned my body, her foot lifting as she prepared to walk on the muddy bank. "It's really not—"

"It is." I shook my head, hearing the protest before she could get the words out and striking it down. I turned my back to her, stepping as close to the water as I dared without getting my own boots wet. "Get on."

"I am perfectly capable of walking, this feels silly." She sighed, setting her hands on my shoulders.

"We've been over the reasons this makes sense. So you shouldn't. Feel silly, I mean. I'm more than happy to be of service." I reached back and gripped her thighs, giving her a boost up my back before hooking my arms around her legs. She was warm and soft, though her calves and ankles were shockingly cold from the water. She was stiff at first, but gradually allowed herself to lean comfortably against me. It made my heart thump happily behind my ribs.

Back at our simple camp, I set her down on a log before squatting near the low flames to tend the steaming pot, hoping my heartbeat wasn't audible to her. The raging pulse in both my ears and my pants was very distracting, and it was my own fault.

Once her feet were thoroughly dry, Hailon put her boots back on and set up our meager bedrolls near the flames. We both curled up cross-legged on our blankets to eat, the little tin bowls cupped in our hands in the heavy quiet. Bugs trilled, frogs sang. The creek babbled gently in the distance. It was peaceful.

"I'll wash up in the morning," I offered.

Hailon nodded, her blinks slow and eyelids heavy.

Dark had fallen completely, and the stars were bright overhead. My brother Rylan was an expert at charting their movements and knew all the stories associated with them. I'd picked up plenty just being around him but was far from as knowledgeable due to how much time I spent in Hell.

"Do you have a favorite?" I asked, looking over at Hailon to find her gazing up at the sky as she shifted her bedding around so she could lie down. The little wooden horse was in her hand as she snuggled in. I was fairly certain she kept it in her pocket at all times. Her thumb rubbed along the gold-tipped ears.

"My aunt Sal told me all about the stars. She has the cycles down to memory too. We plan a lot of our medicine making around the sky."

"Aunt Sal sounds like a lot of the witches and mages I've met." A faint lift to the corners of her mouth assured me that she wasn't offended by my words. I wasn't yet certain she was a witch, but one of the men had flung that word at her as a slur. "My brother has studied the stars for hundreds of years. He's got an observatory at his school in Revalia, even. Fancy telescope and everything."

"Wow, that's …"

"Incredible," I agreed with her unspoken awe. "It's truly marvelous. He's very dedicated."

"Sounds like it."

"How many brothers do you have?"

"Six."

"Are you all close?"

I started to nod, then shook my head. That still didn't feel right, so I ended up shrugging. "We don't spend much time together anymore. Everyone has their own adventures happening. Rylan and Vassago are here on Earth. Tap manages the crossroads. I'm here and there. Ipos, Bas, and Sitri are more like me. Mainly in Hell, but they have their own places they venture off to as well."

"I always wondered what it would be like to have a sibling."

"For us, there was a lot of madness. But joy too. We get along well, when we see one another. You mentioned your Aunt Sal?"

"Yes, she's my only family. I've lived with her since I was small."

"Oh. Can I ask why?"

Hailon breathed in slowly through her nose. "I know what she told me, I know what I remember ... and I know that neither of those are the whole truth." She rubbed the smooth gold parts of her carved horse more intently. "I know that I had a mother, but I couldn't tell you what she looked like or the sound of her voice. I don't know anything about my father. I've been with Aunt Sal since I can remember, and she's been a dedicated parent to me."

"But?"

"But ... I also get the feeling that she never wanted to be. That I've long overstayed my welcome, despite it being out of necessity."

"Oh."

"She and my mother were friends, so she's not actually my blood relative. Something happened. I don't know what exactly, but my mother left me in her charge and ... that's that. I appreciate all she's done, but I worry my presence has stolen away the life she wanted for herself. She's mentioned things, over the years ..." She bit the inside of her cheek. "I try to be sure to give pieces of it back to her where I can. It's probably not enough, though."

I didn't know what to say to that, so I kept my silence. Her worries weighed on me, as well.

"Do you have parents?" she asked. "Demons aren't born, right? Not like people."

"No. My brothers and I, we fell."

"You were angels?" Her tone was curious, not surprised, which was intriguing.

"Once, yes." I did not elaborate, and she did not press. Truth was, the years before the fall were becoming more faded all the time. I worried that soon I wouldn't recall them at all.

"Is it difficult to be hundreds of years old?"

I barked a laugh at the unexpected question. "No. Not really. Time moves differently between the realms. It's faster here than in Hell, for example. And slower here than in the fae world. I've seen many things, learned much, but still have infinite things to explore."

"That's a lovely way to look at life."

"I agree." My heart thudded behind my ribs. Sleepy, introspective Hailon succeeded in winning my affection just as fiercely as her stubborn or violent sides. I settled for keeping my eye on her, but my fingers ached to curl around hers.

"Is there anything you're not telling me about this summoner contract?" she asked, the question abrupt but her tone soft. I could understand why she'd be distrustful.

"I don't believe so. You owe me nothing, if that's what you mean. I'm here because you summoned me, though also because I want to be. Should you banish me back, I could return if I wanted and had the opportunity, but my duty to you would be considered fulfilled."

"You don't have a duty to me, as far as I'm concerned."

"Be that as it may, that's how summoning a demon works. There are certain rules. I agreed to help you. So I am."

She sat thoughtfully for several minutes, gave a solemn nod, then rolled fully onto her back and raised an arm, pointing between several stars. "The Stallion. That's the one that comes to mind as my favorite."

It took me a moment to catch up to her topic shift, as I'd honestly forgotten I'd even asked her a question about the stars.

"Hmm. Tell me the story? I have a feeling your version of the tale is a little different than mine."

"Maybe you should tell me instead. I think yours may be more accurate given how much older it likely is."

"You first. Please?"

"Alright. The Stallion consists of those seven stars there, the ones that look like a winged horse if you squint just right. He was born a regular horse, in the wild lands. One day, the humans came and settled the area, and they captured all the beasts they could, him included. They tried to make him plow the fields. They tried to make him a war mount. They tried all the jobs for a horse there were, but none suited him. Until one day, a man needed to get an urgent message to his father. That day, they discovered he was best suited to *run*."

"Yes, I like this one. Go on!" I propped my chin on my hands and watched her raptly.

A smile was evident in her voice as she continued with the story. "After that first time, they sent him short distances without a rider. He was even faster that way. They started to joke that he knew how to fly without wings. Also, money had a way of finding its way into his saddle bags, and when turned out to pasture, he found several caches of hidden treasure. For all those reasons, he became quite valued by the humans."

"Wait," I interrupted, "does your version have a tragic turn in it?"

She shook her head. "No. This one is a happy story."

"Oh good." I clapped just my fingertips together so there was very little noise from my cheerful applause and settled in to hear the rest.

"The stallion spent his years running messages back and forth from human settlements, accepting his pay in affectionate nose scratches, apples, and carrots. He was well loved and eventually partnered with a beautiful mare and sired several foals."

"Naturally."

"When he got to the end of his life, there was no other horse that could compare, though his children had all trained to take up for him after he was gone. Some went far and wide so that more settlements could benefit from their talent. When he died, as a gift for all his service, he was blessed with golden wings and asked to continue carrying messages through the heavens."

"Does your version say that falling stars are him on a mission to make a delivery?"

"Yes." I heard her smile again, and it warmed me to know

retelling this had pleased her. "And also, that thunder is his hooves, strong winds the breeze from his wings, all that. If you hide any treasure, you're supposed to ask him not to find it so that it's still where you left it when you return to claim it. Yeah, I think that's my favorite."

"I like that one too." I didn't mention how that was the one I'd always identified most with, because that's essentially what my job was. I was the messenger, the traveler. I was a demon version of a flying horse. I even had a trick to make money appear when I had none. The similarities were striking. But there was no family or retirement or heavenly reward waiting for me. Soon, there might not even be a messenger job.

"There's a horse back home, his name is Jacks. I like to pretend he's one of The Stallion's descendants."

"Why's that?"

"He's constantly causing trouble. Hates to be penned. Loves to run more than anything. Very fast too. He's a handful."

"Yours?"

"No, he belongs to a friend. But I like to bring him treats now and then."

There were several long moments of silence, just the fire crackling and the night breathing around us.

"Hailon?"

There was no response. I propped myself up on my elbows and looked closer, finding her eyes closed and the hand holding the little wooden figure relaxed. Her chest rose and fell in a steady, slow cadence.

I quietly banked the fire and settled myself for sleep.

I'd have to tell her my favorite another day.

CHAPTER 8
SEIR

"I'M NOT GETTING on your back, Seir." Hailon shifted the pack on her shoulders—something else I'd tried and failed to reason with her over—and strode with purpose straight for the road, not even looking back to see if I was following. "But thank you for braiding my hair."

Stubborn, wholly independent Hailon was back and unbending after a full night's rest, it seemed.

I'd done as I said I would and washed the dishes in the predawn hours while gathering more berries to have with some hot grain porridge. Then, after we'd eaten, I'd cleaned up again and made sure she applied the healing ointment before sliding her feet back into the too-large boots. Finding her a suitable pair was at the very top of my list, even above locating us a horse or wagon, though either of those things would make our journey much less physically demanding.

After she'd been fed and had made a quick sojourn back to the creek to freshen up, I'd been brave and asked if she'd like me to braid her hair. Endless decades of practicing on myself, my brothers, and many others had left me skilled in weaving plaits for every function. Getting her uneven raven locks out of her face and away from her constantly questing fingers had been my absolute pleasure. Never mind the closeness such a thing afforded. The trust.

I wanted to pamper this woman who had seen nothing but an iron bed with a thin mattress, a worn sheet, and mistreatment the last several months. To my bones, I believed she deserved *everything*. That I was the one responsible for giving it to her. Those kinds of thoughts nagged at me more than I wanted to admit and had nothing at all to do with the fact she'd summoned me.

We were on our way early, while it was still pleasant, and the sunrise painted orange and pink all over the horizon. My traveling companion was efficient in her preparations for the day, which I appreciated. Breaking camp was a fast team effort and there was little fuss about anything. It was nice. Hailon was a wonderful travel companion all the way around.

The cool morning breeze and dew on the tall reedy grass too quickly gave way to full, brutal sunshine and no air movement at all. In fact, the day was a very close duplicate of the one before. Just one foot in front of the other until a quick stop for lunch that left me aching to throw Hailon over my shoulder so her subtle limp was no longer an issue and I could be assured of her comfort. I wanted to know what it was about her that made me itchy in this way, but I also enjoyed the mystery of our connection enough to leave well enough alone ... for now.

The road was barren of travelers all day long, and we were walking at a pace meant to consume the long distance, so conversation between us was sparse. I was completely drained of enthusiasm by the time the small village finally loomed into view, something I wouldn't have thought possible even a few short days before.

"I truly hope they have an inn," I mused, wrapping my tail around my waist under my shirt.

"Ignus had to have stayed somewhere," she answered thoughtfully. "Though in truth, I always suspected there was some kind of brothel he was utilizing, not necessarily a reputable inn. He always came home much less prone to violence than before he left. Calmer."

I choked on the breath I'd taken, then laughed in earnest at her assessment. She spoke her mind plainly, and I appreciated that about her very much.

"You're very observant, Hailon."

"I didn't have much to keep me occupied other than watching people," she admitted, voice low but firm. "It was sometimes entertaining, though I did it mostly to figure out a way to stay alive. Maybe to escape."

The anger that had quelled to a simmer in my blood perked up once more. Our footsteps in the gravel of the road were the only sound for several long beats.

"I always appreciated when his trips here coincided with research days. At least then I was able to get some rest without healing someone."

"Research days?" Just the sour taste of the word in my mouth made me feel like finding a necromancer to bring them back again so I could have another slower go at their useless corpses. I'd met one once, near where my brother Tap lived. Interesting fellow with a biting, dark sense of humor. I made a note to ask after him next time we spoke.

"How you found me in the den, with the men? That was a research day. Most of them weren't like that, though. That day was unusual."

"*Everything* about that was unusual, Hailon," I scoffed. "And that's coming from someone who lives in Hell."

She cracked the smallest of smiles, glancing over at me with those entrancing eyes. "I suppose you're right. But usually, they were just experimenting on me. Gathering samples." Her fingers absently reached for her hair but stalled, finding the braids.

"Samples?" I asked, the word coming out more like a growl.

"Blood. Hair. They wanted to see if they could replicate my healing gift. Make a potion or something like that. To sell to people. It was always ridiculous, honestly. Seven of them to just one of me. I did my best to fight back but it didn't take long for them to wear down my strength."

I bit the inside of my cheek so hard I tasted blood, and my fingers itched for a blade to throw. Then something else she'd said rose through the anger. "Seven? By my count, we only left five bodies to burn."

"There were two others that would usually come for those days. I don't know why they weren't there."

My breath stopped. Stragglers could not be discounted. "Can you describe them to me?"

Hailon gestured with her hands as she told me about the two men I'd be returning to Olinbourg for once I'd delivered her safely home. "One is short, stout. Dark hair cut short. Dark eyes, mustache. Some kind of councilman." I ground my teeth together. "The other looked quite a bit like Dr. Lang. I think they might be related, but don't know for sure. He always spoke quietly but liked holding me still." Hailon stopped walking and blinked hard. "Do you think they'll come after me?"

"I don't know. What was the ranking order of those men? You said the big one was in charge?"

"Yes, Ignus led the group, as far as I could tell, because it was his house, but Dr. Lang and the councilman had the power. They were all careful not to say too much around me most of the time, but occasionally something would slip. Do you think they might see what happened to the others and just ... go away? Stay clear of the area so they aren't connected to that house?" Her tone was hopeful, but I heard the undercurrent of worry.

"Perhaps." I didn't have words of comfort to offer. Men, especially the kind that would participate in the trafficking of people and experimentation on live subjects, weren't exactly the kind I would expect to have high moral standards. But fear was a fantastic motivator. If they thought they might also end up dead, walking away would be an attractive option.

At long last, the little settlement came into view. First came a few outlying farms, though not many fences to separate them. Fields of pale-green grain, very like the roadside grasses, waved in the gentle breeze. The road split off toward them but never widened.

The town was an open one, with a single main street. I scanned the signs hanging over the doors on the buildings gathered around the center of town, finding what I was looking for with measurable relief. I'd hoped for a town large enough to host a clothier so we could find Hailon some things that fit her more appropriately, especially her boots, but we weren't going to get those things here. However, a hot meal and a real bed would surely lift her spirits after all the walking we'd done.

"There's an inn after all," I told her, pointing at the building with a sign depicting a scythe and a barrel. "Come on. Let's get something to eat and find you a bed to sleep in."

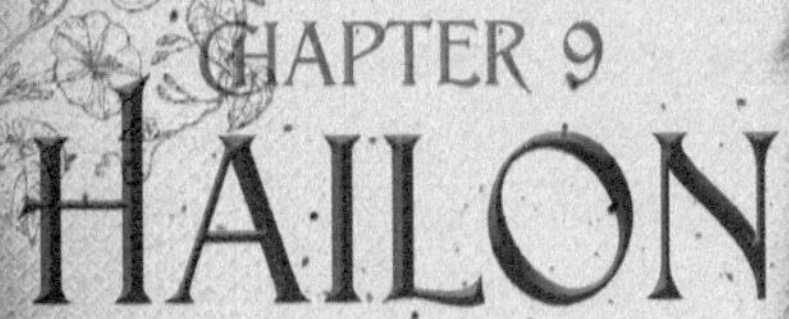

CHAPTER 9
HAILON

THE CLIENTELE INSIDE the little inn stared as we crossed the floor toward the man behind the bar at the rear, but nobody moved to challenge or even paused in their conversations. My skin tingled, unappreciative of all the stares. I was grateful for Seir's presence and seemingly effortless understanding of how to navigate this situation.

"What can I do for you, traveler?" the grizzled innkeeper asked.

"Any chance you have a room available?" Seir asked, forearm on the bar as he casually surveyed the room.

"Some food and drink aplenty, but no rooms, I'm afraid. We're full up tonight." The man drew a tankard of ale from a tap without looking away from Seir's face and placed it in front of him.

"Are there any other places that rent? We can pay, of course." Seir raised the brew and drank deep. I wondered if these gestures were some kind of tavern or inn code; some secret language I was not privy to. I also wondered if I should be offended that I was not included despite clearly standing right beside Seir.

The innkeeper shook his head. "No, sorry."

A man down the bar leaned back, raising his voice to get Seir's attention. "Ms. Welling runs a house down the street, if you're looking for a bed." He smirked, eyes traveling from my face to my chest. "Could probably even make some extra coin lending her out for the evening. Looks like she's handled a good tumbling in her time. Always nice to have a fresh ...*face* around here." He winked at me after waggling his eyebrows in suggestion. My stomach turned.

Seir's head turned toward the man slowly, his palm digging into the left side of his chest. I could feel the cold shift in his temperament and tensed in response. The last thing we needed was to cause trouble or draw attention to ourselves. "Is he a good customer?" Seir asked the innkeeper, though his attention was fully on the other man.

"Kalob?" The innkeeper snorted and flung a smudged white towel over one shoulder after wiping down the bar in front of himself with it. "Nah. He's at least two weeks behind in credit and first to provoke a fight." The innkeeper, it seemed, was participating in lighthearted banter about a loyal customer. Seir, on the other hand, was not.

Faster than my eyes could track, Kalob had been provided a fist to the face and was wearing both his ale and Seir's, his face dripping and shirt saturated. The tankards were reduced to nothing more than shards of earthenware on the floor courtesy of the man's face. As casual as could be, Seir used one hand to smash Kalob's cheek against the wooden bar, then pinned him there, forearm pressing across his neck. Kalob's hands flailed, only stilling when one of Seir's daggers pressed into the soft area under his chin. He was bleeding, soaked in ale, and clearly stunned at how he'd ended up in such a state.

"Seir!" I gasped, at the same time the innkeeper shouted, "Hey now!" Several men across the room cheered.

"Is all your clientele so crass?" Seir asked him. "This is a terrible first impression if I'm being honest. No manners at all."

"He didn't mean nothing by it," the innkeeper insisted, hands up as though surrendering.

"Of course he did." Seir's eyes finally met mine, and they were brutally red. His smile was sharp, and he didn't hesitate to show all his teeth. "Apologize to the lady."

"My mistake," Kalob gritted, face turning reddish purple. Seir's blade poked in enough to draw blood.

"It's fine, let's just go." I reached a hand out, placing my palm on his arm. "People are staring." I could feel it, and it made me itchy. I was flattered—more than, honestly—but this was not how I'd envisioned our evening going at all. I just wanted dinner, maybe a hot bath, and a bed. "We don't want to draw attention to ourselves, right? We should leave."

"Not until he apologizes properly."

"I'm sorry!" he wheezed. Seir leaned in close to his ear, whispering something I couldn't make out. Kalob nodded, at least as much as he was able to. "I'm very sorry, good lady. I meant no disrespect. I sincerely apologize for insinuating you might be a"—his air choked off even further—"whore."

The innkeeper's eyes shifted between us, and we'd drawn the attention of all the nearby tables by this point as well. "He's done what you said, now let him go, yeah? He didn't mean no harm. He's just an idiot who doesn't know when to mind his mouth."

Seir released the man, who wasted no time stumbling his way out of the inn, coughing the whole way. Another round of cheering went up, along with loud peals of laughter. It would seem several other patrons had their own issues with dear Kalob.

"Did you?" Seir asked the innkeeper, the point of his blade now aimed his direction. It bobbed as Seir talked, bouncing between the innkeeper's throat and chest.

"Did I, what?"

"You poured me a drink straightaway. Where was your hospitality for her? Did you mean to be welcoming, or did you mean harm?"

"Oh, I ..."

"Do the women of this town not drink your ale? It's certainly not the worst I've tasted, but I have to wonder if it's of such bad quality you'd prefer it not cross the lips of a lady." He tapped the point of his dagger against his chin. "Were you insulting *me* by allowing me to drink it, or were you insulting *her* by not offering any at all?"

Despite the hot rage pouring from his body and the terrifying tone of Seir's voice, I did not fear him. My heart was pounding in my chest mostly out of anxious anticipation. He seemed erratic, though still very methodical. It didn't make sense, but I'd seen him take out a threat, and this was not the same. This was something more like ... playing with his food.

I scanned the room, finding that the only women present were clearly working in one way or another. There were two laughing and playfully being tossed from lap to lap at tables near the windows, their bodices cut low and their skirts pulled high enough to show stockings and garters. Two more were delivering food and drinks from large trays. Women were not patrons here, only men. I very much doubted Seir had missed such a detail, but it felt important.

The innkeeper hustled to fill a cup for me, but in his haste, it was mostly foam.

"Thank you," I said, not wishing to inflame things any further. I took a drink, and it was refreshing if only because it was cold. My whole body was on high alert, and I wanted nothing more than to follow the hateful man out the door. Seir had shown several features that were not fully human, and I had no idea whether that was going to become a serious problem for us. "Whatever point you wanted to make, you've made, it, okay? Let's just go."

"In a moment." Seir took a deep breath and sheathed his dagger. The energy of the bar relaxed, everyone returning to their own conversations as though what had just happened was completely commonplace. No wonder Ignus got along so well here.

"Can I do anything else for you, sir?" the innkeeper asked, clearly trying to get us to leave his establishment peacefully.

"Who can I speak to about a horse?"

He shook his head. "No horses to let or sell around these parts."

"Not even for gold coin?" Seir asked, accepting the cup as I pushed it toward him. The bright hoppy taste turned my empty stomach.

"No sir. All our animals are working stock, needed for the harvest before winter comes."

"Unfortunate," Seir grunted and finished the ale, the innkeeper startling when he smacked the empty tankard on the bar. He sighed, fishing coins from a pouch at his waist. His tail was twitching irritably under his shirt, like a snake coiled inside a sack, ready to strike at the first temptation of release. "And information? Do you have any of that?"

"Possibly."

"I heard a rumor about a healer in a nearby town."

I was sure I turned bright red, standing right there listening, acting like I wasn't the subject of his questioning, but I appreciated the way Seir had approached his information gathering.

"Aye. I don't know anything for certain, but there's been talk of a woman who can cure just about anything, for the right price."

"Keep talking."

"Word has it she's mountain folk. Has a unique talent. You know the kind—not a witch, exactly, but something close. Should you find yourself in Olinbourg, look for the house near the square with the lattice windows."

Seir placed a coin on the bar, but kept it covered with his hand.

"Any clue who I might want to speak to when I find this house?"

The innkeeper glanced around before leaning in, trying to maintain some illusion of privacy in the busy room. The coin was traded, and he started talking. "There's a man who comes here sometimes, he brings grain for my ale and sour mash. Bartering is commonplace for nearby townsfolk, as you surely know. Everyone has something to trade."

"Of course."

"He goes by Ignus. Allegedly, it's his healer."

I clenched a fist at the insinuation I belonged to him. I'd been his captive, his unwilling participant. But I'd never been *his*.

"Does he travel alone?"

"Occasionally there's another man with him. Bookish type, skinny with glasses." That had to be Dr. Lang. "They generally seek ale here and company at Ms. Welling's, but so do many."

"Indeed." Seir put down another coin. "Apologies for the mess. We'll be on our way."

"Safe journey to you," the innkeeper said reflexively. I could tell by his face there was no actual care for our well-being behind his words. Seir turned from the bar, and I followed, right on his heels.

He kept right on walking once we were outside, headed down the street towards where we'd find Ms. Welling's brothel.

"What happened back there?" I asked, the madness replaying in my head.

"He disrespected you." Seir's powerful jaw clenched, and he swiped at his chest again. "They both did."

"You could have ignored him. Now everyone in there knows what we look like, that we like to cause trouble."

Seir shook his head. "Who will they tell? Besides, these people won't remember tonight for long. And if they do, descriptions both of us and of what happened will be mightily embellished, especially if it's the innkeeper or Kalob sharing the tale." Seir rolled his shoulders back, intentionally forcing some of the residual tension out. "He's lucky I didn't end his miserable life right there at the bar. Would have been simple enough."

The words came so easy, like such an act was no big deal. And I knew he meant it, every word. I huffed irritably, and Seir stopped mid-stride.

"Are you upset?"

"Yes, a little. We need to be more cautious. That inn had only men for patrons, and I know you noticed that as easily as I did. By calling the innkeeper out, by making Kalob apologize instead of just going along with things, you forced us into the center of attention, and we were already obviously outsiders. We need to be inconspicuous, don't we? What if it wasn't Ignus who arranged everything? What if we're being watched? Someone took me before, they could just as easily take me again." My tone had gone high and panicky. That was it, I realized. That was what I was afraid of more than anything.

"No, they couldn't." Seir looked me square in the eye, his hand rising to my shoulder. He moved slowly, so I could see what he was doing.

"Couldn't what?"

"Take you again. Nobody will take you anywhere you don't want to go ever again." His eyes glowed, and those sharp teeth ground together just enough for me to forget how to breathe.

Seir inhaled, forcing the muscles in his shoulders and fist to relax a fraction, though this upset was still palpable. The hand he'd put on my shoulder rose further, palm resting along my jaw. It was intimate and kept my focus completely on him. "I'm sorry to have put you in a position you didn't want to be in, but I will not apologize for what I did. Nobody should treat you like that, Hailon. It doesn't matter if it's some drunk in a shitty village inn." Another inhale, and his body finally unclenched. "But I suppose you're right, we should be more careful. And I'm happy to have all the fun on my own, but should I not be around or you'd prefer a turn, simply use your clever little blades, yes? Or perhaps borrow mine, it served you very well before. I'm sure you can do as much damage as I can and probably in less time. It would have a much larger impact coming from you, as well." He smiled at me, his eyes no longer red but back to their gold with a green ring, and all frustration was gone from his body language.

I didn't know what else to say. His mercurial mood should have been scary, but I understood it. And I was strangely honored by the gestures he'd displayed at the bar, even if it made me anxious. It had been so effortless, the way he handled things there, the same way he'd taken care of Ignus and his friends.

Nobody had ever stood up for me like that before. And now he'd done it twice.

"I will. Remember my knives, that is. Someday." I'd have to practice though, because I'd simply been too stunned by what was happening to consider doing anything myself. "Thank you."

A smile spread across his face. "You're welcome."

The sun had set completely while we were inside the inn. Most of the windows along Main Street were well lit by lamp or candle, and the moon provided a cool, white glow to the road.

As we approached what was clearly Ms. Welling's, given the red scarves tied to the posts on the porch and the rowdy laughter coming from inside, a woman leaned against the second-floor balcony rail.

"You folks the reason Kalob Brown ran out of the Scythe like his hair was on fire?"

Seir looked up at her, unable to hide his smile. "Perhaps. Though he didn't exactly introduce himself properly. He was having a bit of trouble breathing while we were getting acquainted."

She laughed, her voice rich and gravelly. "Good, he's needed someone to set him straight for a while now. We appreciate your service, stranger." She leaned over the rail, ample cleavage on display, though she could hardly help it given the gown she had on. She looked between us, analyzing the way his body was positioned in front of mine, just slightly off to one side. Her posture changed, her face set in a kind smile. "If you're needing a place for the night, Widow Callahan might be able to help you. She makes the best peach cobbler around and has a soft spot for young couples on their way through to visit family, like you all." Her eyebrow raised suggestively, and I nodded that I understood what she'd said. "Just head out of town on this main road. She's got the little homestead past the stone well with a green fence and chickens in the yard." The woman gave a wink and went back inside, leaving us staring after her, then at one another.

Seir turned to me, his eyes full of mischief. "Shall we go see if the widow is up for some company?"

CHAPTER 10
HAILON

"I BREAK MY FAST early, so don't worry about making noise if you're up and about. I'm usually awake before the roosters, much to my dismay. There's a special kind of joy to be had with a late morning lie-in, but I just can't seem to make my bones or my bladder understand that." The kind woman led us to a sizable barn at the back of her property with a lantern in her hand. "You're welcome to come up to the house for some biscuits and gravy whenever you're ready. It's an awfully long way to Ravenglen, I'm sure you'll be wanting to get an early start."

"Thank you, ma'am." I smiled at her, weariness tugging at my bones. "And thank you for sharing your supper with us, that was quite possibly the best cobbler I've ever eaten." There was no lie there, either. She truly had a gift. The woman at the brothel hadn't exaggerated.

"It's my pleasure, really. I'm so happy you enjoyed it!" Her gait had a bit of a limp to it as we crossed the uneven ground of the yard. "We get enough visitors passing through with the Scythe only having those four little rooms to offer that I went ahead and installed some facilities out here too." She winked at me, a grin on her face as she pulled open an oversize door on the side of the closed-up barn. "Was a kindness to myself as well, with this aging body of mine, truth be told. Feel free to use what you need. Water's straight from the pump, so it's cold, but it's clean." She gestured to a small bathroom right inside the main door.

"This is perfect, thank you very much for your hospitality." Seir did one of his fancy bows, his hair brushing the floor. When he stood back up, there were several pieces of straw tangled in the curled ends.

"Well, aren't you something?" She chuckled, lighting a lantern for us from the one she carried. "There're blankets and whatnot up in the loft. I leave the animals out in the pasture to mind themselves until it gets a little colder, so you won't have to worry about waking up snuggled with a goat or chicken."

Seir actually looked a bit disappointed at that. "Do you know of anyone looking to let or sell a beast?" he asked. "We'd be grateful for a way to travel a little faster."

She shook her head in a rueful way. "Sadly, no. We're a small community and only breed as many beasts as we can afford to keep. Lately that hasn't been many."

"Thank you," I said again, and she excused herself out the same big door we'd entered through. "Do you think we're going to run into a lot of this?"

Seir rubbed at his chin. "I don't know. I expected at least one farmer would be willing to part with a beast for the right price."

"Will our food and lodging set us back much?" I wasn't sure how much money we'd started out with exactly, but I knew my contribution wasn't nearly as significant as I'd hoped for it to be. The way he'd tossed around gold coins without reservation at the inn made me nervous.

"She gave me the coins back after you told her we had to get to Ravenglen to care for your sick aunt. That was a good addition to the story, by the way."

I bit the inside of my cheek, wondering how long it would take him to realize that bit about my aunt wasn't just a line to make our cover story more credible.

"Don't worry about money. Even if we run out of coin, I'll figure out a way to get us more. It'll be fine."

"We could sell some of the silver or jewelry." I nodded. That's why I'd taken it, after all. "We'll have to offer again tomorrow, just to be polite."

"Yes, of course. She's doing a very good job for someone on their own with a property like this. Did you see how fat the chickens are?"

I couldn't help but smile at his wide-eyed amusement. "How could you tell? They were all fluffed up and roosted for the night. Even a skinny chicken would look large."

"They're *very* well fed," he said seriously, nodding as though this were very important. Then he seemed a bit crestfallen. "We had roasted chicken for dinner."

It had been delicious too. Very comforting. Widow Callahan could open her own tavern as far as I was concerned and make an absolute fortune with her home-cooked meals. Seir's frown deepened. "Oh. Yes, I'm guessing one of the flock was what we ate, if that's what you mean."

He sighed. "Perhaps they *should* get overnight cuddle privileges with guests if they're also going to be their meal."

There was a moment of quiet while he contemplated the sad fate of farm-raised fowl, and I shifted my weight, legs tingly and exhausted. He hadn't been nearly so conflicted with the wild birds near the cabin.

"Do you mind if I ..." I gestured for the bathroom.

"No, no. Go ahead. Take the light."

"Will you be able to see?"

He grinned. "I'm well acclimated to the dark. I'll be fine."

I took the lantern down from the nail it was hung on and closed myself inside the tidy little bathroom. I washed the grime off my hands and face and rinsed out my mouth before deciding a hasty cloth bath would be better than nothing. There was a small tub made from a watering trough, but I had no desire to submerge myself in icy water.

When I was done, I made my way up the stairs—bless Widow Callahan for her ingenuity born of necessity; a ladder would have been far less friendly—and found Seir had spread out two blankets over some nest-like indentations in deep drifts of hay.

His grin was wide and infectious. "This will be very restful, I'm sure of it. Here, like this." He basically fell into one of the blankets and wiggled around until he was comfortable, his movements exaggerated for humorous effect. His tail thumped along in a contented way as he curled up, his strong, lean body once again reminding me of a cat. I had no idea how he could continue to move like that after the walking we'd done. My limbs had all started to feel like they were weighted with lead before we even left the dinner table.

I shook my head, but my heart had lightened watching him. He found joy in the strangest of places. I was happier he was with me all the time.

"Hailon?"

"Yes?" I removed my boots and the thick socks with a grateful sigh and laid down.

"If I ask you something, will you be honest with me?" He pillowed his head on his hands, looking at me as though about to share some gossip like Sal sometimes did after we wound down from a busy day.

"I guess, sure."

"I understand if you don't trust me enough to share something so personal, though I wish you would. Trust me, I mean."

Words stacked up on one another, clogging my throat. I had a protest half-formed, reasons I shouldn't. But the truth was that I did. I had no reason not to. To have so much faith in a demon I'd only known a few days left me feeling as though I were standing on a cliff, preparing to jump, and I wasn't sure why.

"I do." My voice was breathier than I intended. I cleared my throat and tried again. "I trust you."

His sharp smile appeared for a brief moment. Even that was growing on me. It was no longer strange, just endearing.

I shifted around in the little nest, copying his position. With my head on my bicep, my nerves ignited as I met his eye and shared the truth. I pulled at a piece of straw that had poked up through the weave of the blanket.

The corners of his eyes pinched with sincere concern. "I can understand anyone would want to return to their home, especially taken the way you were. But you also said you have to get back for your aunt?"

"Yes."

"Because she's not well?" I nodded, and he frowned. His tail seemed anxious, winding and unwinding around his leg. "I'm sorry."

"It's not your fault. She's been sick a very long time."

His expression was contemplative but open as he mulled over this information. "How long have you been gone?"

Dread curled around the lovely dinner in my gut, leaving me cold. *Too long.* "By my count, seventeen weeks." I'd never been away more than a single week before, and that was when Sal was far healthier. My trips into the mountains for rare herbs and flowers were always carefully scheduled around times I could afford to be away—generally those coincided with her healthiest times. I never left unless I could have Merry from the grocers or Gerald from the candler check in on Sal when they made deliveries.

"Do you use your ability on her?" he deduced quite wisely.

"Yes. Routinely."

"How many healing sessions has she missed?"

"Eight. Almost nine." The long silence was heavy.

"I will do everything I can to get you home quickly."

Something behind my ribs expanded at his solemn expression as he made the promise again, at the way his hand reached for mine across the borrowed blankets and squeezed my fingers. His thumb idly traced along my knuckles, and my throat clogged again. I breathed in through my nose, heart aching with every beat. I'd known this demon a length of time that could be calculated in mere hours, but he'd shown me more care, kindness, and loyalty than almost anyone else in my entire life had. "Thank you."

He smiled and wriggled around some more, fluffing areas of hay here and there. "I should go wash before getting too comfortable." He bounced back to his feet, wading through the straw. He disappeared down the stairs, leaving the light behind.

My mind was tired but spinning, trying to compartmentalize everything that had happened since Seir appeared in my room. I hardly knew how to handle several days of decent meals, good sleep, and a trustworthy constant companion.

I curled my legs up tighter to my chest, the straw bed indeed quite comfortable with the help of the thick, clean-smelling blanket. With my head pillowed on my hands, my eyelids grew heavy. Once I closed them to ease the gritty burn, it was already too late.

The sound of Seir coming up the stairs registered in my mind, but I couldn't have moved if I wanted to. My body had given over completely to resting. He blew out the lantern and shuffled around a bit in the straw.

"Sweet dreams, Hailon."

Sleep took me as the warmth of another blanket was gently draped over my body.

CHAPTER 11
SEIR

HAILON WAS STILL curled up in a little ball, her breathing slow and even as I willed my body to relax back into slumber. I'd slept a bit, but it was still hours from dawn. Normally, I'd get up, wander down to the unit desk and check on my assignments. Pop over for an in person visit if needed, write up my reports. It was a comforting routine, if boringly predictable. I absently calculated how long I'd been gone, finding it still far less than a shift cycle. I also wondered if I faced any kind of reprimand for being gone, despite having been summoned.

Turning on my side, I allowed myself several long minutes of watching the little human as she dreamt, my thoughts tangled and distracted.

Her hands were tucked under her cheek, her knees drawn up close to her chest. I wondered if I should perhaps have given her a third blanket the way she was curled up. Her slight form moved with every breath she took, a slow expansion and deflation. Even sleeping, she was lovely.

I, on the other hand, was a mess since having come topside. I was sleeping even less than usual despite my vigorous activity. My chest ached at odd moments, sometimes so fiercely I worried I might be ill. Even the smallest notion of approval from this fierce woman brought me pride so intense every part of my body responded.

Every. Part.

I scrubbed my hands across my face and turned away from her, scrunching my eyes closed. I'd had my share of lovers, but none of them ever affected me in such a way. It was a slow, delicious ache from the moment she looked at me until I saw the first breath of a smile. There was no relief from the crushing pressure of wanting to make her happy or being sure she was fed and cared for. And I might not ever have been summoned before, but I knew this was not part of that contract. This was different. I just couldn't explain how or why.

Had circumstances been even slightly different, Kalob would not have survived our encounter. His joke had been anything but funny, and the slight to her honor had struck me in a deeply personal way. Which ... was odd but not altogether unwelcome. The fierce little creature needed someone to take up for her, and that might as well be me.

After tossing and turning for perhaps another hour, I finally relented and climbed out of the little hay nest. Down on the main level of the barn, organization seemed to be an afterthought. Tools were scattered down a long workbench, many rusty or broken. Bales were stacked in a way that would be dangerous for the widow should she pull the wrong one first. So, grateful to have a task to focus on, I got to work.

By the time the roosters stirred, the large cubes of hay had been moved around into much more sensible stacks. I'd also repaired a set of shears missing their spring, fitted a new handle on a hatchet and had organized several sets of tools by size and type. Everything needed a good grinding and oiling to fend off the rust, but that was a problem for another day and someone else.

I left the barn as quietly as I could once the faint orange of dawn seeped through the cracks in the walls and roof, not surprised when I found the widow tossing grain and scraps to the fowl.

"You're up early," she said by way of greeting.

"I don't sleep much."

"Mmm. I understand that all too well. Would you mind drawing the water? I need to fill that trough."

"Of course."

"Did you find the loft suitable?"

"It was perfect, thank you again for your generosity. We'd love to repay your kindness." I patted the coin purse in my pocket, but she shook her head.

"I'm sure we can find an arrangement that suits. Keep your money. You have a long way to travel once you leave this place."

The next hour or so went like that, the pair of us moving in companionable quiet until she found me a little task to do, one that she always did given normal circumstances but was happy enough not to have to manage herself.

"Blessings to you, young man," she sighed, clapping her hands together to dust them off. "I promised you biscuits and gravy. I'll go heat everything up for you if you want to fetch your lady friend."

"I'll get her in a moment," I said, walking back to where the chickens were all contentedly pecking at the scratch in the dirt.

I sat down among them, offering some of the treat from my palm.

As luck would have it, Hailon wandered out just as a hen decided my shoulder was a decent place to stand. I also had one on each knee, eating from my hands.

"Good morning," I whispered with a smile, finding her adorably rumpled, though I could tell she'd made an attempt to put her hair to rights and had washed her face—her collar was still wet.

"Morning," she grumbled.

"Did you sleep well?" The chickens fled in a flurry of feathers and noise as I spoke normally and made the slightest movement with my body.

"Well enough." She looked around. "How long have you been up?"

"Not sure. But I've been productive."

"I see that. You're making friends?" She gestured to the chickens as I got to my feet.

"Apologizing for making supper of their sister."

"Ah. Have you been up to the house?"

"Yes, but I haven't eaten yet. The biscuits should just be coming out of the oven, in fact. Are you hungry?"

Hailon nodded, covering her mouth as she yawned. "Yes, actually. And I'm very much looking forward to eating her cooking again after last night."

We stopped back at the barn before heading to the house. I gathered our packs, which I'd left near the stairs, then followed Hailon across the grassy yard. Widow Callahan had the first batch of biscuits in a towel-lined basket on the table and was busy rolling out more dough when we joined her.

"Good morning! Please, help yourself. Tea's fresh."

We thanked the kindly woman, Hailon watching her with rapt interest as she used a wooden rolling pin to flatten the dough on a big slab of butcher board, then cut it into neat circles with the rim of a small drinking glass.

"Won't you join us?" I asked once she'd closed the oven door with the fresh pan of little circles safely inside. I couldn't help feeling badly that the woman was still on her feet instead of resting.

"Yes, I think I will." She smiled gently, her gait increasingly hobbled as she crossed the kitchen.

Hailon's head tilted to the side as Widow Callahan spooned a decadent berry jam onto a steaming biscuit.

"Forgive me for asking, but do your joints ache?"

The widow laughed openly. "Only always. Nothing much helps for long, especially when there's weather coming. Another blessing of getting older, I suppose."

Hailon finished her food and carried her plate to the sink, washing whatever she could despite weak protests from our host.

After drying her hands on a towel, she pulled out the freshly baked batch of biscuits and set the pan on the stovetop.

"Shit!" Hailon hissed, cradling her hand to her chest as she turned to the faucet.

"Are you alright?" I asked, already on my feet.

"I bumped the pan is all, just a little burn. I'm clumsy in the kitchen, always have been."

"Here." The widow got to her feet, retrieving a pot of ointment from one of the cabinets. "I burn myself all the time. This one will help."

"Thank you." Hailon applied the salve, turning back to our host. "I'm sorry, I seem to have taken too much." The widow scooped the ointment back from Hailon, rubbing it into her hands.

"No problem at all dear. My hands are rather dry, this will fix them right up."

"Can I ask what kind of ointment that is?"

"Just a concoction my granny swore by. Beeswax and calendula with a little arnica mixed in. Not often we get a healer 'round these parts, so we make do ourselves. Heard tell of someone over in Olinbourg, but that fella who comes to peddle her ability isn't the good kind." Her mouth pinched. "I worry about that healer."

If she only knew how right she was. Satisfied that the crisis was managed, I sat back down and helped myself to another serving of breakfast, unsure where our journey might lead us after we left this place.

"Do you know where we could get some better boots for her? I'm afraid the ones she's got aren't suited for long days of traveling."

"They're fine really." Hailon frowned. "With the extra socks, I don't slide as much."

The older woman watched us with amusement. "Afraid those kinds of things are scarce until you get up to the Valley. Plenty once you do, though. I make a couple of trips a year to keep myself well stocked on everything I can't get between here and Olinbourg." She scanned Hailon head to toe. "You could always check with the girls at the bawdy house, but I'm guessing spare boots are not a likely find in their closets. I'd offer you some of my own to get you by, but I'm betting they'd be far too small."

"That's alright. Thank you anyway," Hailon rushed to say, cheeks pink.

She nodded, then flexed her fingers several times, a perplexed expression on her face. "Funny. My hands don't hurt near as much now. Perhaps I should use that ointment more often."

Hailon offered a gentle smile, and I wondered if she'd done something neither the widow nor I could see.

We helped clean up, and the kind woman put together a whole separate pack of food for us, along with more blankets and odds and ends for camping that she claimed were taking up space in her cupboards. We were well outfitted thanks to her generosity.

"Better used by you folks than rotting away here. Hope they serve you well."

Unable to stop myself, I threw my arms around them both. "This is so nice!"

The woman's laugh started as a rumble but turned into a full-bodied cackle. She had tears leaking from her eyes she was laughing so hard by the time we all let go of the hug. "I don't think I'll forget this visit of ours. I'll have to thank Scarlet for sending you my way. She's always keen on a batch of my cobbler."

She never did take any of the coin we offered, but she'd find a little stack of coins in one of her tool drawers one day soon, and the silver candlestick in the pail of grain for the chickens when she went out to feed them their dinner.

I hoped it made her laugh.

CHAPTER 12
HAILON

WITH YET A third pair of socks, a mismatched set borrowed from the widow's pile of mending, my boots were nearly a perfect fit. My feet were snug inside the leather as we made our way down the dirt road toward the Emankor Valley. I was grateful, because the blisters had burst, and I now had rudimentary bandages over the raw skin on both heels. At least I had the ointment.

Seir mumbled to himself, his thumbs laced through the straps of his pack, and his normally jovial expression pulled tight in concentration.

"We'll find an inn soon, probably," I assured him. "There may be towns not shown on that little map, besides. Honestly, I'm surprised that last one was, since it's so small."

He turned to me, tense expression melting into a smile. "Perhaps, yes. If not, maybe we'll run along another way-house. There's not much out here, and those are mainly intended for weary travelers with no other option in places such as these."

I lovingly remembered of the little cabin we'd left behind. The soft mattress, hot water bath, and plentiful food. We were definitely not as badly off as we could be, but the comfort and luxury of that place would stay with me for a very long time.

"Are you familiar with all of Cyntere?" I asked. I thought I knew the answer, being that he'd found me so easily in Olinbourg and seemed to know where Ravenglen was in comparison.

"No, not all." He kicked a stone with the toe of his boot. "I've visited some places, but my way of travel is not something that requires good directional ability."

"I'm not sure I understand."

He quirked his mouth to the side and glanced at the sky, as though searching for the words to formulate his response.

"You understand how portals work?"

"Yes. They're like doorways to other places."

"Exactly. And sifting? Or jumping?"

"That's where you can move somewhat long distances, right? Just by thinking of the place you want to go?"

"Yes!" He clapped his hands and did an interesting little hop, clearly pleased with my answer. "You know a great deal about many things, Hailon Derne. While those two are very, very handy for fast movement, they don't need anything other than minimal information to work. I was able to find you in Olinbourg, for example, because I knew of a nearby portal. Had you not told me the name of the place, I wouldn't have found my way back easily, not even having your face as my focal point." He flashed a wide smile, as though pleased he'd managed to get that key information out of me when it was most important. "And when we were leaving, I was going to use my ability to take us where you needed to go based on how I remember Ravenglen ... feeling."

"Feeling?"

"Yes. Every place has a certain way it leaves an impression on you, wouldn't you agree? I think of that as how a town or region feels. Sometimes it's a certain smell, or the way the wind moves through the trees. The color of the sky ... could be anything." He gestured to the sky with a flourish, his long fingers splayed wide. The lacquer on his nails had gotten so chipped it was nearly gone altogether. I wondered what he'd used and if there was a way for him to replace it soon. I rather liked the black gloss on his tan hands.

"That makes sense." I accepted the water flask he offered, resisting the urge to make a face when he smiled and bobbed his head encouragingly. We'd made some progress as a traveling pair. He'd taken to suggesting things that would keep me more comfortable, and I was doing my best to not be quite so eager to ignore my needs in the interest of traveling faster.

"So going by foot is a lot harder, for obvious reasons." His ears reddened. I could only assume that meant he was embarrassed. My ears burned terribly both when I told lies and when I was feeling shame about something. "It seems I underestimated how scarce horses and wagons might be, to start. I'll admit I was excited by the notion of journeying slowly, but this much time by foot wasn't really a consideration. I expected to have my wings, if nothing else."

"I feel like somehow that may be my fault," I muttered.

He frowned at me, the abnormal seriousness in his golden eyes intense. "Not at all. We'll figure out the reason soon enough. My point is, I'm not used to having to navigate much. Directionality while being bound to the ground is an added layer of difficulty I should have anticipated but did not."

"You don't have to know what direction you're going when you jump or anything?"

He shook his head, the flush that had started in his ears deepening and spreading to his cheeks as well. "No. Portals, sifting, those are a simple exercise in trust and visualization of your destination. There's no walking, planning for camp, or tracking the way the sun and stars move required. And with wings, one can gain a distant perspective on things from the sky. Walking is far more complicated."

"Ah. I see." We fell into a quiet lull for a while. I thought about how little I'd ventured beyond my sleepy town settled up against the northern mountains. Despite that, I'd learned how to find north by the stars and to stay put if I ever wandered too far into the woods. I knew the sun rose in the east and set in the west, and the phases of the moon. A demon, one who didn't even spend a significant amount of time on Earth wouldn't have much reason to know those things. "Can I look at the map?" I asked. "When we stop for a rest, I mean."

"Of course." Seir smiled over at me, but his normal lighthearted personality was weighed down by his thoughts.

"I DON'T THINK anything on here is very well scaled," I said over a mouthful of the dry biscuit-like bread the widow had packed for us. "But that would be difficult with anything drawn this small. It seems to heavily favor the southern area too. There's not much at all over near Vincara, and Austern is almost an afterthought altogether." I turned the map his direction, tracing with my finger. "I think if we follow this line, the water, that's probably our best bet."

"Agreed." Seir studied the little map a bit more, then rolled it up and put it away. "We should be able to follow alongside that creek or river until it disappears into the mountains. Once it starts to curve, we can go the opposite direction into the Valley and then north."

"And avoid the ruins." I nodded, glad to have some kind of plan even if that meant I was walking another several days.

"Sadly, yes." He frowned. I understood his personality enough now to know that missing out on a vengeful spirit haunting a crumbled castle was almost certainly a terrible disappointment. "The closer we get to that many villages and towns, the more likely we'll encounter wagons and other road traffic, perhaps even multiple roads to choose from." This notion perked him back up, and we continued on until it was time to make camp again for the night.

Sitting around our little fire after a hasty rinse in the frigid stream with yet another version of campfire stew, I finally asked a question that lingered in the back of my mind.

"What is it that you do, exactly?"

Seir grinned, breaking off a chunk of the hard bread with his teeth and stirring it into the contents of his bowl to soften before answering. "I'm a prince. I have twenty-six legions under my command, though I don't often use my title or my men these days. Because of how I'm able to travel, I'm mainly a messenger and given far more freedom to do what I like than many."

"Is it like how humans have kings, princes, and all that?" I used some of the softened bread to soak up the last of my soup, wiping the bowl clean before I ate it.

"Sort of." He illustrated a ladder with his hands as he listed titles off, top to bottom. "There are kings, dukes, princes, marquises, then earls, knights, and presidents. But the designations aren't necessarily like they are here. For example, my brother Ipos is both a prince and an earl, and my other brother Tap is both a prince and a great president. You can be awarded several legions on a whim or have them taken away if someone else needs them more." He shrugged. "It's loosely merit based but also not. Every last one of us has a unique talent, and no single one of us is in charge, though a few have taken to management much better than others." He smiled, a secretive lift to his lips.

"So, you're both in charge of legions and also ... not in charge?"

"Yes! Exactly." He nodded, clearly pleased with my understanding, which if I were being honest, was less clear than before I asked. "Hell is like anywhere else. There are lots of things happening, plenty of people looking busy all the time. Things going on everywhere, but everyone is stuck in their own little life. Not much has clear reason or explanation beyond your individual area or assignment. Not even if you ask, most of the time. Does that make sense?"

"I suppose so."

"Would you like to practice my sigil once or twice?" He was almost hesitant in the way he asked, scooting closer to my bedroll with a stick in his hand. "Just in case? You did a lovely job of it before, but you were copying from the book, right?"

"Yes. I should probably learn how to do it without an example to mimic."

He beamed and drew it out in the dirt. "You try."

I found my own twig to use and copied his mark. He'd made it look so effortless, but I needed lots of practice. I drew it several more times, making sure I had the twists and lines the same way he did.

"Here." He came over and knelt behind me, his body pressed against my back. I held my breath as he placed his warm hand over mine on the stick, directing the flicks and swirls. My pulse pounded in my ears, the same electric feeling passing between us everywhere he touched me. I was suddenly hot despite the chill of the evening.

"It reminds me of a cloud, a little bit," I said, tilting my head to the side. I'd thought it was a circle, but there were little bumps and spots where the design narrowed.

"Wings." The word was warm against my hair. My chest ached again at the reminder that something so important to him had been suppressed somehow, and I didn't even know why or how to fix it. "The outline is wings, then through the center is my name, more or less." He stayed there for several long minutes, his heartbeat thumping against my shoulder blade, voice rumbling against my ribs as his hand directed mine. It took everything I had just to keep breathing somewhat normally.

We drew his sigil over and over again in the dirt, until I could do it without the example or his help. To my amusement, he used the tip of his tail to brush the designs away when we ran out of space, so we could start again.

Finally, he was satisfied with my proficiency and returned to his own blanket. I frowned, something right under my ribs burning like my dinner wasn't sitting well.

"Should we practice a circle too?" he teased. "Are you tired of me? Ready to send me back now that you know exactly how to draw it out?"

"No, not quite yet." Truth was, I already couldn't imagine a day without him. Banishing him away from me was the furthest thing from my mind.

"That's good." His voice dropped to just above a whisper. "I'm not ready to leave."

"Are the sigils all similar?" I asked, uncomfortable in the silence that had fallen between us.

"Yes and no. There's a general idea that runs through them all. It's a language. It would make more sense if you knew that alphabet going into things."

"Will you teach me?" I blushed hard as the words came out of my mouth, then somehow more, when he responded.

Seir bowed his head, rolled his wrist several times in a posh wave and then looked straight through me, leaving a strange mix of anxiety and heat pooled in my stomach. "I'll teach you whatever you like, my lady. All you need to do is ask."

CHAPTER 13
SEIR

I SLEPT MORE THAT night on a thin bedroll next to a dying fire under the stars than I had since that first night at the little way-house cabin. I would always fondly remember the pallet she'd made for me out of the bed's soft blankets.

My intriguing companion had my name and could easily write my sigil from memory, which brought me more relief than I'd thought it would. If we were somehow separated and she attempted to summon me, I could return to her.

I liked the idea that she could bring me to her side whenever she pleased. A lot.

The notion lightened my feet as we efficiently broke camp and started down the road once again.

"Is it odd that there aren't other travelers out here at all?" Hailon asked after our lunch stop, a crown on her head made from a chain of white and purple daisies. She'd made it while we ate our increasingly mismatched food. It was whimsical and suited her, though she'd donned it with endearing hesitation. It was almost as though someone had made her afraid to be playful. I hated that for her and swore to always encourage her to enjoy little things like flower crowns.

"Yes," I answered plainly. In truth, the lack of other traffic had been increasingly worrisome. There hadn't been any other people on the road since we'd left Eddington, and even then, none of the wagons had been going the same direction we were. The lack of friendliness with those sparse interactions felt odd as well, the more I thought about it.

The Emankor Valley was a whole group of little villages and towns, a whole area rich in farmland and commerce. To see nobody coming or going at all on what had to be a main road between it and the southern towns was very noticeable. Additionally, the ill temperament of the horses we did encounter was unusual. Surely they couldn't all be that unhappy.

The second day headed north along the river, trees became more closely grouped together along the sides of the road, and I could feel the incline of the road changing as well. The smell of the water nearby was stronger, though we had yet to really see it unless we wandered a reasonable distance off the road.

Conversation had fallen off once again, as we focused on one foot in front of the other. Thankfully, the weather had become cooler and there was a nice breeze.

I stretched my arms out wide, then followed that with my wings, prompting a startled squeak out of Hailon.

"Sorry."

"It's alright. I just saw them in my periphery and ..." She trailed off. "I can't believe I'm saying these words out loud, but I'm used to seeing your tail moving somewhere around your legs. But the wings are right at eye level, so they surprised me."

Amused, I flexed them, a nice stretch and relax so the tip of the one nearest her touched her shoulder, like a fingertip tapping to get her attention.

"Hey." She brushed me away with her hand, but a relaxed smile graced her mouth.

"How do you know so much about demons?" I tried to reach for my magic, to encourage my body to lift from the ground, but nothing happened.

"Aunt Sal." Hailon looked away from me, her focus on the road straight ahead as she spoke.

"And the magic?"

Hailon's hands rose to her hair, the nervous habit she had of tugging at the uneven ends as I'd neglected to offer braids before we left our rough camp. "She's a wise woman."

"So, she knows more than most?"

"Yes." Her eyes flashed, her expression serious again. I missed her smile. "She prepared me for every possibility she could think of, especially when my healing gift revealed itself."

"Then the real question is more 'How did Sal know?'" I said the words in a playful way, wings still out wide and getting their own workout while we walked.

"I have no idea. But she taught me about demons and angels. Some about the fae too. The history as we knew it about them all. Witches and magic in all its forms, and how we could both recognize and use it."

"Is your aunt a witch?" I asked, excited and intrigued. "Are you?"

"Sal may be, but I don't think her power is very strong if she is. Her magic is more in skill as an herbalist."

"And you?" I prompted again.

Hailon shrugged. "I don't know. I'm not talented in anything other than my healing ability, but my only teacher in that arena was Sal, so who knows."

"Well, the good news is I know several, so if you find yourself near Revalia and you'd like an introduction at some point ..."

"That's kind, thanks." Red dotted her cheeks. I enjoyed that nearly as much as her smile.

"Are there no other healers in Ravenglen?"

Hailon shook her head. "Sal was the first in a very long while. I guess everyone used to wait for a traveling healer to come through a few times a year before her."

"Was she born there?" I asked. Something about this situation wasn't adding up for me, but the ins and outs of human city life were not my area of expertise.

"No, we moved there after my parents left me with her."

"I see. And Sal's good with medicines?"

"Very. She can take herbs and flowers and turn them into a syrup or tincture to battle whatever the ailment is. I was out doing the seasonal gather when I was taken." She paused, eyes unfocused like she was recalling something, but it was fleeting. "Between Sal and I, we keep everyone well—as much as we are able, anyway. Nothing is foolproof." There was sorrow there, I could see it in the way her eyebrows pinched together. Any good healer lost patients. It was just part of things, though that didn't make it any easier when it happened.

"That sounds very like a couple of my sisters-in-law. So do you have a shop in the city?"

"No, just our house." Her mouth pinched. There was something there she wasn't ready to share with me quite yet.

The road started a noticeable climb shortly after, the path getting narrower and the embankment up the side down to nothing more than rocks and trees.

"What are we climbing to, I wonder?" I muttered mostly to myself, keeping my body closest to the edge of the dirt road. Hailon stuck to the centermost point of the path as possible, the road rising up with a steep slope down either side.

The wind had begun to blow more aggressively as well, great gusts chasing up pine needles and leaves and dirt straight into our faces. It almost felt personal, which was ... odd. I tucked my wings down, but didn't yet stow them away.

"Let me have your pack, Hailon." I reached out a hand for it, trying to see as far ahead as I could. The perspective seemed unusually narrowed, like something was blocking us from seeing more than perhaps a hundred paces.

"I've got it," she argued, thumbs hooked into the straps as she trudged forward, watching her feet.

I frowned, uneasy. Everything felt off. The weather, the trees. The way the road had suddenly narrowed and climbed several hundred feet with no relief to either side without a painful slide down through the trees. My tail whipped around, seeking the source of my agitation.

Our pace had slowed, Hailon's breath had become labored because of the incline.

"Here," I said, pausing to dig out a waterskin for her.

"I'm okay. Let's just keep going."

"No, you need to have a drink." She accepted the jug from my hand in a gesture that could only be called a snatch, and I was rewarded with a sassy swig and side-eye as she drank deep.

"Satisfied?"

"Not hardly. What else can you offer me?" I winked at her, just to continue the banter. To my amusement, the corner of her mouth twitched as she shook her head. Flirting with her was as easy as breathing, and I only wanted to do it more often the longer we were together.

"Let's just keep moving, ridiculous demon. This place makes me uneasy."

"Agreed." I scanned the trees, seeking a reason for the watched feeling. Still, there was nothing obvious. Then it hit me. "There are no birds. No insects. It's too quiet. There's magic here."

"You're right." Hailon's voice was barely above a whisper as we stopped walking and both looked around. "What *is* this place?"

"I'm not sure. Let's not linger. If I had to guess, the place where the road curves can't be too far off. I expected us to hit it by nightfall."

As I slid the waterskin back into my pack, I stepped closer to the outer edge of the path. The soft soil gave under my foot, and I flung my wings out wide. A gust of wind pushed me further from the center of the road, then, with one leg dangling off the side as I tried to right myself, I was no longer on the road at all.

Wondering how I'd managed such a thing, I was a clumsy mess of limbs and wings, desperately trying to grab the dirt with my fingers to slow myself down or grab a little tree with my tail. Hailon shouted my name from somewhere above me as I tumbled down the embankment, narrowly dodging trees and taking a fair beating from the stones that happened to be in my path.

I skidded to a stop at the very bottom and could only watch in horror as Hailon began the treacherous descent herself.

CHAPTER 14
HAILON

"Well, this is embarrassing." Seir grinned up at me, the smile fading into a wince as he tried to shift his weight. "You were much more graceful than I was getting down here."

He wasn't wrong there. I'd slid down the rocky embankment entirely on my feet, which was much more than I could say for him. It had taken far longer than I liked, but with the help of the skinny new-growth trees, I'd managed not to fall or hurt myself on the way down.

"Stop moving," I ordered sternly, dropping down to my knees at his side so I could better examine the wound. My stomach pitched and rolled when I spotted the pointed shard of bone on the outside of his skin instead of the inside, where it belonged. "Seir, your leg." Then I saw the blood blooming across his shirt. "Oh, *fuck*." I whispered the curse, but he heard it clearly enough.

The tan skin of his face had paled in a worrisome way, his breath coming in sharp pants as he propped himself up on his elbows, wincing. "Can't be all that bad, right? Just bandage me up, and we'll be on our way. Surely there's a way to get back to the road. Oh." He grunted as he pulled his shirt tails out of his trousers and then above the bleeding. There was a branch of some kind protruding from the center of his body, in the crease between two of his abdominal muscles. His eyes closed and his head tipped back, nostrils flaring as he dragged in slow, measured breaths.

I swallowed, throat dry as my shaking hands hovered over the limb, unsure where to start. "I don't think it's going to be that easy."

He leaned up, slowly moving his eyes from my face back to the concerning injuries. "Isn't that terribly ... inconvenient."

My eyebrows slammed together at his detached assessment of the situation. Break aside, he had to have some pretty serious scrapes from the way he'd skidded down the rocky hill. Was he already in shock? I'd seen his desensitization to things like hot pots in action, but could he be immune to mortal physical pain altogether?

His wings had been out when he started to fall, and they were folded awkwardly behind him now. I peered closer at the way one was bent and realized with no small amount of horror that it wasn't a branch that had punctured the demon. It was a bone from his own wing.

My hands shook, bile rising hot and sour in my throat as I tried to figure out how exactly I was going to help him. I could fix it. I could. It would just take some time.

I glanced up in time to see his eyelids flutter and kicked out a foot so that his pack slid enough to cushion his head as he fainted.

"Saints and devils," I swore, leaning up toward Seir's face. I slapped his cheeks, willing him to regain consciousness. He gasped and coughed several long seconds later, his gaze unfocused when his eyes finally opened again. "Hey. You with me?"

"I'm here," he said, still sounding breathless. He inhaled deep, and I could actually see him become centered. "I've been hurt plenty, but this is something new." He grinned again, back to himself enough to be thrilled by the prospect of a novel experience, even if it was not a good one. He was truly bizarre, but I admired his pluck.

I handed him the pack strap. "You'll want to bite down on this."

"I will?" He looked at the fabric, then back at me before placing it between his teeth. I appreciated the blind trust he was putting in me because this was likely going to hurt.

"On three, okay?"

Seir nodded, and I put my hands on either side of the break, heart bruising my ribs it was pounding so hard. Of all the wounds and illnesses I'd healed, bones broken in this way had always been my least favorite thing to manage. My gift could knit them back together on the inside, repair the muscle and flesh given enough time and energy, but I had to do the hard part by hand first.

"One, two ..." I gripped and pulled, twisting the limb and forcing the bone back where it belonged all in one hasty, adrenaline-fueled motion. It used nearly every muscle in my upper body to accomplish, but it seemed to have done the trick. I had yelled with the effort it took, the birds and other small creatures fleeing from the trees at the abrupt sound.

At least down here there *were* such animals. Perhaps the strangeness was limited to the road itself.

Seir hadn't even cried out but stared at me with his eyes wide and his chest heaving as I dug around in my pack for some cloth to tie it with.

He spat the strap out, bewildered but not angry. "Three, Hailon. You said on *three*."

"Sorry. Too many experiences with a patient backing out at the last second forced me to adapt a work-around. Telling you that ahead of time would have ruined the element of surprise." He blinked at me. "How does it feel?"

"I honestly have no idea how to answer that."

"I'll heal you up, but we have to get somewhere I can focus first. Don't go anywhere."

He chuckled, using his sleeve to blot the sweat from his brow. "I'll do my best to stay put."

I stood and turned around, trying to assess where we'd landed. Hopefully there was somewhere we could shelter for the night nearby, somewhere I could work safely … fast.

Trying to keep Seir within sight, I walked in the direction of the sound of water. We'd need to clean ourselves up, in any case, and there might be some fresh berries or maybe even fish. I was not a great hunter, but between the forest and fresh water, there was bound to be something useful.

I walked until the top of Seir's head was barely visible over the stones and timber as the ground sloped down toward a reasonably sized stream. It was likely the one on the map, the one we thought we'd been following the whole time, but at this point I was unsure about much of anything on the little scrap of parchment.

"That'll do nicely," I muttered aloud, carefully stepping over obstacles toward a grouping of large boulders. The largest of them had a natural curve we could easily fit underneath even standing up and a flat area below. If nothing else, we'd be out of the elements should another rainstorm come through.

Making a quick pass, I used my boot to scuff the smaller rocks and sticks out of the way, creating a somewhat smooth floor for us to sit on. We could lean against the wall of rock comfortably, and if I started a fire, the smoke would vent and some of the heat would still be retained. It was just about as perfect as it was going to get given the circumstances.

I returned to Seir and grabbed both of our packs to take over first. By the time I got back to him again, he was already sitting up on his own and fiddling with the hasty bandage.

"Leave it," I scolded gently.

His expression was a mix of guilt and chagrin when he looked up at me. "Sorry. Just curious."

"Think you can make it over there with my help?" I pointed.

The demon was his normal unflappable self. "If you let me lean on you, I'm sure that won't be a problem."

Seir looped his tail around my waist, and I ducked under the arm on his injured side, using the strength in my legs to get him vertical. His stomach wound was a bit of a hindrance, but we were able to make slow progress toward the shelter. I watched the bleeding carefully, pleased that it had slowed. I might have time to fix him properly after all.

"Thank you," he said after we'd successfully lowered him down again.

"I'm going to make a fire before we get started. I never know exactly how much it's going to take out of me, but bones are difficult. We'll need to remove ... that." I gestured vaguely to his midsection.

He looked down, hands hovering over the wound. "I'm fine, really. Embarrassed, mostly. It's my fault we're in this predicament, after all. If you slide my pack closer, I'll start assembling supplies while you work on the fire." He was almost somber, which was more worrisome than the injury itself. I'd never seen him so serious. It made my chest feel tight.

I did as he requested, leaving both packs within his reach as I gathered stones to make a fire ring and enough wood to keep us warm through the night.

The adrenaline kept me moving, busily getting things in order for us to be somewhat secure while I healed him. The rush started to wane as the first sparks took the dried grass I'd use as kindling. My hands gained a tremble, and a cold sweat broke out across my body, leaving me feeling clammy.

"You're very skilled at that," Seir complimented quietly. "You've prepared us a comfortable dwelling with hardly more than stones and branches. I should make us something to eat."

"You'll do no such thing! And I don't know that I'd go that far, but I appreciate the compliment." I sighed, sitting down next to him. I was mentally readying myself to pull his broken wing out of his body, and he was worried about food and the comfort of a fully stone shelter.

"You don't give yourself nearly enough credit, Hailon. Now or … ever. At least not that I've seen."

Here we were again with the flattery. I shook my head. Even bleeding, the demon simply couldn't seem to help himself. Not that I minded, of course, it was just very foreign.

I excused myself quickly and dashed to the water where I washed my hands as best I could and wet down the cleanest of our extra cloths.

"Are you ready?" I asked. He'd gone even paler than before. There was no more time to waste.

"I'm at your whim, Hailon. How do you want me?" The way he arched his brow told me he'd intentionally chosen words that lended heavily to innuendo. I understood then that he was exaggerating his flirting—his humor was a way to cope.

"It's okay to be afraid," I whispered, and his bravado faltered. His smile slid from his face, and I could plainly see the worry in his eyes.

I lowered him to his side, heart thudding heavily every time he so much as held his breath in discomfort. Once he was as positioned as well as I could get him, I sat myself between his body and the stone wall, sending up prayers to whatever deity might be listening that I could use a little bit of help with this task.

"On three," I said softly, wrapping my fingers around the tip of his wing, one foot on either side of where the exposed bone stabbed through his back.

"I'm not falling for that again," he huffed, fingers flexing against the dirt floor, like he was trying to claw his way through to brace better.

"Your choice. One, two ..." He scrunched his eyes closed, and I pushed with my legs and pulled with my arms. The nauseating sucking sound his flesh made as the bone pulled free drowned out my final count. He hadn't done more than pull in a harsh breath to indicate he felt what was happening. "Okay. It's okay." I crouched over him, one hand trying to staunch the bleeding at the front, the other from the back. I closed my eyes and reached for my ability, channeling the power through my hands.

Beneath the layers of his flesh, my magic sought out what it interpreted as *the bad* and began to remove it, which sped healing. First came sealing up the little bit of organ that had gotten nicked. It was something very much like a human kidney. Then came stopping the bleeding. I could do the finer work on this, his wing and his leg all at once, I just had to get the urgent issues taken care of first.

"Hailon." Seir's voice was soft, one large, warm hand covering mine over the wound in his abdomen. I looked away from where my hand covered the hole in his back and found his eyes golden, glowing. "Thank you." That hand lifted, cupping my face as he gave me a weak smile that went straight through to my soul.

Then, he passed out cold.

CHAPTER 15
HAILON

"SEIR!" I SHOUTED his name several times. "You're not dead, you ridiculous demon. You're going to be fine." I repeated the words as though my insistence would ensure they were true. I was reassured, however, when I found his heartbeat strong under my palm, and his breathing steady. "Don't do that again!" I said fiercely when his eyes opened, tears prickling and a lump in my throat.

The injuries I could deal with, there were logical steps I could take to repair flesh and bone. But I didn't know how much blood volume a demon had, their pain tolerance, their healing capabilities. What if I'd missed a compromised organ and he was bleeding to death on the inside? I spiraled into panic, my breath coming as pants and vision going blurry.

He sat up, both hands gently cradling my face. The feel of his warm, calloused skin grounded me. "Hey. Look at me. Hailon." I met his eye, finding the same concern I was feeling reflected back at me. "I'm *fine*," he insisted. "Okay? Really. I've survived much worse than this with far lower standards of care. Everything is going to be alright." I nodded but didn't have complete faith in his assessment. He was still too pale, and his face had a sheen of sweat on it. "Do you trust me?"

"I've already told you I do."

His mouth eased into a gentle grin. "I know, I remember. I just like hearing you say it." He brushed away a tear from my cheek with his thumb. "I promise, if I were worried, I would tell you. Okay?"

We stared at each other for several heartbeats, the intensity of his gaze making my pulse stutter, breaths providing less oxygen. Finally, I managed to nod.

"I ... need to keep working."

"Of course. How can I help?" He drew his hands away from my cheeks, and I realized the intimate gesture had left me more reassured than I expected.

We negotiated a way for him to lie comfortably where he was, at least long enough to set the bones in his wing.

"You will heal some on your own, right?" I asked, using one of the wet cloths to wipe away the dried blood on his back before gently lifting his broken wing.

"Yes. Even if you did nothing else, I would be well enough to continue on my way in a few days, though perhaps with a splint on my leg, a noticeable limp, and lots of soreness. Here, allow me." He pulled the mangled end of his wing over his hip and, without any hesitation or warning, snapped the crooked bones back into their proper places. His jaw was clenched tight, but he fixed it himself with brutal efficiency and barely a grunt of discomfort.

My stomach rolled, and my mouth dropped open. "How ... Why would you *do* that?"

He shrugged, looking both wings over as best he could before closing his eyes and rotating his shoulders in a circle. The wings retracted to their place within his body, leaving me stunned and speechless once again. The physiology of demons was otherworldly and fascinating.

"Do you need a break?" he asked.

"No." I considered changing my mind but let the fantasy of resting go. "No, I'd rather finish."

"Let's get me up to sitting against the wall so it's easier for you, yes?" He pulled his body along the floor with his hands until he was leaned up against the stone. "There. May I?" He reached for one of the clean cloths and swiped the remaining blood away from his abdomen. "Lean forward." I did as he asked, and he used a clean corner of the cloth on my face, thumb and forefinger of his other hand holding my chin steady. "I made a mess of your face when I touched you before." His words were soft, his touch gentle.

"That's okay." I shivered and had no way to disguise it. The corners of his mouth lifted, the gold in his eyes burning as he stared right through me.

"All done," he said, the spell between us breaking as he lowered the cloth and sat back.

Face flushed with heat, I shifted so I sat cross-legged at his side, and pulled the injured leg onto my lap, scooting as far under him as I could so I could stretch one hand to his stomach wound. Seir flinched gently away from my touch.

"Okay?"

He flushed. "Yes, fine, it's just a bit ... awkward."

"Sorry. I can try something else instead."

"If you're comfortable, it's fine. That's not what I meant." He covered my hand with his over the ripple of muscles on his torso, using the other to pull his cloak and then mine over his lap so my arm had something to rest on. "I don't mind you touching me, Hailon, that's not the problem." The depth of his tone made my chest ache.

As I realized what he meant, where my arm rested, I blushed harder than I ever had before and stuttered some incoherent words. He was amused by this, his smirk potent.

I struggled to focus but did my best to pull myself together. "Are you ... feeling faint at all?"

He gave me a smile full of sharp teeth. "No. I'm perfectly conscious and feel nearly normal, believe it or not."

I relaxed under the smooth rise and fall of his breath. "That's good. Do demons have the same amount of blood as humans?"

My hands rested lightly over the bandage on his leg, which had soaked through but had since started to dry.

"Upper-level demons like me have slightly more than humans do. Lower-level demons are far smaller and have less." He watched me with curiosity as I removed the bandage and carefully cleaned what blood and debris from the wound I could with one hand. He was still holding the other against his stomach and seemed very disinclined to release it. After setting the wet cloth aside, I summoned my magic again.

My skin tingled as my magic feathered along the edges of the broken bone. There were still some rough places, but there wasn't much to be done about it now. Breaks that happened as the limb twisted were nearly impossible to fit back together exactly right again. Hopefully between my help and Seir's innate demon healing, he wouldn't be left with any lingering issues.

"Can you shift?" I asked.

"You want me to try now?"

"Do you think it would help? I just thought maybe, it would reset some of the injuries ... I don't know. Is it worth an attempt?"

He shrugged and closed his eyes, his horns slipping out against his scalp. Whatever came next appeared to be taking a whole lot of effort. Then he hissed and reverted, shaking his head.

"That won't work. It's very difficult to find my magic. Probably the same thing that's keeping me from being able to fly. It's no different than it was when we first left the house in Olinbourg."

"Okay, sorry. I was thinking ... Well, it doesn't matter. Can I have my other hand back now?" He raised his but gave me a look that reminded me of a sad puppy. "Take a deep breath," I instructed, moving down toward his foot. I placed a knee on either side of his leg, using my arm strength to make one hopeful tweak by pulling on the leg and turning it a little, aiming for the bone inside to align just a little more naturally. Seir grunted but was still as stone. "Sorry."

"It's alright."

I glanced up at his face as I resettled myself at his side, surprised to find him watching with fascinated interest instead of showing any indication of pain. "I don't mean to be crass, but you do *feel* pain, don't you? I honestly can't figure you out," I asked, thoroughly confused at the signals I'd been getting from him.

Seir smiled wide, tipping his head back against the stone. "I do. Acutely, in fact. I've just learned to disguise it well. Showing discomfort or weakness is not of any benefit in Hell." When I looked closer, I could see the light sheen of sweat dotting his forehead and collarbone again.

"Nor here," I muttered.

"Mmm. In any case, I think perhaps the amount of time I've been away from there is changing me a bit. Everything here is much more potent than there. Pain included."

"Is that strange?"

"I don't know." He swallowed and exhaled slowly through his nose as though trying to distract himself. "I've never noticed a change when I traveled before, but that doesn't mean much. I've never been injured like this outside of Hell. My time in the fae realm was mainly for leisure. When I fight, I don't lose, so ..." He shrugged and leaned his head back against the wall, eyes closed.

"The fae realm?" I asked, both curious and glad to have something to keep him talking about as a distraction.

"I had a good friend there for a long time. He and I spent many an hour fixing the ills of the worlds from the bottom of an ale tankard."

"I see." I forced more magic through my hands, requesting that the bone knit back together, that it be strong like it was as it bonded. "Had?"

Seir sighed and bumped his fist against his chest twice before raising it in a gesture of reverence. "Yes. Van has gone on to the Tombs of the Elders to be with his wife. Not long ago, my brothers and I helped his son Ris reclaim the throne."

That sounded like an interesting story. Unfortunately, I was slipping into the healing trance too far to be a decent conversationalist. It was an odd between-realities state when healing was this intricate. I was in my body but also merged with my magic and therefore not really either one. My surroundings were something I was aware of, but I couldn't always react to them, nor did I really see them. Fortunately, Seir seemed to have run out of energy for chatting and had relaxed against the wall with his eyes closed, breaths slow and measured as I focused.

He smiled wide when I reached my hand back out, and after brushing his lips against my palm, he leaned into it, holding my hand against his face. He looked all the more like a cat, marking me. Seir rested there for a moment before greedily pressing my hand back to his abdomen. Both of his hands flattened mine against his warm skin, trapping it there.

I stared back at him, skin tingling where he'd kissed it, the whole series of gestures having left my pulse pounding and me breathless.

"Alright then," I said, trying to shake myself back to the task at hand. I closed my eyes and submerged myself in the healing. Colors burst behind my eyelids as I made the first touches.

Aunt Sal's chronic sickness was always a particular shade of violet. Cuts, bruises, sprains and most broken bones, those things were green. When I was helping an illness leave the lungs, my magic felt yellow. More serious diseases felt blue or purple. This, however ... This felt orange and red, even a little black around the edges, and I wasn't sure what these new colors meant. Physiologically, Seir was not all that different from a human—tail, wings, and horns excepted, of course. But these new colors reminded me again that he was not, no matter how close he seemed.

Time became a fluid thing as my mind focused only on what my magic was feeling and not what was going on around me. I trusted Seir would alert me if anything needed my attention and was able to fully relax into my power, letting it guide itself through the slow, meticulous repair of bone, muscle, and skin. Behind my eyes, I could see *the bad* curling up like burnt paper and dispersing into the blood as tiny particles of dust. I couldn't actually see it, but I always pictured that the tiny motes that remained were exhaled with the person's breath as they circulated through. I worked to stitch everything together like I was embroidering the detailed storybook kingdom tapestry I'd made for the big wall in my bedroom.

I'd been so frustrated with Aunt Sal for prescribing such a tedious task as a way for me to hone my patience and craftsmanship when it came to stitching, but the end result after countless hours of labor and skeins of thread had proved her right. Lying in my bed every night for years, I made up a new story about the people I'd sewn, the castle, the surrounding farms, while falling asleep.

"Hailon?" Seir's voice penetrated my deep focus as I worked on getting his skin to line up just right, to minimize any scarring. "I think that's enough. You've done a wonderful job, but you need to be done now. Hailon, *stop*." Urgency laced his tone, and I felt his fingers wrap around my arm and pull me into his body as I swayed, everything around me going gray.

CHAPTER 16
HAILON

Coming out of the fog in my mind was like swimming through Aunt Sal's split pea soup. My ears popped and gave a high-pitched ringing noise as whatever had been clogging them cleared away.

"Easy." Seir frowned at me as I sat up from where I'd been pillowed in his lap on our cloaks. He clutched my sleeve in an effort to ensure I'd stay upright. "If you faint again, we'll be even, but I'd really rather you didn't."

"I'm okay. It's almost done. I just need ..." I left the thought half-formed, scrunched my eyes shut, and sewed the last several invisible stitches.

His voice was tight and pitched low, as though trying not to alarm me while being very concerned. "Leave it. You've done plenty. We can work more tomorrow if need be, but for now, I need you to—"

I raised my hands to prove I'd stopped and opened my eyes, the night now fully dark as the fire burned low. Seir visibly relaxed as I sat back, resting my weight on my elbows.

He drew up his leg, bending and straightening it again, testing it out. "Are you sure you're alright?"

"Yes," I said stubbornly. "I'm fine." But my irritated tone couldn't cover the way my muscles failed me when I tried to get up.

Seir scrambled to his knees, scooping his arms under mine while sliding me toward the wall. He gazed down into my eyes, his thumb smoothing across my cheekbone. "That was dangerous, Hailon. I was afraid you pushed too far. Perhaps you did." The ring around the pupil in his eyes was extra green, the little wrinkles in the space between his eyebrows deep as he frowned down at me. His eyes dropped to my mouth, then he pulled away, taking my breath with him.

"I'm fine," I repeated, as though doing so would make it true. I was well and truly worn out, though I didn't think I was in any danger.

He propped me up with a pack on either side of my body before shuffling over to add logs to the dying fire. I inhaled greedily, desperate to fill my lungs with the air I'd been unknowingly depriving them of while he was so intimately close.

"You do incredible work, I must say. I'm good as new." He paused to probe at his stomach with his fingers as he walked around near the fire, flashing me a wide expanse of tan skin. "Thank you. You honor me with such a generous use of your gift." He bowed low, one arm over his chest, reminding me of the day we first met as the tips of his hair brushed the dirt on the ground.

"It's nothing."

"It's the furthest thing from nothing," he huffed, offering me some water. "I'm going to make you something to eat, you need to replenish your strength."

I shook my head. "Not hungry."

He scoffed. "I don't see how, after all that. We haven't eaten much of anything since we stopped midday. You're surely starving by now." As if to agree, my stomach gave a whine. "See? It will only take a moment."

"What about you?"

"I snacked from our packs while you were working. I offered you something several times, but it was like you couldn't hear me."

That sounded right. His injuries had pulled me in deep. Had I not been in a safe environment, anything could have happened, and I wouldn't have noticed until I came out of the trance.

"Sorry."

He gestured wildly with his hands as he spoke. "No need to apologize for that. We have some dried meat still. I could make a quick stew. There's cake, but they're getting rather stale and don't taste right without some tea. But I can make tea too! That's fine. That's a good idea, actually. Or—"

"Don't bother with any of that on my account. I just need sleep. I'm too tired to eat."

Seir blew out another rough breath. "Are you truly going to refuse me the honor of taking care of you after what you just did for me?" His hands were on his hips, his normally jovial expression pulled into a frown, eyes strangely sad. "It took you *hours*, Hailon. Several, in fact. And my leg might be better than it was before. Still, you would deny me reciprocation?"

Something in my exhausted brain found his indignant tone amusing. Confusion pulled his brows even further together as I laughed. "Just for now, demon, not forever. Can we discuss this after I rest?"

He capitulated with a heavy sigh. "Fine. I'll give you the terms of my repayment tomorrow. I'll have you know I rarely make deals. They are so much work and for what? That's more my brother Rylan's thing, he's always loved the art of crafting a good contract. I simply don't have the patience most of the time, but this? This seems like an appropriate situation on which to put conditions in writing." He pounded his fist into his open palm, so unusually serious I laughed out loud again. His mouth dropped open, then twisted into a grin. "You are a truly perplexing creature, Hailon Derne."

"I know." I resisted the urge to throw his words back at him, no matter how true they might be. Knowing him, he'd take it as a compliment. He embraced his mercurial nature more than anyone I'd ever met. "What?" I asked, seeing his lopsided smile as he continued to openly stare at me.

"I deeply enjoy hearing you laugh. It's a truly beautiful sound." As I sat there with my mouth partially open at his admission, Seir shook his head and set to organizing our little camp so we could go to sleep like he hadn't said anything of such significance that I was sure I'd remember it for the rest of my life.

After arranging the logs in the fire to his liking, he approached me again, face far too close for several heartbeats. His eyes searched mine and blood pounded in my ears. He was close enough his breath feathered against my skin, his hair grazed my own. He'd done several things since tumbling down the hill that I should have been far more offended by than I was. He was behaving like we knew one another far better than we did. Like he was preparing to kiss me.

What was more, I wanted him to.

I had time to inhale, the weak protest I'd half-formed stuck in my throat. Then thoughts fled as I found myself lifted against his body. He'd slid one arm under my thighs and the other across my back with his fingers splayed wide, palm cradling the back of my head. The overwhelming desire to cry passed through me with shocking urgency. A lump clogged my throat and tears burned my eyes. The care and comfort in the way Seir held me struck some part deep down inside me I hadn't known was so desperate for such a gentle touch. He lowered himself to his knees and laid me down with my head resting on one of the packs. He made a pillow for himself with the other, then pulled me against him again, my shoulder pressed into his chest. Tossing our cloaks wide, he spread them over us both as makeshift blankets. Seir snuggled in then, his nose in my hair and his arm loosely draped across my waist, hand palming my hip.

My pulse spiked, his spicy scent filling my nose. But the weight of my exhaustion was too heavy to do anything but relax into him.

"There's no need for this." I wiggled, turning onto my side so I could crawl a respectable distance away. "I can—"

"Shh." He clucked his tongue and pulled my back snug against his chest, our legs nested, and his arm banded even tighter across my hips. His tail loosely curled around my ankle for good measure. His breath moved the hair along the back of my neck as he spoke, and I barely managed to keep myself from shivering at the sensation. "Sleep. I promise I have no untoward motivations tonight. Let me keep you warm. Let me protect you while we rest."

Even half asleep, my eyebrow raised. I hadn't missed the careful way he'd qualified that his motivations were pure *tonight*. He was getting bolder and taking any chance to touch me he could get. But ... he also never failed to respect my boundaries. And more often than not, my chest felt hollow when he pulled away.

Besides, I did honestly feel safer with the barrier of his body between me and the dark forest. He was pleasantly warm too. "Fine. For tonight."

"Thank you." His deep exhale betrayed significant relief. "Sleep, Hailon. You've more than earned it." I felt the briefest little kiss against the back of my head, then his fingertips dragged through the tangled mess of my hair, making my scalp tingle and my body relax into a puddle. My heart throbbed behind my ribs, heavy and hot. I fleetingly worried I'd done some kind of damage to myself healing him after all. Maybe the orange, red, and black magic was dangerous. Only time would tell.

As I blinked heavily, hardly able to hold my eyes open any longer, I saw that the moon had risen, nearly full and silvery over the trees. Through the open side of our stone shelter, the moonlight made an arrangement of shadows that was oddly distinct. I squinted, trying to clear my vision. My exhaustion left me wondering if I was really seeing broken columns and other remnants of a structure, not just odd piles of rocks and sticks.

I realized once my eyes closed for the final time that we hadn't taken the wrong road after all; the map was plainly incorrect. With my energy totally depleted, I couldn't even tell Seir what I was seeing, and it was too late to leave. The best I could do was wrap my fingers around the forearm draped over my hips and squeeze.

I was about to find out firsthand if any of the stories were true after all.

We were in the ruins.

CHAPTER 17
SEIR

Hallon twitched in my arms, a high-pitched whine leaving her throat.

"Shh," I soothed her, using my fingers to comb through her hair some more. That always relaxed me, and she'd liked it before, so it was worth a try. I'd almost suspected a sleep paralysis demon was visiting her, but there was nobody else around that I could see. Besides, I doubted they'd try anything with me nearby, outranking them as I did.

At some point in our sleep, she'd spun and was now facing me. I had absolutely no complaints about that. Her arms were tucked up against her chest, her hands curled into fists under her chin. An intense frown plagued her even in dreams, and she tensed as though doing battle with something I couldn't see.

"It's alright," I muttered, smoothing out the lines on her forehead and between her eyebrows with my fingertips. "Shh. It's okay. I've got you. Rest easy." I tugged her closer, hoping that the warmth and security of my hold helped. I pressed my lips to the place the lines had been, whispering oaths of protection directly into her skin. With the arm that was caught between us, I loosened her clenched fingers and held them with my own, feeling the thud of her steady heartbeat against the back of my hand.

I breathed the cool night air and the scent of her hair, far more content than I had any right to be. The beat of her heart matched up to mine, and I reveled in the relief that gave the incessant burning in my ribs. Other, lower aches just had to be ignored.

Before I realized I'd fallen back asleep, I was startled awake by my own snoring.

I detested the thought of leaving Hailon alone, especially since she was finally sleeping peacefully, but the fire was nearly guttered again, and if the chill of the stone we were lying on was seeping through my clothes, it would definitely be an issue for her.

The moon was still high, but dawn couldn't be too far off. She'd worked for hours fixing my wounds, her focus so all-consuming I'd been both awed and concerned. I understood why she'd been such a prized commodity for those detestable men, and I was happier than ever to have removed her from such a vile situation.

I inhaled deeply once away from the stone shelter, filling my lungs with the rich smell of the forest at night. Dark soil and acidic pine mingled with dew as my hands and tail gathered sticks enough to revitalize the fire and leave a small pile to the side. I filled our small pot with water at the creek, taking a moment to wash my hands and face while I was there. It was on my way back that I saw it. The clear form of the castle that had once stood proud in the place we'd sought shelter.

Pillars and doorways revealed themselves in the moonlight, vines trailing up and over ancient walls, disguising them from daytime view.

Curiosity piqued, I adjusted the cloaks so they covered Hailon better and put the pot on some stones near the flames. Then I walked back toward the place where I'd landed after we slid down the hill. The more I moved, the more I could see of the once glorious structure illuminated by the moonlight.

Mentally reassembling the fallen walls, I approached the craggy remnants of one with reverence and placed my palm along the edge. With my boot, I scuffed some moss away, finding flat stone underneath.

"I wouldn't leave either," I admitted out loud. Realizing what I'd said, I hastily added, "If I were king of this place, I wouldn't want to leave my lovely home either."

"Smart amendment," a low voice replied from the shadows beyond the ancient doorway.

Stepping back in surprise, I stared as a tall figure came into the splash of moonlight on my side of the ancient fallen lintel. He had a stern expression on his face, and long brown hair pulled back in three tight braids. A linen shirt and what looked to be leather pants encased much of his brawny form. One hand gripped the hilt of a sword, pulling it free from the leather sheath draped over his hips. The longer I stared at his face, the more fiercely recognition tugged at me.

"Oh! Hello. I've spent enough time with the fae to know I should take care with my words in a place such as this."

"You shouldn't be here, human—friend of the fae or not." He frowned, shifting his weight in a way that put me on alert.

His blade swung through the air, whistling as it passed close to my face. I twisted my body and crouched in one smooth movement, retrieving my smaller blades from the hiding spot along my back as I took several steps back. I regretted having taken off my sword belt to sleep.

"Well, to be fair, we really didn't *choose* to be here. Honestly, we were actively avoiding the ruins altogether, but our map has several things all wrong.

"Is that so?" The large man and I faced off, my little daggers fending off his sword as he danced me around the open area between the crumbling walls, sword cleaving the air near my body the whole way.

"I swear it. I can show you, if you like. Seems the artist was either having an off day when he drew it out or was setting up anyone who found it for disaster."

"You shouldn't have come here." The clang of his steel clashing with mine vibrated through my bones, invigorating me. I'd caught his blade between the X of my daggers, and a joyful laugh bubbled up as I stepped back again, releasing his weapon. He grunted, the frown on his face intensifying.

"This is fun! I've not had such a worthy opponent in a while."

He growled, slashing and lunging at me in earnest. I chucked as I turned, getting a running start toward one of the more stable-looking wall fragments. I used my momentum and the help of a fallen pillar to launch myself to the top.

"I swear! We aren't here purposely. We're on our way north. The road got odd once it started to climb. There shouldn't even *be* hills here, according to the map. It felt like we walked into some strange magic. I got too close to the edge of the road, and it gave way. I fell down the hill, and here we are." I shrugged. "I'm Seir." I stuck out my arm, an invitation for a handshake that he did not and could not accept from so far below me. His head cocked to the side, his eyes squinted in a glare, but he said nothing further. "You're stone kin, are you not? You remind me quite a lot of a gargoyle I know in Revalia. Also, I'm not a human, actually." I waved at him with my tail and brought forth my wings, making a point to display my horns as well. My wings still needed a bit of mending from the fall, and I couldn't fully shift, but it worked well enough to show him what I was.

"A demon?" He growled again, my true nature clearly more insulting than if I were only a human.

I put my hands up, gesturing that I meant no harm, though admittedly as I was holding daggers, the gesture didn't have the impact I'd hoped for. "I'm no danger to you, nor, I hope, you to me. I'm only here to help my ... friend"—I gestured to the glow of our fire and the sleeping silhouette of Hailon near it—"get home. Then I'll be on my way back to Hell." My stomach clenched as I said the words, the nagging ache in my chest flaring to a bright burn. Even the word *friend* tasted wrong, like I'd eaten a handful of ashes. "Well, I might stop by d'Arcan to see my brothers first. They'd probably be cross if I didn't, and I wouldn't mind seeing everyone."

"Who is this stone kin you know?" he asked, taking several steps toward me, his blade still raised, but his body no longer tensed to strike. It did not escape my notice that he'd never actually answered my question.

"Well, I've met nearly the entire clan now, I think, but you resemble Magnus very strongly, particularly in the eyes. Are you kin to him? General Aurichal?"

"Who is your family in Revalia?"

I grinned, believing I'd gotten through to him that we were not enemies. After putting my blades away, I used my extended wings as a buffer and jumped back down to the ground, landing a few paces from him.

"My brother Rylan runs the Collegium d'Arcan. Vassago is there with him now as well. And their lovely mates, of course."

The man blinked, his entire countenance softening. His head tilted again, his dark-brown eyes roving over me as though weighing how much of a threat I might be. Abruptly, he shoved the sword back into its sheath and put his hand out. His fingers clasped mine with a grip that went a step beyond firm. "I'm Coltor. Magnus is my father."

"It's nice to meet you." I vigorously shook his hand with both of mine, unable to contain the smile that spread across my face. I was thrilled to not only have found the ruins, but an acquaintance of this kind. "I've had the honor of meeting your sisters as well, they're both forces unto themselves."

His face twitched into a knowing smile. "Indeed."

"What are you doing all the way out here?"

He shrugged, arms crossed over his chest as he relaxed his stance. "This is my post."

"Big draw for trouble, is it?"

"You'd be surprised. Usually just brigands or wayward travelers, but occasionally a demon wanders through."

"Ah." I chuckled and put my wings away.

"The odd feeling on the road you got is the wards. Most people turn back. Those that don't are left to deal with me."

"Oh?" I smiled at him, but his face was stone serious. "Oh. Oh! Are you the ghost of this place?"

The gargoyle dipped his chin in confirmation but said nothing further.

"Seir?" Hailon's voice called out, her tone edged with stress.

"I'm here!" I called, turning back toward the stone shelter. "I put some water on not long ago, I could make tea? Something to eat? She's sure to be starving by now. Won't you join us?"

Coltor scanned the area then gave a short nod, following me back to our little camp.

CHAPTER 18
SEIR

HAILON WAS STANDING near the fire, both my cloak and hers wrapped around her shoulders. "Seir, I need to tell you something," she said as I got closer. Urgency laced her hasty words. "As I was falling asleep, I could see shapes. Pillars, and walls. I think we're inside"—she paused, eyes widening as she took in the large man following behind me—"the ruins." Her multicolor eyes darted between us.

"I agree! I came to that conclusion myself not long ago when I started wandering around. This is Coltor. He's the big scary haunting thing that keeps people away from here." I turned to him. "There are lots of wonderful stories about you!"

"Good," was all he said in response. He seemed a little rough around the edges, hard to make smile, but I wasn't going to hold that against him.

"Ah ,,, hello," Hailon said, eyes wide as she stared at him. Coltor dipped his head in response.

"You must be famished by now, yes? I'll fix us something to eat."

I went ahead to the packs and got started pulling out supplies. Hailon and Coltor stared at one another.

"Your companion is a demon," Coltor commented, pulling some stumps inside to serve as seats. "But what, exactly, are you, my lady?"

"Me?"

"Coltor is a member of the stone kin," I explained.

"Stone kin?" Her eyebrows pulled together as she joined me at the packs, helping to gather what meager supplies we still had to assemble a meal.

"Gargoyles and grotesques," Coltor said, standing once again. Like I had during our little exercise session, he showed his wings in illustration. The abrupt movement made Hailon step back.

Coltor's wings had fierce spurs on the tips and appeared to have more bones between the membranes than mine. They were the same leathery skin, however. Most of my brothers had at least some feathers on their wings, but not me. I was like Coltor, with bat-like smooth ones.

"Gargoyles like the statues?" she asked, eyebrows pulled together in confusion. "What's a grotesque? What's the difference?"

"Nothing, if you ask most of us. Some disagree, but they're wrong." He retracted his wings. "I'd demonstrate further, but I haven't been able to shift properly since ..." He stepped toward her, looking down into her face with a menacingly curious expression.

He was larger than me, bulkier, though not much taller. Compared to her, however, he was quite a bit bigger and intentionally hovering in a way that put him in a position of dominance. I didn't like it. In fact, it made all my protective instincts scream.

I pushed my way between them, my favorite blade in my hand and pressed to the large artery in his throat before he could blink.

"She's not your enemy, stone man. But if you approach her like that again, you will be mine. Do we understand one another?"

A smile twitched at the corner of his mouth. "I see. Apologies." Coltor stepped back from us both, hands up in a gesture of surrender. "You'll have to pardon my manners. I'm out here for long stretches with no socialization. I'm afraid I get a little rusty with how to interact politely. What can I call you, my lady?"

Hailon blinked, glancing between us before responding. "I'm no lady," she said shaking her head. "My name is ... Hailon." I could tell she'd changed her mind last minute from offering her surname instead. She stuck out her hand, and he accepted, his much larger one engulfing hers as he gave it a gentle up-and-down shake.

"Pleased to make your acquaintance, Hailon. Would you both excuse me for just a moment?"

"Of course."

He looked at me for approval, and I nodded tightly. Coltor stepped away from the shelter, his footsteps crunching over the debris on the ground as he went in the direction of the creek.

"He's ..." Hailon's face scrunched up as she searched for a descriptor. She gave up after a long pause and just shook her head before adding the herbal mixture we'd been using as tea to the hot water.

"How are you feeling?" I asked, gently directing her by the shoulders to one of the log seats.

"Fine. Still a little tired, but I'll manage. I can help."

"You will not. I have it well in hand." I dropped a kiss on her hair and attempted to reassure her with a smile, but just as quickly as the surprise faded and some softness crept into her gaze, it sharpened again as Coltor came back into the shelter.

"Perhaps this would be of use?" he asked, holding out a large fish he'd already cleaned as well as some wild herbs.

"Perfect! Thank you." I accepted the generous offering as he scooted the largest stump to the far edge of the fire, allowing Hailon as much space from him as he could without leaving the shelter again.

"So, Coltor, why exactly are you posted here? What is so worth protecting in a ruined castle?" I asked him as the fish began to cook on a flat rock over the flames. The tea was steeped, so I poured them cups and drank my own directly out of the pot.

"How do I know I can trust you, demon?"

I shrugged. "You don't. But that is mutual, is it not?"

"I suppose." The large man sighed and sipped at the hot brew. "You said you had dealt with the fae, before."

"Yes. Quite a lot, actually."

"Then you understand how precious some doorways can be."

"Certainly. My brother Tap is stationed at the crossroads, and he can barely manage a day off now and then, let alone—" What he was saying without actual words sank in. "Oh. Yes. I can see why you would want to deter people from wandering through here, if that's the case." There were portals here then, permanent ones embedded into the very materials of the old castle. Entry points to the fae realm or perhaps other places entirely that needed to be protected. Shame we couldn't make use of them to get Hailon home.

Satisfied, Coltor nodded. Hailon watched us with open fascination as I shared some news I'd gathered the last time I was in Revalia, then other small talk until the fish and the tinned vegetables I'd added to the fire were finished cooking.

We ate in companionable silence, Coltor expressing his thanks and honestly looking like he'd finally relaxed a little by the time we were done.

Hailon rose, dishes collected in her hands.

"Leave those," I told her, taking the stack from her hands. "I'll wash them."

She let me take them without argument, her eyes never leaving Coltor's face. The behavior was unusual for her and had my awareness tingling even as I stepped aside to scrape remnants of our meal off the plates and into the flames.

"Consort with many demons?" Coltor asked, forearms resting across his knees. His tone was light, but she stiffened.

"No. Just the one."

"Hmm. How do you know so much about them and magic, but you've never heard of stone kin before? How is it that you felt the effects of the wards of this place but were still compelled to enter? Why exactly are you traveling with a demon in the first place?" Coltor's tone had turned antagonistic again, and something inside me roared.

There was a meaty, squelching sound as one of my blades embedded itself in his thigh. He growled and yanked it free, examining it with shock. Surprise and anger pulled his eyes wide as blood stained the leg of his trousers.

"Seir!" Hailon scolded, rushing to Coltor's side. "That's uncalled for."

"Mind. Your. Tone." My voice came out as a rough snarl, and my hands shook from the rush of rage. I gestured to where Hailon already had her fingertips on the edges of his wound. I didn't care for the fact she was touching him at all, let alone on his leg like that, but I pushed the jealousy down when she glanced at me with fire in her eyes. "See? She's helping you and scolding me. She's *not* your enemy. And I'd prefer we remain friends, but that won't be possible if I have to remind you again."

Coltor raised his hands and relaxed his body, shedding some of the tension that had accumulated in his shoulders. He handed my blade back to me, bowing his head. "Apologies. I meant no disrespect. I'm truly just curious. I don't mean to be interrogatory. It's very odd that you would feel the effects of the wards yet continue on. What else are you capable of, my lady?"

"I have a healing gift," she said, the glare she threw at him as cutting as my blade. "I was taken from Ravenglen, sold to a man in Olinbourg because of it. I was held captive, routinely abused for my gift. In an act of desperation, I summoned him to help me escape, so I can get back to my home. My sick aunt." She spat the words, and I watched his face transform.

"Apologies." He shifted, head bowed. "Truly, I should not have assumed anything negative. I'm sorry that happened. Are your captors—"

"Dead," she said with finality.

"Good." He studied her a moment. "The two things together … you're a null, then."

My fingers brushed the handles again from the small twitch she gave at the word. I still couldn't truly explain why I had such aggressive responses where she was involved, but it wasn't something I could envision going away.

"Been a long time since we've seen one of your kind," he added.

"A what?" she asked, stepping back to her seat. His pants were stained, but the wound was cared for. "That word doesn't sound friendly. And who is 'we'?"

Coltor shrugged. "Stone kin, mages. I'm sure the archives at the council chambers in Revalia have more information on when exactly the last one like you was discovered, but as I recall from my schooling, it's been a very, very long time. Your gifts are unique, like your eyes. They're a dead giveaway."

"My eyes?"

The stone kin nodded again, then got to his feet. "The coloring. Split irises are not unheard of, but only nulls have four colors like that. Means your heritage is unique as well." He frowned. "Did you not realize?"

Hailon shook her head tightly. "People stare at me for lots of reasons, I assumed my eyes were simply one of many."

"Mmm."

"What exactly does a null do?"

"Magical … consumption. Often with a side effect of canceling out ambient abilities tied to said magic." Hailon contemplated that description, her mouth opening then closing again without any words appearing. "Are you able to shift?" Coltor asked me.

"Not fully. Not since I came to Earth."

"You mean, not since you've been near her."

"I ..." I frowned, calculating.

"My ability to shift disappeared yesterday afternoon. When exactly did you fall down the hill and into the area protected by the wards?"

I looked to Hailon. She blushed a bright red, something like embarrassment crossing her face. I hated that she felt shame around something she likely had no control over. And we couldn't be sure it was her fault in the first place.

"You think *I'm* doing this? That I'm responsible for blocking your magic?" She gestured vaguely between him and me.

"Yes. I believe you are. You truly didn't know?"

She shook her head, a pained look on her face. "No. My gift has always been healing. I've never heard the word *null* before, or had anyone mention that I ... consume magic." Her face scrunched up like the word tasted bad.

"It might have been intentionally kept from you. Or perhaps nobody knew." He shrugged.

"To what end would it be kept a secret?" she asked.

"I'm no expert, but imagine you were in a place where mages are," Coltor explained. "Assuming your presence works on them as well as it does on our ability to shift or fly, it would render them all powerless. That's a very coveted gift to have, if you can control it." He tilted his head to the side. "No less incredible, but also quite dangerous if you can't."

Hailon swallowed hard, and I shifted closer, itchy at her discomfort.

Coltor turned his attention to me. "I don't doubt she's in capable hands with you, demon, but be watchful. She's valuable beyond gold to some."

She was valuable beyond gold to *me*.

My blood bubbled hot under the surface of my skin, remembering how I'd found her in the first place. How she'd been taken. What she reported they were doing to her; sampling pieces of her to examine. She'd assumed they were trying to copy her healing gift, but what if it was more than that? What if they knew what she was? Such an ability would make for a disastrous weapon.

"I'll get her home safely," I swore, but that didn't seem like enough. I wanted to commit myself to her protection from any harm, eternally.

Coltor nodded. "I'll attempt to send word out, perhaps I can ease your journey a bit. No promises though; resources out here are quite thin."

"Do you have contacts in Ravenglen?" Hailon asked.

"I may be able to trade some messages. Again, no promises. What did you want to know?"

"There's a wise woman there, her name is Sal. She's my aunt. I just need to know if she's alright."

"I'll see what I can do. If I find anything out, I will try to pass word along. I'm not allowed to leave this place until my post expires."

"When will that be?" I asked.

He smirked and gave a rueful grin. "When it happens, I'll let you know. Nobody else is very keen on taking this kind of assignment."

I understood that more than most.

Hailon's shoulders relaxed, and she inhaled the first full breath I'd seen her take since she'd woken. "Thank you. Thank you very much."

Coltor inclined his head politely. "Can I see your map? Perhaps I can make some much-needed corrections."

I pulled the small square of parchment out of my pocket, and he scowled at it, using a bit of charcoal from the fire to scribble over the inconsistencies.

"You will be protected here," Coltor promised, gesturing around himself, indicating the bounds of the ruins. "Beyond this place, take the east road. Keep to the valley. The grasslands further out are full of trouble."

"Thank you." I accepted the parchment back, and he turned to go.

"Head north from here once the sun is up. Follow the water. There's a glade with several springs, and the forest there is a bountiful place. Rest and replenish your food if you need to. After that, go directly toward the sunrise. The water will no longer serve you, it dead-ends in the mountains. Nice to have met you both. Safe journey, I hope we meet again."

"And you." We shook hands, and he disappeared into the darkness, leaving us staring at one another as the fire crackled and dawn broke in shades of peach and gold over the horizon.

CHAPTER 19
HAILON

BREAKING CAMP AND moving north was a simple affair. We gathered our belongings after putting the fire out and walked along the bank of the little river in companionable silence.

The odd weather and lack of wildlife we'd experienced on the road because of the heavy magical wards was nowhere to be found down here. Birds sang, insects buzzed, and life thrived in every direction. The morning sun was warm, but the season had noticeably changed since we crossed into the bones of the old castle. Gone was the heat we'd experienced the first few days of our journey. I smiled. Autumn was my favorite.

Aunt Sal was a fan of spring, when everything started to sprout anew and the earth came to life again after months of snow and frost. I, however, craved the serene return to the earth that happened in the fall. I loved the way everything turned over, tucked itself in and prepared for a long nap.

Maybe I was just more tired than I wanted to admit.

Perhaps a quarter hour of walking later, the forest opened up into a broad glade. Coltor's vague description hadn't been adequate. This place was a glorious oasis, hidden from prying eyes by dense trees and rock formations. Wildflowers of all colors and types mixed in with the tall grasses, and someone long ago had taken the time to lay out a walkway of flat stones in patterns around a series of five springs of varying sizes and shapes. Three of the pools were steaming into the heavy morning air.

"Hot springs." I sighed, every bit of dirt and grime suddenly much heavier on my skin as the prospect of a real bath dangled in front of me.

Seir made a whooping noise and bounded off, startling the birds into flight. He went from pool to pool, testing their temperatures.

"This one," he said, pointing at the smallest but steamiest spring. "This is the one I'll be using." His grin was wide, his excitement infectious. "Come on!"

Setting our things down to the side of the path made of flat stones, Seir quickly gathered more rocks and started up a fresh fire.

"Are we staying that long?" I asked.

He blew gently into the sparks he'd created in the kindling, getting a strong flame to glow around a twig before responding. "I have no expectations or plans," he admitted. "I know you want to get home as quickly as you can. A fire is always a good thing to have, in any case, and easily put out." He started adding bigger and bigger pieces until the flames were well fed. "I wasn't sure how recovered you truly were, to be honest. You didn't sleep much compared to the effort you expended yesterday, and what little you got seemed less than restful." Seir stood, dusting his hands off on his pants. "I thought about making it a requirement in my repayment terms that you allow me to carry you, but—"

"I'm fine." My knee-jerk response had him lifting an eyebrow. "Really. I could continue on right now if we needed to. On my own feet even; no carrying required." That eyebrow arched even further, his head tilting forward in challenge. "I *could*, I said. Not that I wanted to. Or that it would be easy." I frowned, realizing I really wasn't in very good shape, and not resting now could result in me having to take twice as long to recover later. "I suppose I wouldn't mind lingering in a hot bath for a bit before we do anything of the sort."

"Was that so difficult?" he teased, fishing out the towels we'd inherited from Widow Callahan's linens and a cake of soap. "Besides, I don't have paper or ink so that, too, will have to wait until we return to civilization. I'll have to humbly request that you take my suggestions for recuperation into consideration before rejecting them out of hand."

I opened my mouth to protest but shut it as quickly. There was nothing unfair about his request, in fact it was designed to benefit me more than him. My reactionary nature was defensive, but I was trying to school it a little better around Seir. His intentions were never malicious. "I'll do my best."

He smiled wide. "Can't ask for more, then, can I?"

As I gathered our mutual dirty laundry, he dashed around and gathered wood for the fire. I tested the temperatures of the pools, finding the one he'd chosen far too close to scalding for my liking. The one next to it, however, felt perfect.

"We'll wash everything, yes? We can string it up to dry while we eat, after." He looked around thoughtfully, hands on his hips as he evaluated the potential of the rocks as laundry racks.

"What will we wear?" I asked, blushing as I pictured the pair of us sitting around in just our skins.

"The towels, I suppose. Cloaks?" He squinted as he considered this option. "No, they'd be terrible against even damp skin." His hands and tail stayed busy as he carted our laundry to the small walkway between the pools, plus the towels and the soap. When he stripped off his shirt without warning I turned around and started walking toward the trees.

"I'm going to see if there are any shampoo plants growing here. For our hair."

"Don't go too far."

I was deep in the shade of the trees when I heard the telltale splash of water. Had he really been about to strip right there in front of me? My mind spun through several scenarios as I hunted among the low-growing foliage for the broad-leafed plant I'd come looking for. As far as I knew, that plant didn't grow unless it was intentionally nurtured in a greenhouse with constant high heat and humidity, but perhaps I'd get lucky outside the cool climate of Ravenglen.

After several minutes of searching, I abandoned the search. However, I noted that there were brambles and berries growing all over the place, and we would do well to come back here to collect berries.

I paused, watching from the shadows of the trees. Seir's back muscles knotted and rolled as he scrubbed the soap between his hands. He was indisputably beautiful. There was not a muscle underdeveloped on his lean body. Even from a distance, I could make out what seemed like infinite white scars standing out in relief on his bronzed skin. Freckles were also generously sprinkled along his shoulders like they were across his nose and cheeks. The two contrasting colors looked like a galaxy of dueling stars spread across his skin. I wondered how exactly a demon developed freckles in a place where there was no sunshine, my thoughts less and less linear the longer I stared. In that moment, Seir turned enough that I could have been spotted, had he looked closer. My heart pounded, but I still didn't step out into the sunshine.

My eyes caught next on his mysterious tattoos. The odd greenish lettering ran across his back at the top of his shoulders and continued all along his front just under his collarbone and down his breastbone. I squinted as though that would help me see them better, startling when he glanced my direction again, a concerned look on his face.

I flushed with heat, heart thudding heavily in my chest. I turned to the side and blinked several times, realizing my hand had strayed to my breast. Guilt and shame pressed in. I was not a voyeur, but here I was, spying on him. After a moment, I turned back again, unable to stop myself.

A bird flapped right above me, making Seir spin to look a third time. I had enough presence of mind to step out of the trees, making it appear as though the bird had fled because of me.

Seir caught my eye and smiled broadly as I came ever closer to the pools. "Any luck?"

"No." I shook my head hard and stepped near the pool, purposely avoiding looking into the water where he was standing. "Plenty of berries, though. For later."

Boldly unashamed where I was self-conscious, Seir spread his arms out wide, leaning back slightly in the water. "That's alright, the soap isn't so bad. Isn't this wonderful?"

Face hot, a faint pulse between my thighs, I forced my hands to start working on undoing the ties on my clothing. "I can't wait to soak. Could you ..."

He scanned me, then turned away. "Oh. Of course."

I quickly shucked my clothing and stepped down into the spring. My assessment had been right; this one was perfect for me. At the edge where I entered, I was covered up to my ribs. If I moved to the side a bit, there was a seat or shelf of some kind in the stone, low enough that if I sat, I was submerged all the way to my chin. If I ventured further in, I could stand and be covered to my shoulders. I walked around until I found the deepest part, going all the way under for a moment so my hair would get wet.

Seir pulled the pile of laundry close, dipping them in the hot water, then scrubbing in the same soap we were using on ourselves.

"I can do mine," I protested as he pulled mine over too.

"Nonsense. I'm already working on it. Just relax." He cracked the little cake of soap into two pieces. He kept the small one for himself and gently tossed the other part to me. His eyes never left the garments, his movements methodical and well-practiced.

"Do you enjoy doing laundry, then?" I asked, standing deep enough my chest was covered, working some of the lather over my arms.

His smile appeared, but still, he didn't look up. "Not particularly, but I'm very good at it. It was my assigned duty for nearly a hundred years in my old unit."

I froze. "A hundred years?"

His eyes lifted. "Yes. The alternative was latrines. I'll take dirty clothes over toilets any day." He finally focused on me, and his expression changed. The gold in his eyes seemed to glow, and his gaze dipped before darting back to my face. "I'll ..." He gestured vaguely, then moved the sopping clothing from the rock path between our pools to the one on the opposite side, so he was no longer facing me.

I turned, too, for whatever good that would do. I moved to a shallower part of the pool and scrubbed myself from the top down, motivated to get the layer of dirt and grime that had accumulated the last several days off my skin. Things only got truly revealing when I raised my legs out one at a time to wash them down. Glancing over my shoulder, I could see his back tensing and relaxing as he worked.

I washed and rinsed my hair three separate times. The uneven length left from the number of clumps removed for samples bothered me. Once, it had been a source of pride. Long, soft. Well kept. Now it was an ugly distraction.

Lost in thought as I combed through the knots with my fingers, I stared off at the trees, trying to picture myself the way I'd been before I was taken. I was most certainly smaller now, thanks to the lack of care and feeding Ignus and his lot had provided. My hair was dry and uneven, the same with my skin. My hands traveled from one end of my body to the other, assessing, measuring. I was whole, but I was changed.

"I'm getting out," Seir's quiet voice warned, breaking me out of my reverie. I sank into the water up to my throat.

His bare feet tapped across the stones as he carried the clothing past me to the colder pools. Towel knotted around his lean waist, he squatted down and proceeded to rinse, scrub, and smack the garments until their cleanliness met his satisfaction. Again, I watched him, fascinated by how his tail accompanied his hands in the labor with no visible effort or thought … and also how it no longer seemed strange to me.

Peaceful was the word that came to mind as he crossed back in front of me with the wet clothes, then laid them all out on some of the larger stone formations.

There was no resting for him, it seemed. Once that was done, he stoked the fire and started some tea in the big pot. Then he wandered off toward the trees, still barefoot in just a towel.

"Won't your feet get dirty? Or cut up? What will we do then? I'm not sure I can carry you!" I teased.

I was rewarded with a rich laugh. "Don't underestimate yourself, Hailon! You're dangerous, remember? That includes strong."

He vanished into the trees, and I finished up, getting out and into my own towel as quickly as I could, all too aware that he would be within his rights to look his fill at me as I had of him.

As I turned around, my eyes met Seir's, the pile of berries he'd collected in the end of his towel spilling to the ground at his feet.

"Sorry, I didn't mean to sneak up," he rushed to say, one hand out defensively. His eyes darted up and down my form, then over to the trees, a fierce blush lighting up his cheeks. But everything stopped when he dropped his gaze toward the ground again. "Hailon, what's happened to your leg?"

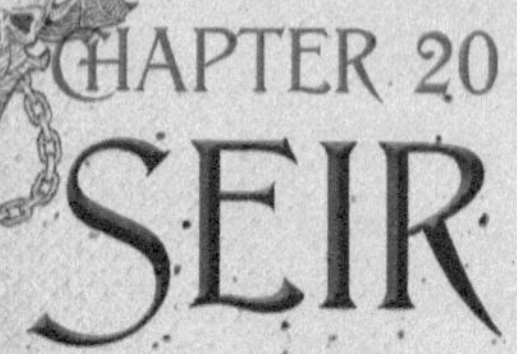

CHAPTER 20
SEIR

"IT'S NOTHING," SHE said casually, as though the black and purple streaks were completely normal.

"That is not nothing," I said, dropping to my knees to take a better look. The injury was fresh, angry. I worried briefly about blood poisoning as I examined the damage, but the red streaks were contained enough that seemed unlikely. "Why do I feel as though that's something I'm going to be repeating often with you?"

"Seir, truly. It doesn't hurt much at all."

I glanced up at her, finding a cross between annoyance and amusement on her face as she held the knot in her towel together with her fingers.

"How can something that looks like that not be painful? And where did you get it? Were you hurt yesterday?" Guilt pressed in, fierce and hot. She'd been so concerned about me, about my healing, that she'd neglected her own injuries completely. And so had I. "I'm sorry, I should have—"

She heaved a sigh and put her hand against my mouth to silence me. Her doing that while I was on my knees before her sent a riot of thrills through my veins. I tensed, worried she could see right through me, and considering a hasty escape back to the trees so I could take a private moment to … relax.

"You didn't do anything wrong. I'm fine. Honestly."

I narrowed my eyes and started collecting the berries I'd dropped. "Explain so I can understand. Please. I'll beg if need be, I'm already on my knees."

"You're absolutely ridiculous." She finally let go of her towel, the knot holding steady as she put her hands together to make a bowl and accepted the berries.

As we walked over to the fire, I was unnaturally aware of her stride, the way she favored her injured leg a tiny bit. She'd had a limp for most of the time I'd known her, and that, too, was my fault. There were hot embers trapped under my ribs, burning in a way that was increasingly worrisome.

She tipped one of the water flasks to her mouth, shaking it after only getting a few drops. "It will be gone in a few days."

"Something like that will not resolve in just a manner of days, Hailon. Saints, it looks like you hurt yourself the same place—" I choked on the air in my throat, understanding pressing down on me like stones. I reached for her towel, pulling the edge to the side with a finger, exposing a similar mark on her stomach. I spun her, finding bruising on her shoulders, some old and yellowing, leftover from when I first helped her escape. Others the same fresh red and purple.

"Hey! Stop that!" She yanked the cloth from my fingers and pulled it back tight, cheeks reddening as she stared me down.

"I'm sorry, I wasn't trying to be forward," I apologized, suddenly mortified at what I'd done. "I wasn't trying to see—"

"It's fine," she snapped, knuckles white where she clung to the fabric wrapped around her.

Understanding dawned, and ice slipped down my spine. "That's the cost, isn't it." Her lips thinned and she wouldn't meet my eye as she dug around in her pack. "Your magic, the way you healed me—that's what it cost you to do it." An almost imperceptible nod. Cold rage rumbled under my skin, my chest aching. "You should have told me, Hailon. I wouldn't have let you—"

Her head snapped my direction, fury burning behind her eyes. "It wasn't *up* to you. You needed healing, there was no time to waste discussing such things. I helped you. I fixed it. I knew the cost and willingly paid it. Just like I did for the frog. Just like I did for Widow Callahan, though I had to be clever about that so she thought it was the ointment. It's no different than what I've done for the hundreds of others before that."

I struggled with what might be the right response. If I let the brash words of frustration I held behind my lips burst free, I would surely lose any goodwill I'd built with her. If I said nothing, I was sure to go mad. My demon was close to the surface but was stifled from releasing. My horns ached to be let out, and my eyes were almost certainly glowing. Hailon squinted at me but showed no fear over my outburst. If fact, she'd put her shoulders back and raised her chin, her indignance prepared to go to war with my accusation.

I reached out, grabbed onto her shoulders and pulled, folding her into my arms.

"What—"

"Shh."

Her cheek pressed against the skin over my burning, pounding heart. I closed my eyes and just breathed, pressing my lips to the crown of her head. She was stiff for several breaths, then relaxed, her hands even rising to hold me back, the touch of her hands welcome against my flesh.

My world settled and, several slow inhales later, my thoughts were orderly, my blood no longer buzzed with heat or the desire to lash out. Everything about her in my arms felt right, and it brought me a profound level of peace.

"Thank you."

Hailon frowned, confusion in her gaze as I released her. She stepped back. "What?"

I reached out, my palm going to her jaw. I loved holding her face like this, and she was kind enough to let me do it despite her frustration. It made me feel connected to her, close. Like we were the only thing of importance in the universe at that moment.

"Thank you," I said.

"What?" she repeated.

"Thank you for making sure my body was repaired so skillfully. I am wise enough to understand that your consent was likely rarely considered where your healing power is involved. I appreciate you doing that for me, though I would have preferred to know that you would suffer for it ahead of time. I never want you to suffer for me, Hailon."

Those perfect lips opened then closed again, shock painting her features in a whole new expression. It was a lovely composition, the tilt to her mouth, the wideness of her brilliant multicolored eyes. My breath stuttered in my chest, and the pain behind my ribs bloomed. I pressed my other palm into the muscle, the ache unrelieved but the gesture itself comforting.

I was so gone for this woman.

"Had it not been so urgent, I might have discussed it with you beforehand." Her tone was low and intentionally measured. "But you're welcome, I guess. I don't feel as though there was much of a choice, really. A simple wood splint wouldn't have done enough to get us back on the road in a timely way, now would it? Not with your shinbone sticking through your skin and your own wing spur stabbed through your gut." She raised her hand, pressing it against mine, her eyes closing for a brief moment as she leaned into my touch.

I smiled at her, my tail winding and unwinding around my leg nervously. "No, I suppose not," I agreed. There was something about her that made me feel joyfully unbalanced. The novelty of it was thrilling in a way that both terrified me and made me feel as though I might be chasing such a sensation for the rest of my life. "Still. Thank you. Is there anything I can do for you? These look ..." I stuck my finger in the joint of her towel again, trying to get another look at the bruising to her middle. She slapped my hand.

"Saints, you're incorrigible. I'm *fine*." Her mood had softened, and I was blessed with a chuckle after she gave a long-suffering groan and a lingering look at the strong shoulders she carried the whole world around on as she stepped away from me.

AFTER A BIT of discussion, we decided that remaining there for the night was far preferable to continuing on at such an odd time of day.

"I hate to lose the time," she muttered thoughtfully while collecting her things. Guilt stained her face, pulling her mouth into a tense line.

"It's only half a day. We'd be no good later on anyhow, and we'd have to find another place to make camp, find food, and sleep at some point. We can make up the time once we get to the Valley." I tried to inject confidence into my tone. "There's bound to be a wagon or horses there, right? There's constant trade between Emankor and Ravenglen." Hailon's head bobbed thoughtfully, and she relaxed a little bit. "My promise to get you home as quickly as I can hasn't changed."

"I know."

We lingered over a lunch of fresh berries and an assortment of edible greens put together in a kind of salad. It felt luxurious almost, to lounge on our blankets dressed only in towels near the hot springs, sipping on tea and snacking while the sun worked its magic on our skin. I was fairly sure we both dozed a little bit, too, which was a beautiful extravagance.

I wished for a lifetime of days like this for her. *With* her would be perfectly amenable too.

When I looked over, Hailon's fingers were tangling in the ends of her hair again, tugging and twisting as she stared off into the trees, one of the dark-purple berries I'd picked staining her lips red as she nibbled on it.

"Would you like me to brush and braid your hair again?" I asked, chin pillowed on my hands as my back soaked up the sunlight.

Her lips curled upward. "Does it bother you that I worry at it? I know I do that, for the record. I can't help myself, it feels … strange." Her voice went wistful. "It's dull and lifeless now, missing in chunks. I used to have beautiful hair."

"Your hair is still beautiful, Hailon." I gathered the comb and the strips of leather I used to tie off the ends and settled on my knees behind her, willing her to hear the sincerity of my words. That I meant far more than just her hair.

Sunlight bounced off the crown of her head, illuminating unmistakably pure-white threads mixed into the dark strands. I kept that to myself, not wanting to worry her. I'd known enough women to understand that commenting on a change in appearance like that might not be appreciated.

I liked it though. She reminded me of a moonflower just beginning to bloom.

Her head tilted back as I began to comb through the strands, her eyes closed and face turned into the afternoon sun. I worked as slowly as I dared to, stretching out the activity so that I could continue touching her. Soothing her. As my fingers brushed against her scalp, her features tightened, and her hand rose to her chest. The heel of her palm brushed against the space right over her heart. The gesture was familiar.

I froze. If she was also feeling the burning pain, that could mean ...

"Are you feeling alright?"

"Fine. I think the greens maybe aren't sitting well. It's happened a few times recently. I wasn't exactly well-fed at that house. Perhaps my body is adjusting back to real food."

My pulse pounded in my ears. Experimentally, I rested my hand on her shoulder. The storm in my chest settled some.

Hailon turned her head to look at me. "It comes and goes though. Sometimes quite suddenly." She frowned. "Are you finished?"

"Not quite." I tidied up my work as I tried to control my breathing. I lashed the ends of the two braids together against her neck, leaving the tails of the tie long, so she could play with them instead of her hair if she liked.

"Thank you."

"My pleasure, moonflower."

Perplexed, she watched me as I wandered away to check on our clothing, a maelstrom of understanding swirling through me.

This lovely little human, this perfect specimen of beauty and violence was more than my travel companion or a fixation I'd developed on this journey earth-side.

She was my mate.

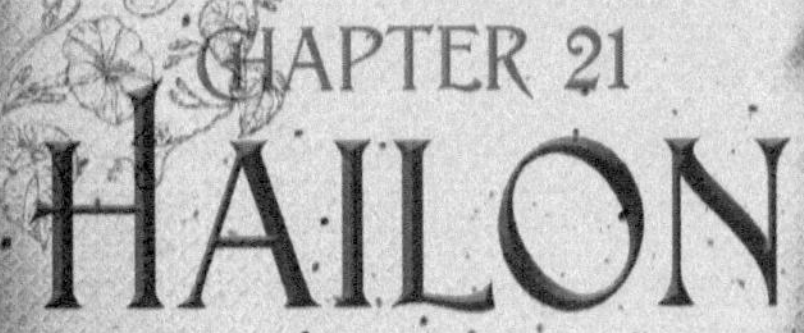

CHAPTER 21
HAILON

"**C**OLTOR COULD LEASE out time in that glade for holidays or health rejuvenation or something of the sort," I said, sad that the little oasis was now several hours of walking behind us.

Following Coltor's changes to our little map, we'd easily found what was the actual main road and had been walking along it peacefully all morning.

"Most certainly," Seir agreed. "I could live there quite happily."

"Doing so could interfere with his posting, though. That might make him grumpier than he already is."

"Guarding doorways like he suggested exist within the castle itself is a very important job. Can't have people wandering in and out of other worlds on a whim."

"People like you?" I teased back, though in truth I was as jealous as I was curious about using portals. "What's it like being able to travel like you do? Portals and things, I mean."

"I'll show you one day," he promised, and my stomach clenched. Whatever I was, whatever negative power I possessed that apparently canceled out other's magic would almost certainly keep me from ever doing any such thing. "Perhaps you should suggest that to him next time we see him? That he build some little cabins to rent out. We could be his first clients." Seir smiled.

"You believe that will happen? That we'll see him again?"

"Of course!" Seir nodded enthusiastically. "People like that are never just a one-time meeting. I suspect we'll see him plenty more times."

"We?" I asked, amused by how absolutely positive he was about such a statement.

"Naturally," he scoffed, releasing his wings and spreading his arms as he jogged ahead and turned around to face me, walking backwards. "Where you go, I go, little Moonflower."

I let that idea linger there between us. I knew that once we arrived in Ravenglen, he was returning to Hell, and the odds of us running into that stone kin man several times over the next few days was infinitesimal. But I had grown very used to being with him, and clearly he felt the same about me. It was nice to imagine a future where we had more adventures, even if the notion had never before crossed my mind.

"Why have you started calling me that?" I didn't mind it, in fact it made my heart skip a little beat every time he said it, but it was odd. "Moonflower. That's two or three times now."

He dropped his chin to his chest, chagrined. "Do you really want to know?"

"Yes."

He pulled his wings tight against his back and stopped walking, reaching for my hair as I caught up to him. "You've acquired some moonbeams in your braids." He showed me the end of one of the two braids he'd given me before we left the beautiful glade. Sure enough, mixed in with the black were threads of pure white.

I gasped and used the pad of my thumb to spread out the

strands, trying to see how many there might be. "When did this happen?"

Seir shoved his hands in his pockets and turned around, starting to walk down the road again. His wings spread wide, he flexed them repeatedly, doing some kind of exercise routine I wasn't privy to. "I'm not sure, I just noticed it myself."

Panic had my pulse racing. "How are there so many? And why are they white all the way to the ends like this? This isn't how hair normally starts turning gray."

Seir watched me rant with a serious expression. "I didn't tell you at first for this very reason. I didn't mean to upset you by pointing it out."

"I'm not so young I shouldn't expect some gray soon, but—"

"How old are you, Moonflower? I've never thought to ask."

"There are three things you should never ask a woman," I scolded him, though in truth I was not offended. It was honestly a surprise to me that it hadn't come up sooner. "Her age, her dress size, and whether or not she's with child."

"Noted." He grinned widely, and I could tell he was calculating something.

"So? How many winters have you seen, then?"

"Clever, but still the same question." I tutted at him, and he laughed.

"What if I start? Three hundred twenty-nine Earth years have passed since I took up residence in Hell. Time is a much more fluid thing where I originated. I don't really know how to calculate how much passed before then. And it also bends and moves differently depending on the realm you're in, so perhaps even that's not an accurate accounting."

I kept my silence for several paces, but there was no need for my age to remain a secret. "I'm thirty-three. Old, by all accounts where I'm from. Spinster-y even."

Seir scoffed. "You're still very spry. What could possibly be the qualifications that would make someone call you *old*?"

"Well ..." I mentally compiled all the things that had been listed off to me over the years, most of them intended to shame or guilt me into some kind of marriage of convenience or admission of failure as a woman. Then I listed them off for him, getting increasingly sharp with my tone as I did.

"I prefer to keep the company of my aunt almost exclusively. I perform a craft that many find questionable. I was educated past primary school, which is mostly unheard of where I'm from, particularly for girls. I have a proclivity for using my blades and prefer pants to skirts. I'm unmarried by choice, having refused most suitors even attempting to court me, but especially proposals that would have only benefitted them and their families, not me or mine. I've unashamedly bedded people I didn't plan to marry, some I didn't even like all that much. I don't have any children and I'm past thirty. The list is quite long, honestly."

He gaped, eyebrows up high and mouth slightly open. "That's madness. Education is a positive thing, no matter who you are. Knowing how to defend yourself is valuable, as is your healing ability. And babies are adorable but terrifying, so I can understand why you weren't interested in jumping into having them or a marriage, particularly with someone you didn't care for. Those contracts are binding." He shook his head fiercely and a hand strayed to one of the blades along his belt. I could only imagine what he was envisioning, but I was certain it entailed violence. He seemed like he was struggling to decide what he wanted to say next. "In any case, I think it's pretty. Your hair," he said quietly. "I call you that because the white reminds me of a moonflower blossoming."

My breath caught and I stopped, the gravity of his casual words leaving me unable to move for several moments.

"Hailon?" Seir turned around, finding me several steps behind him.

"That's ... sweet," I managed. With no hint of insincerity on his part, it truly was. "Are there moonflowers in Hell?"

He chuffed a small laugh and continued on, lifting one knee high, then the other. "There are some gardens there, though my experience with flora and fauna like that is mainly here, or in the fae realm. Between the two, the chances of being injured by pretty plants is much lower here."

I watched him doing knee lifts as he walked, his gait wide and comical. "What is it you're doing up there? It would be wise to take your hands out of your pockets, in any case. If you fall, you'll land right on your pretty face."

Seir spun, grin wide. "You think my face is pretty?" His tail swished happily back and forth in the air behind him, one hand dramatically pressed to his cheek.

I rolled my eyes but felt the heat of a blush on my face. "You know it is."

"It doesn't matter what I know, *you* thinking so is another thing entirely." He flapped around me like a light-drunk moth, teasing and laughing, chasing up great gusts of wind and dust with his outstretched wings.

Then, we both froze. "Seir, did you—?"

He blinked at me and tried to replicate what he'd been doing. On the fourth flap, he lifted off the ground.

"Ah!" he shouted and laughed, crashing into the ground so hard he stumbled to his knees. He somehow turned the fall into a graceful tumble and sprang back to his feet after doing what looked like a carefully practiced roll. "Hailon, you saw that, right?"

Excitement surged through me. "Yes, you were hovering!"

Eyes alight, enthusiasm bubbling over, he reached out and held my face between his hands. Then he crashed his mouth to mine in a kiss that could only be called a smooch. I froze, feeling the surge of electricity that passed between us, a riot of palpitations in my heartbeat. He pulled away, a wicked grin on his mouth like he knew exactly what he'd done but had no regrets.

Then, as I stood there in shock, he took off at a run down the road, mighty wings pushing him off the ground—but only a few inches at a time and only for a moment. Still, he was undeterred. He practiced on and off in different ways until we broke for lunch, then continued again until we set up camp for the night. I was exhausted just watching him, but it was amusing nonetheless. His energy never seemed to flag, and his determination was relentless.

He finally put his wings away when we found a copse of trees to camp in for the evening.

"I'll get some wood," I offered as he assembled some rocks into a ring and collected kindling to get a fire started.

I picked up as much as I could carry and found he'd already gotten a decent flame going when I returned. "What'll it be tonight, soup or stew?" he asked.

"What's the difference?"

"Nothing, really. More water for broth. Just seemed polite to offer a choice."

I shook my head and pulled out my bedding. "As long as it's food, I'll eat it. Hopefully it settles well."

He paused, an odd look on his face before the easygoing smile returned, and he began pulling things we'd taken from the glade out of the pack.

We'd just settled in to eat when thunder rumbled, not far off.

"That doesn't sound good," I muttered, searching the sky for lightning. The clouds were thick, blocking the moon, but puffy and white.

"We'll be alright." He seemed unconcerned but finished his food in a hurry and started constructing a little shelter out of the one piece of cloth we had that was mostly water-resistant. Widow Callahan to the rescue again. I hoped to see her again someday.

Fat droplets began to fall not long after he'd moved our things under the small shelter. I'd wondered about the angle he'd used, but everything was clear when he let his wings out. He shifted around until he was satisfied, and so long as he ducked his head a bit, we could both stay perfectly dry and warm. Even the fire was under enough cover thanks to the end of his wing.

"Your wings have gotten quite the workout today."

"They're often very useful."

"I'm sorry—"

"Don't apologize. It's not your fault." His gaze was unusually stony, his jaw working as he said the words.

"But it is," I argued. "Or at least it seems like it is."

"Hailon—"

I held a hand up. "I'm not saying it's my fault in a way that's intentional, but it *is* my fault that some of your talents don't work right simply because I'm near you."

Seir shook his head. "You don't know that for sure. It's a good theory, but nothing is proven." He grumbled and changed topic. "How is your leg today? Your stomach?"

I pulled up the hem of my trousers. "Better. See? It'll be just as it was before you fell down that hill in a few short days."

He grunted, still unreasonably put out by the bruises I'd taken on for healing him.

"Would you like some tea or are you finished?"

"I'm done." Tea sounded good, but I was already feeling a bit of heartburn from our innocuous dinner. I wished whatever it was that had my stomach so irritated would go away.

Despite the fact it was he who had run, jumped, and flapped the whole walk, I found myself dozing almost immediately once I pulled my cloak over my shoulders and laid down.

"Hailon, I ..." He tapered off, eyes widening when mine met them. "I'll be back in just a moment," he said, disappearing into the trees. It was odd behavior, but sometimes nature called.

The sound of the rain tapping on the cloth above my head was soothing, though the storm was quickly turning into a downpour.

The fire hissed and popped as the drops did their best to extinguish its warmth. The thunder had picked up, the lightning too.

Seir returned and shuffled under the shelter with me.

"Can I get a bit closer, Moonflower? I don't want either of us to get wet. It would make for a miserable night and a terrible day tomorrow as well."

"Okay."

He met me in the middle, so we both had as much space as possible to the edge of the shelter, but the way the drops were bouncing off the ground, we'd both be soaked by morning regardless.

The look in his eyes as they searched mine made me shiver. I could see the desire there, but also the care. He was afraid of overstepping, though he had yet to do so. Not even when he kissed me earlier.

"No untoward intentions?" I asked, voice hushed.

His mouth twitched. "Not tonight." He opened his arms, and we both scooted closer yet, closing the gap between us altogether. "I …" He clearly had something he wanted to say but was holding back. "Are you warm enough?"

"Yes, I'm fine." I closed my eyes, forehead resting against his chest. The thump of his heartbeat was strong and steady next to my ear and under the palm of my hand. He added his cloak to the warmth and then … something else. I cracked my eyes, finding it was darker than it had been.

"Rest well, Hailon." He snuggled his cheek against the top of my head.

"Good night, Seir."

His tail wrapped around my ankle, like it had back in the ruins, his arm resting over the curve of my hip. It was comfortable. Familiar. The burn in my chest finally eased up. I realized that as impossible as it seemed, I was happy.

Wondering what I was supposed to do with that, I drifted to sleep, lulled by the sound of the rain, safely wrapped up in my demon's wings.

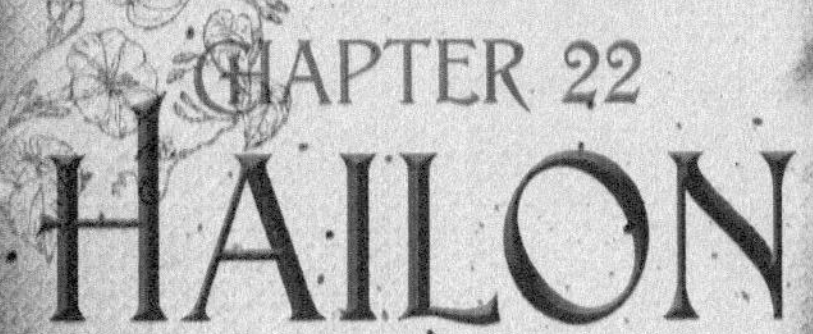

CHAPTER 22
HAILON

"Hailon, come try these on!" Seir was positively vibrating with excitement and had been since we stumbled into Manvil around midday. To say we were both grateful to have arrived somewhere with a wealth of amenities was an understatement. I could also feel how close we were getting to Ravenglen with the shift in the temperature and season. This place *felt* more northern and much more like home than previous towns.

We'd immediately found the nearest tavern and eaten a full hot meal—double servings for Seir—before starting a slow circuit through the bustling shops. I already had two new tunics, a pair of trousers, and a skirt, as well as matching underthings and socks. I had no clue where we were going to store everything, but he was undaunted by such details and kept magically finding space for things in his pack. It probably helped that I wore several of the items out of the shop.

"The boots I have are fine," I argued, terrified of the price tag on such fine craftsmanship.

He scoffed and brought the footwear to me, earning a scowl and wary eye from the cobbler who ran the shop. "Only with *three* pairs of socks. Look, aren't these lovely?" He held up the pair of supple leather boots, his smile wide. "This pair is perfect for you."

"Is it? How so?" I chuckled, taking the boots and allowing him to tug me by the hand back to the little store. The cobbler finally relaxed once we were through the door.

"Well to start, this rich honey tone will look lovely with your eyes." Seir gently pushed on my shoulders, and I sat on the wooden stool. "Then there's the higher arch, and these toggles along the calf."

"It's antler," the cobbler provided helpfully. "The toggles, that is. Elk, if I'm not mistaken. The leather too."

Seir knelt on the floor directly in front of me and pulled my foot to his thigh. Heat flared violently through my body. It was a simple gesture but certainly a meaningful display to anyone looking on.

"This really isn't necessary. I can take off my own boots."

"I know you can. Let this prove once and for all that I'll happily get on my knees for you any time the situation calls for it, Moonflower."

He winked and pulled off the oversized boots, setting them to the side. Next were the socks, which he replaced with a single pair of new ones, a burgundy set I'd fallen in love with immediately for their softness and color.

My blush only deepened the more he fussed. His fingertips lingered on my ankle and calf as he settled the sock over my leg. Then came the boot. His thigh was once again the prop as he slid the leather over my toes and forced my heel down into the sole.

His smile was slow and heated as he checked the fit. I didn't miss the twinkle in his eye when he glanced up at me long enough to wink again. Then he dipped down and pressed his lips to my knee before repeating the process. His shenanigans would have been hindered by the pair of trousers I'd been wearing when we first arrived in town. Lucky for him, I'd changed into the long skirt at the clothing store.

"Seir," I chided, exasperated.

Things had shifted significantly between us since our time in the ruins, and I wasn't sure how to feel about how little I minded. The more boldly he flirted, the more I melted, even if I made a front of scoffing at his efforts. It was so unlike me, but I couldn't even find the will to fight it. It was nice to be cared for. I hadn't had much of that in my life.

"Wiggle your toes around, make sure they're not too tight." He ignored my scolding tone completely. On went the second boot, and he was offering me a hand while still on his knees so I could stand and walk around. Even on his knees, the top of his head came to just below my ribs.

"You need a job, mister?" the cobbler asked, arms crossed as he watched us from near his workbench. "Seems you have a knack with the more persnickety customers."

Seir beamed at the compliment. "Only passing through, I'm afraid. How much for these? We'd be happy to trade you the other pair as well. They're good quality and fairly new, just not well-fitted for her."

The cobbler made a show of considering it, then the two engaged in some polite haggling as I silently marveled at how good the boots felt on my feet. They might have been the best ones I'd ever owned. I hated that he'd been so right.

"Deal," Seir finally said, getting to his feet to shake the man's hand. He rattled the poor cobbler's whole arm, making him stutter in shock.

Seir gathered up our packs, shoved the old pair of boots and the appropriate amount of money at the cobbler, and we were back on our way. He threaded his fingers into mine, sending another skip through my heartbeat. We were in a very busy area, but it felt like he might be doing it for more than just that reason.

"This is fun! I haven't been able to do this kind of thing in a regrettably long time."

"What, go shopping?"

He nodded, looking around for our next stop. "Yes. There are markets in He—" He paused, the crush of people dense and too much attention on us to be comfortable speaking so openly. He dropped his volume and continued. "There are markets where I live, but nothing like this." He stopped, head swiveling as he scanned the wooden signs above shop doors.

"What are you looking for now?" I asked with a chuckle, his buoyant mood infectious. I'd had a good meal, had spent more coin than I'd ever seen at any single time in my life, and could almost guarantee a night in an actual bed was in my very near future.

"Ah!" He tugged me down a short alley, pausing in front of some leaded glass windows.

"A jeweler?"

"Are you attached to the spoons? I was going to see if they would be interested in buying them for the silver. Maybe that little belt, too, for the gold."

"Not at all, that's exactly why I brought them along."

"Good. Stay where I can see you out the window?"

"Sure."

He nodded once, resolutely, then walked into the small shop.

I watched people milling about, banners in red and orange strung up on ledges and signposts. Trees were wrapped in ribbons as well, and there seemed to be an unusually high amount of people out and about, given the size of the town.

A woman with a kind face walked by, and I got her attention. "Excuse me? What are the decorations for?"

She smiled. "The Forage Festival! One of the best days of the whole year." She looked me up and down. "Traveling through, I assume, as you had to ask?"

"Yes, we arrived today."

"You're here just in time, then! Everyone is already setting up, but after sunset, things really get going. There's food and music, street vendors. Enjoy yourself!"

I thanked her as she continued along her way. Seir emerged a few minutes later, jingling heavily with every step. "That was smoother than expected, honestly. All set. What did that woman say to you?"

I appreciated that he'd had his eyes on me. "I wanted to know what the banners are for. There's some kind of festival," I said, gesturing to the orange and red fabric.

"In that case, we'd better secure a room. We can come find some sweet treats after, yes?"

He tugged me along again, and I let him, heart lighter and worries far away.

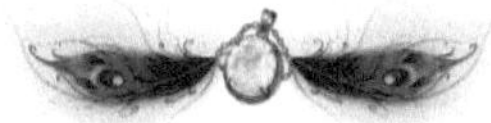

SEIR WAS UNDETERRED in his efforts to find us a room despite the first three inns having none available.

To soothe the frustration, he continued to shop as we made our way down alleys and around blocks and through all the tents and tables that enterprising shopkeepers were setting up on the walks.

In the end, we were able to rent the attic room of the Rusted Rooster. It was at the far end of town, and actually was a preferable location for getting on our way in the morning even if it seemed like a more troublesome spot at first. Besides, the owners were an adorable older couple, and I could tell they didn't get as much traffic because of their location. They were all too happy to help us out.

We had to climb three flights of stairs to get to our lodging for the evening. Seir even had to duck a bit under areas of the sloped roof as we went down the short hall.

"That last flight of stairs was only a little terrifying," I complained. The steps had gotten narrower and steeper as we went up, and the door to the attic itself required a special key. Everything creaked and squeaked as we walked, and I wondered if we'd be resting with the house's ghosts.

"At least there's a private bath," he gestured to the dark room across the hall as he unlocked the door. "And the door locks, which is nice."

"It's private everything, this is the only room up here," I countered.

"They should be charging more for such a privilege." Seir grinned as he strode into the main bedroom, dropping our packs near the little table with two stools without hesitation.

"Oh." I stopped short in the doorway, looking around to see if there was more to the space I couldn't see.

"What's the matter?"

I gestured my arm to the singular—though ample-sized—bed.

Seir shrugged. "I can sleep on the floor by the fireplace like I did at the way-house. No matter to me."

"It's ... a big bed," I found myself saying. My cheeks lit up as I realized what it might sound like I was inviting. "Surely we can both fit and get some decent rest. We did just fine last night, after all."

"Mmm." Seir crossed to the far side of the mattress and laid his long form down, one eyebrow raised playfully. "Care to test it out with me?" He held his hand out in invitation.

"You're ridiculous." I was blushing, I was sure of it. And tempted.

"No," he countered, "I'm practical. Come on. It's a lovely bed. Very comfortable. Perhaps we should nap before we go back out to the festival." He closed his eyes and folded his hands together over his stomach.

That was a temptation for sure. It seemed sleep was the one thing we were constantly chasing, though I was still feeling fairly rested from our extra day in Coltor's glade.

I toed off my new boots and carefully laid myself out as close to the edge of the bed as I could get.

"Come now," Seir tutted, his strong hands sliding under my hip and shoulder. I made a squeak as he pulled me toward the center of the mattress. "No need to fall off the edge. There's plenty of space."

His fingers combed through my hair, and I found myself melting into the mattress despite my anxiousness. "Just a little nap?" I suggested, eyes already getting heavier.

"An hour or so, to recharge our energy for the festivities."

"How can you be sure we won't sleep through until morning?"

"My stomach, for one," he chuckled, fingers delving deep into the strands, short nails dragging along my scalp. "I have a relentless body clock, remember? And I don't sleep much. I'll bet we'll be up and ready for supper without any trouble at all."

"If you say so." My words were mumbled, running together as I dissolved into my pillow.

"I do." Seir's fingers disappeared from my hair long enough to pull the quilt over me.

"You're kind, Seir."

"Oh?"

"Thoughtful. Generous."

"You flatter me, Hailon." He shifted a bit closer, both hands now in the mix, pulling sections of my hair into little braids. "To what do I owe such pretty words?"

"I just ... needed to tell you. For a while, I think I was sort of waiting for you to stop being so nice. To be sure that it wasn't an act. But then I realized it's who you are. Are all demons like this?"

He made a thoughtful noise in his throat. It rumbled through my chest, and I reached up to soothe the slight burn that flared with my hand.

"I'm hardly a rarity, Moonflower, but I suppose not all that common either. My brothers and I decided early that we would do our best to remain ourselves, no matter our location."

"What does that mean?"

"Mostly that I simply refuse to let Hell turn me into one of the beasts it houses. It would be very easy to let it happen, honestly. Seeing ugliness, torture, violence all day every day … it does something to you." His voice grew distant. "Battle. Blood. There's only so much the mind can take before it fractures. But I am still myself, despite all I've seen. Despite my own terrible deeds. The choice to fall was mine, and I stand by it." The mood lightened again, the shroud of despair disappearing as quickly as it had come. "We'll talk about that another time though. Or not. It's not something you need concern yourself with. You've seen plenty of the darkness yourself, after all. Rest now. Dream of savory meat skewers and fluffy candy floss. Perhaps there will be fireworks or those little sticks that sparkle when they are met with flame. We can look for a gift to take to your Aunt Sal. Maybe there's a book she'd like, or a little trinket …"

I drifted away as he pulled his fingers through my hair and listed off curiosities and baubles, wondering what the angel version of him must have been like if this was him after he fell.

CHAPTER 23
SEIR

"COME ON!" I threaded my fingers through Hailon's and pulled her with me through the crush of people.

"You've been hauling me through town all day!" she complained, but there was no bite to her tone. In fact, there was a wide smile on her mouth and wonder in her eyes as she looked at all the activity around us.

"Just a bit longer, I promise. And it was worth it, was it not? You have those lovely new boots, a whole bag full of treats. You got a nap, and—"

"Yes, yes." She laughed, and my heart soared.

Our nap had been longer than an hour but completely needed and well worth it. When I woke, it was to a peaceful Hailon tucked into my side, her head pillowed on my shoulder with my fingers tangled in her hair. I didn't move until she stirred, taking the opportunity to memorize every tiny freckle across the bridge of her nose and sprinkled over her cheeks and the sound of her breathing as she dreamt.

After she opened those glorious eyes, my concentrated study was over, however. She blinked at me twice, like she was trying to decide whether or not she was still sleeping, then when I said nothing more offensive than hello, she bolted from the bed and disappeared into the little bathroom, her cheeks a rather intense shade of red. No matter. I'd been entirely present while she cuddled with me and would remember the quiet moments before she panicked.

After securing our most valued items in a hidden space next to the tub behind the locked attic door, we made our way back out to celebrate with the townspeople.

"Are you going to spend *all* the coin you traded those spoons for?" she teased as I stopped at yet another food stall, this time retrieving us some kind of meat skewer with roasted potatoes sliced in fancy spirals around the stick. We'd had stewed fowl and root vegetables in a bread bowl, fruit covered in a crunchy sugar shell, and I'd enjoyed a couple of tankards of local ale. I was beginning to feel very spoiled, given most of our journey so far.

"Not hardly." The jeweler had been more than happy to buy the pieces, and my pockets were heavier than they had any right to be from our exchange. "Besides, the spoons were yours, Moonflower. What I traded them for belongs to you. Would you like to carry the coin? I should have offered straightaway."

She finished her food and, with a shake of her head, tossed the thin stick into a nearby trash bin. "No. I don't want it."

"But—"

"I took the spoons and the jewelry for just this reason, so I would have money to travel on. So I could get back home. Spend the coin however you like, I'm just glad it didn't stay in that horrible house or benefit those men. If there's some left when we get back to Ravenglen, we can talk about it, but I don't care. It's not mine, even if it is part of what was owed to me for the time I was there." Her somber expression left me regretting I'd even mentioned it as we wandered slowly past a few tables. "Come on." She tugged at me this time, and I followed her willingly.

"Cosmetics?" I asked as she turned over a small tin of rouge in her hand.

"Can I help you, miss?" The heavily painted woman batted her eyes at me, though she addressed Hailon.

"Yes, I'm looking for some nail lacquer."

"Ah! Yes, of course. We have these." The woman displayed several tiny pots, the pigments all in reds and pinks.

"Anything darker?" she asked, subtly glancing at me.

"Darker?"

"Yes, like purple or black?"

The woman pulled a face. "No, we don't carry such colors. No demand for them." She turned a judgmental eye on Hailon, and when she looked back at me, I gave her a smile that included my teeth. She flinched.

"Shame. I'd have liked to get myself fixed up." I wiggled my fingertips at her, the black now nearly all chipped away.

Her mouth dropped open, and she started to babble something apologetic, but Hailon was already halfway to another table.

"She was rude," Hailon sighed as I jogged up to her side.

I was beaming. Hailon had just tried to do something nice for me. It hadn't worked out, but I didn't care, the intent was there, and I was awed by the gesture. In fact, I wasn't sure anyone had taken any interest in how I kept my nails at all before now. The behavior of the stall woman had barely made an impression on me because of that, but I could see it had bothered Hailon.

"Would you like me to take care of her?" I asked, already reaching for my blades.

"What? No! Why would you think I wanted that?" She covered my hands with hers, glancing nervously over her shoulder to see if anyone else had noticed my threat.

I shrugged. "She offended you."

"Seir." This time I was the cause of her deep sigh. "People are rude sometimes. There's no need to threaten someone's life because they were more interested in impressing you than being polite. There's a time and place for everything."

"Impressing me?"

She stopped walking, mouth partly open as she stared at me, incredulous. "Are you being serious?"

I shrugged. "People do that eyelash batting thing to help sell whatever it is they're peddling. Doesn't mean I'll buy it."

"She definitely wasn't just trying to get you to buy her *rouge*, demon." Hailon huffed a little laugh.

"Oh, I'm well aware of that, Moonflower." I winked at her and her cheeks colored, which made it all that much more entertaining. "But I'm here with *you*. I'm not buying anything she's selling, now am I?"

The red color spread to her ears. "Do you threaten everyone who flirts with you?"

"Only the ones who do it in a way that displeases you. Though ... perhaps it should be anyone who does it in front of you? Or at all? It's quite disrespectful."

"Should I feel murderous toward anyone who looks at you the way she was?"

I brightened, a light fizzy sensation careening through my veins. "Do you?"

Her mouth opened, then closed again, her eyes shifting away from my face. If that wasn't confirmation, I didn't know what was, though she didn't address my question. "You don't belong to me," she argued.

"Yes, I do. I said as much the first night we met. Do you not recall?"

"That wasn't— I didn't—" She threw her hands up, faced flushed and normally composed demeanor flustered. I loved every second of watching her unravel, it put a particular kind of fire in my blood. "That's not the point! There's no need to draw attention to ourselves, remember? Besides, there will be other vendors," she said with finality.

"Of course." I grabbed her hand and threaded my fingers through hers, kissing the back of her hand for good measure. "But you do, right? I mean, you think my face is pretty, so naturally you feel a little possessive over other people looking at it? Murderous even?" I asked, earning myself another rough exhale and hidden smile.

It was worth it.

And there were more vendors. So *many* of them. There was no product I could think of missing from the tables and tents and storefronts. It bordered on overwhelming.

By the third cosmetics stand, Hailon had secured us a pot of both black and purple lacquer and brushes to use with them along with a fresh container of healing ointment and a lotion for her skin. Along the way, we'd picked up a variety of interesting foods as well, and she'd enjoyed sampling two different kinds of mead.

Having made a full circuit of the main town square and most of the streets spiraling off from it, we started to work our way back to the Rusted Rooster. Hailon's giggle was free and easy as she drifted from table to table, admiring and complimenting the artisans, her face flushed and her eyes sparkling. She was more beautiful than anyone had a right to be.

I'd replaced the mead in her cup with water after the fourth one, but she was clearly still floating on the alcohol. I'd never been more aware of every eye drawn to her, nor my urge to remove so many men's ability to see.

"Isn't this nice, Seir? One day I want a bunch of these hanging from the roof of my porch, so when the wind blows, I get my own personal symphony." She gently pushed on a glass rod, making it dance around. As it touched the other ones in the set, different tones rang out. She repeated the gesture with another one made from colorful stone slices.

"What are these called?"

"Wind chimes." Her smile was rueful. "It'll be a while though. Aunt Sal doesn't really have a porch to speak of, it's more of a stoop. So, I'll need to get a house first."

I reached out and touched some made of hollow wood tubes and another with various iron animals. I thought the glass ones sounded the best though. "They're very nice."

Hailon grabbed my hand for maybe the tenth time that evening. I loved that she'd gotten so comfortable. "Look! They have cake!"

I laughed at her but claimed one of the small iron tables outside the bakery for us as she purchased a special selection of little bites they'd designed just for the festival.

"I'll get the drinks," I offered after she sat.

"Mead?" she asked, an adorable begging expression on her face.

"No more mead. You need tea. I'm afraid you're already headed for a dreadful headache in the morning."

"You're no fun," she complained, sagging into her chair.

I leaned close to her ear, finger and thumb lightly holding her chin. She tried to hide the shiver, but I felt it run through her flesh. "Now that's just completely untrue, Moonflower. Stay here. I have to go over there to get our tea." I gestured back the way we'd come from, where the wind chime stand sat next to a teahouse.

"I'll be right here," she promised. Her eyes stuttered across someone in the crowd, her forehead pinching. I followed her eyes but saw nothing out of the ordinary.

Hurrying, I placed my order at the teahouse, chatting with the chime vendor while I waited for it to brew so I could keep her in my sight.

When I returned to the table, she was patiently examining the pretty samples of cake she'd bought.

"It's very hot," I warned. "Be careful."

"Okay." Hailon blew over the top of her cup, steam curling toward her nose.

I knew I'd made the right choice as I watched the false energy slowly drain from her. The longer we sipped the hot floral brew and worked our way through the little samples of different cakes, the further she sagged into her seat.

"Which do you like best?" she asked.

"This one," I pointed the little wooden fork at the spiced cake with apples. I liked how the cinnamon danced on my tongue and the apples were just the right amount of sweet.

"Really? The apples are kind of mushy. I think the chocolate."

I traded her the remaining bites so we could each enjoy what we liked more. "Have you had enough?"

She nodded. "Yes. I'm worn out all of a sudden."

"It's been a busy day."

Before we could get very far out of the city square, the music had picked up, and we found ourselves pressed together as everyone around us danced.

I gave her a querying look and she shrugged, offering her hand. I spun her in a very rough version of the dance everyone else was doing, soaking in her smile, her laugh, her light. This was a version of Hailon I wanted her to be able to hold on to. She carried responsibility like a warrior, but I very much enjoyed being able to see her when she was allowed to set it all down and just *live*.

She was perfect in every way. I was surer of it the more time we spent together. Though I would admit, the version of her that I saw wielding my blade at that terrible house would always hold a special part of my heart.

The second song was far slower than the first, but the crush of people was no lighter. I marveled at my luck, smiling as I held her in my arms, her face turned up to the moonlight.

"Oh!" She stumbled backwards, tripping on an uneven stone in the street. I stepped into her fall, catching her in time to keep her head from hitting the bricks of the nearest building. My body pressed against hers, my palm on the bricks keeping us both upright.

"Careful."

She nodded, both of us breathing heavy. Time stopped as she scanned my face, those fascinating eyes lingering on my mouth.

I gave her ample opportunity to pull away, to speak her dissent, to change anything and everything about our situation as I slowly lowered my face. It was like a vice clamped around my heart when my lips met hers. The softness there plus the sweet little gasp of breath as she leaned into me plucked at every bit of tension in my body.

My hand pulled away from her lower back and gripped along the slender column of her neck instead, my thumb tracing her jawline as I mapped her mouth with mine. She tasted like chocolate and cinnamon, her eagerness matching my own as I tangled my tongue with hers. Her fingers gripped the fabric of my shirt along my waist, twisting as she pulled me into her. I sank into her embrace. Our bodies lined up perfectly, like matched pieces of a puzzle. She made the tiniest moan, and I responded in kind, consuming every bit of her I could get as I pressed against her.

I released Hailon on a gasp, my lungs burning for more than air as my body roared, demanding more. She blinked up at me, eyes wide and round, but neither of us could speak a word.

Sound suddenly rushed back in, the whole world appearing from behind the veil that had kept us inside a little peaceful bubble for that moment. Couples spun and stepped just an arm's length away, the music loud, their laughter and raucous energy no longer separate from us.

After several slow breaths between us and an unmentionable struggle inside my own head where I imagined pinning her to the wall and repeating our interlude and then some, I pulled her back to the street. There was a big conversation we had to have before that happened. I had been too much of a coward to discuss it the other night, but now it was necessary.

We waltzed through the crowd again, and I directed us away from the square, only stopping the slow measured spins when we were well enough away to not get caught up in the dance again.

"That was something," she sighed, gazing up at the full moon and sprinkling of stars.

"Perhaps I shouldn't have—"

Her head snapped to the side so she could look at me. "Did you want to?" The flash of hurt in her eyes was too much to bear.

"Yes. I did. Very much."

"Then you should have." She looked away, palm rubbing at her breastbone.

"Did *you* want me to?" I asked, flipping the question around, getting a softened look for my efforts.

"Could you not tell?" she asked quietly after a torturous few seconds of silence. I smiled wide, glad for the enthusiastic confirmation. "Thank you for today," she added hastily. "All of it."

"You're more than welcome, Hailon. It was truly my pleasure."

My heart pounded hot and heavy in my chest. I wanted to ask her a dozen questions about what she was feeling, whether I'd guessed correctly or not. Whether she recognized me like I did her. If she even knew what a mate bond was, what that meant for us.

But I kept my mouth shut, content to have kissed her at all, to have her hand in mine and her taste still on my lips.

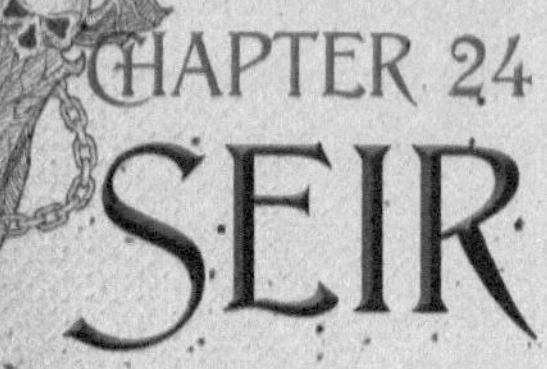

CHAPTER 24
SEIR

I T WAS DIFFICULT to keep an eye on everything in an unfamiliar city, particularly with such festivities going on. My neck prickled with awareness as we got further away from the main focus of the festival, and that was enough to make me wary.

The rush I'd experienced with Hailon in my embrace was quickly washed away as my senses went on alert.

Tables were well spaced and being packed up in many cases the further out we got from the revelry, and the road had hardly any foot traffic. Mostly, we saw people ambling down alleys toward their homes, or someone waiting outside in a doorway or on a balcony for a loved one.

After passing the third dark street, I noticed a man in my periphery. He was hanging back enough to not be overly suspicious, but something about the way he moved had my attention. When he'd slowed, stopped, or changed direction the same as us even after every other person had vanished from the road, I resolved that I wasn't making something out of nothing. Hailon was unaware, smiling softly to herself as we walked the cobbled street toward our bed, humming a tune in her throat.

Just as the fireworks started, I leaned down to whisper in her ear. I hated that I had to dash her beautiful mood.

My closeness and tone must have tipped her off that I wasn't preparing to ask playfully if she wanted to race back to the inn.

"There's a man behind us. Tall. Light hair. Been there for several streets now." I was almost certain it was one of the two men she'd described to me from Olinbourg, but I wanted her to verify. "Play along."

I slid my arm along her waist, inciting a startled noise from her as I spun her around like we were dancing again. To her credit, she was excellent at going along with things. I barely noticed her eyes shift from my face to the side of the street.

The man, on the other hand, was a terrible poker face, and very obviously tensed at our sudden movement.

I kept her tucked to my side as we half-stumbled a few extra steps, playing up that we might have had a little too much to drink and gaining a little bit of distance in the meantime. Hailon's eyes were dilated wide, her breath coming in short gasps.

"I saw him earlier, but I thought I was imagining things. That's the man who liked to hold me still." Stress edged into her tone. "What is he doing here? Do you think he's been following us all this time?"

"Doesn't matter," I soothed her, mouth as close to her ear as I could get it. "Do you have any of your little blades on you?"

"Yes." She swiped her hand across her hip.

"Good. First, we're going to lead him somewhere less populated."

She blew out a slow breath, and I could feel her compartmentalize her feelings so she could fight. "Okay."

I remembered a series of industrial buildings not far from the Rooster, they seemed like the best option for confrontation.

Unfortunately for us, the man was tired of playing along and decided to start closing in before we got to the end of the next block.

"Fancy seeing you here, Jane," he called out.

"You've got the wrong girl. No Jane here." I tightened my grip on Hailon, her head turned down so her eyes weren't visible.

The man stepped in front of us. I marveled at how bold he was given the difference in physicality between us. "That girl has something that belongs to me." He reached out a hand, pointing. I simply stared at it.

"Her? Nah. I don't think so." I turned to Hailon, who was still examining the ground. "Moonflower, do you have anything that belongs to this man?" She shook her head aggressively. "There you have it."

He reached out, his wrist caught in my hand before he could touch her face. "I just wanted to look. Say you're right, I've got the wrong girl. I'll leave, no harm done. But what if I'm right? Worth checking, wouldn't you say?"

Incredible explosions of color and light went off in the sky, rattling the windows in the buildings around us. I stared at the man, weighing my options.

"It's really not a good idea to do this right in the middle of the street. Shall we go somewhere a little more conducive to friendly conversation?"

He looked around shiftily, then gave a short nod, following closely as we walked toward a warehouse-type building with an open grassy yard and a chimney still smoking into the night.

The further we moved away from other eyes, the twitchier he got. I liked watching him squirm, but his actions made me nervous. They betrayed that he might not be alone, that things were not going according to his plans.

"Now then. Who are you and why are you accosting us in the street after such a lovely evening?"

"I'm Royston Lang. That girl there has things that belong to me. Things that belonged to my brother. And I'd put down good money she also had something to do with his untimely death." His hand fluttered against his leg, and he looked around again.

"No," I answered simply.

"Sorry?" He jerked.

"She doesn't have anything that belongs to you. If your brother died, he must have done something to deserve his fate. And her name isn't Jane."

"Listen, friend—"

"I'm *not* your friend." My fingers itched to pull a blade. Hailon was still safely tucked under my arm, her own little dagger palmed in her right hand. She'd brought the one that could be held between her fingers today. I liked that one. I slid the pack off my shoulder and set it on the ground near my foot.

"Be that as it may, that girl was previously under the ... stewardship of me and my friends. I have reason to believe she has something that belonged to my brother."

"Is that so?"

"Yes, my brother and his friends had business in Olinbourg. She was part of a residence there."

"Oh? An employee?" I baited, interested how far this idiot would go thinking he had me on the hook.

"Of sorts, yes!" The man grew excited, thinking he'd won me over with such an argument. He was a fool.

"Moonflower?" Her head finally rose, and I could see the rage burning behind her beautiful eyes. "Do you recognize this man?"

"Yes."

"See! She knows me. There was a little book, maybe more—"

I didn't move so much as a muscle before Hailon stabbed him in the ribs with her dagger. Because of the way the weapon was held, it looked like she'd punched him just before he started bleeding. It was spectacular.

"Oh, dear. Looks like she doesn't want to go with you. Have you done something she didn't care for? Seems as though you have, she's not one to just skewer people like that on a whim." My blood rushed under my skin, lust chasing the adrenaline of the fight. All the facets of her beauty had manifested before my eyes in one evening, and I wasn't sure I was going to recover from such a gift.

He stuttered and babbled, making pointless excuses and lying through his teeth about what had happened back at that house. Hailon was having none of it, and didn't appear to need my help.

"You in particular liked to hold me down while they poked and prodded," she snarled, twisting the blade. "You think I don't remember you?" The man begged for his life while drowning in his own blood, but she wasn't yet finished exacting her wrath over every vile bit of experimentation she'd suffered at his hands. "Your brother's pathetic life came to an end on the tip of his sword," she hissed, gesturing at me. "Meaningless. With no fanfare. They all died in that terrible house, you know. Then we set it on fire. I gutted three of your friends *myself*."

"You? How?" He somehow managed to scoff, and it was by far one of the most brazenly foolish acts I'd ever had the pleasure of seeing someone perform.

Hailon was incensed, and honestly, I understood. To doubt this goddess when she'd already escorted you to death's door? Sheer madness.

"If I had it to do again, you'd all die *slower*." Rage flared in her gaze as she twisted the blade buried in his flesh, then pulled it out. The tall man gasped, clutching at the wound, trying to figure out how to breathe over the blood he was coughing up. "I'd take the same kind of care with you that you took with me. I'd snatch you up from your peaceful life and leave you chained in a cold room with no comforts. Hungry. Tired. Always waiting for the next torture session. I'd poke and prod at your flesh with pointy objects, take little pieces of you away until there was nothing left." Her shoulders sagged and she stepped away from him. "But really ... you aren't worth the time it would take to do all that. None of you. And soon? You'll all be dead anyway, so it won't even matter. I'll go on to live my life, and you'll all be long gone. Where's the other one? I know there's one more, is he following us too?"

"Too important. You'll never find him."

"That's not what I asked you!" she yelled. "Is he following us too?"

He was no longer capable of speech, but he shook his head aggressively. I wasn't sure I believed him.

Now that I'd had a second taste of it, I'd firmly decided that vengeful Hailon was my favorite to watch, though happy Hailon was a very close second.

The life drained from him faster than I'd hoped, honestly. All too soon, the gurgling stopped, and there was nothing left but a wide-eyed corpse on the grass.

Hailon glared down at the body, her rage having left her panting. "There should be a furnace in that warehouse, right?"

I smiled. She was still her brilliant self. "Almost certainly. Come on, Moonflower," I said, slinging the man over my shoulder. "Let's make sure he's not carrying anything important and clean this mess up."

HAILON

I STALKED ANGRILY UP the stairs to our room at the Rooster. "Unbelievable. I've had these clothes all of a day, and they're ruined." Over the last couple of hours, I'd gone from genuinely carefree and happy to afraid. Then I'd embraced my darker side and hurt one of the men who had hurt me.

But blood on my new clothes? That was the thing that pushed my fragile mental state a step too far. I worried about myself sometimes.

Seir shook his head. "Don't worry about that. If I can't get them clean, I'll buy you more. Just leave them by the sink."

I grumbled to myself as I gathered up another tunic to change. Seir lingered by the bathroom door, stance wide and arms crossed.

"Everything alright?"

"No, it's not."

"What—" He caged me between his body and the wall, face impossibly close to mine as his fingers traced down my cheek. I shivered, every nerve alight.

"There is no part of you I don't appreciate. Do you understand?"

His voice was low and husky. "You smell like blood and wine and chocolate, and I have ... untoward intentions, Moonflower. A great many of them in fact. And there's no forest here for me to hide in so I can ... relieve myself ... of them." His jaw flexed and his eyes slid closed, his head tipping back as he took several slow breaths.

I inhaled sharply, understanding exactly what he meant. I stood straighter, which caused my leg to brush against him. He grunted, and I clenched my thighs together. "That's okay. I've had thoughts like that too."

Shock painted his face, and his eyes snapped open. "Hailon. We have to—"

I cut him off, dragging his mouth to mine with the same intensity I'd felt punishing the Lang brother. Want and need were usually very separate feelings when I took a romantic interest in someone, but there was no clear line here. It was both. My chest ached as he devoured me right back, one hand staying on the wall, our position a mimic of how we'd kissed in town against the bricks. The other hand splayed across my mid back, drawing me up against him. We rocked together, the adrenaline of the evening like kerosene on a pyre.

Time ceased to exist as I devolved into nothing more than sensation. My magic reached for every nick and cut it could find on him, repairing, soothing, as his teeth nipped at my lips, then my throat, his heavy breath against my skin driving me closer and closer to madness.

"Stop. Stop, stop. We have to—" He kissed lightly all over my face, then took a step back, panting. He groaned, regret all over his flushed face. "We have to stop, Moonflower. I'm sorry. I want nothing more—sweet saints, I could punch myself right in the *face* for stopping right now—I promise. But there's something we must discuss first, it's important." Then he kissed me again, and I could feel the way he grinned against my mouth as he whined, "I need you so badly." He kissed me again, gently consuming me.

"But we can't. Not until we talk. Go in the bathroom and shut the door. I can't have you yet."

"Promise it'll never happen again and I won't have to kill you over leaving me so needy."

He groaned, low and long. "I swear. And should it come to that, you know I'd happily go to my knees and bow before you, Moonflower. I'd willingly take your blade at my throat. The very thought turns me on, in fact. Can't you tell?"

I could. And he wasn't alone there.

I leaned in and kissed his smile one more time, unafraid of the taste of blood on my mouth, unsure if it was his or mine. Then I shut myself inside the bathroom before I could change my mind.

"Thank you." He barely breathed the words from the other side of the door. I heard him slide down the wall and land on the floor with a thump.

I felt dizzy from the combination of lust and exhaustion flowing through me as I started to undress. I was wound tighter than I could ever remember being and needed some outlet for the desire crashing through my veins. I climbed into the filling tub and reached for myself to soothe the ache.

A light moan escaped my mouth as I rubbed at my aching sex.

"Hailon? Are you …?" Seir asked.

"I'm fine," I responded, already breathless again. I got to my knees in the tub, realizing I had a better way. The tap for the tub was on the side instead of the end, and if I positioned myself just right …

"Hailon?" Seir sounded frantic as another, louder noise escaped me, my body flushed hot as the combination of rushing water and my own hand pushed me closer and closer to the edge. I gripped the porcelain with my free hand, knuckles going white. "Should I—" He paused, and I could hear him press his body against the door. I pictured him listening to the sounds I was making, and it only drove me higher. "Oh, fuck." He sounded absolutely bereft on the other side of the door, and between the persistent throb in my core and the idea that he knew what I was doing, that I was thinking of him while stroking myself, I couldn't hold it back in any longer. I shuddered my release, unable to stop the loud moan that left me. I nearly doubled over as my muscles seized and water splashed as I sank down, the heat of it like a warm embrace as I came down from the rush.

Seir called my name again from the other side of the door, but it was not a query. It was a benediction. My body throbbed again in response. We were even, then.

Once I was submerged in the steamy water, my body finally relaxed.

I wanted to go back to the moments when I was hazy from the mead and everything felt floaty. To the days where I'd forgotten that there were men who might be looking for me at all. I wanted to go back to dancing. To the way Seir's mouth had felt on mine.

In the wake of what was one of the most intense orgasms I'd ever had, my chest ached something fierce. The pain was getting more worrisome as the days went on. I wondered if I should find a healer before we left town. I also felt the ugliness of the evening creeping back up, replacing the joy.

"Hailon?" Seir's cautious voice came from the other side of the door.

"I'm fine."

I washed and rinsed and washed again, trying to scrub away the stain of those men and the memories attached to them from my body.

When the water was completely cooled, I pulled myself out and dressed. I teetered on my feet as I combed out my tangled hair with my fingers, exhaustion finally catching up to me.

When I opened the door, Seir was still seated on the other side, leaned up against the wall.

"Sorry," I apologized. "I didn't mean to take so long."

"That's alright. I didn't want to leave you in there alone. I was considering coming in to check on you if you were in there much longer. The thought of you falling asleep in the water ..." He shook his head. Clearly, he'd cycled through several worst-case scenarios that had bothered him.

"I'm sorry. I didn't mean to make you worry." My heart thudded, heavy and hot behind my ribs. It hurt. I rubbed with my palm and Seir's eyes tracked the movement.

"It's alright. We need to talk about *that*," he said quietly, pointing at me.

"About what?"

"The pain in your chest."

A flash of cold went through me. "You know what it is?"

He looked away, and the fact that he wouldn't meet my eye sent my pulse spiking, anxiety and exhaustion mixing in a toxic way inside my body.

He rubbed a hand across the back of his neck. "It's complicated." Of course it was. I huffed a heavy breath. "It's not bad, Hailon," he reached out, the pad of his thumb running across my cheekbone. His eyes betrayed him though, the gold dimmed. He seemed sad. "Promise. But it is important. You can come in while I bathe, if you want. We can talk."

I declined but stood outside the cracked door longer than I cared to admit, listening to the splash of the water as he washed, the soft noise as he hummed a tune while scrubbing out our clothes. I'd barely moved the handful of steps to sit on the end of the bed when he emerged, hair damp and his clean tunic over his arm.

"I really do need you to teach me your alphabet."

He followed my eyes to where they were fixed to the strange greenish letters tattooed across his chest.

He grinned, tongue teasing along the points of his teeth. "As I told you, I'm more than happy to teach you whatever you like. These just tell my rank as a soldier and Prince of Hell. Nothing mysterious." After pulling his shirt on, he fussed with the fire in the hearth.

"You're stalling."

He nodded and fidgeted, visibly struggling with where to begin. "What do you know about fated mates?" he asked.

"I beg your pardon?"

"Fated mates," he repeated.

"I've heard the term but have never known anyone it applied to. I thought it was another one of those things that ends up in storybooks but doesn't really exist, not for normal people."

"You're not exactly 'normal people,' Hailon. And I'm ... well, I'm not even *people*, really." He smirked, the gesture somehow humble.

"You know what I mean."

"I do." He nodded, then laid down on his back, his feet still on the floor. "Fated mates are a rare and treasured thing," he started. "Two of my brothers have been so blessed. The two that are in Revalia now, interestingly enough."

I stiffened. The chances of that happening ... I was awed. "How does one know they've met their mate?"

"My brothers both said they felt a burning in their chest. That's how it's recorded in several books, as well."

My ribs suddenly felt too tight, the muscles and skin there rigid. His fingers reached out for mine, squeezing. I returned the gesture, which made him sigh.

"Has your chest been burning, Seir?" I wanted to look at him, but I also didn't dare.

"Yes."

"How long?"

"Since I first arrived in that house." He was uncharacteristically quiet, his voice barely above a whisper.

I spun to look at him, and he gazed back at me with such soft-ness, such vulnerability I could hardly stand it. He was a tall, strong man, an enthusiastic force of nature. Yet that look on his face was more powerful than any sword he could wield.

Words failed me as I watched him study the nuances of my expression. He seemed braced for a negative response. I stuffed my initial reaction of disbelief down and instead focused on smoothing the wrinkles in the blanket as I lay down next to him.

"I thought it was the food, too, at first," he said, our faces nearly so close our noses touched. "But now I think it's more than that. Much more."

"What does that all mean? What happens if that's true?"

Seir shrugged. "It doesn't have to mean anything." He pulled one of my hands to his mouth, kissed the palm and set it over the strong, steady beat of his heart. "I believe we all have a choice, even when the fates try to get involved in the details."

"Will it hurt like this forever?"

"No. I don't think so. The bond is making itself known right now, trying to be sure it's ... completed."

"Completed?"

"It's a simple magic. Old as time itself." He looked at me meaningfully, one eyebrow raised. "It's also why we had to stop, before."

A flush washed over me. "Oh."

"Oh, indeed." He smirked, the innuendo unavoidably humorous.

"To be clear, if we were intimate, would that automatically mean we chose to accept the bond?"

"I believe the bond would interpret that as enthusiastic acceptance, yes." He smirked again. "Does that mean you still have untoward intentions with me, Moonflower? That I could have been having the same, all this time?"

I sighed, less put out about his question than I made out to be.

He chuckled, seeing through me. "Just making sure I understand you, is all. Because all you have to do is ask, Hailon. I meant it when I said I'm yours. But I also don't want you to have any regrets. You had to know this part of it to be fully consenting. Though I desperately wish I could have seen your face when you came—"

"Ridiculous demon." My whole body burned at the reminder of what I'd done with him listening and doing the same, the pair of us separated from one another by only a door.

We lay there in silence for several minutes, nothing but the sound of our heartbeats and the crackling of the fire between us.

"What do you want it to mean?" I asked finally. "What would you choose?"

Seir's eyes closed, and he exhaled slowly through his nose. "I'd be honored to have you as my mate, Hailon. I am. I will always be."

"But?"

He shook his head, redoubling his efforts to press my palm to his chest. "There's no but. Not like you're thinking. I understand that the timing isn't optimal. I wasn't looking for a partner before you summoned me. Your circumstances are certainly not of someone seeking out their mate. But the fates laugh at such things regularly. They don't care what else you have going on when it's your turn on their wheel." He exhaled slowly. "*But* ... choosing not to satisfy the bond can lead to madness, Moonflower. It would probably take a long time, but there's a risk. There are pairs that avoid it, even still. And if you're not all in, then we're not taking a chance. I'd rather not risk you resenting me and regretting the bond for all eternity."

"My eternity will be much shorter than yours, will it not?" I asked, stomach woozy.

"Perhaps, yes."

"Just 'perhaps'?"

"Well, to be fair, we've got some investigation to do on you, do we not? With the null thing Coltor mentioned? It's possible your life expectancy isn't all that different from mine."

There was no arguing with that, I supposed. And there he went again with *we*. Like it was his responsibility to help me figure myself out. How could I not appreciate such a thing?

"I know my brothers are looking into that with their mates as well. I've full confidence they'll find a way to keep my sisters-in-law around for a very, very long time. One of them is part fae. Surely there's a way to extend a human lifespan within our grasp."

"I ... We don't know one another all that well," I added, though that felt like a flimsy excuse. In many ways, I felt like I knew him better than anyone aside from my Aunt Sal.

"No, we don't. But I've seen enough to know I'd be beyond fortunate to end up with a woman such as you."

"Now who has the pretty words?" I reveled in the soft smile that earned me. "I don't think I can make a decision about that kind of thing right now."

He looked away, a flash of sadness crossing his face. "I understand. I would not ask you to respond to such a thing in haste."

It felt like he'd moved miles away, despite him being right there next to me. I hated it.

"For the record, I can't think of anyone else I'd rather the fates paired me up with," I said, placing my hand on his arm in a way I hoped communicated sincerity and comfort.

He turned back, the relief in his face palpable. He patted my hand, then lifted it, pressing another kiss into my palm.

"We should get some rest," he said, fingertips tracing down my cheek, eyes staring into mine in a way that made me feel truly seen. He leaned in, pressing his lips to my forehead in a sweet gesture that had me melting. Then he abruptly sat up.

"Where are you going?" I asked, heart pounding as he picked up a pillow and one of the small blankets spread across the foot of the bed.

"I'm going to sleep," he said, gesturing toward the floor in front of the fire.

"Absolutely not." I shook my head. "There's no need for that, it's a big bed, and we're both adults." His mouth twitched as he watched me burrow between the sheets. "Besides, my chest feels better when you're close. I wouldn't get any sleep at all if you were clear over there." I punched the pillow and fussed until I was comfortable on my side. The bed dipped as he slid in behind me, leaving space between us. After he was settled, his tail curled around my ankle.

His breath was warm as it ghosted along the back of my neck, his fingers gently combing through my hair.

"As you wish, Moonflower."

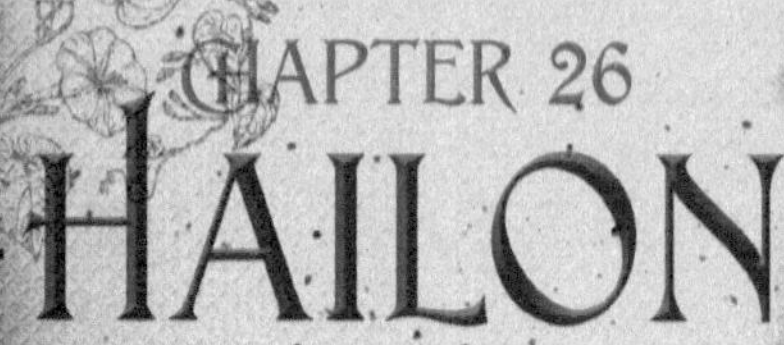

CHAPTER 26
HAILON

FOR THE NEXT two days we zigzagged across the Emankor Valley, going from town to town. Some were quaint little villages where we only lingered long enough to ask after transportation and buy some food or drink, others were towns much like Manvil had been.

It was nice to have hot meals we didn't have to cook ourselves and real beds, but the closer we got to Ravenglen, the more anxious I was about finishing our journey. We left the comforts of the lush farming region for more camping, knowing we were merely a couple more days from finally reaching our destination.

Horses were still too scarce for us to borrow or buy, and neither humans nor beasts seemed particularly fond of us.

Seir practiced as much as possible with his wings as we walked and was able to get up to several minutes of flight regularly. He even managed to sift twice, though neither attempt landed him more than several paces away, and he said it still felt wrong. My leg was nearly completely healed up, and the bruises I'd accumulated at the house in Olinbourg had faded.

There was something kind of beautiful about returning home like a whole new person, despite how I'd left.

We hadn't spoken again about mate bonds, but it was always there, lingering under whatever it was we were actually talking about. I found myself staring at Seir, calculating how we could make such a thing work. After all, we didn't even live on the same plane. Could I go with him to Hell? Would he be able to stay on Earth part time? Would everything change when I banished him and the summoner contract was fulfilled? The questions piled up inside my mind, distracting me from the ones I'd started to be afraid of asking; the ones about Aunt Sal. Had she found anyone to care for her in my absence? Was she still alive? I couldn't bring myself to consider the notion that she wasn't, thought I knew it was very much a possibility. Unfortunately, Coltor's stone kin network had not brought us any news, so I was left to stew in my worries.

Even with my new boots, by the time the sun was setting at the end of the day, my feet were sore, and I was exhausted.

We'd gotten lucky and found a nice, wooded area to camp in, one with heavy rock formations that helped us make a decent shelter. There wasn't, however, any water to be found.

The process of setting up and taking down camp had gotten to be such an exercise in familiar teamwork that we were settled in with a fire and food before I had time to even feel tired.

After eating the hearty soup Seir had cooked for us, I stared into the flames, one thought repeating through my mind, one that had been bothering me for days. It was something I should have taken care of in the Valley, but there hadn't been a chance to seek out a shop. And in truth, I'd thought the persistent thoughts would pass. I turned to him. "Would you trim my hair?"

"Your hair?" he asked, head tilted to the side. "My blades are certainly sharp enough, but how would you like me to cut it? And why?"

"The uneven spots, the missing chunks ... it reminds me of them. Of that house. I'd like to be done with those thoughts. I'd like for all of them to rot without being mourned or remembered. It's what they deserve."

"Oh, Moonflower." His eyes went soft, and he tucked himself behind me. Seir's arms wrapped around mine, squeezing my ribs tight. He rested his chin on the top of my head, his heartbeat strong against my back. He even wrapped his legs around my body, his broad thighs over mine as he bear-hugged me. I melted into the embrace, fighting the urge to cry as my body absorbed his affection.

Seir draped one of our towels over my shoulders, then settled back down behind me, standing on his knees.

"Do you trust me?"

I relaxed, a slow smile tugging at my mouth. "You know I do."

"Just checking. It's been a while since I did one of these, but I promise it'll be my best work." I closed my eyes, the tingle in my scalp a soothing sensation as he combed and tugged and scraped with the edge of his blade. "There's even more white today," he mused quietly. "It's such a pretty color."

Worry filtered through me. I was fairly young to be going spontaneously gray. I worried that perhaps the exertion from healing him had done something unexpected to me.

Bits of hair fell on my blanket and the ground as he worked, circling around me with a serious look on his face as he measured, cut, measured again.

I was nearly asleep and the fire was getting so low it was hard to see by the time he finally sat back on his heels with a satisfied look on his face.

"Feel," he said. "I think you'll like it." He smiled. "I do."

My fingertips explored my new style, finding that the back had been shortened even with the big missing chunk, so my whole neck was exposed, and the ends were even with the middle of my ear. The rest tapered forward at an angle, so there were long points at my face.

"It feels nice, thank you."

"You're welcome." He gathered up what he could of the hair and tossed the remnants into the fire. "Would it be rude of me to request payment for services rendered?"

"Probably not. Depends on what you're asking for." I found myself blushing, going along with this playful demon's game.

"Nothing too taxing. Just ... a kiss."

He'd gotten very close, his hand resting on my cheek like he had a habit of doing, his breath feathering across my face. Despite all my reservations about jumping into something like a mate bond, I trusted him. I was not afraid of him or his intentions. So, I pulled my bravery up around me like a comfortable blanket and let myself have something I wanted for a change.

"Take what you're owed then," I goaded. His tongue teased across the points of his teeth before he lowered his face, lips pressed almost chastely against mine. "That is not a kiss. Where is the demon I met the night of the festival?" I teased, taking both control and his face in my hands, covering his mouth with mine.

Seir grunted in surprise, lurching forward against me, hands protectively curving around my ribs. I licked at the seam of his lips, earning myself another growl as he opened for me, all too eager to devour me once I'd shown my intent.

He lowered us down so I was on my back beneath him, all his hard angles pressed up against me. Heat coursed through my veins as he pulled his lips away from mine and slid them across my jaw, then down my neck. I could feel his need pressed against my stomach, and gasped when he nipped at my collarbone with those sharp teeth.

"Hailon ..." His eyes were molten gold, dripping with desire as he pulled back far enough to gaze down at me. They roved over my face, my throat, fingertips tracing across my skin and leaving a fiery sensation in their wake. "I need you to know that it makes no difference whether or not you've decided you're mine. Of course, I'd prefer it that way, but even if I'm not ... I'm yours. I have been since you summoned me into that terrible little room in Olinbourg.

"Banishing me back to Hell won't undo whatever bond cracked wide open inside me the second I looked into those incredible eyes of yours. I spoke the truth when I told all those men I belonged to you. I did. I do. I always will." His eyes were soft, pleading as they took in every detail of my face. He placed light kisses at the edges of my mouth, the tip of my nose, my forehead.

Emotions backed up in my throat, threatening to choke me.

He'd shown me more kindness, more trust in a couple of weeks wandering the realm than anyone else in my life had ever done. Seir had always given me full agency over myself, believed what I stated were my limits, and protected me. Without question, he had offered his help and had never asked for anything in return.

"Seir, I—"

"Don't. I didn't say that because I was trying to prod you into a declaration of your own. I just needed you to know." He kissed me again, thoroughly and completely, rendering me speechless and somehow also removing most of the executive function from my body. I was nothing but a boneless mess incapable of coherent speech.

He gave me a grin that would haunt my dreams when he pulled away. Then, he placed his hand over his heart. He let it rest there a moment, then brought his fingertips to his lips, then mine. The green in his eyes was intense among the glowing gold, and I understood the gesture to be some kind of oath the way he delivered it. Despite the soft tilt of his lips, the movements were intentional. Reverent. My heart ached it was pounding so hard, the sweet gesture nearly too much for me to manage.

I closed my eyes, reveling in the cacophony of pleasurable sensations crushing down on me, the feeling of his body against mine, the taste of him on my lips. I was hovering right on the edge of committing to the biggest decision I'd ever make. And I was definitely leaning in.

Then something shifted, and everything felt too light, too cold. The weight and sensation of him touching me was ... gone.

I opened my eyes, and abject panic settled in. My chest felt like someone had filled it with the coals from the fire, and I instantly started sobbing. Everything hurt as I rushed to sit up.

"What's happening?" I asked, but nobody was there to answer. "Seir?!" I looked all around the camp, in the darkness along the trees, even up in the sky. But it wasn't a trick.

I was alone.

Seir was gone.

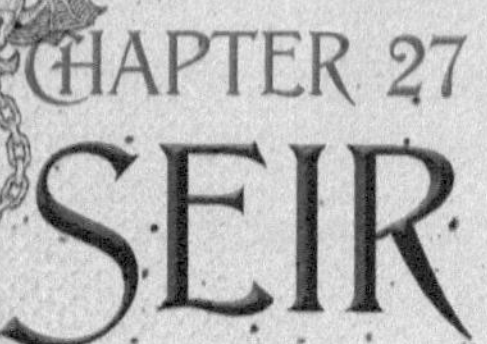CHAPTER 27
SEIR

"NO. NO!" I spun in a circle, staring up in horror at a black ceiling and dark walls instead of a starry sky or the trees around our little camp. "Fuck!" I swore, the oath out of my mouth before I could temper my emotions. I curled into myself, the mate bond burning so intensely I worried it might turn me to ash from the inside out. It clearly did not appreciate the sudden distance between me and Hailon. I wondered fleetingly how there were mates who existed at long distances from one another for years or decades. Though it did make sense why they went mad if they tried.

"Is there a problem, Seir?" my unit leader asked, a dark eyebrow raised as he assessed me from behind his desk. Keplar was a hulking figure, a shadow demon of massive size and imposing personality. He'd always been fair, however, and seemed wholly disinterested in posturing for the sake of feeding his own ego. Not for the first time, I thought he and Magnus, who was in fact a stone kin general, would have gotten on famously.

I forced my body to straighten up, though I couldn't make myself remove my hand from where it clutched at my shirt over my heart.

"Sir, hi. I was in the middle of something, and—"

"You've been absent for more than a full shift cycle without checking in."

I did a quick mental calculation, realizing I hadn't been keeping track since early in our journey, and he was right. "I'm sorry about that, it wasn't intentional. I talked to Meg, she sent a note—"

"Yes, I got the note. Unfortunately, because you were gone that long with no further communication, summoning you back was my only recourse. I'm owed a debrief on your whereabouts and activities, at the very least."

"Of course." I tensed, unsure how to speed things up and cursing myself for having gotten comfortable being gone, not calculating the time difference from the start. I was wasting time in Hell while Hailon was alone, potentially being followed. I had to get back to her as quickly as possible.

"Well? Start at the beginning."

"I was summoned for the first time. Sir." I couldn't help the excitement that bubbled up, getting to say that.

"Oh?" He raised a bushy black eyebrow in curiosity. "Go on." He leaned forward, scribbling a note into a large journal with a pen that looked comically small in his hand.

"A human summoned me, and I am providing them aid." My instinct was to be as vague as possible, to leave out names or even descriptors. I wasn't sure why, I'd never not trusted Keplar, but something deep inside wanted me to keep Hailon a secret. It physically hurt not to declare her as my mate, so I wasn't sure my tactic would be possible to maintain.

"And that has required more than a full cycle? Nearly, what, two earth weeks to accomplish?" He frowned, gesturing to the chair facing his desk.

"Yes, sir." Had it really only been two weeks? That seemed like such a short amount of time to have passed, and yet I felt like I'd been with Hailon for far longer.

"Have a seat, Seir. You're making me nervous."

"Sorry, sir. But yes, we're traveling, and it's been quite slow." I stared at him, catching the moment where he processed what I said.

"Travel has been *slow*? For you?" He barked a hearty laugh, shaking his head as he made another note. "I do miss your particular brand of humor when you're gone."

I schooled my expression, making sure he was looking me in the eye before I continued. "I wish I was embellishing, sir, or making a joke. But I'm not. My powers aren't functioning like they normally do, not since I was summoned. I can't sift or jump, and portals will not activate for me. Even flight has been out of the question. Only in the last few days can I even hover a few inches for a short distance."

He frowned even harder, flipping through the pages. "Says here you came back shortly after you were summoned."

"That's factually accurate." I remembered all too well the unfortunate series of events where the water had spilled on the circle, forcing me back to my apartment when all I wanted to do was stay. To defend her. To talk to her. "The circle was broken."

"But no banishment."

"Correct. I took a portal back. For what it's worth, when I returned, they were doing a very good job of trying to summon me again." I was significantly stretching the truth there, but he didn't know that. Or perhaps, he already did and simply wasn't calling me on it. It was impossible to know how much detail the command leaders actually had access to in their seemingly infinite information.

"Tell me why I should consider letting you finish whatever this side mission might be instead of keeping you here and punishing you for forgetting to check in. I understand summoning bonds have their own rules, but I need my men at their posts. I need to know what's going on."

"Apologies, sir. I just need a little more time. I'm trying to return someone to their home. They were taken, kept against their will."

He made a thoughtful noise as he closed the thick journal and slid it to the side. "You're a good soldier, Seir. You never argue, always agree to take missions nobody else will. Even with this last promotion, you've been more than happy to pick up the balance when asked. So, I do recognize that this is odd behavior for you. I'm honestly not sure how to react."

"I'm sorry, sir. None of this was intentional."

He folded his hands together over his notebook, staring at me intently, clearly searching for any kind of dishonesty. "I believe you," he finally said. "What should I do?" He cracked a smile, and it gentled his stern expression immensely.

"Let me go back, sir." I grunted as a flare in my chest took me by surprise. His eyes drifted from my face to where I was rubbing at the burn. "Please. If punishment is still part of that equation, that's fine, I'll accept it."

"I can understand needing to see something through." His head tilted. "What's going on there?" He gestured to my hand. "Need to see the medics?"

"No sir, I think I have it under control." As much as one could, anyway.

He cracked another smile, but it faded quickly, his eyes narrowing. "How much more time do you need to complete your errand?"

My heart ached. I'd known my time traveling with Hailon was coming to an end, but I'd never really thought about how quickly it might actually be done. "A few days, maybe a week. But—"

"I can give you three days. Then we need you here. Nonnegotiable. I don't want to have to summon you back again, the paperwork is a huge pain in my ass."

I nodded. I didn't see another choice, and that should be ample time for us to arrive in Ravenglen. "Sir—"

"Three days," he reiterated, pointing at me for emphasis, "then you report back here for reassignment or there will be serious consequences."

"Understood. But I need to ..." My heart stuttered. "Reassignment, sir?"

"Your particular skill set has become obsolete, I'm afraid. We're going to have to give you a new set of duties. You're my most reliable prince, Seir. I'm loathe to lose you, but my hands are somewhat tied. Unless you can make an intriguing proposal, your travel talents are no longer needed here in the office. They would, however, be rather useful out in the wastes."

I stared at him, unable to find words to convey my disappointment. The wastes was, as the name reflected, a place where things were sent in order to do nothing more than decay.

"Respectfully, I'm your *only* prince, sir. My brothers are assigned to other command or are no longer active in Hell. I would like to remain active, but as a significantly less full-time resident."

He smirked. "I see. This summoner. They're a potential mate, then?"

I was momentarily stunned, though perhaps I should have expected his expert perception. "Sir?"

The sigh he gave was deep and long. "You insult my gifts, Seir. And my capacity for empathy." He sat back, arms crossed. "Bring me a proposal. I'll do what I can from this side, but I cannot push anything through unless you return. On time."

"Understood, sir." My heart beat faster, optimism having returned full force with his words.

"Good. In the meantime, report for ten lashes with ..." He consulted his papers again. "Asim. Hall 73."

"Got it." Asim and I were friendly enough.

"Check in with the desk on your way out. Go take your lumps so you can finish whatever it is you're doing. Then get back here—*on time*—so we can figure out where to put you so your skills are not totally wasted, no pun intended, and so you can pursue this mate situation. Lucky bastard. Perhaps all of us should make a habit of venturing out once in a while." He chuffed and waved his hand in dismissal.

I didn't hesitate. As a test, I even sifted a reasonable distance, letting out a victorious whoop when I found it just as easy as it had always been. Practicing on Earth, I'd been able to do tiny leaps but not without an intense amount of effort. I was able to sift through the many halls until I arrived at Asim's designated torture room as smoothly as a stone skipping across a lake.

"Seir? What are *you* doing here?" Asim looked very much like the goat-headed demons depicted in a variety of artwork found on Earth. He had human hands, but cloven hooves for feet and a tail much like mine.

"Ten lashes punishment," I reported, not bothering with formality before pulling the tails of my shirt from my trousers and yanking it over my head. Then, I braced my hands against the low stone table off to one side of the room.

He grunted in surprise, sorting through the available devices hanging from the wall next to his desk. "Ah." He consulted the scroll sitting on his worktop. "There you are. You got here fast, not that I'm surprised. What have you done to earn a punishment?"

"I missed checking in for a full shift cycle. A little side work on Earth. I got summoned!"

"Really? Congratulations! First time, right?"

"Yes, first one. Very odd feeling, still not sure if I liked it or not."

Asim chuckled and clapped my shoulder in a friendly way. "Good for you. Are you back then?" He shook out the long coil of whip he'd grabbed off a peg and did a test crack. The noise was painfully loud in the confined space.

"No, I have to go finish up once I'm done here. I'm in a bit of a rush, actually."

He snorted. "Got a hot date waiting for you topside, then?"

I smiled wide, and Asim blinked. He'd been joking, but I was all too willing to take the opening. "Yes, actually. I'm pretty sure I've found my mate."

He made a choking noise. "Really?"

"Yes! She's the one who summoned me, though it's a bit more complicated than that."

"Of course it is. To have that kind of luck is a gift, friend." He shook his head. "Alright, let's get you gone then. Ready?"

"As I'll ever be." I took a deep breath and closed my eyes, trying to keep my muscles from tensing too much. I had taken fewer lashes than many demons I knew over the decades, but enough to know that the more you braced, the more it would hurt. I started sweating in anticipation, but a blow never came. I glanced over my shoulder as Asim crossed the room again, selecting a different tool from the wall.

"Turn around. Hold your arms out, palms up." he instructed, and while I was a little confused, I obeyed. Asim was no longer holding a whip, but a small metal rod that appeared to be steaming. "Count the lashes for me if you please."

He struck my forearms with the rod with enough force for the skin to sting, and the heat of the metal left red burn stripes in its wake. A few were worse than the rest where they overlapped, but still barely enough to draw blood. By the end, it looked like I'd gotten into a fight with a disgruntled hellcat more than anything.

"Are you sure this is adequate?" I reached for my shirt, confused. Burns weren't something that hurt, particularly for me.

"The requirement is that lashes be served, not that they be debilitating. It is at the discretion of the assigned torturer what tool and force to use. It's there in the conduct code, section 3, part

8.4." He cracked a small smile. "I believe I've served a punishment proportionate to your infraction."

"Thank you, Asim."

"Off with you then! Find me when you return, dinner and drinks on me? I want to know all about this adventure and your mate."

"Sure thing!" He waved as I left the little room, immediately sifting into my apartment.

I'd taken most of my valuables when I left the first time, but I scooped up my remaining few pieces of jewelry, another knife, and quickly changed into a clean set of clothes. Once I was done gathering everything I wanted, I headed toward the hall of portals at a sprint.

It was with a pang of guilt that I mostly ignored the people who attempted to greet me, and it wasn't until I was nearly past it that I remembered I was supposed to sign out where I'd left that note when I went topside the first time.

"Hi, Meg. I'm out for a few more days. Mission earth-side, Keplar knows."

"I warned you about checking in, didn't I?""

"You did."

"Worth it?" she asked.

"A million times."

She smiled, all her sharp teeth starkly white against her deep-red skin. "Alright. I got you down. Have fun."

"Thanks." I finished my run to the portals, debating my options.

I had no idea where the closest one might be to our camp. The only one I knew of for sure was in the ruins, and I hadn't even seen it while we were there. There might be one in or near Ravenglen, but I'd never been there. I could use Hailon's face as a focal point, but if there wasn't one near her, I might end up somewhere completely unfamiliar and take longer than necessary to get back to her.

The vast hall stretched out before me; the possibilities endless in the infinite doorways.

Then I smiled, realizing I could manage several things at once. I hurled myself toward a very familiar and reliable portal not all that far from where we'd camped, relatively speaking.

The portal turned me inside out and sideways, but I enjoyed every moment. I could travel again. I loved dreaming of the possibility that I could potentially bring her with me like this one day soon, take her to the fae realm to visit with King Ris. With me to Hell, even, to see my little apartment and the parts of it that weren't actively participating in torture. I allowed myself to fantasize of a time where I could go everywhere, just as I always had, in the blink of an eye, only better. Because Hailon would be at my side.

My smile had returned with the daydreaming, and it widened as the portal dumped me out on the familiar grounds of the Collegium d'Arcan.

CHAPTER 28
SEIR

I WAS ABLE TO walk right through the doors of the main build-ing of my brother's magic school, which honestly left me a bit concerned for the state of the school's security. Not all that long ago, a fae had sifted himself past all the wards and stolen a priceless book directly out of a classroom. As I strode down the hall, I filed that away as something to periodically surprise test once things had settled down a bit. If nothing else, it was a surefire way to get under my brothers' skin, which was one of my favorite things to do.

A quick peek in the dining room revealed the room was empty, though I could hear the clatter of dishes being washed back in the kitchen. The lingering smells from whatever delicious food had been served had my stomach rumbling. A real meal would not be amiss, particularly one of his head cook Grace's, but I didn't have the time.

I went straight for Vassago's classroom next, the one the book had been taken from. I happened to get lucky and found both of my brothers and their wives ensconced there.

"Seir?" My sister-in-law Greta was the one to see me first, as she was standing at her worktable across the room and had a clear view of the door. I'd startled her, but she recovered beautifully, the vial in her hand not having spilled a single drop.

Everyone's head turned to follow her stare, so I strode in, waving.

"Security is lacking at your school, *Stolas*." I used my brother's old name to further prod at him. He went by Rylan now, had for quite some time, but he'd started as Stolas ages ago and now used it as his surname.

"Clearly, if someone of your caliber just wandered in," he shot back, grinning. "What brings you here?"

"Do any of you know much about nulls?" I asked.

"Hello, Seir. How are you? I'm lovely, thanks for asking. Just traveling through?" my brother Vassago teased, setting down his book. He rose from the armchair he'd been sitting in as I got close, tying his long hair up with one of his favored silver ribbons. As always, his silver and white clothing was posh and pristine. He pulled me in for a quick embrace, the thump of his hand on my shoulder a welcome familiar presence.

"Yes, hello to you too. I'm in a bit of a hurry I'm afraid. I don't mean to be rude. What do we know about nulls?"

"Not much, except they're exceedingly rare," Rylan frowned, head tilted. He was the dark to Vassago's light, his long hair loose and clothing black. "I'm assuming you've met one?"

"Yes, I believe I have."

"Well, bringing them here is an option, though—"

I shook my head. "We are operating under the assumption that she cancels out all magic near her, so I'm not sure if that's a good idea."

"She?" Rylan's wife, Calla, piped up, interested in this new development.

"How close does one have to be for that to happen?" Vassago asked.

"*All* magic?" Rylan's curiosity was piqued, his own book set off to the side in favor of our hasty conversation.

"I'm not sure. For either question. We've become somewhat acclimated to one another, enough that I can use my wings some again."

"You lost your ability to fly?" Rylan frowned.

"Yes. And fully shift. I think given enough time, it's possible I could even bring her through a portal, but we're not there yet, and as it stands, I can't activate them anywhere near her."

"That's ... significant, Seir. Your abilities are completely inaccessible?" Vassago asked.

"It's not her fault. Besides, when I first met her, I couldn't use my wings at all, now I can at least hover."

"Fascinating," Rylan rubbed his chin with his thumb and forefinger. "A null. I'll ask Magnus to check the archives, surely there's something there."

"That's what his son said."

"His son?" Calla asked, so intrigued by the conversation she'd moved to the slightest little edge of sofa cushion.

"Yes, we came across Coltor Aurichal in the ruins of Emankor. In our presence within that space, he also couldn't shift. It was he who suggested she might be a null, as well."

"You met Magnus's son?"

"The Emankor ruins?"

"What kind of distance before it's not effective?"

Questions poured out from all sides, and I laughed as I raised a hand to quiet them.

"One at a time, please!" I chuckled, holding my hands up in front of me as if that would help me ward off the barrage. "I truly am in a rush, besides. I wasted far more time in Hell than I wanted to, and she's camped by herself in the empty grassland between the Emankor Valley and Ravenglen. It's possible we're being followed, though I've seen no signs." I hadn't seen any in the first place, however, which left me doubting my ability to detect such a thing accurately.

"Camped? You're truly traveling like a human?" Vassago's head tilted, amusement playing across his features. "Is that why you're smudged with dirt?"

"These clothes are fresh," I argued. "But yes, truly." I grinned back. "It's been a wonderful experience!" Both of my brothers smiled back at me, and in that moment, I felt truly understood. New things were few and far between for creatures such as us, and I had always appreciated them more than most. "In any case, I wanted to see if there was a way to help her control her power. If she could turn it off, or even just relax the strength, that might be very beneficial. But to answer your questions: yes, yes, and I don't know. Coltor seems nice enough, or did at least once we established we weren't enemies. Indeed, the ruins. They're fascinating, and I'd love to go back one day. And I'm not sure if it's all kinds of magic. So far, it's been effective on me and a stone kin but not on the powerful wards set around the ruins. We didn't have accurate measurements to test distance for her range. So. Can you help?" They all stared. First at me, then at one another. I raised a finger. "Also, I'm pretty sure she's my fated mate. Everything about me feels a little strange since I met her, and my chest is absolutely killing me right now. So really anything you can offer to help is greatly appreciated."

Rylan and Vassago exchanged a knowing, open-mouthed look, and their wives perked up even further, particularly as I scrubbed my fist pointlessly across my shirt, trying to east the ache that refused to let up.

"Well, you could have *led* with that detail, Seir." Vassago shook his head.

"Your mate?" Greta asked, coming around the table she was working at while wiping her hands on her heavy full-body apron. I wondered what chemicals she'd been working with, what intriguing new alchemical solution she might be crafting. But it was not the time.

"Yes, I'm fairly positive. We're both having the pains. She summoned me!" I said proudly, not elaborating on the details of the fond memory.

"Right," Rylan said, blinking slowly as he stared at me. "Bring her here. It's a risk, but we can surely manage the consequences. At the very least, we can take some measurements. Perhaps the stone kin can make a suggestion for the rest. Magnus can check the stone kin archives for records about nulls, and I can consult on the mage side. There's bound to be something there."

"Perhaps Ophelia can help?" Calla suggested, a kind smile on her mouth. "She's invited us to visit, should we have a need. We could bring her with us? If she had no effect on the wards around the ruins, perhaps that's the safest place for her this close to the city?" She raised an eyebrow, clearly interested in such an experiment.

"She didn't overpower the wards at the ruins, but we both felt their effects. Once inside, she cancelled out Coltor's abilities the same as mine."

"I'll check my books as well," Greta offered. "There's bound to be something in one of those old tomes about muting or suppressing a power like that."

"So long as it doesn't also hide her healing ability, that would be great."

"Healing ability?" Vassago asked. He'd wandered over to his own table and was messing with a series of small mirrors.

"Yes, she fixed me right up. I broke my leg and had a wing bone puncture my gut on our way into the ruins." They all just stared at me. "It's a long story, but she was taken from her home in Ravenglen for that ability. Taken to Olinbourg and kept prisoner in a house there. Forced to use that ability for her captor's profit."

Calla gasped, but I could also see the rage in her start to manifest. She was an earth witch; a very powerful one. The ambient tendrils of green smoke dispersing as she exhaled told me how upset the idea of Hailon's situation made her.

"They're all dead now, though," I reassured her with a friendly pat on her shoulder, and the tendrils disappeared.

"Good."

"Well, except for one. But we could definitely take him, should he show his face. In fact, he's some kind of councilman. Perhaps you could put out an inquiry?"

"Of course." Both my brothers focused on me as I relayed the description Hailon had provided.

"Hailon was very helpful there, actually," I said proudly. "Took my dagger and dispatched three of them all on her own. It was beautiful."

"*Your* dagger?" both Rylan and Vassago asked at the same time.

"Yes, my favorite one! She just grabbed it right out of my hand." I waved my arm around in illustration of how she'd slashed and stabbed, my heartbeat a proud thump behind my ribs.

My brothers exchanged shocked looks, sharing a whole conversation with their eyes. It ended with them both smiling.

"Is that her name?" Greta asked. "Hailon? That's pretty." Greta was a stone kin and Magnus's niece, actually, which made her Coltor's cousin. But she hadn't known much of anything about her heritage until very recently. She was also part fae, the daughter of King Ris.

"Take this," Vassago said as he came over. He handed me a mirror the size of my palm.

"Same words?"

"Yes, same as always."

"You know I don't have any luck with these," I told him, grimacing. "I've broken what, six?"

"Nine, actually," he corrected, "but we need a way to get in touch. I should've made you another ages ago, whether I was frustrated with your inability to keep them intact or not. Be careful with this one, yes?"

"I was careful with the others too," I pouted, realizing I was acting every bit the petulant little brother but unable to stop myself.

"Be *more* careful. Keep it wrapped and in your pocket or something."

"That's where I had it the last time," I muttered.

"What was that?" Vassago asked, head tilted to the side, arms crossed.

"Nothing."

"You said she's waiting for you?" Calla asked gently.

"Yes. I have to go. Thank you all! Once I get her home I'm supposed to return to Hell pretty much immediately." I frowned. The more I realized I actually had to be separated from her for an unknown amount of time, the less I liked it.

"You're going to leave her there?" Vassago asked.

"I have to go back to complete the summoner contract. Also, so my unit leader can process my reassignment. So, I can be here more. With her."

"Will she be safe where you're going?"

My heart clenched. "I think so. It's her home. She's trying to get back to a sick aunt." Doubt began to fester.

"Oh, poor thing!" Calla gasped.

"But you said she was taken from there?" Vassago's forehead furrowed. "We could send someone, perhaps. Just to keep an eye."

"You have someone in mind?"

My brothers looked at one another. "Surely one of the stone kin could, if we can't?" Vassago suggested.

Rylan agreed. "We'll ask."

"She's not afraid to use her blades," I assured them, as much as myself. "And she's as stubborn as the day is long." I found myself smiling.

Vassago nodded good. "And you have the mirror."

"We'll look into the archives for you in the meantime," Rylan promised.

"And I can help make the arrangements for her to meet with Ophelia."

"Ravenglen is not all that far, especially if you can find a nearby portal to have us use. But wings would be effective enough for that distance," Vassago offered. "Even if we aren't able to fly the whole way."

"The horses are strong," Calla said. "We can also send the carriage with someone."

Rylan agreed, and I could see all the gears turning as they started to formulate a plan.

A warm sensation different from the burning ache I'd been feeling since being pulled away from my mate infused my chest. My brothers and I had been very close once, before we all went our separate ways and got lost in our own little lives. It was nice to have their direct support and affection.

"So lovely to see you again," I said, rushing to give each of my sisters-in-law a quick squeeze and kiss on the cheek. "See you soon!"

"Hands off my wife!" my brothers both chided me, but I was already out the door and on my way to the courtyard.

Nerves had my stomach tight in the seconds before I concentrated my will and deployed my wings, relief flooding me as I found my magic right where it belonged.

I leapt into the sky, joy at being airborne again rushing through me as I pointed myself east, toward Hailon, and a future I was willing to do anything for.

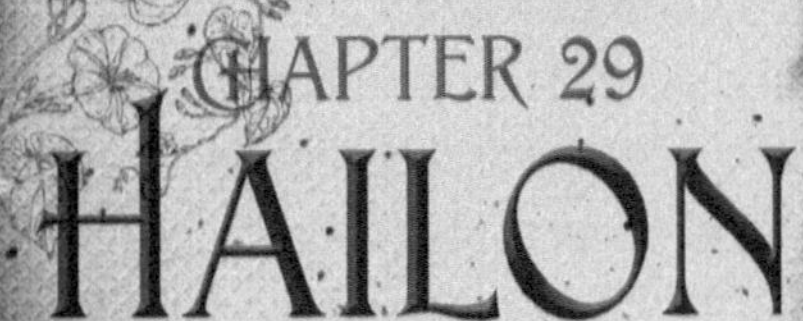

CHAPTER 29
HAILON

NOTHING AT ALL had made sense after I realized Seir vanished. My whole body ached, my chest most of all. Every emotion was exposed and raw, my reactions exaggerated and completely out of my normal range.

After regaining control of my ragged breathing, I cycled through everything he'd said and done that day. If he'd decided to up and leave, surely there would have been signs. If I'd missed them, I wanted to know how.

I thought back to the declaration he'd given me, the sweet fingers to mouth and heart gesture. With the stain of his abrupt absence, both struck me as him possibly saying goodbye. The notion brought a fresh wave of pain, my body stuck in a terrible feedback loop thanks to the irritated mate bond. But when sense returned, I discarded such an idea. That kind of behavior didn't align with the Seir I knew. Besides that, I hadn't banished him. He himself had made a big deal out of the fact that he was supposed to stay with me until that happened.

I stared into the fire, sorting through more and more outlandish scenarios. Perhaps he'd sifted elsewhere? But that wasn't possible, not unless he'd suddenly figured out how to make all his powers work again, and at full strength. Flying? Still very unlikely, unless he'd figured out how to vastly improve his ability without telling me. None of that seemed plausible.

"Get it together," I told myself when I could finally function, swiping away some stray tears with the back of my hand. "You've been through far worse than this."

I fed the fire. I assembled our belongings so that if daylight came and he wasn't back, I could continue on my own. I ate more than my share of the dried strips of root vegetables that we'd purchased from a vendor in the last town in the Valley, stretching out the time it took me to consume each one, mentally chanting that by the end of every next piece, Seir would pop back into existence next to me. My manifesting was unfortunately unsuccessful.

If nothing else, the time alone gave me a chance to explore every possible feeling I had for the demon while I tried to decide what my next move would be. It was not a surprise when my heart told me with quite a lot of certainty that Seir had burrowed deep, and I simply could not picture my life without him in it. Besides, before he'd left, we'd been on a sure track to completing the bond.

Or at least I thought we had.

Frustrated with myself, I turned my attention to planning. Should I continue on my own toward home? Wait a day? I could always try summoning him.

"That has to be what happened," I mumbled to myself. Nothing else made much sense.

I worried myself in circles. Was he in trouble for being gone? Would he be punished if I tried to summon him back again? Could I even do that? I swallowed some dried beet, discarding any notion of taking that step unless I had no other choice. Ravenglen was only two more days or so, I could surely manage that myself.

Eventually, the adrenaline was completely gone, and I found myself blinking heavily against gritty eyes as I stared into the sky, right at the constellation of The Stallion. My hand strayed to my pocket, where the little carving stayed most of the time. I pulled it out and stroked along the smooth golden parts, the action soothing.

I managed a few fitful hours of sleep before waking up fully alert, heart pounding behind my ribs. The bond was burning, and nothing I did soothed the pain, though moving around did seem to help. Deciding I was not now—and had never been—a damsel waiting to be rescued, despite what had happened at Ignus's house and craving any kind of relief I could get, I packed up our bedding. Then I set about making breakfast. Seir's favorite hot grain cereal and tea seemed reasonable and was the little bit of familiarity I needed to truly re-center.

"It'll be okay," I reassured myself as I wandered near the trees, hoping to find some berries.

The small insects were extra loud and troublesome, flying too close to my face and ears as I scavenged a mere handful of what were probably tart blackberries.

Daylight was still a ways off, but when I emerged from the shadows, a faint orange glow lit the horizon.

My heart sank. He'd been gone all night.

I went through the motions of cooking, eating, cleaning. Mentally, I tried to do some calculations as to how much time had actually elapsed since he disappeared. Seir had been very clear that time moved differently in other realms, but I didn't know what exactly that meant. Did time in Hell move slower? Faster? It could be days or weeks there, but only minutes here and vice versa.

My heart thumped painfully as I finished packing up, stealing my breath and sending me to my knees. Something was very wrong, and I had no idea how to manage it. There was nobody here to help me if I was sick or dying. My own power wouldn't even do me any good.

I managed only a little squeak as the pain intensified, forcing my eyes closed as I focused all my energy on continuing to breathe. Then everything went black.

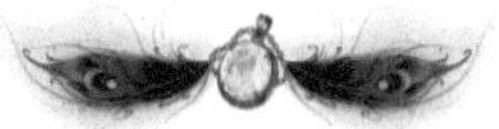

THE WORLD SWAM into focus, far brighter than when I'd lost consciousness. My body was quiet, which was an incredible relief. I dawdled a bit longer, hoping that the lack of discomfort meant Seir was close by, but he didn't appear.

Deciding it did no good to stay and wait, I shouldered one pack on my front and one on my back and forced myself to start walking. Before long, the little stand of trees where we'd camped was no longer visible behind me.

The road was empty still—which most days was frustrating, but today was a relief. I continually willed a demon to drop from the sky, and that would have been incredibly awkward for anyone else to witness.

The hours passed in a blur, my mind simultaneously preoccupied with making sure I kept putting one foot in front of the other and being sure I was distracted by my increasingly stressed thoughts.

If Seir was in Hell, was he being tortured for his absence? If so, it would be my fault. Would it be possible to offer myself up in trade to take his punishment? I wouldn't hesitate to accept if so, but it could be *anything*. I felt tightness across my ribs as I went down that terrifying mental path and forced my thoughts elsewhere. Getting back to Ravenglen. Checking on Aunt Sal. Anything to keep me from envisioning the painful possibilities he might be suffering.

I walked until the sun had started to slip down the horizon again, and I was feeling weak and shaky before finally stopping to eat. There was a lovely little meadow with tall trees and a sprinkling of wildflowers where I stopped to camp.

Autumn had a firm grip on the weather now, the leaves on the trees turning orange and yellow, painting the forests in vibrant color before they gave up and fell off the trees completely. The late afternoon breeze ruffled the tall grasses and my hair, and for the first time all day, I wasn't upset I had so much of my body covered by the insulating packs.

I frowned. It was my favorite time of year, and yet I couldn't find it in me to enjoy it.

The container of water slipped from my fingers before I could take a drink as my hand spasmed. "Shit," I swore as the sudden pain caused the precious contents to spill all over the dirt.

Something ticked over in my brain as emotion swamped me again. I kicked and swore, tears tracking down my face again which only made me angrier.

Once the pain resolved, I had a startling sense of clarity. He was my mate. I needed him. I *wanted* him.

I wanted the bond satisfied so I never had to feel like I had while he was gone ever again. But it wasn't just about the bond or the painful side effects. We belonged together. I wanted him to be mine. I wanted people like those men in the tavern or that cosmetics vendor to get put in their place when they disregarded me standing at his side. Seir was kind, generous, attentive. He never asked me to diminish myself—the opposite in fact. He always honored my wishes. He'd done more for me and treated me with more kindness than anyone else in my life.

As my thoughts spiraled out, creating a list far longer than I could have hoped arguing for the logic of our pairing, I heard it. A heavy sound beyond what a bird could hope to achieve.

Hope flared and I looked up. In the distance was a man-sized creature with wings, coming from the direction of the camp where I'd begun the day. I stood, gasping as the torrent of feelings washed over me again. Then, they turned sour, sending a shock of cold through my body, nausea rolling through my gut.

It was like he'd hit an invisible wall in the sky. His body was limp as he plummeted, wings uselessly tucked to his sides.

CHAPTER 30
HAILON

"S EIR!" I CALLED out, headed for where he'd fallen at a dead run.

I didn't see him hit the ground, but I could only imagine the damage such a fall would cause. He'd done plenty just slipping down that embankment at the ruins.

My breath ran short as I sprinted, his form nothing more than a dark dot on the road at a distance ... until it wasn't.

"Hailon!" he called out, suddenly no further away than perhaps the distance of a few city blocks from me. I could see the panic on his face until he spotted me, then everything transformed to pure joy. His arms went out wide, the interesting glide he was doing about a foot off the ground steady as he beat his wings. He hit me at full speed, grabbing me up in his arms then folding his wings around me for good measure. "Are you crying? I'm sorry. I'm so sorry," he breathed the words into my hair, peppering my face with kisses between words. The warmth and smell of him put everything inside me at ease. "I was summoned back to Hell to report to my unit leader." The fire behind my ribs was doused, and

I no longer felt as though I might drive myself mad with thoughts I couldn't control. "I came back as quick as I could. I didn't mean to go. I didn't mean to. I'm sorry. I'm sorry." He was babbling and clearly at least as distraught as I had been.

Then he took a few steps back and fell to his knees in the road. Panic stopped my heart for a moment. "Seir?" My eyes went wide as he literally crawled the short distance between us. "What are you doing? What's wrong?"

His eyes met mine, full of glimmering sincerity. "I have no right to ask this of you, especially since I have to return to Hell once we get you back to Ravenglen, but know that I am yours, Hailon. In every way. I just need to be near you. I swear, I'll figure out how to come back to you as fast as possible, every time. When I do, please let me stay by your side." He pressed his forehead to my stomach, his hands wrapped around my hips. "Let me love you the way you are meant to be. Adored. Cherished. Please, my dangerous little Moonflower, let me show you how good of a mate I can be to you."

It was the tremble that gave me away, the slight twitch in my flesh that had him gazing up with the gold in his eyes glowing. Fear shivered through me, worry that I was not worthy of this sweet demon, that this was all too hasty. That somewhere along the way, he would decide I wasn't enough or that I was too much trouble. That the fates had made a mistake.

"How did I manage to summon a demon such as you? What have you done to me?" I exhaled long and slow, then plunged my fingers into his curls, giving the slightest tug as I swept through the strands, forehead to neck. I continued to stroke his hair like he was so prone to doing for me as he relaxed into my touch. The longer I stayed silent, the harder he dug his fingers into my hips, his forehead into my middle. The longer I delayed answering because I was speechless, the harsher his breath became.

"Please, Hailon. Don't make me go on without you for eternity. I don't want it if you're not there with me. I know I said I could walk away before, that I could be okay if you weren't mine even if I was yours. But I don't think I'm strong enough."

I sniffled, unable to hold it in any longer. He pulled back to look and reached up to wipe away the tears streaking down my cheeks. "Will you carry me, then?"

All worry fled from his face, leaving behind the youthful exuberance that was his very essence. "Yes. Every step. I've been telling you that since the day we met! You just have to stop arguing about it and let me."

I laughed again, feeling whole and centered. "Ridiculous demon. Get up." He all but jumped to his feet and tangled his arms around me. "Seir?" His eyes shimmered, shifting subtly between gold and red. "Are you okay? You really weren't hurt when you fell just now? How did you land? Were you in trouble in Hell?" The idea he'd been physically punished for helping me made my stomach roll with guilt. I raised a hand to his face like he had a habit of doing to me, and his eyes closed. A breath leaked slowly from him as he relaxed under my touch, and he held my hand in place with his own on my wrist.

He turned his head slowly, kissing my palm as it slid over his mouth. "I'm fine. So much better now, actually." His expression became pinched, pained. "But I was worried about you. You're okay?"

"I only passed out once," I whispered. "Now we're even."

He stilled. "What? Why did you do that?"

I shook my head, wondering why I'd mentioned it at all. "It was fine. I felt really ... odd while you were gone."

"Elaborate, please?" He was frowning, deadly serious.

"The bond was ... really upset." I wasn't sure what else to say.

"Yes, I felt that too." His hand rubbed at his chest. "But you fainted?"

I nodded. "Only once. The pain went everywhere a few times. Like a flare through my whole body. Like I couldn't control my muscles. I don't know how else to describe it."

Seir grunted, still frowning. "I was definitely more uncomfortable than I have been."

"Wait, you didn't answer me. Were you in trouble?"

"There are consequences to disappearing from your post for a full shift cycle and forgetting to check in, even if you're summoned and leave a note," he said cryptically. "But I'm fine."

My emotions shifted violently, my fear for what had happened to him manifesting as anger. "If we're going to be mates, you must teach me the rules of your job so I don't accidentally get you tortured by summoning you back in the middle of something important! Because I almost did, but then I didn't because I didn't want to make things worse, so I was just out here, by myself, going crazy!" I found myself shouting. "And you *must* teach me your alphabet! Soon!" I rushed to inspect the parts of him my hands could get to, looking for any injuries or damage. "And I need to know how time works other places, so I know how to convert that before I start to worry or start walking by myself, and—" I'd started gently beating my fists against his chest to emphasize my points, my anxiety bubbling over as subtle violence.

"Aw, so you *were* worried about me." He smiled down at me, all too smug as he brushed some hair away from my face before resting his hand over my fists, stilling them. He didn't relax his grip on me overall, however, the other arm still lashed tight across my back while his wings cocooned us in their hold as well.

"No." I huffed a breath. He was right, but I was feeling indignant.

"Liar."

I opened my mouth to argue but couldn't formulate anything clever fast enough. Seir, however, planted a thorough kiss on my lips as quickly as he could. "I missed you too."

I squeezed my hands against his forearms, eliciting the smallest intake of breath from him.

"You *are* hurt." I reached for his shirt, pulling it up so I could find his hurts and fix them.

"It's nothing—hey!" His chuckle was rich, full of amusement as I pulled his shirt off altogether. I circled him, then took his hands into mine and turned his arms over. At my grunt over the new collection of angry stripes, he said again, "It's nothing. Really. *Hailon*." He used that tone on me, the serious one that made every cell in my body pay attention. "I'm fine."

"You're not. I can fix it, just hold still—"

Instead of letting me gather my thoughts and reach for my magic, Seir crushed his mouth to mine. Then he reached for the tails of my shirt, pulling it up and over my head in one smooth motion.

"What are you doing!" I squeaked.

"Checking you for injuries. Fair is fair, right?"

"I'm not hurt!" I protested.

"You could be. You said you fainted. Did you fall? Did you land on your side? Your back? This delectable ass?"

"Seir!" My blood pounded in my ears as he gripped my backside with both hands, mouth sealed over mine once again.

"Tell me to stop, Moonflower. I'll listen. I'll always obey your commands."

Our bare chests plastered together, his warm voice rumbling through me, I took the final leap. "Why would I do that?"

He grunted, sounding strained. "I need you to be absolutely sure, Hailon. This is no small agreement."

"I'm sure, Seir."

I felt his hesitation and ended it for us both, once and for all. I leaned into him, enticing him into a long, luxurious kiss. His hand came to cradle my face as our tongues tangled and his breath mingled with mine.

My hands shucked my trousers and then worked on his, earning me another surprised grunt, but also a smile, though he never pulled away from our embrace or the kiss. I used my hands to position his along my thighs, and he understood right away what I wanted. He lifted me up, my center against his stomach.

"This will not be sweet," he warned.

"I never asked for sweet."

"But—"

"I'm fine. I want this. I want you, Seir." I took his hard cock in my hand and guided the tip to my opening. A noise rumbled through his throat as I swept it back and forth through the moisture already gathered there before seating it properly. I reveled in the burn as he slowly lowered me down, his eyes fixed to mine as we both gasped at the sensation of him entering me for the first time.

The sounds of my harsh breath and pounding heartbeat were all I could hear as I adjusted to the way he filled me up.

"Hailon." My name was a prayer on his lips, his cheeks flushed with color and eyes soft as he gazed down at me.

I put my hands on his shoulders and used the strength in my thighs to move a bit. I was rewarded with Seir following my example, his wings tightening even further around me in a way that allowed them to provide stability so I wouldn't fall, even if he let go of my legs with his hands. His mouth met mine again, our moans exchanged through mutual breath as we rocked.

"I'm going to shame myself," he panted, nipping at my neck with those sharp teeth. I clenched against him, earning another moan. "Hailon, no. *Please*, don't do that, I can't—"

I moved my hand to grip behind his neck, angling my hips so that I could guarantee if he was close, I would be right there with him.

"Fuck," he swore, the word drawn out and harshly whispered, the heat of his breath and the slight graze of his teeth against my neck beyond erotic. "You have no idea how many times I dreamt of this, Moonflower."

"Those untoward intentions again?"

He groaned. "I was having thoughts constantly, trust me. We've just had far more important things going on."

My whole body felt like it was on fire, but the spot in my chest that had been causing so much trouble most of all. As the tension low in my womb finally released, I cried out. I worried I might be dying the way my ribs burned, but I couldn't bring myself to care. Seir's thrusts became rough, frantic. His eyes rounded as he gazed down at me, the gold and green flashing to red and back again as his face pinched with strain and bliss. He rested his forehead on mine as he exhaled hard, body shuddering against me.

"Thank you, Hailon. I swear I'll be a good mate."

Chests pressed together, our hearts pounded the same rhythm, the heat and ache gone completely. Only after I wriggled in request did he set me down on my unsteady feet.

Seir smiled, placing light kisses all over my face before turning to gather our assorted discarded clothing. "Come, dangerous creature. Let's get back to your camp, I'll tell you everything I can while I make you dinner as an apology for leaving at such an inopportune time." He kissed me again and again—cheeks, lips, throat. He even hovered in the space between my neck and shoulder for a long moment, inhaling slowly. "Though this return greeting certainly makes me think it might have been worth it."

My cheeks flamed again, and I batted at his shoulder. He chuckled as he nuzzled into my neck, then squeaked as he pulled me back against him, his tail winding around my waist as he lifted us both with his powerful wings and glided us the short distance back to the meadow.

CHAPTER 31

HAILON

"HOW ARE YOU using your wings so well this close to me all of a sudden? That's much better than before you left." I set out our bedrolls, trying not to be awkward about putting them next to each other. "Not to mention you were able to catch yourself when you fell."

"I'm not sure, though I'm quite pleased about it. That landing would have been awful otherwise. Hopefully soon I can fly properly with you in my arms."

"We'll see."

Gliding had been kind of fun, though a bit intense at first. I couldn't help but picture myself frantically clinging to him as he kept rising higher and higher into the sky should he get that skill back.

"I nearly forgot!" He pulled a pouch out of his pocket and produced several pieces of jewelry, each with a fancy gemstone. "I don't have much to offer you at the moment, but if any of these strike your fancy, it's yours."

My heart stopped, then resumed beating at a heavy pounding. "I don't need a ring."

"I want you to have one, Hailon. But we can wait to choose a set, if that suits you better?"

I hadn't considered anything of the sort, but now such a thing seemed incredibly attractive.

"My brother could enchant them for us if you like."

A ring seemed to make everything very official, very quickly. I was not averse to the idea of marriage, but I hadn't adequately prepared myself for that step. Seemed strange, to go straight to accepting a mate and avoiding marriage, but my mind wasn't always logical.

"These are all lovely, but there's plenty of time for that later." There was one with a chip of obsidian, the stone a rough triangle shape imbedded in the metal band, that I picked out to look at closer. "Where did you get them?"

"Same place you got the rings in your pouch, Moonflower." Bodies, then. I should have been put off by that, but I understood. If nothing else, he wasn't wasteful. "Except that one." He grinned. "I've had that one with me since just after I fell."

I gasped and handed it back. "Why don't you wear it? If you've had it that long, it must be precious to you."

He turned it over in his palm before putting it back into his pouch with a shrug. "Never was much for rings, I guess. And that one in particular is too small for my hand. I kept it because it was unique, but it was never really for me." He put the pouch back into his pocket and went over to the fire.

He'd managed to find a couple of small fowl in the high grass and carefully removed them from the hastily made spit they'd been roasting on.

Seir prepared our plates and presented mine to me with a proud smile. "Should be tasty enough, though I wish I had some seasonings." He dropped down next to me, sitting cross-legged on his bedroll.

I was reminded of our first meal together in the little cabin outside of Olinbourg. The meal was much the same, though I felt completely different from that woman who had been weak, hungry, and unsure of how to get home again.

"You alright?" Seir was watching me closely, his own food going untouched until I took a bite.

"Fine. Just thinking about that first meal we shared."

He grinned, tearing into a leg quarter from his bird. "You were so hungry. I was very impressed at your appetite."

"Impressed?" I asked, choking a bit as I laughed at his moony expression.

"Absolutely. You are indeed a dangerous woman, Hailon. You were so beautiful taking your vengeance in that house. I'm fairly certain I fell for you the moment I saw you, but watching you take my dagger from my hand and dispatch those men?" He heaved a dreamy sigh. "Then you wanted to argue with me about helping you leave, carrying you, all of it. When you sat down at that little table in the cabin, I expected you to pick over your plate, but you dove in wholeheartedly and ate more than me."

"I should feel embarrassed about that, probably."

He shook his head, eyes wide and tone earnest. "No, not at all. I would have found and cooked a dozen more birds if you'd wanted them. You deserved—*deserve*—to eat your fill at every meal. To be satisfied in every way." I blushed, and as though he just realized what he'd said, he smirked. "You went without even your most basic needs being met for months, after being taken, held against your will. It's all mad, honestly, what you went through. I was just excited I could provide something to help you feel better, to start to heal."

From most other people, his words would have felt over the top. But he was being completely genuine, and it warmed me.

"Feels like a long time ago."

"It does." He paused to chew. "I owe you an apology."

"Another one?"

"Many," he nodded enthusiastically. "I should have been keeping better track of the time. I should have prepared for being called back if I didn't check in. I'm sorry I left you here all alone."

"How does time move in Hell?"

"Much slower than here. I was there perhaps a couple of hours."

"It was most of a day up here."

"Oh! Speaking of." He dug around in the pocket of his trousers and produced a small mirror. "Something else to teach you. I needed to use a portal to come back, and the best option took me through my brother's collegium. I can't wait for you to meet them." He smiled wide.

"Your brothers?"

He stood, clearing our now empty plates. "Yes, and their wives. I have options for you, Hailon, should you want to explore your powers more. There are people who can help us figure out what it might mean that you're a null. After you see to your aunt, of course."

"Okay." Excitement bubbled in my chest. I'd never really dreamt of a life beyond our little house in Ravenglen. We had our routines, Aunt Sal and I, and life was often difficult, even if we never strayed outside of them. But now ... it was wonderful to have options. I could understand completely why Seir took such enjoyment out of novel experiences. I didn't realize how small of a box I'd been living in before getting this odd chance to wander the realm with him.

"You'll get along with my sisters-in-law perfectly. You're all birds of a feather."

"In what way?" I chuckled as he maneuvered my body into a fully horizontal position, wrapping his arms around me as he lay his head on my stomach.

"You are all very powerful women." I could feel his smile. "Rylan's wife, Calla, is a tremendous earth witch, and Vassago's wife, Greta, is a talented alchemist. I think in some ways they are stronger than my brothers." He turned his mouth into my shirt, gently kissing me through the fabric before winding his fingers up under the hem. "And I think my brothers enjoy that fact. I know I do."

"You do what?"

"Love knowing you could take me out if you wanted to, Moonflower." He shivered, and heat flooded my veins as he slowly moved his hands and mouth up my body, taking my shirt with him as he went.

"You think I could?" I asked, voice shaky as he stopped to lavish my breasts with attention, the alternating heat of his mouth and chill of the night air making me squirm.

"I *know* you could." His voice had dropped to a growl and his horns had slipped out, both of which made my thighs clench together. Then he playfully bit around my nipple, and I gasped. None of this deterred him, however, on his quest to divest me of my clothes altogether. Then he stripped at my request once I was feeling overly exposed.

He bent one of my legs up, then the other, and settled his broad shoulders between them.

"What are you ...?"

"Having my dessert. Everything was a bit rushed before, if you recall. I'm dying to know how you taste. Now I finally have an opportunity to find out."

My eyes rolled back as he started to feast on me, his wicked tongue tracing along the edges before teasing inside. His hot breath and satisfied groans had me arching into his mouth, directing him to where I wanted more attention. He slung a forearm over my hips to keep me in place as he worked a pattern over my sensitive nub that had me making sounds deep in my throat. My hips moved on their own, but he just applied more pressure to keep me exactly where he wanted me. He'd bring me right to the edge like that, getting me to the point where my thighs were shaking and I was whispering curses like prayers, then stop, only to lick me from top to bottom and back again, spearing me with his tongue again and again ... then starting over.

It was torture.

"Is this my punishment then?" I asked, panting.

"Do you deserve punishment, Moonflower?" he growled before plunging his fingers inside me and sucking on my clit. "What is it you've done?"

I reached down and grabbed his horns with my hands, relying on them to keep me grounded. Seir growled, alternating licks and sucks while pumping two fingers in and out of me.

My thighs clamped around his ears, and I unintentionally pulled on his horns, the sensation intense as I came with a roar.

"Most delicious dessert I ever had," he mumbled, looking up at me with eyes glowing gold, his mouth shiny as he licked his lips.

He held me steady until the shaking stopped, then dipped his head again, lavishing the curve of my waist and hip with kisses and nips from those sharp teeth of his.

Seir crawled up my body enough to press his chest against my stomach, then he slid his hands under me. His warm palms dragged down my back, fingers sinking into the flesh, pulling me closer, lower as I moved down the blankets. He bit along the edges of my breast playfully, making me twitch. I didn't get very far, however, as he had me in a tight hold, tracing firmly from my shoulders to the curve of my ass.

Seir paused, turning my body slightly to the side, balancing me on my right hip. "What ..." He frowned as he rubbed a fingertip over the thousands of tiny pinpoint scars that dotted along my skin. They were hard to see unless you were right up close or intentionally felt for them.

"They don't hurt," I whispered, sad to have lost the passionate moment to my marks. "Not even at first. They just show up."

"They just appear?"

"Yes. One for every time I use my healing power."

His eyes snapped to mine, a mix of lust and concern swirling in the gold as he continued to explore the dots that were arranged in an oddly geometric pattern across my ribs. The tiny scars were positioned roughly in lines that followed my ribs, but also in noticeable sections that sometimes curved like a wave or swept up like an illustration of the wind. There was even a section near my spine that was mostly vertical. I hadn't ever been able to puzzle out the reasoning behind the patterns, and it was only recently that they had spread from the left side to the right. I often wondered what would happen if or when I filled up every inch of skin on my body. Would I die? Would they start cramming into the empty space until I was one solid scar?

"There are so many, Moonflower. You've given so much." He breathed out slowly through his nose, my marks clearly weighing on him. He scanned them again, tracing the edges with one finger. Then he smiled. "They look like wings a little. The way they're settled just over this area."

"You think so?"

"I do." He gave me one of his soft smiles, the kind that stole my breath when they appeared, because they were a peek into the depth of his soul. When he drew an outline around the left side again, I felt what he meant about the shape of a wing. It wasn't all that different from the outline of his sigil.

Seir's hand splayed across my stomach as he gently kissed my marks, light feathery brushes, over and over again. His fingertips seemed restless, flexing against the soft flesh along my hip, digging in further as he discovered the softness there. His hand migrated south as he moved up toward my neck with his mouth, the playful nips back, his breathing heavier, intention clear.

My body began to tingle when he rolled me off my hip and onto my back, his mouth instantly finding mine and wasting no time consuming me. I shivered as his fingers stroked the skin to either side of my clit, trapping it between them.

He pulled away from my mouth, groaning deep in his throat. "Can you take me again, Moonflower?" His one hand strayed to his cock, pumping lazily as the other teased me further, one digit dipping just barely inside, leaving me desperate for more friction.

"Yes," I breathed, knowing I was going to be sore but not caring. That was tomorrow's problem to manage.

"Good." He maneuvered me where he wanted me, bringing my ankles to his shoulders as he sat back on his heels. He employed both hands to lift me by the ass, positioning me carefully across his thighs.

Then he smiled as he raised himself up on his knees, and I swear my internal temperature went up thirty degrees. He pressed into me, entering slowly as he continued to lean forward until he was fully seated inside me, and my knees were up by my face. Palms on the blanket next to my head, his glowing eyes slipped closed as he released a long breath. The slow ache as my body adjusted for him once again had me whining.

"Okay, beloved?" He froze, his own chest heaving but his eyes concerned.

"Yes," I repeated. The word came out on a moan, which was all the provocation he needed to continue.

Our first coupling had been frenzied, desperate. This time, Seir very clearly was being slow, deliberate. His tail tickled along my legs, up and down the calf on one side and then the other before wrapping around my right leg, the length of his tail twined around my limb like a snake.

"I'm not going anywhere," I teased, but the impact was diminished greatly by the breathiness of my voice.

"Oh, trust me, I know you're not. You're all mine right now." The gentle rocking pace he started had my eyes rolling back because of the angle he was at, that delicious spot near my entrance getting perfect friction. His jaw flexed and rolled as he set a torturously slow pace. I felt every inch as he moved, his cock pressing all the way in and then pulling nearly all the way out.

He lifted his torso up a little, balancing on a single hand. The other he brought to his mouth, making painfully prolonged eye contact with me as he sucked on his fingers then delved between us to circle my overly sensitive clit.

"Seir. I can't. It's too much, I'm going to—"

"Don't threaten me with a good time, Moonflower." He increased the pressure as well as the speed of his fingers, my body hovering right on the edge. "We have all the time in the world. I'm willing to see exactly how many times you can come for me."

"Move. Please." He'd stopped rocking his hips, but I wanted that too. I needed it. And I needed him to stop talking like that, because it was doing something to me I didn't expect or know how to manage.

"I like you greedy, Hailon." He stared down at me, eyes glowing bright gold, satisfied smirk on his mouth. The low tone of his voice rattled through me, the way he said my name causing a sharp increase in my arousal.

"I'm not greedy," I managed to argue though panting breaths, but it was too late.

He chuckled through a groan as I detonated, a wild noise tearing through my throat as my body clenched around him.

Seir leaned down over me again, holding my face in his palm as I breathed my way back to reality.

"You are, little Moonflower. But I like it." His thrusts were harder, more intentional as he whispered to me, pausing to lace my collarbone with gentle sucks. "I like when you take what you need." His hips flexed almost brutally, and I was somehow hurtling toward another climax as he played every part of my body like its master. "Love when you tell me exactly what you want. I'd give you anything, you know. The whole world. Just ask."

I was reduced to moans and ashes as my body incinerated itself from the inside out once more.

"Fuck." His rhythm became disjointed, and his jaw twitched as he chased his own release. "I was going to take my time, draw things out. But I can't resist. You feel too good." Eyes closed and face turned to the sky, he gasped as he spilled inside me.

He carefully slid my legs from his shoulders, pinning me to the blanket and smothering me with more slow kisses before leveraging himself off.

The fire crackled as he found a cloth and wet it with some of our heated water.

"I can take care of myself; you don't have to do that." I sat up and tensed my legs, drawing them together when he returned, clearly intent on cleaning me up.

His head tilted to the side, and he gave me a playfully chastising look. "Open." I relaxed my thighs. Seir cleaned me up with gentle reverence, then wandered off toward the fire again. When he returned, he brought cups of tea with him and some of the dried fruit I'd hoarded in my pack. He pulled a blanket over our legs as he settled down next to me. "I thought you'd have learned by now that I take care of what's mine, Hailon, particularly you. Are you alright?"

"I'm lovely. You?" I wasn't brave enough to look at him and was more than thankful for the cup of tea to bury my blushing face in.

"I could die right now, perfectly happy. Though I'd rather have an eternity of repeating that, if it's all the same to you." This new side of him was a pleasant surprise, at least to my hormones. It was no small relief that my chest was no longer on fire, but the way he had my heart racing was a new complication to manage.

"You're different since you went back to Hell." My brain still felt more than scrambled, in the best way. My eyes were heavy, too, and I knew that sleep was chasing me.

He chuffed into his own mug. "It's not Hell's fault, Hailon. I've been different since I got into you." I choked on his words, spraying the blanket with my tea. Seir only laughed, thumping my back helpfully as I coughed. "Sorry. That's my fault. Here, for your safety." He took my cup and laid us down, my head pillowed on his chest and his fingers running through my hair.

I shook my head but found myself grinning. Everything was new, somehow, and this little bubble of peace with us inside was perfect.

Even if I sometimes choked on my tea.

CHAPTER 32
SEIR

WE LINGERED LONGER than we should have breaking camp in the morning. It was clear neither of us wanted to leave the pretty little meadow where so much between us had changed. But we were too close to our destination not to go.

I made breakfast while Hailon packed away our bedding. We were down to our last changes of clean clothing again, and being in the grasslands with limited water was an excellent argument against staying.

As was the ticking clock for me to return to Hell.

When we finally started down the road, Hailon grabbed for my hand, linking her fingers through mine.

"Did you want to try flying?" I asked.

She shook her head gently. "We don't have to. We're pretty close now. We could glide a little, but ..." She hesitated, the road ahead of us stretching out both long and short.

"I understand."

"We should probably fly while there's nobody else on the road to save time. I'm both anxious and afraid to get back." I squeezed her fingers.

"We can in a bit. We've got time enough."

"Hailon, I have to go back."

She nodded solemnly. "You said. When?"

"I have to return before sundown two days from now, if my calculations are right. My unit leader probably won't summon me the moment the sun sets or anything like that. I do feel pressed to go voluntarily, however. He made it seem as though if I did, he would be able to help me quicker." I swallowed, already trying to figure out a loophole, not wanting to leave. "If it comes to that, if he summons me—"

"It won't," she said firmly. "We'll get you back on time. I don't want you to be punished for no reason. I want you to come back as fast as possible."

"I would bear it though. For you." The temporary pain of whatever consequences Keplar would enforce would be worth being sure she was safe before I went. "I've likely already faced something similar. If I need to stay a bit longer, I will."

Hailon sighed. "There is no need for self-sacrifice, Seir. We've established I can mind myself well enough." She wasn't wrong, but I hated the very idea. "How long will you be gone do you think?"

My heart sank. "I honestly don't know."

"What if I banished you, then immediately summoned you again? That would restart the clock, right? What could they do then?"

I stared at her, awed at her thought pattern and doing my best to think of the most accurate answer.

"Never mind. I'm being ... I don't even know what this is." She blushed and looked down at her feet.

"Hey. Don't do that." I lifted her chin with my finger. "I can't promise it will be easy, Hailon. Or how long it will take to sort things out. I wish I could. I wish I didn't have to leave you here to do it at all. I'm sorry."

"It's okay. I still would have chosen the same." She gave me a gentle smile. Her words quelled the building storm of fear and worry in my chest.

In the silence between us, I ran through what felt like the most implausible of proposals to take back to Keplar. Nothing seemed the right fit, though.

IT WAS EARLY afternoon when Ravenglen proper loomed into view beyond the pastoral outlying farmlands. First came the needle-like church spire, then the other tall buildings clustered in the village center. It was a bustling place, the people busy, smiling. It appeared on all counts to be thriving.

Hailon had been quieter than normal most of the day despite my efforts to woo her out of her thoughts. It was clear she was anxious over returning on top of dealing with our new bond and needed some time.

I understood that just fine; going home was never a simple prospect, even when it was somewhere you wanted to be. Somewhere you belonged. I didn't know if that described Hailon's relationship to Ravenglen or if home was simply wherever her aunt was. She had explained to me more than once her concern over her aunt's well-being in her absence, and I hoped Sal was as hearty as Hailon, and that they could be reunited quickly.

In truth, I was nervous too. I didn't know exactly what this meant for us, but I did know I was not looking forward to saying goodbye to this woman, even temporarily. Hell as a whole held little appeal for me after my recent adventures topside, and without her by my side, I worried I'd be terribly bored. Lonely. I enjoyed everything about her company even before the mate bond and the complications it added. I didn't want to go back to the bland life I'd had before she'd disrupted my routine, not even part time.

Her stride took on more speed once we passed through the broad, tall lintel welcoming us to Ravenglen. There was not a wall nor a fence, but rather a welcoming archway woven from tree branches over the road at the edge of town. Little ornaments made of flowers hung from it, and some bits of colored glass. It was quite charming.

"Everything looks incredible," she commented as we got into the bustling town center. "It's cleaner, brighter almost. No more empty storefronts—there were several when I left." Her head tilted. "Memory is an odd thing."

Hailon had a singular focus as we walked through the busy village. Several people stopped to stare; indeed, a considerable number did a double take when they saw her. I was not altogether pleased with the way so many faces pinched in recognition. It looked like they'd tasted something sour which made no sense at all. A healer with her gifts surely should have been missed all this time. Nobody came to offer their condolences, however, which seemed positive. Hailon didn't acknowledge the behavior at all, though I'm sure she saw as much of it as I did.

We walked all the way across the relatively large town to a quiet neighborhood with tidy cottages and flocks of fluffy chickens roaming free from yard to yard. Hailon stopped in front of the one home on the street with herbs in the front planter beds instead of flowers. The roof had seen far better days, and everything looked like it could use a coat of fresh paint, but it looked very quaint. Cozy, even. It seemed quite well maintained for a home with an unwell inhabitant. I hoped that was a good sign.

Hailon seemed a perfect balance of relieved and nervous as she stood in front of the faded blue door. Her hand lifted and dropped again, and she finally looked at me, really looked, for the first time since our stop at midday. "Thank you," she said. "For bringing me all this way. For getting me home."

"You're welcome." I offered a smile. "Thank you for letting me come along instead of immediately banishing me back to Hell."

"I did send you back right away. Accidentally," she kidded, the corners of her mouth lifting.

"You did." Neither of us had the heart to say out loud that soon enough she would have to banish me for real, whether either of us wanted her to or not.

Hailon looked at the door. She stood on her toes and tried to peek in the window. Still, she made no move to knock or reach for the knob.

"And now you're the one who's stalling, Moonflower. Go on. Don't get nervous. We finally got you here." I gestured with one hand what I hoped was encouragement.

"Right." She lifted her hand and knocked, the pattern a particular cadence. A secret knock, perhaps, that only the two of them used. For some reason, that silly little detail made me smile.

The door opened, revealing a petite woman with graying dark hair. "Hailon?" She glanced between us, shock widening her eyes.

"Aunt Sal?" Hailon's words were steeped in disbelief. "You're okay! Better than okay. I'm so happy to see you! But how?" She reached forward, pulling the older woman into her arms for an enthusiastic hug. I could see tears of relief shimmering in her eyes.

"You're here. How are you here?" Sal asked, weakly patting Hailon's back, before pulling away from the embrace. "Come inside," Sal said, poking her head out the door after ushering us in, as though gauging to see how many of the neighbors had seen us.

A warning tingled under my skin. That was an odd reaction for an aunt who should have been sick to the point of being on death's door to ask of a niece who'd been missing for so long. She also didn't seem particularly excited. I could make allowances for shock, but this woman's response to Hailon's homecoming felt all wrong.

"I'll make us some tea," Sal said, perpetually moving her body away from Hailon when she got too close.

I stood near the door with our packs, allowing Hailon to absorb being back in her home without my interference. She gazed around, wonder in her eyes.

"Everything is just as I remember." She smiled at me, and I did my best to nod reassuringly. I had my eye on her aunt, however, and that seemed mutual.

"Are you going to introduce me?" Sal asked, measuring out loose tea.

"Oh! Sorry, I got distracted and forgot my manners. Aunt Sal, this is Seir. Seir, this is my aunt Sal."

"Pleased to meet you." I threw an arm across my chest and gave a deep bow. "Hailon has had much to say about you."

"Has she now?" Sal all but scowled when she looked at her smiling niece.

"Indeed. She's been very worried about you."

"Mmm." The noncommittal noise rubbed me wrong.

"How are you so well, Sal? I've spent all these weeks worrying that the worst might have happened! We've missed nine treatments by my count. Don't misunderstand, please, I've never been so happy to be wrong. I'm elated to see you up, and so vibrant! I can't remember when I last saw you so hale and hearty. I just don't understand *how*. We've relied on me healing you for so long, just to keep you relatively functional. Did you find a new tincture or medicine?"

Sal's tone was cold, and my hand strayed for a blade without any conscious thought when she looked my mate in the eyes and said, "You really shouldn't have come back here."

CHAPTER 33
HAILON

M Y HEART SANK, the cold edge of fear skittering down my spine. The way Sal said those words ...

I huffed a rough laugh, emotions a muddled mess. "Where else would I go, Sal?" I stared at my aunt, but the woman in front of me was suddenly unfamiliar. "I got back as soon as I could. Did ... Didn't you miss me? Didn't you wonder why I never came back from the mountains?"

Sal sat in her favorite chair after handing out the tea. There was a small basket next to it with the same collection of yarn and mending inside there had always been. The plants lining both the front windows were perhaps a bit more overgrown but seemed mostly unchanged. The tapestries on the walls, the stacks of books on the floor in front of the full shelves ... everything was the same. But it wasn't.

I could feel it now that the rush of excitement had waned, the feeling that the house had moved on in my absence. I no longer fit in this place, not even in the partial kind of way I had before.

Sal sipped at her tea, then set it aside with a sigh. "There's nothing for you here, Hailon." Her eyes met mine, and again I got the impression I didn't know the woman I'd lived with all my life.

"What?"

"Did you notice the healthy new fields on your way in? The way everyone is smiling in town? How nobody looks hungry?"

"I—"

"*I* did that." Her sudden snap of anger, the way her fist went to her chest, was so unlike her, I flinched from the movement.

"I don't understand."

"I did my part," she said quietly, as though she'd repeated the words to herself several times before. "I cared for you well. Thirty years is enough. More than. I did my duty to your mother, I kept my promise."

Seir shifted his position, but I was rooted to the floor. Ice flowed through my veins as I absorbed her detached tone.

"You did, Sal. And thank you for that. You always did well by me. You taught me everything I know. I thought it went without saying, but I cared for you too. I stayed in this house because you needed me. Because that was the only way to guarantee you'd stay alive—"

"But *you* were what was wrong with me!" she barked. "Me and the whole town. When you would go into the mountains, the springs would start to flow freely, like a clog had released upstream. Every fountain in town would go from a little trickle to a full bubble. Fields were irrigated like no other time. Plants, animals, people—all would perk up when you were away from town. Did you know that?"

"There was always talk about the springs being unpredictable, but—"

"I tracked it. For *years* after I first got a hint that there was a pattern. I had to be sure. You were my best friend's daughter, after all, and I could be signing my own death warrant if I was wrong. But I wasn't. Something about you is toxic, Hailon. You suck up any magic around you like a black hole." She shook her head. "I couldn't be your source any longer. And I needed my own life! I sacrificed my own relationships and youth to tend to you."

"Sal." The lump in my throat was hard to swallow over, let alone try to speak over.

"I did everything I could think of to get you to leave on your own, Hailon. Nothing was ever enough to convince you to just *go*, even with the whole town torn between fearing and despising you. It wasn't enough that the town thought you were a whore. Not enough that they thought you were responsible for several people dying under your care. You took the abuse they dished out and still *helped* them." The sour expression on her face made it seem like such a thing was far from her comprehension. "Despite it all, you kept trying. So I had to find a different way. It was common knowledge you periodically went to collect herbs in the mountains, I just had to make sure the right person found out you'd be out there alone."

Tears prickled, the words like punches. My breath was loud in my ears, the pain that stabbed at my insides every time I breathed reminiscent of the angry bond but much sharper, like I'd inhaled shards of glass. When I opened my eyes after blinking to clear the tears from my vision, Seir had moved from his post near the door. He was leaning over Sal with his horns out and sharp teeth bared, tail wound around her throat and dagger in his hand.

"Be *very* careful what your next words are," he warned, voice low and menacing. Every dish in the kitchen cabinets rattled. "You're lucky you're still alive after a confession like that."

"A demon?" she gasped, eyes and mouth both wide.

I took the few steps separating us and put my hand on Seir's arm. "It's alright. Let her go."

He snarled, the noise aimed at her, not me. He unwound his tail from her throat and took the smallest possible step back from her.

"Do you know where they took me? What they planned to do with me?"

"All I did was casually mention to Gerald when he dropped off the candles that week that you were off on one of your excursions. You went all the time! It's not like it was a secret. What he did with that information is none of my concern."

"Did you look for me, Sal?"

"Of course. There was no way to know what happened to you. For all I knew, you ran off or got eaten by a bear in the woods. It was just coincidental timing that a traveling merchant happened to be in town then and had mentioned he was looking for a healer for his town and the neighboring villages down south."

"But neither of those things happened to me, Sal. I was taken. By that merchant. All because you gossiped with Gerald."

"None of this was easy for me, Hailon. I felt like I had no other choice."

"No other choice." The blood in my veins had frozen solid. "You could have left, Sal. You could have *talked to me*. Instead, you sold me out." The words came out of my mouth in my voice, but I was numb. The shape of them felt wrong on my lips. "You knew that information would end up in the tavern. You all but hand delivered me to men you knew nothing about, including their true intentions."

She scanned me up and down. "You look no worse for wear."

Those words made something inside me break. Wild energy pulsed behind my right eye, a rage like I'd never known flooded through me. I put out one arm to bar Seir from surging forward, a wild growl rumbling through him. I understood his motivations, but this was my fight. I reached the other hand forward, Sal's pulse fast against my thumb as I held her by the throat. She didn't move. There was a slight flinch at the corner of her eye, but she held steady, staring right back at me.

"Three men snatched me from the woods. For weeks I was bound, hooded, and kept in a wagon." I took a small step closer so I could keep a grip on her and bend down a bit. I held eye contact with her as I spoke, wanting her to feel every word. "After that, I was kept in a small, cold bedroom in only a thin nightgown. I was chained to the bed by my ankles so I couldn't escape. I was forced to use my gift over and over. My captor was cruel, and he profited while I suffered."

She flinched again, what might have been a flash of guilt crossing her face, and it was the fuel to the fire inside me.

"Seven men routinely experimented on me. Sampled everything they could think of. Blood. Hair. Nails. Skin. I was cold, hungry, exhausted, and battered. No sunshine. No happiness. And do you know what I thought of?" Her lips parted the tiniest bit. "You." Tears prickled again, ones born of anger and disappointment. "I was worried about *you*. About getting back here, so I could heal you. I calculated the weeks I was being tortured in missed treatments." I scoffed, voice gone rough from how loud I'd been yelling.

"Hailon, listen." Sal put her hands up as though surrendering.

"I'm not done!" I shouted.

Sal jerked and scooted back, my hand now a claw around her throat, her pulse thrumming against my palm like a hummingbird. The lines in her face suddenly seemed more noticeable, her gray hair more pronounced. The glow I'd admired in her face had faded to sallow gray.

"I was so desperate to escape my situation that I pickpocketed a spell book from one of my captors. If he'd noticed, I could have been killed, but I had no other choice. Those pages held instructions for how to summon a demon. Turns out, that was the best risk I ever took." I felt Seir's hand on my shoulder, his tail slowly winding around my leg. "He got me back here as quickly as possible. For *you.*" I laughed then, the sound wild, unhinged. The inside of my body felt too light, too free. I was worried that I was very much not okay, but the notion was slippery, sliding away from my grasp as quickly as it came.

Finally, I released her throat. Sal coughed, looking as though she'd aged ten years since we arrived. "I guess you were right about one thing, though. We came back here for nothing." I turned to Seir. "We could have stayed in that lovely little cabin for the rest of our lives. Lingered in the hot springs another day, wandered around those quaint towns in the Valley for a week. It wouldn't have made any difference." The concerned frown on his face made my head hurt. I sagged, all the strength I'd gotten from the anger gone.

Sal held her head up, meeting my eye. "For what it's worth, I'm proud of the strong, capable woman you've become. I knew you'd be okay no matter what happened to you."

For some reason, that hurt worse than anything else she'd said.

I roared, a feral sound of rage and agony that originated from somewhere beyond my physical body. Seir stood at my back, every muscle tensed, waiting for the slightest signal that I wanted him to act.

"Where are my things?" I asked when I could coherently form words again.

"Your room."

"Do. Not. Move."

I met Seir's eye and communicated with a slight nod that I wanted him to guard her before moving through the house to the small room that used to be mine.

Dust motes filtered through the slant of orange afternoon light coming through the tattered curtain. The walls were bare. My bed was right where it had always been, but it was covered in a plain white cloth. There were no pillows, no blankets. It had been dressed for long-term storage, to keep the dust off, not for use. I supposed I should be grateful that she hadn't moved in someone else yet. In the far corner of the room was a trunk and a couple of crates. It seemed a pitiful collection to represent someone's whole life.

I went over to the pile of things, pulling out a book, a dress. My eyes were wet again, and my heart squeezed so hard I could hardly breathe.

After having survived out of a pack for so long, I was surprised and disappointed that none of it brought me any sentimental feelings at all. It was mostly useless garbage.

I dug around in the trunk for the few items of clothing I knew I'd regret leaving. My old boots had been taken from me by my kidnappers, and the knife I always used for plants had ended up somewhere in the woods, which still made me sad.

I went through the crates, taking out my books, a small jewelry box. I looked through the piles once more before deciding I had everything of value. It was a sad little collection, but all the other things could be replaced. I wrapped everything in my wall tapestry and looked around one last time.

"I owe you no kindness," Seir snarled at Aunt Sal as I came back into the room. "You're lucky to still be breathing."

"I took everything I want," I said, putting the bundle inside my pack. "Burn the rest or sell it. Makes no difference to me." I turned to Seir. "What did she ask you?"

"The secret to demon summoning," he answered, crossing his arms. "If we happened to still have that little spell book."

"I've just been trying for so many years," she lamented, appealing to my pity. Unfortunately for her, I no longer had any. "I made myself crazy trying any method I could find. None of the books or pamphlets had it right. Nothing worked. But you managed it! You!" She scoffed, as though I were some inept fool for whom such a thing should have been impossible. "If I'd been able to do that, been able to bring your mother back, I wouldn't have been so desperate. Things could have been different! I wouldn't have been driven to do such a thing—"

"Are you saying my mother"—my vision narrowed, the overwhelming emotions of the visit rising again from where they'd finally settled—"was a demon?"

"Not full-blooded, no. Her mother was a demon, or that's what she was told. But I always hoped it would work, if I could have managed to figure out the right way."

Sal rose and retrieved a small notebook from her bookcase. "This is what she left for me, when I took Hailon in," she said, showing us both a worn piece of parchment. "For all the good it did me." The whole page was written in a language I couldn't read, signed with what looked like a sigil. Seir reached out and took the paper, scanning it with a frown before putting it in his pocket. He just stared Sal down when she opened her mouth to protest. Sal accepted the loss. "Her name was Wyn. I loved her. And I did my best to honor the promise I made her." She nodded, convincing herself that there was truth in those words.

I turned for the door.

"Moonflower?" Seir asked, a perplexed look on his face.

"I traveled all this way, terrified I'd get here to find her gravely ill or already dead. The reality is honestly so much worse." I laughed again, the sound humorless and edged with anger. "This kind of betrayal … I don't even have words for it. But I won't do to her what she did to me. I'm better than that."

"I'm not," my demon was quick to respond.

"I need you to be. For now. She lives. For now."

He huffed a breath, showing her his teeth one more time before turning to grab our packs. "I will honor this command because you gave it. And because it is only *for now*."

Sal flinched but didn't apologize.

I turned back one last time, Sal's bitter face burning into my mind along with all the words she'd flung at me. Then I bestowed the best curse I could think of on her and turned to leave the place that had been my home my whole life for the last time.

"I hope you have the life you deserve, Sal."

CHAPTER 34
SEIR

HAILON WAS FAR more magnanimous than I was. I'd have killed that horrible woman on the spot halfway through her speech about how Hailon had ruined everything. As it was, I had half a mind to keep record of everyone who so much as looked at her sideways so I could have a few words with them. To start, at least. After that, my blades could finish the conversation. Or hers. That might be better, truth be told—then they could see for themselves just how dangerous she *really* was.

I smiled. Yes. That would definitely make me feel better.

A glance at my mate left me concerned. She was withdrawn, quiet.

"Are you hungry, Moonflower? Let's go find something you've missed while you were away. We've time enough for some food before we continue on our way. Unless you want to try to find somewhere to rest?"

"I don't think I can make any rational decisions right now."

"Food then," I nodded, threading my arm through hers.

Hailon might have been upset, but she still knew how to find several of her favorite food vendors as we worked our way through town. I got a glimpse of her previous life I wouldn't have otherwise gotten while both filling our stomachs and keeping her momentarily distracted.

The meat skewers from the little open brazier set up outside the butcher shop were truly divine, and I wished I'd bought at least twice as many when she left me at a little wooden table situated just off a main sidewalk and disappeared into what looked like the back door of someone's house. When she returned, I was presented with the largest baked potato I'd ever seen. I stared, marveling at the plate in front of me.

"I was a little worried they'd no longer be serving. It's later in the day than I've ever been. They often sell out." She pushed around the toppings with her fork, the brief moment of happiness she'd found already fading away. "I didn't know what you'd like, so I got everything."

I was salivating just looking at the very dressed-up humble vegetable. "What is 'everything'?"

"Butter, soured cream, cheese, crispy pork belly, spices, and spring onion." She pointed with the tines of her fork, then scooped up a hearty bite. There were no words for what I felt when I got my first taste, but she seemed less than moved.

After that, we found dessert in the form of deep-fried batter dusted with powdered sugar and sweet spices from a little cart on wheels. I playfully dotted her nose with the fluffy sugar.

"Feeling any better?" I asked. I was still positively murderous, but I could tell that's not what my Moonflower needed. She had moved into grief and needed a bit of space to breathe around that shift in her emotional state.

"I haven't been this full in a while, if that's what you mean. I'm grateful none of those vendors refused to serve me. I was worried they might. None of them even seemed to recognize me, though. Perhaps after a busy day, all faces look pretty much the same."

I clenched my teeth, and she soothed me by putting her hand over mine. "Was it always like this? The hostility, I mean."

Hailon shrugged. "It does seem a bit more obvious than before, but maybe I've lost my knack at ignoring it while I was gone. Like Sal said, lots of them thought I was trading more than medicine. Even after a winter where sickness spread through most of the town, and we made enough medicinal syrup and chest rub to share with them and their families. Even though our clientele was mainly women. Rumors work like that, unfortunately. One batch of negative gossip claiming you're in the skin trade with even the slightest bit of questionable evidence, like your spotty dating history and resistance to marriage ... and suddenly you're everything they always thought you were. Especially when you can't save everyone who comes to you for help. Sometimes it's too little, too late, but when the surviving family is angry, painting someone who was helping as at fault for their loved one's death is inevitable."

Frustration simmered in my veins, along with several new questions about this town. "You mentioned before several reasons the town looked down upon you but this ... I'm sorry, Hailon. That's not fair."

She shrugged. "It doesn't matter." She stopped walking and after a long pause said, "We should stop by the grocers. Get some supplies to take with us."

"We're leaving?" I confirmed.

"There's no point in staying. Best to move along."

"You have everything you need from this place?" I didn't want to let on how relieved I was, but if we hurried, I could maybe get her safely to Revalia before I had to be banished. "Let's go then. We can get a ways down the road before we need to sleep."

She nodded and led us down several streets, the third of which dropped us out at a main intersection with a fountain. People were gathered around it, talking in panicked tones about how the water had slowed down. Their chatter was too muted and mixed, but we made out several little pieces, all of which pointed blame at Hailon.

"My sister saw her earlier, walking through bold as anything. It must be her!"

"The wise woman won't let her stay, don't worry."

"We can't go back to how it was before! I refuse!"

Slowly, we stepped backwards, into the shadows of the narrow alley we'd come down and pulled our cloaks from the packs. Donning them with the hoods up wouldn't be too suspicious as the evening chill deepened and would afford us a little bit of anonymity.

We avoided getting close to the fountain and turned to the right, walking quickly toward what looked like a large stable. Only a handful of horses were still left out to graze, the rest assumedly having been taken into their stalls for the night.

"Jacks?" Hailon called, heartened to recognize one of the animals. "Is that you, handsome?"

The horse raised his head from the grass and flicked his tail as Hailon approached the fence. She stretched out her fingers, and the horse pressed his nose close to Hailon's hand.

"Good boy. How have you been? I've missed y—" The horse whinnied, eyes wide with terror. He nipped at Hailon's hand, and not in a playful way. Then the horse tossed his head and kicked his hind legs out. "Hey, hey. It's alright, it's just me. Jacks? It's ok—" The other horses spooked at his aggressive reaction, and all of a sudden, there were six or seven horses all braying in alarm, bucking and stomping, causing a ruckus. Several hands started talking loudly in the stable, and it was surely only moments before one or more of them came out to see what was going on.

My heart squeezed, watching the very last bit of light vanish from my sweet mate's eyes.

"They're right," she said, tears in her eyes as she looked over at me. She tugged me along, the pair of us escaping down the street before we could be seen by the hands as the cause of the mess in the paddock. "The problem is me. Whatever this magic is that makes me the way I am, I'm sorry," she choked, sobbing silently as she ran.

She threaded through twisted alleys and crossed busy streets without hesitation. It took several beats for me to realize that while she certainly was trying to escape the stables, the hatred of her by the townspeople and perhaps even herself, she was also running away from *me*.

My heart broke for her.

Panic set in when I couldn't find her for several long minutes. There were too many narrow little alleys and buildings she could disappear behind, and I had no idea how I would locate her if she truly didn't want to be found. The bond could get me pretty close, but in a city like this she could be feet away but inaccessible because of how the roads and buildings wound together.

I nearly walked by her, standing eerily still next to a mountain of discarded pottery behind a series of shops.

"Hailon?"

"I'm sorry," she repeated.

"I know, Moonflower. It's okay. I'm not going anywhere. Please don't disappear on me like that again."

Her tortured eyes met mine, and it set me on edge. I had to bite back the urge to let my horns and wings out.

"It's not fair," she said quietly, kicking out a foot. A broken pot slipped from the stack and shattered further when it hit the ground. Hailon stared at it, then looked around. The end of the alley was made up of brick walls, all part of the neighboring buildings. She picked up two teapots, one missing a handle and the other missing a spout. Hailon threw them, one at a time toward the bricks. "It's. Not. *Fair.*"

She took off her cloak, gathering more broken pottery. One at a time, she worked out her hurts while hurling the clay against the bricks. "I didn't ask my parents to leave me with her. I didn't ask them to leave me at all." *Smash.* "I helped everyone who came to me, even the ones I knew called me a charlatan or a harlot behind my back." *Smash.* "I grieved the loss of every single person who died in my care, knowing I did my best and it wasn't enough. Even when the families still blamed me." *Smash. Smash.* "I ignored how people looked at me. The things they said. Because I knew whatever they thought of me wasn't true." *Smash.* "I listened to Sal, always. Respected her." *Smash.* "I *loved* her, would have done anything for her, and she set. Me. Up." *Smash. Smash. Smash. Smash.*

Chunks of beige and reddish pottery flew around us, Hailon's breathing harsh as she rushed back to the pile several times. Her words devolved into screams as she broke a dozen more pieces. Finally, her energy flagged, and she started to slow down. "I suck the magic from everything around me." *Smash.*

"Don't say—"

She wheeled on me, fury in her eyes like I'd never seen. I hadn't ever really doubted she could take me out if she wanted, but in that moment, I was certain of it.

She was truly my perfect mate.

"You can't properly shift around me. Or fly. I'm probably *feeding* on your powers right now, and we don't even realize it."

"I don't care," I said. She had turned to throw more pottery but spun back. "I'd give everything up for this," I said, gesturing between us. "For you. I don't need to shift or fly or sift."

"I'm not worth that kind of sacrifice, Seir. I'm a … magical void. It will never stop."

I stepped closer to her, gently but firmly taking hold of her upper arms. "You are far more than that. To me, you are *everything*. Never say that again." She blinked at my tone and sagged, dropping the last pieces of pottery she'd picked up at her feet. I took her face between my hands and crushed my mouth to hers, willing her to feel how serious I was. "I'd rather be flightless for the rest of my life and be near you than be able to shift freely and have to go without you, Hailon." I wrapped my arms around her, relief flooding through me when she finally held me back.

"I'm sorry."

"No more apologies, beloved. You're perfect just as you are. And for the record, I think we can have both. We simply have to figure out some details." I picked up her cloak and put it back on her, assessing the mess she'd made. "This is nicely done." She dropped her chin to her chest. "Do you feel better for it?"

"I think so."

"Then it was a fantastic way to work out some frustrations without killing people, and that's something I suppose you should be proud of. I can think of another," I joked, "but it would have been very awkward to stop and get naked with you in the middle of the street, wouldn't you say?" She shook her head, a tiny flicker of her humor showing. "Come on. Take me to the grocers, then we can leave this place behind." I laced my arm through hers, ensuring that she wouldn't leave me behind again.

CHAPTER 35
SEIR

THE GROCERS WAS off one of the main streets near the center of town. As we approached, I realized it was a storefront spanning a full block, not just a small shop. They were more like a general mercantile, with everything from lumber and clothes to books and food, but they'd been "the grocers" for so long, that's what they stayed to the townspeople.

Hailon pulled her hood up but hesitated as we got near the doors.

"I'll wait around back. Meet me there when you're finished."

"No. I'm not leaving you alone anywhere in this town. We'll be fast."

Her mouth tightened, but she nodded. I pulled open the door and let her in first, marveling at the variety of things the large shop carried.

"Those are my favorite," Hailon gasped and crossed to a small table displaying a crate of squat orange fruit that looked a bit like a tomato. "Persimmons. But the season is very short." She sorted through the pile to find a few to her liking. "You have to wait until they almost look spoiled."

"I can't wait to try them."

We weren't terribly far from Revalia, but I wasn't sure how close we were either. We gathered apples and potatoes, carrots and a small slab of dried meat.

"It's a good thing we both enjoy stew." Hailon sighed. A petite woman with bright orange hair approached cautiously. "Merry?"

"I thought that was you!" the woman whispered, glancing over her shoulder before reaching out to squeeze Hailon's hand. "Are you finished shopping?"

I nodded that we were, and she helped ring us out. "Meet me out behind the store, okay?" Wary, I frowned at her, and Hailon was making a similar face. "You can trust me."

We agreed, and by the time we'd rounded the corner, the little woman was bustling out the back door of the shop, bags in her hands and a smile on her face.

"Here, please, take this."

"What is it?" Hailon asked, perplexed.

"Some of it belongs to you and some is food we can't sell. I don't have enough space to keep it all myself, and I hate seeing it wasted. You're leaving, right? You need supplies."

"I ... Yes, thank you."

"I always knew you'd come back." Merry's head bobbed, her orange curls bouncing wildly. "You were always kind to me, Hailon. Honestly, I never saw you be anything *but* kind. To anyone. What they say about you ..." She frowned. "It's not true. I know it."

"Thank you, Merry." Hailon cracked a weak smile. "You always did a good job, looking in on Sal for me when I left for the mountains. I'm sorry for the trouble. I didn't know—"

"Of course you didn't. You don't need to apologize." She dug in her pocket and produced a key. "There's a hunting lodge west of here. Take the trail that leads out of town near the cemetery, not the main road. It's far enough out it'll be late by the time you get there. Stay as long as you need to. Just leave me the key somewhere

I can find it when you go. I promised Mr. Grummond I'd go tidy it for him before elk season starts."

"Why are you helping us like this?" Hailon asked, eyebrows drawn together.

"Because you helped me. My mother. My sister. We would have all died three winters ago of that terrible cough if not for you. You fixed my brother's broken arm last summer when he fell out of that stupid tree he was specifically told not to climb. You saved us, time and again, and you didn't even want proper payment. Plus, Jacks loves you. That should be enough by itself, honestly. That horse doesn't like anyone but me, except for you."

The smile slipped from Hailon's face. "Not anymore."

Merry grabbed Hailon up in a quick hug. "Well, I bet if you spent some time around him again, he'd love you just the same as he always did. You had him properly spoiled with apples and carrots when you left." Merry's face went serious after she broke the hug, and she glanced around again. "Go on. Get out of here before they find you."

"They?" I asked.

"The ignorant rabble who believe Hailon is to blame for all their problems. I heard rumblings when I came past the tavern earlier. They've already been drinking, so it's safe to say they're looking for trouble."

Hailon took the key and squeezed Merry's hand. "Thank you, Merry."

"You're welcome. Now, get gone." She turned to go back inside. "I'll see you again, one day."

"Should you ever want to leave this place, I believe Revalia would welcome you," I said. "There's a big school there, d'Arcan. My brothers run it, tell them you know us."

"I'll remember that." She smiled and waved as she ducked back inside.

"How about that, Moonflower? A little bit of luck found us after all. The good kind, this time."

She nodded, and between us, we crammed all the things Merry had given us into our packs. Then we took her advice, leaving Ravenglen behind.

THE PATH THROUGH the woods was narrow and almost disappeared in places, but it led us to a small hunting lodge just as Merry said it would.

It was a similar configuration though only perhaps half the size of the little way-house cabin. It was a welcome respite, nonetheless.

When we finally arrived, the moon was high in the sky despite the sections of path I'd done my best to glide down with Hailon in my arms. I could manage that much fine, but not for long distances. It had been a quiet walk, my heart sore because my mate was so distant and sad, but I tried to allow her the space she needed to process everything that had happened.

"I'll work on the fire so we can eat and heat some water for bathing if you want to get us a bit more organized?" I offered.

She nodded and sat on the floor, the assortment of items we had collected on our journey slowly expanding on the rug around her.

Off to one side was the wooden strongbox Hailon had liberated from that terrible house, the cooking gear and all the other gifts Widow Callahan had sent along with us, and the clothing and few other items she'd taken from Sal's. The food Merry had sent, however, was a substantial pile. In addition to what we'd bought, we were set for a week as far as bruised produce and dented tins went.

"Oh." Hailon's voice dropped to a hushed gasp. "This must be what Merry meant when she said some of this was mine. I thought I'd lost this forever." A smile tugged at her mouth, but it didn't last. "She must have gone into the woods looking for me." Tears shimmered in my beloved's eyes as she held a small knife. "I've had this for my herb work since I was seven." The handle looked to be made from cherry or another reddish wood, and it fit in her hand like the branch it was carved from had sprouted there. The metal of the blade was pitted and thin after so many years of use and re-sharpening. It definitely needed some loving attention from a bladesmith, but I could see that holding it again was like gaining feeling in a numb limb—effortlessly comfortable. I felt the same way about my favorite dagger.

"I'm very glad you got it back." I accepted it from her to take a closer look. "I'm also happy to find you have an ally like Merry."

"She was always good to me," she said with a nod. "Probably as close as I got to having a friend, really."

I frowned into the growing flames of the fire. "I'm going to go get some water."

As I pumped water into a bucket, I decided I would never even come close to forgiving Sal for all she'd done. And I would find comfort in making creative plans for her demise until I could either obtain permission from Hailon to follow through or get it done without her knowing it happened.

"We never even used these," Hailon said sadly after I'd filled the large pot over the flames with water so it could heat. When I turned, I found her holding up the little pots of nail lacquer.

"There's time yet," I grinned, taking them from her. "No time like the present, in fact. That's going to take a while to heat, and we can feast on this lightly bruised fruit for days." I sat next to her and took her fingers in mine. I used the purple color on her, the act of perfectly painting each of her nails like a meditation. "Nobody's ever shown such fire trying to do something kind for me like you did at that market, Hailon. I like you jealous as well as greedy." She opened her mouth to protest, cheeks bright red, but I didn't leave her time. "Give me your other hand." She complied, wet nails splayed wide over her knee. "I'll be back long before this needs to be redone," I assured her.

"Promise?" she asked. I looked up to find her expression melancholy.

I put the lid back on the pot and held her face between my hands, sure to both give her my full attention and get hers in return. "It doesn't matter what they do to me, understand? I'm coming back. As soon as I possibly can."

Hailon nodded, and I started painting my own fingernails with the black lacquer as she turned back to unpacking. She pulled a bundle out of the bottom of the bag that had been mine, eyebrows drawn together. "What's this?"

I'd meant for it to be a surprise, perhaps for her birthday or Yule. But today was as good a day as any.

"Open it."

She looked at me suspiciously but pulled off the outer layer of cloth. The second layer came up and she stopped, mouth dropping open.

"They're beautiful." She found the little hanger and pulled the small set of wind chimes up near her face. I'd selected a set that reminded me of a stained-glass picture that hadn't been assembled yet. Hailon pushed the center bar, creating a pretty tinkling noise. "When did you have time to buy these?"

"You were waiting for cake, and I was getting tea."

She stared at me, disappointment creasing her brow. "All I got you was nail lacquer."

Her earnest expression had me laughing. "I *love* my lacquer. And you got me much more than that, Moonflower. You've given me everything I never knew I was looking for. Besides, that very night you also got me a substantial serving of righteous vengeance, don't you recall? I feel like that more than makes up the difference." I leaned in and kissed her, taking my time with it as I felt her soften beneath my fingers.

I gently held her chin with my thumb and forefinger, mapping the shape of her lips with my own, breathing her gentle exhales and tasting her with my tongue. I was committing everything to memory, so I'd have something to think back on once I left her for Hell. I didn't care how short the separation might be, I wanted to always have such things freshly available in my mind. When I pulled back, the frustration was gone from her eyes, and her cheeks were flushed with color.

"Are there any other surprises?" she asked. "I'm not sure I can handle any more today, though these are really wonderful, thank you."

"Actually ..." I got up and dug in my discarded pants pocket, producing the little round mirror. "I showed you this before, but we got distracted before I could tell you about it. This is a scrying mirror. You can use it to get in touch with my brothers if you need to."

"Don't you need it?"

"I can find another way to get to them from Hell if I have to. Or perhaps Vassago can make one for you. Hopefully we'll either have made it to Revalia or be close before I have to leave, but it's worth knowing how to use it either way." I settled in next to her, then earned a squeak as I pulled her into my lap instead. "Speaking specific words activates the magic. I want you to practice them with me, they're in the old language like my sigil."

We started with the first word, the unusual tongue curl at the end throwing her several times. I clapped proudly once she got it right. The second word was easier and only took her a few tries. We practiced putting the two together, then moved onto the third, which was a very simple single syllable.

"Alright, now all together," I said, and she recited them all perfectly. I kissed her on the cheek with a loud *smack*.

"How will we know I said them right? What if whatever in me that cancels magic effects the mirror too?"

"My brother has a mirror as well, and it will activate if you did. I'm hopeful we'll get lucky and the mirror is a kind of magic you don't affect, but we'll know shortly. We don't look alike, my brothers and I. Vago is the pompous sort, very posh. White hair, silver clothes—"

"Miss me already, Seir?" Vassago asked, and his face came into view inside the mirror. As I was behind Hailon, it was her face he saw in the glass. "Hello, there. My apologies, you must be Hailon?"

She was too stunned to speak. I could understand, the magic required to do such a thing was nearly unfathomable, and I'd been used to being able to use it for a very long time. Finally, she found her voice again. "Yes, hello."

"It's a pleasure to meet you. To what do I owe the honor?"

"I was just teaching her how to use your little mirror."

"My *little mirror*?" Vassago scowled lightly, every word properly enunciated in his irritation.

"I'm leaving it with her when I go back. Just in case she needs something."

"So, it's not *all* magic that's affected by her then. Rylan will be pleased to have some new information to obsess over. When do you leave?"

"I'm supposed to be sent back by tomorrow evening."

"I see."

He turned his attention to Hailon. "Please feel free to use the mirror any time. I'm near one in my classroom most days, but there are others throughout the collegium as well. I'll let the rest of the house know, so they are never ignored when they alert. We're here for whatever you need." He swept an arm across his chest and bowed his head gracefully.

Pompous prick. His precise, gentlemanly gestures had always made me smile, and this was no exception. At least until Hailon blushed, and then I rolled my eyes as a tiny thread of jealousy worked itself under my skin.

"Thank you, that's very kind."

My brother smiled, eyes shifting to me. I could see the wheels turning behind his eyes. "Have you made it to your destination?"

"We're on our way to Revalia, actually."

"Is that so? I thought you were bound for Ravenglen."

"My business there was finished much faster than expected," Hailon said.

"How wonderful. We'll be very happy to see you both." Vassago smiled, then shifted his eyes to me again. "We could easily come retrieve you, if you'd like. Save you some travel time? There are several options for that, in fact. Some with wings, some without. Though I understand there may be a bit of a ... complication with flying where you're involved, Hailon."

"Yes, chances are high that anyone trying to use shifting-based magic within close range of me would find their abilities either gone or limited."

"There are certainly other ways. In any case, I look forward to visiting with you in person soon." Vassago nodded and turned his attention to me as Hailon excused herself for a moment. "The carriage as well as someone with wings can be on the way shortly, if you think that's wise?"

"I do. Thank you, Vago." Relief swept over me. Hailon would be protected one way or another. "We're in the woods outside of Ravenglen. I have until tomorrow evening, but I wasn't sure that was enough time to cover the whole distance on foot. We haven't had much luck with horses—they seem bothered by Hailon's power. But having someone with her when I cannot be would offer great relief."

"Understood. We'll think on that, perhaps there's an incantation that we can use ..." His gaze went distant and thoughtful.

Hailon returned, and we discussed how she'd know if they were trying to contact her through the mirror.

"Like a scream? That's terrifying." She frowned.

"But effective," Vassago defended his choice. "Kettle noises are ignored, I've found."

"Fair enough," she muttered.

"Thank you, again, Vago." I waved to my brother and then swept my fingers across the glass, ending the conversation and cutting the magical link. "See? Nothing to it."

"Sure." She muttered the words under her breath a few more times. When I was sure her quiet words weren't going to accidentally activate the mirror again, I put it to the side, setting it on one of the packs.

I took her hands in mine. "Swear that you won't hesitate to use it."

"You'll be with me. Or they will, right?"

"That's the plan but swear. Please," I insisted, unable to shake the slithery sensation of nervousness under my skin. "Use the mirror. Summon me back. Whatever you need to do, you do it. Do not hesitate. Promise me."

"I promise." She sighed, shaking her head. "You're very bossy, you know. I took care of myself among those people my whole life. I survived that house for a long time. I just have to get to another city at this point, one where there are demons and mages and stone kin, right? Everything is going to be fine."

"I know you did. And I know how capable you are. I'll accept being a little bossy if it keeps you safe." My lack of humor made her fall serious as well.

"Why does the mirror work near me? That doesn't make sense."

"There are many kinds of magic. You didn't deactivate the wards around the ruins, either, and you felt their effects. Those are similar things. Maybe you don't have any effect on enchantments, only innate magic."

"I wish I understood this more." She pinched the bridge of her nose.

"We will figure it all out," I promised. "You have a mage and a mystic already looking into things. Not to mention an earth witch and an alchemist."

"Your brothers? And their wives?"

I smiled. "Yes. We're all just as curious as you, Hailon. We want to help." I waited for her to digest my unspoken words. She had a family. Support. She didn't have to go through any of this alone, even if I had to leave for a bit. I stood and found the hot water was steaming, so I added it to the tub, tempering it with cold until she told me it was perfect.

Hailon slid in, knees tucked to her chest in the small space.

"Head back," I instructed, pouring a pitcher of water over her hair. It was nearly half white, the strands turning at a fascinating rate.

She washed her body as I worked on her hair, her silence a good indication she'd slid back into her thoughts.

"What did that letter say? The one Sal gave you. From my mother."

"I'm not sure. Not completely, anyhow. I think it's written in fae."

"Fae?"

"Yes. For all the time I spent with Van in that realm, I didn't pick up more than a few words of the written language. I can make out tavern menus pretty well, but beyond that, I'm useless."

"Why would she write it in fae?"

"That would be an excellent way to encode her message if she was trying to keep secrets, beloved. Don't worry though, Vassago's wife can help with that."

"You don't have to do all this for me."

She felt so far away again. I hated it. I thought the bath would help, but she was still frozen, stuck in her mind and detached from her feelings. "Perhaps not, but I *get* to, and that's a thrilling new development I'll happily take advantage of as often as possible." I winked at her, and she softened a fraction, standing up out of the water so I could wrap her in one of the respectably fluffy towels the lodge stocked.

"Are you finished here? We should get some rest."

She surveyed the clutter all around her and yawned. "I suppose. What about you?"

"I'll be awake long before you. Plenty of time then."

I scooped her up, depositing her on the bed before going around the room to extinguish the lights. As I slid in behind her, she relaxed into me. I wound my tail around her ankle, my arm across her hip, the other stroking through her hair.

I dozed off looking forward to a day where I didn't have to sleep any other way.

CHAPTER 36
SEIR

I TWAS STILL dark outside when I opened my eyes to find Hailon tucked into me like a little spoon, just as we'd fallen asleep. The desire to breathe her in, consume her taste, rode me hard. She was so peaceful though; I couldn't bring myself to wake her up.

Instead, I buried my face in the curve between her neck and shoulder, the sweet smell that was uniquely her branding itself into my memory, my hand palming her hip instead of dangling over it. My tail tightened around her ankle as I settled.

I realized it was inconsistent of me, but I couldn't help vacillating wildly between being confident she was going to be perfectly fine without me here and utterly anxious at the prospect of having to return to Hell.

As I lay there ticking off mental boxes, reassuring myself she would be secure either in or near Revalia, she turned over, crushing her face to my chest and breathing me in just as I had done to her.

"Why are you awake?" she asked, voice rough with sleep. Her hand rose to my neck, and I captured it with my own, bringing it to my mouth and kissing her palm.

"Normally, I'd already be up and about. Stoking the fire. Thinking about how soon is too soon to start breakfast."

"Mmm."

After a few minutes, her breathing evened out and I slipped from the bed to do just that—the fire part at least. Reviving the flames brought some much-needed warmth and light back to the room. I was fine seeing in the dark, but the loving way the glow bounced off Hailon's features was unmatched. I'd stared at her plenty in such light during our travels.

I filled the big pot with water as well, ready for my own bath.

Hailon cuddled her body into me immediately when I laid back down. My heart thumped happily behind my ribs, the bond pleased by our closeness.

"I didn't mean for you to leave," she complained sleepily.

I brushed my lips across her forehead, fingers stroking through her hair. "Just taking care of the fire. It's cool this morning."

"Mmm. Can you go back to sleep now?"

"No. But you can."

She shook her head. "We're working with limited time today, though, aren't we?" She covered a jaw-cracking yawn with her hand.

"Yes, but you need to be rested. Right now, there's nothing going on but this," I argued, closing my eyes and resting my lips against her forehead as I slowly pulled my fingers through her hair.

Her hands were restless and started working under my tunic. My muscles tensed as her fingertips crawled up my stomach and danced along my ribs. I copied the gesture, and she squirmed a little, cheeks flushing pink.

"I like touching your skin," I whispered, dragging my hand along the tiny scars that decorated her back along the ribs. "Tasting it." I pressed my mouth to hers, a surge of lust hitting me as she breathed a light moan while kissing me back. Her leg rose, hitching over my hip, and I suddenly desperately wanted out of my trousers. I traced my way up her leg with my hand, stopping at the top of her thigh.

"I like those things too."

I groaned into the curve of her neck and allowed her to take her time exploring while she kissed me, her fingertips leaving tiny fires in their wake as she touched every inch of me she could get to. She traced along my tattoos, then down the valley between my stomach muscles. She poked gently against my ribs, counting them before tracing along the hollow of my collarbone. Then she dipped her hands under the waistband of my pants, and I had to pull away from her clever mouth. "You're dangerous, Little Moonflower."

She rose up in the bed on her knees, pulling off the tunic she'd gone to sleep in. To my immense pleasure and distress, it was the only thing she was wearing at all.

"Hailon. Please." I wasn't even sure what I wanted, but I was begging. I didn't care.

The beautiful creature shimmied my trousers off my body and decided immediately to end my existence on this plane when she settled herself between my legs and lowered her mouth to the head of my throbbing cock.

It was an exquisite kind of pleasure, the way she worked me with both her hands and her tongue. I was seeing white behind my eyelids with every stroke, the alternating sensations of heat of her mouth then the cool air of the room plus her rotating hands impossible to keep up with. There was no boring topic in the world I could have thought of that would have kept me from getting that tingle down my spine, the warning that things were going to end all too soon.

"No, please," I groaned, reaching for her. "Not yet."

She released me with a pop, rising to her knees after a long lick, and that was beautiful torture. Hailon settled herself on top of me, using her own hands to guide me to her wet center without so much as a blink of hesitation.

"*Fuck.*" I heaved several breaths, holding her hips still so she couldn't move. She wiggled side to side a little, getting a better position on her knees. When I was finally able to open my eyes, I found my goddess peering down at me, pleasure etched into her face. "Anything," I offered. "Anything you wish for, my queen. I will get it for you."

She smiled, a patient, gentle grin and started to rock, her weight shifting from her toes to her knees. Her hands settled against my chest as she moved, head thrown back and breath coming in short pants. Her eyebrows drew together, and I felt the moment her body decided to tease her with the first flutters of her impending release. I was barely keeping myself together, jaw clenched and body stiff, as she controlled our rhythm. I used my tail to slip between us, teasing at her sensitive clit as she clenched around me, her pace becoming more aggressive as she chased her orgasm.

"I think you're going to kill me, Moonflower," I gasped for breath, praying I could hold out for her, the pleasure rocketing down my spine like a bolt of lightning. "It will be a beautiful death."

"Seir!" Hailon's head fell back, and she lifted up a bit as she found her release. Her fingertips dug into the flesh of my chest, and part of me hoped she'd leave me marked. My thoughts went white as my own pleasure chased through my body, the squeeze from her core too much for me to battle.

I pulled her down for another lengthy kiss, both of us slick with a sheen of sweat despite the chill in the air.

Once the temperature caught up to us both, I retrieved a fresh cloth and cleaned us up. She huddled under one of the blankets from the bed as we made a picnic in front of the fire out of some bread and cheese Merry had sent. The pair of us were quiet but happy as we broke our fast.

Then, somehow, I was kissing her again, and she was moaning beneath me on the rug.

I would never get enough of her, I was sure of it, but I was thankful we were getting a chance at a bit of a head start on eternity.

"I SUPPOSE I should start putting things away," Hailon sighed, pulling on a pair of trousers and a tunic.

We were both refreshed and ready to move on after another quick trip through the bath.

"I know you're right, but there's no need for such haste." I used my finger to lift the hem of her shirt, getting a decent glance at a strip of her stomach.

"Stop that." She rewarded me with a small chuckle. "We need to get on the road."

I groaned. "I suppose you're right. Places to be, people to meet, and all that."

She squatted down and picked up a stack of her things so they could be transferred to the pack she had open on the bed. As she stood again, the weight wasn't balanced. Everything tipped, too quick for either of us to catch. As the strongbox hit the floor, it made a ticking noise.

"What was that?"

Hailon went to her knees and opened the lid. The top edge of what appeared to be the bottom of the box was tilted up.

Her hands flew as she took everything we'd already gone through out of it, piling it to the side before lifting the thin piece of wood that had served as a false bottom. She gasped at the contents hidden underneath.

There were three small, worn notebooks and an assortment of tiny bottles.

"That prick," she swore, lifting out the bottles one by one. "Hair. Nails. Blood. These are Dr. Lang's precious *samples*. And his research notes."

I stared, horrified. We'd had this with us the whole time and had no idea.

"Keep those hidden, Moonflower. They could give someone a reason to continue his cruel research." I felt my blood heat at the very idea. "His brother wanted more than that little spell book. I'd bet anything he was looking for this box. What was hidden inside of it."

Hailon flipped through the notes, nose wrinkling more and more the further she read. Eventually she slammed it shut and tossed it back inside the box.

"Why would they have been trying to summon a demon, though?"

I shrugged. "Maybe they thought one could help them find the missing piece to their research. Maybe they wanted to barter for some magic item to replicate your power. Wouldn't have worked though, that's all against the rules. Whatever demon they might have managed to call up would have either told them to go fuck themselves or given them something fake and taken their offering back to Hell. And they wouldn't even have been punished—summoning contracts don't work like that."

"Their offering was me." She frowned deeper.

"No, not quite. Your spilled blood in the circle was the offering. Maybe their own rotten souls, too, but never you." I took her chin between my thumb and forefinger, gazing deep into those unique eyes. I looked between them several times. "Your eye …"

"What's wrong?" she asked, nervously searching my face.

I pulled out the scrying mirror and had her look in it. "What do you see?"

"My hair is so white," she lamented, combing it back with her fingers before leaning in to look at her eyes, one at a time. "I don't ... How is that possible?" She took the mirror from my hand, gazing at one side and then the other, her cheeks growing pink, her breathing more rapid. "Seir?"

Her right iris appeared to have turned ninety degrees. The bright blue that had once been on the left side of her eye was now at the top, and the opaque yellow from the right side had shifted to the bottom. They were slightly off center, which made me wonder if they were somehow still moving.

"I don't know, beloved. Do you feel any different?"

"No. I feel fine."

"Your vision?"

"No change." She handed the mirror back to me and gazed into the distance. "At Sal's, when I got really, really angry, I felt ... something. I figured it was because I was so upset. What do I do? What does this mean?"

"I don't know," I repeated. "But I think getting you to Revalia has become urgent for more than my own selfish reasons."

We packed up, working in hushed tones as we set the lodge to rights. Hailon hid the key under a little ceramic pig stationed near the door, and we said goodbye to our second little cabin haven, urgency tingling under my skin.

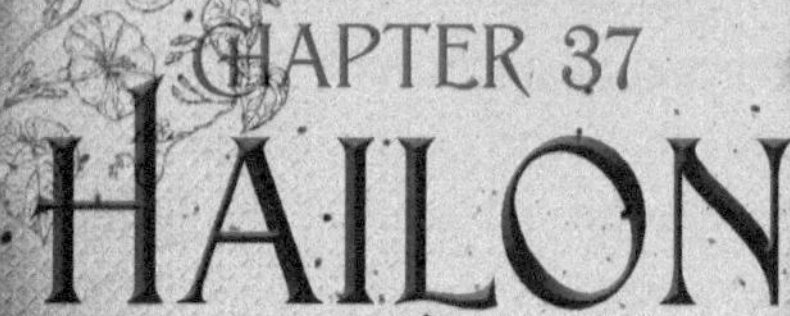

Chapter 37
HAILON

"WE'LL USE THE mirror," Seir said, "when we stop to eat. See who they sent and guess how close they might be." Our fingers were linked together, and he pulled my hand up near his face to drop a kiss on my palm.

"Alright."

He was mostly talking to himself, completely focused on getting us as far down the road as possible. We'd used his new ability to glide on and off for the distances he could manage without it becoming cumbersome and walked the rest.

After leaving the little lodge behind, we'd covered a lot of ground, but our time was truly running short. We seemed to both be feeling the invisible clock ticking, like at any moment he could disappear again.

"I'll be fine out here by myself. If it comes to that," I offered again, for perhaps the third time. I was trying to convince myself as much as him.

"I'd rather that not happen. I'd rather someone be with you, Hailon. The councilman is still unaccounted for."

"I know." And I did, but from what I'd seen of the man, he wouldn't be much of a challenge to me in my current, healthy state.

"Give the notebooks and samples to Rylan. There are a lot of very studious minds in that school. I'll bet they can make heads or tails of what those men were after with their … experiments … and whether it would actually work or not." He made a sound deep in his throat, teeth showing in distaste. "Rylan reports to the mage council, besides." His head tilted to the side. "I gave your description of the councilman to my brothers. Perhaps they'll get lucky. Though I'd really prefer nothing be done to him until I can be present, his punishment should be left to you for the crimes he committed."

"You seem very confident he'll be easy to find. Quick to capture."

He smiled at me, but there was an edge to it. "Men like that are often blinded by their own ego. They never believe they'll be caught, so they make mistakes, not realizing others have started paying attention to them."

"I hope you're right." A sense of calm washed over me at the idea of being able to put to rest that whole part of my life. With no other dangling threads, no more of those men still alive and able to show up unexpectedly, I might be able to truly move on. Have a whole new life.

"Do you have a proposal for your unit leader? Something good?"

Seir smiled. "Yes. I think it could be perfect. Plenty of time here with you and enough time there that I get to keep my tail."

"Your tail?"

He swung our arms between us, a smile gracing his handsome face. "When a demon commits to living anywhere other than Hell, they must sacrifice some of their demon features. My teeth would become more blunted, and my tail would disappear, so I appeared as human as possible if I came here full time. Rylan and Vassago seem unbothered by the cost, but I'd like to keep them if I can."

"It would definitely take me some time to get used to you without them," I mused. "When we first met, I remember thinking how strange it was to see your tail move, to think it was normal. But now ..." I shrugged. "I prefer you as you are."

He smiled wide and kissed my hand again, several little smooches to express his appreciation for my compliment.

It was well after midday when we finally found a place to stop and eat. Seir almost immediately pulled the little mirror out of his pocket once we'd set our things down.

"Oh no." He looked crestfallen, staring at the little piece of glass in his hand.

"What's the matter?"

"My brother is going to be very cross with me." He didn't elaborate, but rather started speaking the words to activate it. The first attempt wasn't successful, nor the second or third.

My heart stuttered when I saw the terrible crack nearly halfway down the mirror as I peered over his shoulder.

"May I see it?" He handed over the mirror and started pulling out food for us. I tried to mend the mirror with my healing magic. I'd never tried to fix an inanimate object before. Unfortunately, the glass seemed resistant to my magical stitches.

I tried the words myself several times, unsure why a crack would disable the magic in the odd communication device altogether. If it did, that seemed like a terribly fragile thing to put such powerful magic into.

"Hello?"

I gasped, nearly dropping the device. My heart pounded, both from the near tragedy and from the relief of having reached someone. A man with black hair was looking back at me in the mirror.

"You did it!" Seir cheered, taking the mirror back from me. "Rylan, hello. We've been on the road most of the day. I wanted to see if we might be getting close, or if the escort was—"

"Seir? Is that you? Something's wrong with your mirror."

My gut twisted.

"Hello? Can you hear me?" Seir paced, holding the little glass carefully in his broad palm. Frowning, he came to stand next to me.

"Vago!" the man called. "Something's wrong with it."

The man with black hair was replaced in the little piece of glass by his white-haired brother, the one I'd met.

"Hello! Vago, can you hear me?"

"Seir?"

"Yes! The mirror is cracked, but I—"

"Damn. I'll bet he's broken it. That's ten now." He shook his head. "I'm glad the stone kin already—"

The connection disappeared. "No! Wait!" Seir growled in frustration. We both tried the words several times, but the mirror never worked again. "He's going to strangle me. I can't seem to keep myself from breaking these things, no matter how carefully or close I keep them." He sighed and took a hearty bite from an apple. "Perhaps you can convince him to make us both a new one. I went a couple of decades without before this one. He's much less likely to deny you, as I'm the one at fault." When we stood again, he slipped the mirror into my pocket, where it clanked hard against my little horse carving.

"We'll see."

We didn't linger once our stomachs were full and our bodies rested enough to push on.

If we trusted the map, Revalia was not terribly far from Ravenglen, but we'd learned to be wary of the scale and organization of it after the detour into the ruins.

The trees became denser all around us the further we traveled, and I could feel it was going to be a truly cold autumn night from the moisture in the air.

As the sun started to slip down the horizon, the threat of evening coming on, we both heard it. Wingbeats, far too heavy to be any bird. Seir's smile returned, a weight lifting from his shoulders.

The sound suddenly stopped, and the dark form in the sky appeared to plummet, just as Seir had. We looked at one another, both debating running toward it. In the end, we only walked a little faster, a carriage drawn by two stout working horses a closer priority. It stopped several paces from us, the horses thankfully unmoved by my presence from that distance. I thought of Jacks, how he hadn't reacted until I was nearly touching him. I could only hope that these beasts were used to magical presence and my nature wouldn't be an issue for them.

One woman was driving the horses and another climbed out of the carriage. A man, a very large one, came jogging down the road right after, his large wings tucked close to his back. Even from a distance I could see the fierce bone talons at the tips.

"Well met, travelers!" one of the women called. She, too, was quite tall. She had long dark hair and stood a full head over the smaller, golden-haired woman.

"They sent a full cavalry," Seir joked. "Greetings to you, friends."

"Always good to see you, Seir." The big man shook Seir's hand and then drew him in for a hearty hug. "My lady." He bowed at me.

"The pleasure is mine," I replied politely, surprised to find I wasn't nervous to meet these strangers.

"Thank you for coming." Seir's gratitude was evident in the solemn expression he wore as he bowed.

"Couldn't refuse a good adventure," the blonde one said, smiling widely. "We heard you met our brother Coltor?"

"Indeed."

"Our condolences," the smaller woman joked. She turned to me. "I'm Lovette. That's my sister, Imogen." Imogen raised a hand in a gentle wave.

"Nice to meet you both."

"We were told you might need an escort back to Revalia?"

I nodded, unsure what to say.

"They warned us about your magic, but some things you just

have to experience to believe. Felt like a brick wall when I hit it." The man did not seem at all put out by this, in fact he was beaming. "Luckily I've learned how to take a fall." He stuck out a hand. "Alright, my lady? I'm Magnus. We're happy to have found you."

There was no mistaking the strong, angular features of the man in particular. Coltor was indeed his father's son. The larger woman, too, resembled him plainly. The smaller woman had softer features, all light to their dark, including her friendly, open expression.

"Hailon," I confirmed.

"Shall we go?" Magnus gestured with his arm toward the carriage. "I'm sure you're a bit anxious to get to the city? Your brothers mentioned something about a short timeline."

"I'm ... not coming," Seir said. My mouth dropped open and my chest felt like he'd dropped a boulder on it. I knew our time was short, but I'd let myself get comfortable, to pretend he would get to stay with me. "I'm sorry, Moonflower. It's time. I can feel it." He scrubbed at his chest, my heart aching behind my ribs just the same. "I'm trusting you with my mate, Magnus."

The men made steady eye contact, and the smile slipped from the gargoyle's mouth as he gave a solemn nod. "I understand, demon. If it brings you peace, your brothers have done the same. She will be safe with us." They clasped one another on the arm, a hushed conversation passing between them. There were lots of wide eyes from Magnus and several nods, then a smile before they embraced one another quickly and separated.

"Don't mind us," Imogen said, and when I glanced over, she was very casually cleaning one of her weapons with the tail of her shirt.

"Right, we're only here for decoration, I suppose," Lovette teased, arms crossed.

Seir's face lit up, and he strode to them, pulling them both in for a hug, one in each arm. "I know you wouldn't have come if you hadn't already accepted such heavy responsibility. Thank you."

"Aren't you sweet?" Lovette patted him on the shoulder.

"You all have my eternal thanks." He pulled me off the road, going several paces away from the gargoyles into the softer dirt. A single little purple daisy was still blooming near his foot, the kind I'd made a crown out of one of our first days together.

He plucked it, then tucked it into my hair, fingertips lingering on my cheek. He sighed deeply, golden eyes sad. "I need you to banish me, Moonflower."

CHAPTER 38
SEIR

HAILON TUCKED HERSELF into my body, arms wrapping around my middle. I held her back, arms tight around her shoulders, my tail wound securely around her leg.

"You're safe with them, and that's all I've wanted since the moment I figured out what was happening to you in that house. I feel very confident nobody would survive crossing you unless you wanted them to, but I'm not willing to take the risk. And I'm very thankful there are others I know will look out for you in my absence." I breathed in deeply, face nestled in the space between her neck and shoulder, trying to bolster my courage to leave.

"Ridiculous demon. As you said, I can take care of myself."

"I know you can, Moonflower." I kissed her forehead. "But my point is you shouldn't have to. You *don't* have to. My family can be your family. They already are."

She glanced over at the gargoyles patiently waiting by the carriage. Her lips parted again, but instead of the argument I thought was coming, I got a very gentle kiss. "Thank you."

"Truly, it's been my honor, Hailon."

"That sounds ominous." Her arms tightened around me. "That sounds like goodbye, Seir."

"I don't mean it to." My stomach lurched. I could feel the echoes of the preparations being made to summon me back in my bones. "Make me a summoning circle, Moonflower. Show me how well you can draw my sigil."

"I don't want to." Her voice was weak, throat constricted with tears.

"I know. But you must. It's the best way to ensure I can come back to you quickly."

After several more breaths, she pulled away with a sniffle and picked up a stick the size of her arm.

In the soft soil, she executed a perfect summoning circle. My pride flared when my sigil appeared next, well drawn and including several little marks that were her own flourish in the strokes. She pulled my dagger from its sheath and poked the tip into her finger, dripping three little drops onto the ground in the very center of her art before handing it back. I licked the remaining smear of blood from my blade and put it back in my belt, the flavor as bright as I remembered on my tongue.

"You have to say the words, Hailon."

"I know." She sniffled again. Our eyes met, and she threw herself back into my arms, my strong mate clinging to me as desperately as I held onto her. "Come back to me," she whispered.

"I will," I promised. "I always will, Hailon, I swear it. No matter what happens, I will come back to you."

She nodded into my shoulder and slowly measured out the next several words, the ones that would send me away from her. I closed my eyes, breathing her in, and captured her mouth in a kiss.

Then my arms were empty, and my chest ached.

I was in Hell.

"GLAD TO SEE you back," Keplar greeted me from behind his desk. "On time, even."

"Sir."

His eyes roved my face, and he sighed. "So? Is everything resolved with your summoner?"

"No," I said plainly. My bond was raging, I didn't want to be here, and I didn't want to waste time pretending about it.

"You're not finished?"

"I completed her request, and she banished me back, so technically the summoning contract is complete. But no, I'm not finished with her."

Keplar sat back in his chair, eyes narrowed as they focused on my hand rubbing over my chest. "Shit."

"Sir?"

"You're sure about the bond?" he asked, cutting right to the chase.

"Yes."

"And it's been completed?"

"Yes." My blood flared, every time Hailon and I had satisfied the bond flashed through my mind.

"You have my congratulations."

My eyebrows drew together in confusion. "Thank you. Sir."

He crossed his arms, looking for all the world like he was preparing himself to have his day ruined. "So tell me, what have you come up with? What do you propose?"

I laid out the vague ideas I'd had, Keplar becoming more and more intrigued the longer I talked. "Do you think any of that's possible, sir?"

He'd taken at least one full page of notes, and he scanned it again, giving a slow nod. "I don't see any issues at first glance. It's actually quite brilliant. I imagine Tap will be grateful for the assistance."

I smiled, the first one in what felt like a long time. "I hope so."

"Let me get the paperwork going on this. You know that's always the hardest part."

"Yes, sir." My heart thumped, but I was wary. This felt too easy. At what point would I learn the catch to getting what I wanted? "What's the trade?"

"Trade?"

"We're demons, sir," I said. "Respectfully, none of us do a single thing here unless there's a benefit to us. We don't take bad deals. So, what is it that makes this situation a deal worthy of you accepting it?"

Keplar sighed, then started to laugh. His smile was infectious, his chuckle a deep, resonant boom as it rolled around the room. "You're smart, Seir."

"I'm not sure I've ever been accused of that, sir."

He shook his head and leaned forward again, weight on his elbows. "I'm not losing you altogether, son. You're going to get what you want, at least as far as I can manage. I don't see any reason this won't work to everyone's advantage, honestly. You get your time on Earth with your mate, I get to keep my best traveler instead of losing him to the wastes, and your brother gets a little help. There's no part of this deal that isn't advantageous."

"And?"

Keplar laughed again. "*And* I look like my unit has its shit together. That we're performing above expectations." There it was. "Maybe I get a little push for my next promotion."

"Happy to help, sir."

"Go on then, get out of my office. I have a stack of papers to sign so we can make this happen. Make yourself useful in the meantime.

Pack up your things and turn in anything that belongs to the unit at the desk. After that, report to the reassignment office."

I stood so fast my chair scraped across the floor and sifted directly into my apartment. There wasn't much left to be packed, so I made quick work of it, putting my clothes in one bag, odds and ends in another. The rest was unit assigned and could be dropped with Meg at the desk.

I was far more hopeful than I thought I would be as I made my way through the halls. Keplar had probably barely had enough time to find, sign, and file the paperwork.

To my surprise, my unit leader was already there when I arrived at the reassignment office, discussing things with the studious little demon behind a massive desk with a chest-height counter in front of it.

"There he is now. Seir, this is Rune."

"Pleased to meet you."

"Don't leave, Keplar," she said, voice raspy. Black smoke puffed from her throat when she spoke. "If you want me to rush this, I need you here to sign off."

Keplar gave a loose salute and sank his body into one of the big chairs that faced her desk.

"Have you spoken to the crossroads demon about this plan?" she asked me, eyes focusing on me over the tops of her glasses.

"Not yet, but I can take a portal. I feel confident he will be in agreement."

"And the stone kin ally?"

"Already discussing with the council—or will be shortly."

"Good. And you'll still be able to be here, to do your job, at least part time?"

"Yes, I'll be able to portal back and forth quite easily." I left out the part where that might only work in theory, at least temporarily. Surely we could figure out a work-around if need be.

"Any special demands?" She seemed skeptical as she looked over the paperwork one more time.

"No. Except that my ability to be summoned be restricted. I can make a list of the summoners I'd approve of. And that I am able to stay with the same unit. I don't want to change command, I want to stay under Keplar in perpetuity."

Rune's eyes swept from me to the paper and back again. "Fascinating. For a prince, I expected much less flexibility." She used a special quill to sign the documents in glowing red ink. "Go, speak with Tap. Make it fast. We'll be waiting."

I grinned, bursting with pride. It still felt too easy, but hopefully that meant it was simply a good plan. "Thank you!"

I dashed for the hall of portals, going through the familiar one that would transport me to the place between places, the origin of all gates. I went to the crossroads.

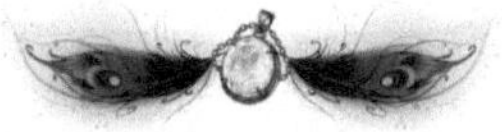

TAP STALKED BY the portal I stepped out of, stopped, and spun on his heel. "What are *you* doing here?" A smile graced his face, and he pulled me into a quick hug. Tap was a similar build to me, though more slender thanks to his less physical job. He'd cut his dark hair very short since I'd last seen him and added several new rings to each ear. His gray eyes were tired behind his round spectacles.

"I have a proposition for you."

He groaned. "Walk with me. I don't have time for any of your schemes, Seir. You know this. I'm barely dug out of the weeds from when I attended Rylan's wedding. And the stone kin have a massive project for me. I can't run off to visit the fae or go in search of a hidden treasure—"

"It's nothing like that, brother, I promise." His shoulders relaxed. "How's the portrait coming along?"

Tap turned a glare and a frown at me. "I'll finish it up one day," he insisted. "You'll see."

"I have faith in you, brother." I slapped his shoulder encouragingly.

The portrait was a running joke between us, though a sore point for Tap. When we'd first fallen, all of us had struggled to find fulfilling hobbies as we adjusted to our new lives. Tap eventually landed on sketching and art. Unfortunately, his assignment to the crossroads left him no time to work on anything like a portrait. Even if he'd had the time, his attention span had become increasingly divided because of how every hour of his day went. He was torn between twenty things at all times, monitoring doorways, making sure that things stayed where they belonged. And that didn't even address all the animal familiars he was in charge of managing or the hundreds of deals that regularly crossed his desk.

"What's this proposal then?" he asked, handing me a cup of ale and grunting as he sat down on a worn leather chair.

"You're not still sleeping in that, are you?"

He simply stared back. "And if I am?"

"You need more rest, Tap."

"I get what I can."

"It's not enough." Worry for him had long since infected my thoughts, and visiting always reminded me that he was not taking care of himself.

"Are you here to hen peck then? We've had this conversation at least the last seventeen times you visited."

"Actually, I'm here to offer some relief."

"Oh?" He perked up a bit. "How so?"

I gave him a brief version of my plans, measuring my enthusiasm against his careful questioning.

"And you think it will work, truly?"

"I do." I grinned at him, pouring him another ale from the seemingly endless bottle that always sat in the same spot on his little table.

"I don't know what to say. I've always held it together, but this past little while ..." He frowned, chin going to his chest as he shook his head. "I'm ashamed to admit I feel as though I'll never catch up again, never feel like I'm on top of things. I don't have time to reorganize or train someone to pick up some of the weight, never mind filing all the deals that are stacking up. I'm barely keeping the familiar bonds in order." He heaved another sigh, adjusting his spectacles as they slid down his nose.

"That's not shameful, Tap. It's alright to need some help. I'm sorry I wasn't faster thinking this one up. Truth be told, I've been trying to find a way to help you for a very long time."

"I know. I appreciate you for it." He stood, the weariness twice as apparent as when I first arrived. "Alright then. I'll send my approvals over and requisition some things. I'd be grateful for the help, and I trust you can manage without my guidance. You've watched me do the job here more than most."

"I have. Sorry I can't stay longer, I'm rather hopeful to get back quickly."

"Back?"

"Oh! Of course, I haven't told you that part yet. I've found my mate, on Earth. She summoned me! I think you'll like her. There may be another wedding for you to attend at some point in the future, so it's best we get some of these things straightened out sooner rather than later. You need a holiday. A real one."

I dragged him in for another quick hug, then dashed for the portal back to Hell, leaving him standing there with his mouth hanging open.

HAILON

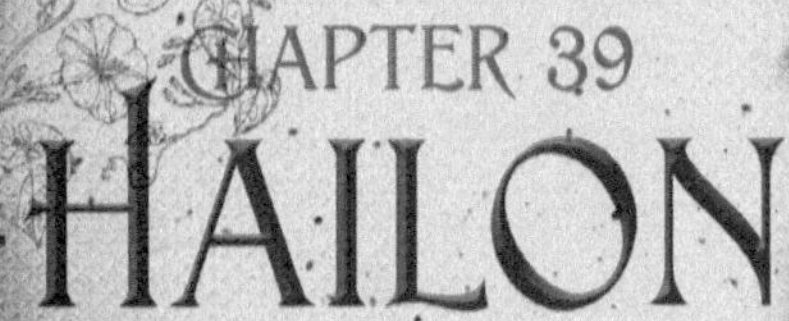

IT FELT LIKE there was a hole where my heart should be. One that was full of hot coals.

"I'm so sorry," Lovette said kindly, her hand resting on my shoulder. She'd wandered over as I stood there stunned. She led me toward the carriage gently, not bothering to fill the space with small talk. "I can only imagine what it must feel like to have to do that to your mate."

Magnus appeared, carrying my packs. He loaded them inside and, after a brief rearrangement, they decided among them who should ride inside with me first and who would drive the horses. Magnus would be flying just far enough behind he wasn't affected by my power.

And so, I found myself seated inside a strange carriage with a stone kin woman named Lovette, headed toward a city I'd never been to, to meet two more demons, a witch, and an alchemist after having banished my mate back to Hell.

It had been a very busy day.

"I'll bet this is really strange for you." Lovette smiled at me gently. "Sorry about that."

"Compared to the last several months, this at least feels somewhat exciting. I've rarely traveled by carriage, and I'm going to a city I've never been to."

"That's a nice way to view it. Is there anything you'd like to know about us? I realize it must be a leap of faith to go with us after such a short introduction."

I appreciated her understanding, but I felt no sense of distrust for any of them. "I've met your brother, so at least you're not total strangers. Seir trusts you, and I trust him."

She nodded. "We came as quickly as we could but had no idea how long the trip might take, considering your abilities. It seemed best to send those of us who could fly and fight. You can, too, by the way."

"What, fight? I definitely can't fly."

Lovette laughed, the sound like tinkling bells. I warmed despite the fact that she was laughing at me. I could tell it wasn't malicious, just good-humored.

"I don't doubt that part, if you're anything like the rest of us. No, I mean you can trust us. I know that's asking a lot since we just met, but you can." Her golden hair bobbed as she nodded, smiling encouragingly. I made a noncommittal noise in my throat. "They—the demons I mean—said you have a healing ability?"

I shuffled my hands under the layers of my cloak. I was plenty warm, but it was good armor. "Yes."

"We're getting such a wonderful array of healers in Revalia! I'm the main one for the conclave, that's the stone kin settlement. It's outside the city, but not far from it. I run the infirmary there. I hope to be able to see your skill in action one day. I've seen Rylan work, his wife, Calla, as well. And Greta is a marvel, she's quite gifted with elixirs and the like."

"I'm not sure my ability is anything to look at, honestly, but I'm happy to demonstrate."

"I'm much the same. I'm skilled with the healing part, but my gift is more about being able to remove the fear and anxiety people feel while injured. It's terribly helpful in some situations. May I?" She extended her hand.

"It probably won't work," I apologized in advance but stretched my hand to meet hers.

The woman's fingers were warm as her hand closed around mine, but I felt no different. My insides were still half-twisted and my pulse a little elevated thanks to the bond being upset and unusual situation I found myself in.

She frowned. "Can't say I'm not a little disappointed. I've never met anyone it didn't work on before."

"May I?"

"Sure." Her eyes were bright as she clutched my hand.

I pushed my magic out, checking for anything that needed fixing. Lovette was healthy, and the stone-kin physiology was as close to human as Seir's demon makeup was. All I found were a few nicks and cuts on her hands. But my healing touch was powerful enough that she noticed and looked down when I repaired the little imperfections.

"Marvelous! Thank you. Those little cuts are always terribly painful when I apply antiseptic to patients." She pulled a package of cookies from her pocket, offering me one. "They also mentioned Coltor suggested you might be a null." She chewed her own cookie, eyes narrowed as she looked at me. "I think he might have been on to something."

"Do you know anything about nulls?" I savored the spice in the gingersnap she'd given me, appreciating the way it burned in my nose.

"Not much, unfortunately, mostly that they are very rare. My father tried to find some information in our archives, but there's simply not much on record. Their—your—existence is kept as hidden as possible. That kind of power is deeply coveted, and usually by the wrong kind of people. It's not very safe to be a null."

"Mmm."

"Hopefully Ophelia will know more."

"Ophelia?"

Lovette's smile returned. "She's one of the oldest of our kind, a sorceress. Most of us have trained under her at one time or another. She knows much that the rest of the world has forgotten. A bit temperamental, perhaps, but mostly wonderful."

Lovette took over the conversation for quite a while, chattering about daily life at the stone kin conclave. It seemed that both of Seir's brothers had mated and married women with some stone kin heritage as well, and there had been quite a bit of tension and trials in all their lives for the last year or so. Then she changed topics and left my head spinning.

"My father is better at recognizing kin than I am, but it feels like you may have some blood as well."

"Stone kin blood? Really?" That was quite possibly one of the last things I'd ever expected her to say.

"Yes, it's a very particular sound. I'm not sure how else to describe it. It's like an extra tone in your heartbeat, the way the blood moves. It's a resonance that other kin can hear. It's a good way to recognize one another in sticky situations."

"And you can hear that in me?"

She nodded. "It's faint, and there's other noise mixed in there too, but yes." That was truly unexpected. "Can I say, your eyes are just stunning, and the white hair suits you."

"Oh. Thank you." I blushed, painfully unused to genuine flattery from other women.

Lovette leaned forward to get a better look. "I've never seen anyone have four colors before. And not ever where two colors were top and bottom." Her head tilted as she inspected my face.

"That's all new, actually," I confessed. "My hair started turning white shortly into our travels. As for my eye ... the color is vertical as recent as the last day or so. The blue used to be on the left."

"Oh." Lovette sat back, thoughtful. "Well, perhaps Ophelia can help explain that as well."

I didn't know what else to say, but the compliments were very sweet.

We stopped after a while to water and rest the horses, stretch our legs, and get a quick bite to eat. Lovette swapped out with her sister for the next part of the ride, as Magnus refused to give up his vantage point in the sky.

Imogen was not nearly as keen on conversation as Lovette was, which I didn't mind at all. My brain felt mushy from all the information I'd taken in, not to mention everything that had happened. The rocking of the carriage was also doing an excellent job of lulling me to sleep.

"Thank you," I muttered, resting my head against the wall, "for coming to meet us. It took Seir and I two weeks to get from Olinbourg to Ravenglen. I was not looking forward to that much more walking. Especially with how the weather is turning colder."

Imogen chuffed a light laugh. "I'd bet not. We're happy to do it." She pulled out yet another blade and started polishing it. She caught me watching her careful but well-practiced motions. "I can't help myself," she laughed, the sound a low rumble in her throat.

"Oh?"

"I'm the forge mistress."

"I've never seen a blade made," I admitted. "But it seems a fascinating process. I have one that needs some care."

"I'd be happy to take a look. Do you have it here?"

I nodded and dug through the packs, pulling out my worn herb knife with a smile. "I've had this since I was a child. It's seen a lot."

"I can tell." She accepted the knife reverently, holding the handle with her palm on one hand and the blade with her fingertips of the other. "Any more sharpening may leave you with nearly nothing." She frowned, turning it back and forth, looking at it from all angles. "But I'll see what I can do once we get back to the city."

"That's very generous, thank you."

She nodded and went back to polishing. I found myself struggling to keep my eyes open and rested my head against the wall of the carriage.

"You can sleep if you need to, there's a ways to go yet."

I let my eyes close, staying in that dreamless, disembodied kind of in-between place where you're not sure if you're more awake than asleep or the other way around as the carriage bumped down the road.

After what felt like just a few short minutes, I was startled awake, heart racing and ready to fight as every cell in my body screamed I was somewhere I was not supposed to be.

CHAPTER 40
HAILON

I GOT OUT OF the carriage, heart pounding against my ribs. The urgency to flee pressed on me, though Imogen had done her best to explain that it was just wards when I woke up panicked. Lovette wasted no time knocking on the door.

"Isn't it very late?" I whispered since speaking loudly felt like an invitation for disaster.

"It's alright. We're expected," Lovette said, smiling as a wizened little woman opened the door. She was short and squatty, wrinkles carved deeply into her face. Lovette made a happy noise and bent down to give the woman a hug. "Hello, Ophelia."

"Hello, my girls! Magnus. Come in, come in." The little stone kin woman ushered us into a cozy hut.

I found it odd that Magnus lingered at the back, clearly uncomfortable, while his daughters entered without any hesitation at all. Thankfully, the urgent feeling the stone kin's wards had woken me with disappeared once we were across the threshold.

"Have a seat, get comfortable. You"—she turned to me, her wrinkles rearranging a bit as she scanned me head to toe—"you take that one." She pointed at a seat to the right of what I could only assume was her favorite chair. "What is your name, dear?"

"Hailon Derne."

"Derne. Hmm." Ophelia squinted, looking at me as she measured the name. She didn't come up with anything familiar I supposed, and she shrugged. "Nice to meet you, Hailon. Shame your demon couldn't join us."

"Sorry?" I stuttered, surprised at her statement.

"It is a demon, yes? Your mate. Another one of the creatures that are so drawn to this city."

The stone kin looked from one to the other, all grinning in amusement. I gathered quickly that Ophelia was not one to mince words.

"Yes, his name is Seir. He had to return to Hell. Temporarily, at least."

"Mmm. Odd times, odd times," she muttered cryptically.

"We appreciate you meeting with us, Ophelia," Lovette said. "Apologies that it's late. We were rather anxious to get back."

"No trouble. I wasn't sleeping anyway. Tea?"

Imogen reached for the tray. "I'll pour."

Ophelia laughed. "If you're not in the mood for my whiskey, Imogen, just say so."

Imogen chuckled as she started pouring the steaming brew into laughably tiny china cups. They were disproportionately small compared to her hands, not to mention Magnus's. "You'll have a roomful of unexpected overnight guests if we start drinking now. Been a tiresome ride."

"That wouldn't be so awful, now would it?" Ophelia asked.

"I thought you didn't like visitors?" Lovette teased, giving the old woman a wink.

"I enjoy the *right* ones from time to time." She turned her attention to me again. "Now you. Let me get a good look at you." She spun completely in her seat so she could hold my face between her hands. Her soft fingertips brushed some wisps of hair away from my eyes. It was a gesture so full of gentleness that tears prickled. I'd never known a grandmother, but she embodied the kind of energy I expected from such a person. Ophelia turned my head back and forth, examining it in the light. "Been a long, long time since one of your kind graced my doorstep."

"My kind?"

"We'll get there, my dear. Drink your tea. I've a table to sort." She got down from her chair with a grumble and went over to a little alcove behind the kitchen. Under a stained-glass window was a table, and on the table was a curious assortment of items.

Lovette gave me an encouraging wink. Imogen just leaned back in her seat, eyes closed as though she were going to take a little nap. Magnus sat stiffly in his chair, looking like he could actually do with a good serving of whiskey.

Out of habit, I pulled the little horse carving from my pocket and held it in my hand, stroking the gold parts. The smooth metal under my fingers never failed to calm my nerves.

"Come over here, Hailon."

I stood, obeying immediately. They had all impressed very firmly that Ophelia could be dangerous if disobeyed or provoked. Magnus had reinforced this sentiment, but with much more urgency, and he'd been borderline distraught that he hadn't brought some kind of candy for her. I didn't understand his wariness, as all I'd felt from her was kindness so far, but perhaps my gauge was off.

She stood me in front of the table of random oddities, her hands hovering and adjusting something here and there. There was a small pile of salt and a mix of crystals all spread out from one another. Herb bundles and sand. Shreds of paper.

"Hold this." She handed me a bell. "Ring that please."

I shook the little bell by the handle, but the clapper only made a dead clanking noise. Ophelia gazed up at me and nodded, shifting around several things on the table. She turned a chunk of amethyst upside down and traded a decent-size piece of rose quartz for a smaller one of jade and a polished round tiger's eye. She shuffled the order of things, stepping back when everything was to her liking.

"Again?" she prompted.

I was prepared for another dull *clank* but was rewarded with a vibrant clear tone.

Ophelia beamed. "Good, good." She put her hand out. "The little carving you have, may I see it?" Reluctantly, I handed over the little horse. The ancient stone kin set the figure on the sill of the window behind the table after giving it a thorough examination and friendly pet. "Now. Let's just …" She collected tiny amounts of sand and salt and a sliver of the jade that had broken off. She put all those in the smallest cauldron I'd ever seen, and once the candle under it was lit, added two pinches of the shredded paper. "Your hand?" I held it out to her, and she pricked the tip of my finger so quickly I barely saw her move. Two drops went into the cauldron. "Would your demon have been upset about that, do you think?" she asked cryptically.

"Sorry?"

She grinned and waved a hand. "Never mind, never mind. He'll be sad to have missed it, I'll bet. But it's nice not to have to tell someone to mind their manners."

Perplexed, I put the pad of that finger between my lips and sucked the sting away, still unsure what exactly she was talking about.

"Vassago wasn't that bad," Magnus chuckled. "It was Rylan who really got offended by it."

Ophelia made some singsong sounds in her throat, clearly amused by the memory of Seir's brothers reacting to her drawing blood from their mates. There was an odd comfort in knowing others had come before me through this strange ceremony.

The mixture started to smoke, first a billowy cloud of gray, then the smoke turned yellowish, and a square shape took form.

"What's happening?" I whispered, stepping back when I realized that faces were forming, like a portrait being painted in puffy smoke.

"It's alright." Ophelia nodded. She reached over and patted my shoulder comfortingly, the other three stone kin still rooted to the chairs in her living room.

A woman's face took shape first. Her smile was soft, her eyes too. Her cheekbones were prominent, and there was something about her hair that seemed unusual, but I couldn't put my finger on quite what. The man was tall, broad. He had an impressive beard and expressive eyes. He also had what appeared to be slightly pointed ears.

"Who are you?" I muttered.

The man looked shy, almost ashamed, as though he could actually see me standing in front of him, hear my question.

The woman turned his way, smiling up at him as though he'd hung the moon. He turned and pressed his forehead to hers. It was then I realized what was happening with her hair. She had tiny horn nubs on the top of her head. Then they both turned back to the front.

Realization dawned, a flush running through me, first cold, then hot. These were my parents. The people responsible for bringing me into the world. The ones who vanished, leaving me with Sal.

And I didn't even know them well enough to recognize them.

There was an odd rumbling noise, and the woman touched her collar, where a necklace chain disappeared under the fabric. I heard the sound of wood cracking and looked over just in time to see the front and back halves of my horse carving fall in opposite directions on the wide windowsill. What looked like a black rock fell out from the center.

My gut swooped and I took another step backwards as the portrait began to lose integrity. I was thankful that there hadn't been much to our meal on the road as I grappled with what exactly any of this meant.

"Well. That answers that." Ophelia dashed her arm through the remaining smoke and opened the window wide, retrieving the black stone that had fallen out of the carving.

I was grateful at least one of us understood what had just happened, but it certainly wasn't me.

"I believe this belongs to you." Ophelia dropped the smoothly polished obsidian into my palm. It was on a chain, set in a band of plain silver.

"A necklace."

"*Her* necklace, I'd wager," Ophelia said sagely, watching as I retrieved the two halves of my little horse. My heart hurt, the little item one of the only things I'd maintained from my childhood that had always brought me comfort. It had been taken from me in that horrible house, and I couldn't have been more grateful to have found it in the lockbox. "Perhaps we can find a way to mend it."

We reconvened in the living room, the three other gargoyles quiet as they watched the whole situation unfold.

"Those were my parents."

"Yes, yes." Ophelia reached forward and refilled her tea, making a face as she discovered it was lacking whiskey.

"You didn't know them at all?" Lovette asked, expression empathetic.

"No. I was left with my Aunt Sal by my mother when I was three. She never spoke of my father at all. I don't remember either of them. I was too little I guess."

"That's unfortunate," Magnus said. His voice was deep and resonant, even when he was speaking softly. "I recognize your father. I'll have to search my memories a bit better to be sure, but I believe he has roots in the grotesque house. I can check the records, of course."

"Thank you. Sal said my mother's name was Wyn. That she had some demon lineage."

"The perfect marriage of all the bloodlines is required for a null to be conceived. It's why there's so few of you. People get very uncomfortable when magics mix that powerfully." Ophelia nodded sagely as though this statement explained everything.

"All the bloodlines?"

"Human, stone kin, witch, demon, angel, and fae."

I attempted to process this information but found myself stumbling. "You're saying that I'm ... all of those things?"

Ophelia smiled. "Yes, dear girl. There's no telling how much of any of those elements is needed, but yes. Your mother clearly has demon genes, and your father some fae. I can hear the stone kin blood in you as well. You're a healer, so that likely accounts for the witch part. The angel bit gets tricky, but it's a requirement too. No null can exist without them all being present, at least somewhere down the line. A null has the ability to balance the magic of the world outside themselves by being composed of a perfect balance of magic within themselves."

Except I wasn't balanced. And I had no control over that terrible power.

"I'm sorry," I apologized, head spinning. I put a hand to my forehead, willing the dizziness to stop. "I'm not feeling well all of a sudden. I'm not going to be very good at answering questions or puzzling much of anything out right now. I'm ... tired." *Tired* didn't quite convey how much it felt as though my brain might start to leak from my ears soon, but it was the best I could do. I'd rested in the carriage, but even my bones felt weary.

"Of course, of course. It's very late, after all. Let me get you set up in my guest room, dear." Ophelia got to her feet and disappeared into the back of the hut. I hadn't expected there to be more than one bedroom in the little building. After sleeping on the ground so much, the soft couch would have been perfectly wonderful.

"We'll be back in the morning," Lovette assured me as they prepared to leave. "Unless you want one of us to stay?" She and Imogen exchanged a look, and I could see a whole conversation passed between them in a matter of seconds.

Imogen nodded. "This is all very unusual, I'm sure. A lot to take in. But you're safe here. Ophelia might be one of the oldest of us, but nobody crosses her. She's still very capable."

"Thank you. I'm sure I'll be fine."

Lovette squeezed my hand, making sure I saw the reassurance in her face before stepping away.

Ophelia came bustling back in. "Your room is the one to the left. The bathroom is the center door, and my room is to the right." She gestured vaguely.

"I appreciate your hospitality."

"I'm happy to have you here with me, dear, you're quite fascinating. We have much to discuss, but you need some sleep so you can get your bearings first."

"Any requests, Ophelia? It's market day. We can stop on our way in," Imogen offered.

"I'll bake some bread and brew the tea. The rest I leave up to you. Muffins are never amiss, nor chocolate. Or some of those crispy sausages you sometimes bring." She licked her lips as though already tasting it.

"I'll take care of it."

Ophelia shooed me to bed while she cleaned up. I washed my face and took care of my necessaries in the adorably small bathroom, then tucked myself into the little bed in the equally tiny guest bedroom. It was cozy, and the size of the room made it feel like the house itself was giving me a hug.

Even with no tail wrapped around my ankle, I fell asleep in no time at all, comforted by the muffled homey noises Ophelia was making in the kitchen.

CHAPTER 41
HAILON

I'D BARELY MANAGED to wash my face before the gargoyles arrived back the following morning.

It was just Lovette and Imogen, and I felt a bit as though I was intruding on a private girls' morning when I came out of the bathroom to find them all huddled around breakfast on the low table in the living room.

"Hailon, good morning!" Lovette got to her feet and came over to me, ushering me back to join them. "We brought a little bit of everything. Do you prefer coffee? Tea? There are muffins and some fancy pastries. Imo and I had a lovely time running through the market right when everything opened. We got first choice of everything we wanted!"

"Coffee would be quite welcome, thank you." My stomach growled as I took in the veritable buffet they'd set up. They chatted and laughed, nobody shy about grabbing and sharing the food. I felt an odd mix of being included and like I was watching as an outsider.

"Did you fly here?" Ophelia asked.

"We did, and do you know what's interesting? It wasn't until we hit your wards that we were stopped."

"Really?" I asked, perplexed by that.

"Hmm." Ophelia poured herself a cup of tea that was half whiskey. "My wards are many layered. I've had the benefit of decades to get them to where they are. Perhaps they are just containing your power."

"Was it like that with Coltor?" Imogen asked.

"I'm not sure. Seir couldn't fly yet. But within the wards at the ruins, neither Coltor nor Seir could shift."

The sisters looked at one another and got up from their seats, each standing behind a separate part of the U-shaped furniture arrangement. They each released their wings, both moving carefully so that they didn't knock into any of Ophelia's things.

"Oh," Lovette said, surprise in her tone. "That's very strange."

"Yes, it's like that part of me is empty."

"Well good, that's something we know for sure now, anyway. Sit down, girls." Ophelia turned to me. "Tell me about yourself, Hailon."

I choked on the bite of cinnamon muffin I'd eaten. After I'd successfully chased it down with some of the strong coffee, I asked, "What would you like to know?"

"Tell me about your abilities. As best you can."

I explained my healing power, how I could feel *the bad* with my magic and remove it.

"She fixed some little things on my hands in the carriage like it was nothing," Lovette attested, showing her hands.

"Have you found limitations to it?" Ophelia asked, very obviously looking at the fresh pink marks on my own hands. I suspected very little got past her.

"I don't think it works on anything inanimate," I added. "I tried to mend a cracked mirror, and nothing happened." Though that wouldn't stop me from trying with my little horse when I had a chance. "And something big, like a broken bone or deep sickness, requires lots of focus and energy. I'm often not really aware of my surroundings when it's like that."

"Mmm. You didn't know about the other part?"

"No, not until we met Coltor in the ruins. We knew Seir couldn't shift or fly, but not why. It wasn't until we met up with Coltor that we had an explanation. I'd never heard the term *null* before he said it."

"And your eye? What happened to cause the color shift?"

I took a deep breath, the sting of what Sal had said still fresh. "I was very, very angry."

All three of them made thoughtful, understanding sounds in their throats, heads nodding as though this was the most logical thing in the world.

"It's interesting that you don't have any feeling as far as that power is concerned," Lovette said, dusting muffin crumbs off her fingers. "How are you supposed to control it when you can't even tell it's there?"

Ophelia turned to me, eyes squinted with thought. "Hailon, have you tried on that necklace yet?"

"No, I put it away." In truth, I'd been a bit afraid of it. Too much about my mother was a mystery, I didn't know what such an object might do.

"Would you mind getting it?"

"Of course." I retrieved it from my pack in the guest room and held it out to her as I sat back down.

"No, no. Put it on."

I did as she asked, the stone somehow warm against my skin despite the fact that it had been nowhere with outside heat. Now that I was wearing it, I could feel a low vibration tingling just under my skin. I plugged both ears with my fingers and wiggled my jaw, trying to gently rub away the itchy sensation there.

"It feels ... strange."

"Lovette, do you mind seeing if you can shift now?"

Lovette got to her feet and stood behind the furniture again, putting her wings out and then closing her eyes. "Oh!" She beamed and transformed from her human self into a slightly larger version with a grayish-green stone skin and fierce claws where her fingernails were, fairly feline paw feet, and brutal fangs.

"Lift the necklace by the chain, away from your skin please?" I did so, and Lovette immediately shifted back into her human form.

"Ouch." Her hand went to her forehead.

"Sorry!" I apologized.

"Not your fault."

"Fascinating indeed. May I take a closer look at the stone?" I took the necklace off and handed it to her. She turned it over and around, up and into the sunlight streaming through the window. "Imogen, would you mind?"

Imogen reached for the necklace and did the same kind of thing, twisting and turning the quail's egg sized stone around in the light. "It's in the stone, not the setting. It's mirrored."

"Yes."

"Care to share with the whole class?" Lovette asked, daintily sipping her tea as she glanced between the two.

"Whoever made this necklace inscribed a powerful incantation directly into the obsidian. It's covered by the metal they set it in. They reversed the letters so that their power is turned the correct direction as viewed through the stone."

"And that ... stops me from blocking magic?"

"Would seem so." Ophelia smiled. "It's something to get us started at least. Now, you can go into the city, if nothing else. Just don't lose that necklace."

Imogen handed it back to me. "I'm sure there's an apprentice or two at the conclave I could conscript to craft a duplicate or two. We'd need Rylan to do the incantation though."

"It can't be that simple, can it?" I blurted, unexpectedly angry about how easy that seemed. "If it were that straightforward, why was the necklace hidden in that horse? Why didn't anyone know? I've had it with me since I was a child but couldn't make use of it. What if I'd *lost* it? It was *taken* from me not all that long ago, I'm ridiculously lucky it wasn't thrown away or sold off for the gold on the hooves."

Ophelia patted my hand in an effort to soothe me. "Hailon, would you look at me, dear?" I snapped my head her direction and her eyebrow went up as she took a good scan of my face. "Safe to say anger's a trigger then."

"I beg your pardon?"

"Your eye. The color has shifted a bit more."

I jumped up and went into the little bathroom, staring at myself in the mirror in stunned disbelief. The colors were now somewhere in the middle between vertical and horizontal.

"What happens when it gets to completely opposite where it started? How and why is that happening in the first place?"

"Good questions, but I'm afraid I don't have any answers for you."

"What about my hair. Any idea why it's turning white?"

Her head tilted to the side. "When did it start?"

"A few days into our journey."

She shrugged. "Perhaps a side effect of your mating bond waking up. Access to more or new powers can cause changes like that." Her eyes went squinty. "Was there anything else left for you like the horse?" Ophelia asked.

I retrieved the strongbox and brought it into the living room. Imogen gasped when the box opened and the obsidian blade dagger was revealed.

"May I?"

"Sure." I handed it to her. "It's not mine, I took it from the place I'd been held captive when we escaped."

"Oh, I disagree." Imogen smiled widely. "It's definitely yours." She handed it back to me and I accepted it by the handle. The weight felt off though, the grip too large.

I shook my head. "It's not comfortable."

"We can work on that. If you don't mind parting with it for a bit, I can take both this and your knife back to the forge with me."

"I have no attachment to it." I set the dagger in the box and moved around some of the papers, pulling out the sheet that Seir had taken from Sal. Under the paper was the little obsidian chip ring I'd told him I liked. Sneaky demon. My heart squeezed, and I allowed myself a little private smile as I looked at it.

"Seir said someone can help me with this? It's the letter my mother left with my aunt." That title for Sal tasted bad now. I resolved to finding something else to call her in very short order.

Ophelia leaned in for a better look. "Yes, our lovely Greta is part fae and understands the language very well."

"She can go to d'Arcan, right? Since the necklace works?" Lovette asked.

"Yes. And I think she should, after we try a few things." The smile on her face made me nervous for the first time since we'd met. "Would you mind sitting here in front of me, Hailon? On the floor. Take the necklace all the way off first, if you please. I'd like to use my hands on you, if you don't mind."

I did as she asked, both stone kin sisters leaning in with curiosity as the older woman gently put her fingertips against my scalp. There was no sensation from her touch other than warmth. She tapped and pressed, frowning in concentration as she stared into my eyes.

"Put the necklace in your hand." I obeyed, clasping it tightly. "Can you send out your healing magic with the stone against your skin?"

I closed my eyes and tried what she suggested. My magic was right there waiting when I went to draw on it, full and vibrant. I pictured it like a glass of water, and this time, it was so full it was mounded over the rim but somehow not spilling. I'd never felt it as clearly or as fully before.

"Do you need any healing, Ophelia?" I asked, the hum beginning to irritate, like there were bugs wriggling under my skin.

She chuckled, the sound raspy and dry. "Of course I do, my dear. Comes with the territory for my age."

"It feels like I need to purge some of my magic. I've never felt it so full. Do you want me to use it?"

"Not yet. Drop the necklace."

I did, and the relief was immediate. My magic felt normal, no more overwhelm. The hum was gone, and I felt like I could take a deep breath. "Feels like it usually does."

"How odd." She frowned and picked up the stone herself, examining it again. "It's an amplifier, but it needs to be tempered. Perhaps it was calibrated for whatever null came before you. Imogen, the dagger please?" Ophelia put the obsidian dagger in one of my hands and the necklace in the other. "Try now."

Heart pounding, I closed my eyes and reached out again but immediately pulled back. It was as though I'd been burned, my power a pan on a hot stove I'd grabbed the bare handle of. I dropped both items, unable to speak and panting.

"Sorry, sorry." Ophelia put her fingertips back on my head and soothed the sting away. "Not together then, noted." She thought again. "If you don't try to access your healing ability with the dagger, what happens?"

Lovette hopped up again, and I held the dagger loosely in my hand.

"I can't find my magic at all," Lovette frowned. I set it down again, and she shifted with ease.

"Odd indeed," Ophelia said. "One item to enhance each power." She nodded, as though this made perfect sense. "They just need some calibration. That's all," she muttered, mostly to herself.

"But the dagger was in a city on the other side of the realm. How could it possibly have been meant for me? If I hadn't been kidnapped and taken there, then what? I stole it when we left because it looked expensive, no other reason."

"It found you." Imogen's words were clear and intense, despite the low volume of her voice. "It would always have found you, eventually."

"That's her gift," Lovette explained, seeing my blank expression. "We don't argue with Imogen about anything to do with blades."

I still found myself resistant to accepting the ease with which such things were coming together, but perhaps that was the most reasonable explanation after all. I had long since stopped trusting in the fates, but given the last few weeks, there was enough evidence to make me reconsider.

Ophelia tried several more things to trigger something inside me, some kind of sense that would allow me to feel and control the nulling ability. Morning spun into afternoon, and after a break for lunch, she had me trying a new set of things, including reading off spells from an ancient tome. The absolute lack of success there proved, if nothing else, that I was not a witch, even if I did have some witch blood in my veins.

"I've tried everything I can think of for something like this. The girls will take you to d'Arcan. The demons can help, and Greta is there. She can read your letter. There will be good guidance there, I'm sure of it."

I gathered everything Seir had suggested I take to his brothers, and we started toward town.

Answers were closer, but still felt far away, and as we made our way down the road, my thoughts inevitably strayed to the demon I couldn't help missing.

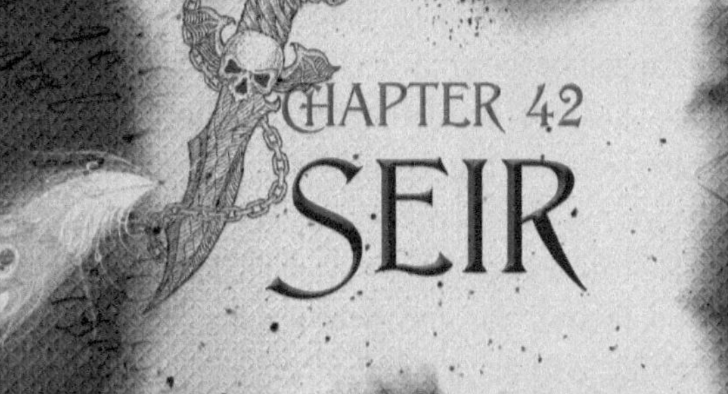

CHAPTER 42
SEIR

I WAS TIRED OF pacing hallways waiting for Keplar or Rune to send for me.

It had been hours without any kind of update. I went to the dining hall with Asim and ate tasteless food while I filled him in on how I'd found Hailon. I even managed to bathe, change, and catch a few hours of sleep in the apartment that would soon no longer be mine to use. I made sure my mission notes were up to date and all reports were filed. I wandered the halls, aimless, willing myself to be patient even though that was the very last thing I was feeling.

"Find something to do, Seir, or I'll find something for you. The process is moving as fast as possible, I swear it," Keplar had warned me the last time I'd strolled by his office.

Not wanting to get caught up in anything I couldn't drop and leave immediately, I'd gotten a pass for the archives.

There was a frustrating lack of information on anything I could think to look for, particularly nulls. The only thing helpful I was able to locate was a scroll with a list of known magical nullifiers through history. One appeared every couple of generations or so, but only ever one at a time. Sometimes there was as much as a five-generation gap between them. Thankfully, the scroll I found also contained the known nulls' immediate family trees. I copied it down so I had something to take back to the surface with me to reference against the archives the mages and stone kin both kept. Hailon's name was not in the records, but her mother's was. Wyn was listed as the great-granddaughter of Elowyn, a null who resided peacefully in Vincara for all of her normal, mortal lifespan. No husband was registered for Wyn on the tree, and she was the last entry for that line.

Vassago had spent a very long time at a monastery in Vincara. I scribbled a little note to myself on the parchment to speak with him about it. Perhaps he'd known an Elowyn, not realizing she was a null, or had crossed paths with her at some point.

I turned to seeing if there were any new developments in regard to several demon horde infestations that my brothers had managed in and around Revalia. Thankfully, that whole strange situation seemed to have cleared up since Ris had taken back the throne in the fae realm.

Bored, I wandered between the shelves, picking up a tome here and there, hopeful I'd get lucky and stumble across something helpful if I glanced through enough books and scrolls.

Unfortunately, I found nothing more than boring battle reports, many of which I'd participated in, and instructional manuals for torture.

I'd given up and was walking past the check-in desk when Meg stopped me.

"Did he find you?" she asked.

"Who? Keplar?"

"Yes, he was looking for you just now. Said to send you down to Rune's office. Good luck!"

I turned and sifted, arriving at Rune's office just steps behind my unit leader. He laughed when he saw me. "Anxious?"

"Of course I am, sir."

Rune sat behind her desk, stoic as ever. "Welcome back. Your paperwork has been approved, but"—she held a hand up, stopping my premature celebration—"the boss requires you to bring something to Earth for him."

"The boss?" I asked. Rune leveled me with a stern gaze that I was certain had reduced many demons to terrified puddles on the floor. I hadn't seen Lucifer himself in decades, but we'd never had friction. "Of course. What does he need me to take?"

"He wants you to deliver this to Lilith." She held up a thick parchment envelope.

"She's notoriously difficult to locate, but I'm sure it can be arranged. Is there a time limit?"

"No limit was given, but he impressed a sense of urgency. He requested you specifically, Seir. Any notion as to why?"

I shrugged. "I have a reasonably friendly history with Lilith. I don't doubt she'll see me, that I can deliver this as requested. Once I'm able to find her, of course." I kept to myself that I'd seen her not all that long ago, when she, Ris, and Tap had collaborated on the creation of a series of portals so we could all be a bit more easily connected.

"I see. Report back as soon as it's done. Sooner is better, of course."

I reached across the desk and took the envelope from Rune, finding it dense and heavy. "I'll take care of it."

"Good." What might have been the ghost of a smile crossed her mouth under the black smoke. She turned to the papers in front of her, signing them one at a time in bright red ink before handing them to Keplar to do the same. Then it was my turn to sign. "Here you are."

"Thank you." I looked between them after putting my name down with a flourish in the magical red ink. I finally relaxed when Keplar laughed.

"I need you back to work as soon as possible."

"Yes, sir." My blood was thumping through my body, the need to get back to the surface my only focus.

"Get yourself set up. Check in as often as you can. We'll begin the transfer of door monitoring from the crossroads to your new location as soon as you're set up." He grinned at me and reached out his hand. I shook it. "It was a good proposal, Seir. I'm more pleased than you know that you found a way to stay out of the wastes."

"Me too, sir. Will someone be sent in my place?"

He shook his head. "They wanted your talent, so unless someone presents with similar abilities, they will continue to put in a request that will remain unfulfilled."

I wasn't sure how to feel about that. They were willing to sacrifice a prince to the wastes, but there was no true urgency? What was out there that they needed help with so badly then? Perhaps I could get one of my other brothers to look into it, they generally worked much more on the outskirts than I did.

He tilted his head, a sly grin on his mouth as he watched me process his response. "We'll discuss that another time. Get out of here."

I didn't hesitate. I sifted to the main hall, waved at Meg as I sprinted to the portals, and dove through the one for d'Arcan, done with waiting to get back to my mate.

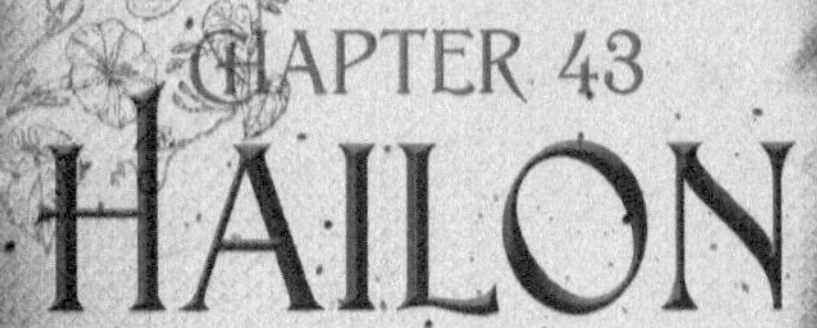

CHAPTER 43

HAILON

REVALLA WAS A beautiful city, flourishing with life of all kinds. I'd never seen the like and could understand why it was one of the most desirable places in all of Cyntere to live now that I was within its walls.

Lovette and Imogen walked me past the outskirts where all the big estates were, then through the center of town and square where the market was held midweek. There were shops of all kinds, a few of which reminded me of the little places we'd visited in the Valley.

"The carriage was otherwise engaged today, or it would have come to pick us up," Imogen explained, watchful as we wandered the city streets. Every now and then, her eyes shifted to the sky, and if I was quick to follow her gaze, I'd catch a glimpse of another stone kin stealthily monitoring things from the rooftops.

"I don't mind walking. It's beautiful here." Even from a distance the cathedral was beyond impressive, and what they pointed out as the observatory for d'Arcan was stunning just in sheer height.

By the time we reached the Collegium d'Arcan, I was overwhelmed. The city was so much larger than it had initially seemed, and there was an endless number of things to take in. The people, the noise, the vendors—it was all lovely, but I wasn't used to the scale of such a city. It was very pleasant to not have to ignore others staring or sneering when I walked by, however.

The school itself was imposing in size but still somehow felt welcoming. As we went through the iron gates, I felt no sense of foreboding like I expected to, despite a large raven swooping near us as we entered the courtyard. The bird dipped down, like he was getting a good eyeful of us all, then he flew off again toward the main building.

The doors opened as we crossed the courtyard, and a beautiful woman with dark hair greeted us, a shockingly oversized cat winding between her ankles before trotting off to go roll in the grass.

"Welcome! I'm Calla." She took my hand between hers, giving it a gentle shake.

"Hailon."

"So lovely to meet you. Please, come in." She hugged the two gargoyle women, gesturing for us to go down the main hall. "You're just in time. Greta's nearly done with a very complicated elixir. Grace is bringing us snacks."

Calla led us down a wide stone hall and into a classroom that took my breath away. There were overflowing bookshelves and supply cases along the back wall, but it was the floor-to-ceiling stained-glass window that stole my attention. It made a rainbow of light in the room, more beautiful and muted than standard clear glass.

Instead of desks there were sofas and comfortable chairs near a stone fireplace, and several worktables spread through the room with a variety of tools and interesting items on their tops.

Seeing our entrance, two tall, broad men—one dark haired and one light—stood from their seats. Another woman looked up from behind a table with chemistry equipment spread across it at the back of the room, a kind smile on her face. Her hands,

1. INVISIBLE

Eva

Sporting events brought out the worst in people. For masochistic but dedicated Cubs fans, that meant painful amounts of drinking. Heading into the seventh inning stretch, the Cubs led by two. Unfortunately, they were down by *four* an inning later. In hopes of hitting the watering holes of Wrigleyville before the sad crowds showed up, our party left the friendly confines of the club level we paid too much money for.

"Can you both watch Callie?" Ellie, my best friend, asked myself and Jace, her sibling.

"Sure," I said.

Callie O'Malley, one of Ellie's sorority sisters, was of Irish blood but lacked any ability to hold her liquor. I resisted a strong urge to smack her as she tried to slam her hand on the hood of a guy's car, fully stopped, to reenact a scene from *Midnight Cowboy*.

I mouthed an apology to the older man in the Porsche. Jace shot me a look like they couldn't believe this bullshit. We did it because we loved Ellie, but neither of us fit in. Jace was better suited by Northalsted's rainbow-flag-waving set of openings. I was much of the same mind.

We arrived at the club. Callie bitched that no one had given her a drink.

"That girl is trying my fucking patience," Jace groaned. "I will not make it. I swear I won't."

I looked at Jace, hands on their small shoulders. "I promise you, friend, we will survive this onslaught."

"Hey, ladies—and Jace!" Dia Hernandez gave a shrill, but inconclusive declaration. "Who wants shots?"

"I'll get them," I groaned, wanting a break.

Jace called. "I swear to god, Eva, if you leave me—"

I waved and departed, looking ridiculous as I approached the bar where a man refused to move. He turned and began to chat me up.

"Oh, a bridesmaid," said the polo-wearing dickhead blocking my free movement.

"Hi," I said.

"No Cubs gear? Are you here with the Giants?" He joked.

"I do not wear sports gear in an act of protest."

"Protest?"

"They have shitty options for women. You mind moving, buddy?" I tried brushing past, something he read as flirtation.

"What are you up to after this?"

Great, a non-sequitur since he's not even listening!

"I'm hanging with my friends over there. It's my best friend's bachelorette. My focus is on celebrating her!"

"Oh, really? Is she the hot little blonde?"

She wasn't. That was Allison Florence, Ellie's teaching coworker. I didn't get along with her well, but her uncle offered the party bus for free since Ellie's future father-in-law was a close friend. For a savings of three grand, I'd get over it.

"Nope. The bride is the one with the tiara," I said.

I expected an offer to buy the drinks. Instead, he stared down my summer dress.

"Well, my place is around the corner—"

As he moved his body slightly, I slid quickly past and bellied up

to the bar. Desperately seeking the attention of the bartender, I practically laid my breasts on the bar top. Men looked, but no one helped me. The intrusive man hovered.

"They don't make them like this anymore," he said.

I felt his eyes boring into my ass. I wanted to turn and yell but remained focused on shutting Callie O'Malley up. My eyes remained on the prize until the man clamped his hands on my hips. I turned to shout, but before I could, someone stepped in.

* * *

Davey

"I knew as soon as they put Rudy on the mound we were fucked," Carlos sighed as we settled into beers at our favorite haunt.

"Maybe you could just buy him out. Does it work like that?" Joe, an old buddy asked.

"I don't think it does, no," I chuckled. "Someone needs to fire House. The man cannot manage a team."

"It's the Cubs," Rudy said. "Every year, you think it will get better."

"And every year it gets worse," I added. "Yet, we're in this toxic relationship and always come back for more."

"I think I know what's *really* happening," Carlos said.

I wanted to listen to his delightful conspiracy theory, but all I saw was a pretty woman with honey colored hair trying desperately to get the bartender's attention. Her tits were the first draw and the reason I became distracted, but I soon trained my eyes on the man behind her looking ready to strike.

"Give me a sec," I said.

Sensing trouble, I quickly ditched my beer and filed through the crowd to find the man gripping the woman's hips from behind.

"Hey, buddy, you want to step off her?" I called.

He turned, enraged, and immediately backed off. I didn't know if it was because he recognized me or appreciated that I had a good

five inches and at least thirty pounds on his skinny little ass, but he backed off.

"We were just… talking."

"Like hell we were!" The woman shouted. "You can fuck off!"

The guy glared in her direction, then cowered in mine, leaving.

I expected a thank you but got none. She turned back to the bar, ignoring me. I tried very hard *not* to stare, but I couldn't help it. She was beautiful. The scowl on her face was more attractive yet. So, when she turned, giving me a look like "you're excused", I couldn't help myself.

"I don't owe you a thank you," she said. "But I do appreciate that you did the bare minimum as a member of society to run the fuckwad off."

I snickered. "Well, I'd hope someone would do the same for me."

"Promise that if a woman grabs onto your hips, buddy, I'll go after her. Sadly, the only woman who would do that is at the table over there that is waiting for drinks, and this bartender could give a flying fuck about me."

I raised my hand, and the bartender nodded and approached.

"What can I get you, Davey?" He asked.

I looked at the woman.

"A round of shots," she answered. "Six lemondrops."

She made a face that showed she found her friend's taste in drinks to be reprehensible, and I laughed.

"Make it nine. We'll be drinking with them. Put it on my tab," I said.

Incredulous, the blonde rolled her eyes. "Sure."

The bartender put in the order.

"Thank you. You didn't have to do that."

"It's a bachelorette party, right?" I asked.

"Correct. It's hell."

I snickered. "Your sister?"

"Best friend," the woman said. "But her friends… they're… a disaster."

"Drinking helps?"

"Debatable."

I waved my friends over. Carlos and Joe popped around.

"This is my college buddy, Carlos, and my best friend since childhood, Joe," I said. "And I have *no* idea why I gave you that backstory."

Except I did. The more I talked, the more nervous I got. It was her big brown eyes. Damn, they were gorgeous. I'd not gotten a smile out of her yet, but I knew it would come if I persisted.

"I'm Eva," the woman said. "And your buddy chased off a dickhead I would have handled."

"He wouldn't have forgiven himself for ignoring it," Joe explained. "He has four younger sisters."

"Oh, big family," Eva said. "Well, nice for you."

"Six of us," I answered.

"Your poor mother." A small smile spread with the joke.

"Indeed."

The shots arrived and Carlos—now closest to the bar—carried them in the direction Eva directed. I watched as she paraded ahead, her hips swaying beautifully. I'd take her home tonight if it *killed* me.

2. WHITE KNIGHT

Davey

EVA WAS A FORCE—ONE THAT DABBLED BEST IN DRY HUMOR AND getting her friends to laugh at her straight reactions. Lacking pretension, she was a blissful reprieve from my usual choice of woman. When she sang a wild rendition of "Bad, Bad Leroy Brown" with the "brides-person", Jace, I was hooked. I didn't ask about Jace's backstory, but they seemed cool enough—if not very overwhelmed in a sea of woo girls.

I helped Eva herd the crowd onto a bus and back down to Streeterville. There was a club in a restaurant basement that some girl Allison swore by. By this point, I was alone. My very married buddies had lives and babies. By eight, they turned into pumpkins. I had no idea what I had gotten myself into, but getting off the ride wasn't in the cards. It had been years since I'd been so attracted to anyone as this random woman.

We piled out of the party bus and provided our surly door greeter our IDs. At thirty-nine, they had no reason to card me. Unfortunately, everyone had to go through the ritual of struggling to pull our IDs out of our wallets. I went last, hoping he wouldn't out me. He gave me a sly smile, shook his head, and went back to his normal grimace as I passed.

"The music is awful. Should be awesome!" Eva sarcastically shouted at Jace.

I shook my head. "It's standard fare."

"Not in London and not where I go."

"What are you listening to at clubs in London?"

"It's more folk music."

"Folk music?" I laughed until she glared, so I covered my ass. "That is… not what I expected from you."

"I forgot which team you batted for momentarily," Jace snickered. "And also, just the general age disparity. What's it like dating a boomer?"

Eva slapped Jace on the arm. "Okay, young person!"

I didn't *quite* know what that meant.

"I'm going to order drinks," I said loudly. "What do you ladies want?"

"If they have whiskey, I prefer MacCallan—they have the 12, I bet. It's decent. Not swill."

I did a double take. She knew her scotch.

"I can manage that probably," I said. "And I will get some champagne sent over for the others. And… water."

By now, Callie was grinding on a dance floor railing.

"I'm too sick of this shit," Jace muttered. "I'm coming to help."

They followed me to the bar where we waited.

"So, why the hell are you here?" Jace asked.

"What?" I laughed. "You and Eva have your hands full as the only adults in the room."

"Sad, I know. I'm only twenty-five," Jace said. "These women are all over thirty—well, I guess Eva's twenty-nine. Anyhow, you sidled in like hot daddy vibes and you're clearly interested in Eva. Yet, you know nothing about her, and she's not given you any indication she's interested."

"Truthfully, I would have no idea how to read interest with Eva," I admitted.

Jace cackled. "Okay, fair."

The bartender arrived, obliging us to two beers, a scotch, and two bottles of champagne.

"I know she doesn't *only* date women," Jace said. "But she just broke up with one she was basically married to—and as long as I've been able to drive, she's only dated women."

I cleared my throat nervously. "Eva?"

"Yes, straight-cis man." Jace patted my back. "Eva is usually down with the ladies."

"Oh, shit, well... anyhow, you all are fun."

I wanted to crawl in a hole and die.

The bartender sent us back with a member of staff to bring the two $300 bottles of bubbly. We carried the other drinks. It felt like a procession—perhaps a march to my social death. I'd gotten so wound up just *seeing* Eva that I'd been silly all night with her. I *flirted* with this woman. David Delphine did *not* just *flirt!* He didn't have to. Women threw themselves at him!

I sat in the only place left—next to Eva—and handed her the scotch.

"I got it," I said.

She smiled and sipped. "Perfect. Thanks. Drinking champagne is *not* my idea of a good time."

"Oh, really?"

"Yes, really. You are still drinking beer?"

"Yup. Is that a knock?"

"Nope. I like the lack of pretension in a man brave enough to both wear that ridiculous watch and chase around a hen party."

"Ridiculous?"

"That watch is worth more than every car I've owned combined. You *want* people to notice it, don't you? If you didn't, you wouldn't wear it."

I examined my watch, supposing she was right. I never considered what it cost. I liked it. I bought it. To average people, that probably wasn't the case.

"What are you doing here, Davey the Mysterious?"

"I found a beautiful woman overwhelmed with herding cats

and decided to help in hopes I might even get a chance to kiss her by night's end, but Jace said that wasn't gonna happen."

"What? Are they going to beat you up?" Eva giggled.

I suspected Jace was all of 120 pounds soaking wet.

"No, they said… you probably weren't interested in people like me."

"Oh…" Her eyes fell to her lap. "Uh… it's not that I don't date men. I am just more *selective* with men. Because… well, they talk a big game, but they're all selfish."

"Selfish?" I scoffed.

"Yes. None of them can go down on a woman properly. They always blame you when they cannot get you off. Don't get me wrong, women can be shady, but straight men are by far the worst at gaslighting you about that."

I arched my brow. "Then maybe you've been sleeping with the wrong men? I haven't had many complaints."

Eva bit her lip. "Are you really coming onto me right now?"

"Are you going to give me a chance or… what?"

"You think your dick will cure me, right?"

"No. I don't mean that. I mean… I find you utterly intoxicating and I've been following you around like a lost puppy all night. I would do literally anything you asked if you let me try."

Her eyes grew wide.

"That's a new one."

"What?"

"No mention of a dick cure. You have my attention, kind stranger."

"My sister is bi. So, I'm aware you've probably heard that sort of thing a million times," I explained.

Eva relaxed. "You, sir, are not what I expected."

"So…"

Eva set her glass down, not dropping my gaze. "Tell me how bad you need me, then."

"Really, really bad," I said.

It killed me to plead. I did not beg. I did not chase, but this

woman had me in a trance. I couldn't put my finger on why I wanted her so much—more than anyone in years. I guessed it was her don't-give-a-fuck-ness and rare smiles that lit up a room. It was also her massive tits and sizable round ass. I wanted to have all of her. It killed me not to.

Eva kissed me, her mouth hungry for whatever it is I *might* provide. It was some sort of test, and I wasn't about to fail this exam. She gripped my shirt rough, pulling me closer in a very sexy, authoritative way. I'd never been with a woman so *demanding* and, yet, I wanted so much more than this. Her full lips and insistent tongue left my cock butting uncomfortably against my pants. Fuck, she was *hot*!

Eva pulled away sternly. "We should get away for a minute."

* * *

Eva

I never imagined myself at almost thirty pressed up against a men's room stall making out with a wealthy man too old for me. But as he played the sub in this moment, I gave over. I was horny, desperate for attention, and intrigued by his devotion to getting me off.

Davey kissed me deeply, plowing me into the stall divider. I moaned as his fingers made their way up my dress to my panties. It was what he *said* and how he *looked* that set me ablaze.

Pulling back, I let him ask, "What do you need, Eva? How can I serve you?"

Serve me? Damn! I was over the edge.

"Get me off. Use your hand to show me you're worth my time."

I didn't talk like this—not to anyone. I'd rarely been in control with my ex. She'd liked to manage the situation as the dominant one. Sometimes, I liked to lose myself in moments like this—to not have to do the work. However, a *man* asking me how he could get

me off was a novelty. Maybe if cybersecurity didn't work out, I could become a dominatrix?

Davey slid his finger over my clit, tormenting me. I threw my head back, banging against the metal divider. His eyes—trained on me—yearned for some sort of sign I liked this. I kissed him again, desperate to keep going. He read this as a green light. I greedily pressed his hand to my pussy with force. I needed this release.

"You want more?" He asked.

"I want you to get me off. You better fucking get me off," I growled.

"Yes ma'am," Davey said.

He freed my breast from my dress with one hand and adeptly ran his fingers over my nipple. With his other, he brought me closer to release, thrusting two fingers inside, then three as I panted harder. I expected a half-hearted attempt to find my G-spot, not this long-fingered adeptness. With each slow move in, he slowly hit my G-spot, making my legs quake. I shuddered. His palm and thumb slapped against my clit, adding to it.

It wasn't that a man never made me cum. It was that a man never made me cum hard like I was about to. It normally took ages to get me to this very point. I moaned louder, gripping his arm tight. I braced, my clit and G-spot now so swollen, I couldn't fight it. I felt a familiar fullness—one that usually took weeks for any partner—then came all over his hand.

My body shuddered, and I screamed. "Fuck! Yes! Oh, shit!"

I knew we were *not* in private and everyone around fucking hated us. I also knew that was the best orgasm I'd had in years. While a series of unfortunate events recently complicated my life, Davey reminded me I was still a sexual being for a hot minute.

"Did you just…" Davey stared at his hand. "Really?"

Is he actually angry right now?

"You've never made a woman squirt before?" I asked, annoyed.

"I have!" Davey protested, "but not like… this."

"Are you angry—"

"No, I'm… I'm surprised. You are fucking wild, Eva."

Someone banged the door.

"Calm the fuck down!" I shouted before gesturing to Davey, "Can you please hand me some toilet paper."

"Oh, yeah. Fuck! Sorry."

He was *rattled*. Had I just scarred this poor man with a healthy orgasm? Just when I was about to give up, he surprised me by almost lovingly working to mop up my wetness from between my legs. He wiped his hand and tossed it all.

"You good?" Davey asked.

"Great, thanks."

Another person banged the door. I left first, annoyed. Davey followed. One man in line whooped at him like he was a fucking God. Meanwhile, I felt all-powerful knowing I'd gotten the better shake, torturing him without returning the favor. I rode high on the ownership of my orgasm.

"What are we going to do?" I asked as we approached the others.

Callie leaned on Jace's shoulder, totally inebriated. The others were nowhere to be found. Jace shot me a look like *really?* I should have felt embarrassed, but why? Men celebrated Davey's ability to make me scream. I'd made him do that—I'd been in utter control.

"The others are dancing," Jace said. "This one needs to go back to the hotel and sleep it off."

"Do you want to stay to herd cats?" I asked.

"I can," Jace said.

I sensed they would rather stay with the annoying straight ladies than deal with Callie O'Malley puking.

"I can help," Davey said.

For once, I was grateful for a man riding in to save me—not that I needed saving, of course.

3. TURNED IN

Davey

Eva tucked Callie into the room she shared with three others. The fact that four women could share such a small room appalled me. Who did that? And where were they from? I figured they weren't from here. I also knew my chances of running Eva off to my place were slim. She'd not want to leave her friends.

"Okay," Eva whispered, finding me by the small entrance. "She's out, her head is elevated, and there is water by the bed."

"Are you turning in or—"

Eva shrugged. "What do you want to do? I feel bad because—"

I shook my head. "Don't feel bad. It may be too forward or even a long shot, but what if I got us a room? Or would that freak out your friends?"

"Ellie will not care as long as she can make sure I'm okay," Eva said. "We cannot fuck here—obviously. But I also need to be back for brunch at noon tomorrow."

"Well, I can get us a room here?" I offered.

"On such short notice? Are you crazy?"

"No."

"You're that desperate?" Eva giggled.

So desperate. I'd not get the image of her cumming all over my

hand out of my mind. It was mind-blowing. The way her eyes rolled back, her nostrils flared, and her legs quaked was a visual symphony. Coupled with screams and moans, I knew it was spankbank material for ages.

"I'll try to get a room," I said. "And… I don't suppose you have condoms?"

"Not a one," Eva sighed.

"I can grab some. Do you just want to wait until I come back here?"

"Text me the room number and I'll meet you," Eva said.

"I don't have your number."

She put her number in my phone and handed it back to me after texting herself.

ME

> Thank you for cumming on my hand.

She laughed. "Okay, well, I am departing. Send good vibes or whatever for getting a room."

It was all quiet at the front desk.

I approached the clerk, "I need a room—preferably a suite. Whatever you have, no worries about cost."

She helped me land a suite with late checkout and sent me on my clandestine pursuit with two keys. My next mission brought me to a 24-hour drugstore. I gleefully raced to the condom aisle, cursing myself for *not* restocking after my last happy night out. To my great dismay, the place was decimated.

"Damn bachelor party season," I groaned.

I'd been cursed. The only options were a regular-sized pack of a cheap brand. I knew they were going to fit too small, but what choice did I have? I knew I could at least get one on and suck it up. Maybe I'd even get a blowjob out of the deal? The possibilities were endless, right?

Hopeful and disregarding the too-small condoms, I planned to suck it up. Stepping onto the elevator, I texted Eva, who replied in an instant.

Boom!

I settled into the hotel room, got half naked, hoping I wasn't being presumptuous, and opened the condoms. It was on.

* * *

Eva

I knew I shouldn't go to a rich man's hotel room at 1 AM. So many things could go wrong, but I couldn't help myself. Tonight, I was Eva the Independent Woman. I was cosmopolitan and living it up in the city after years of boring hermitage. Tomorrow, I'd take the train back to Indiana and go back to my "normal" where there would be no more rich men with a sub kink willing to spend money just to have a chance at fucking me.

Davey didn't disappoint in the whole "spending money" way. He'd paid out a *very* handsome tab I couldn't afford in my unemployed breakup state—thank God. As I entered, I realized he dropped a couple grand on this huge hotel room. He stood from the bed where he sat and approached. The lighting here was better. For a moment, I wondered if I knew him. My thoughts faded as he kissed me. That was ridiculous. I barely knew anyone in the U.S. at this point—certainly not any rich men who grabbed hotel suites for hookups.

"Well, you really *were* desperate," I joked.

The way his tongue pressed into my mouth and how his stubble felt against my chin was somehow magical. He *yearned* for me. His stolen glances and worship of my body thus far emboldened me. I hadn't felt this good about my body in years.

"Take your boxers off," I said. "I want to see what I'm dealing with."

"Why should I if you're still in that dress?" Davey demanded.

"Get naked or I won't."

I knew it would please him. Davey stripped, tossing his boxers aside. The man was *hung*. He was by far the biggest guy I had ever even contemplated fucking. In fact, given my lack of recent experience with men, I worried it was a *problem*. Once more, I tossed doubt aside. This was new and new was okay.

As promised, I undressed, luxuriating as he looked me over like I was an absolute snack. I wondered if he saw my stretchmarks or knew about the war I'd fought earlier this year with my own body. It seemed doubtful as I moved closer. I kissed him and pumped his swollen shaft with my hand. I rolled my fingers over the head, enjoying how the precum felt between my fingers. He couldn't wait to have me.

"I want to sit on your face." I denied him a chance to play with my tits, owning the moment for my own pleasure.

"Yes, ma'am," Davey obliged with no hesitation.

He fell onto the bed, inviting me and not giving a flying fuck about the mess I'd made earlier. I never did this with a guy but was game to try. He gripped my hips as I lowered myself, then dug in like this was a mission. He sucked on my clit *too* hard.

"A little *less* aggressive," I winced.

"Oh, sorry," he murmured. "You taste so good I couldn't help myself."

Davey slowed, licking and sucking more gently.

"Oh, fuck! Good boy!" I moaned, slowly gyrating against his mouth.

That encouraged him. He gripped my ass, hands roving. This was *fun* for him, but I was the one about to cum again. I marveled at his desire to forgo *his* orgasm to please me. He may have been a rare bird, but right now, he was *my* rare bird. Davey wasn't magic, but he presented new possibilities.

"Oh, fuck me," I moaned louder. "God, that's so good!"

I knew he'd want me to say his name. And, after this effort, he deserved a little bit of thanks for his good deeds.

"Yes, Davey! Oh, fuck!"

I came hard and he took it like a champ, waiting for my come down before slapping my ass.

I giggled and rolled sideways, still reeling from my climax.

"Good? Or selfish?" Davey asked.

"So good. You are… really trying."

"Trying and succeeding."

"Uh-huh," I panted.

Davey rolled to face me.

"I want to watch you cum," Davey said. "I want to see your face light up and go wild again. Let me serve you."

Oh, fuck! He said *all* the right things. The man was good at this.

I didn't respond but let him kiss down my neck to my breasts. He licked my nipple torturously, again sending a shock through my body. I grabbed his cock suddenly interested in penetration and the satisfied feeling of pulsing around him. For the first time in ages, I'd have more than my trusty glass dildo, which now had stiff competition—pun intended.

"Want me on top?" I asked.

"Yes, ma'am," Davey agreed. "Whatever your heart desires."

He flipped on his back, reaching for a condom on the nightstand.

I watched him very slowly roll the thing on, then climbed atop him. I took in his girth and length. As I ground against him slowly, he filled me wonderfully.

"Good?" Davey asked.

"Amazing," I confirmed.

"Take all you want," Davey said. "You're in charge."

Did he sense the slight worry I had? Penetrative sex was vulnerable in a way oral or foreplay wasn't. Hands weren't cocks and toys were less threatening. Anytime I did this, I braced for impact; but my trust in Davey grew every time he checked in.

"Fuck, you feel so good."

"You're dripping," Davey moaned. "Fuck. Your pussy's perfect."

"Yeah?" I dug my nails into his chest as I found myself already headed for another orgasm.

"You're flushed. Are you about to cum again, Eva?"

"Yes," I gasped.

"You are so fucking good," Davey said. "You wanna cum for me, baby? Are you a good girl?"

We'd switched roles, but I didn't hate it.

"You think you can play daddy now?" I joked.

"I can play whatever you want."

"Then make me cum, daddy."

Part of it was cringe, part of it was so bad I loved it. As I got close, he bobbed me up and down on his cock, leaning into this power I surrendered in the moment. I threw my head back, screaming his name, and shuddering. I half expected him to cum, but he kept rolling his hips into me, suggesting he was still good for more.

He spanked me. "Good girl."

I grabbed his hand, playfully pinning it back. "You don't get to spank me."

His face showed worry.

"It's a game," I said. "You can spank me until I tell you it hurts. I like it."

"Oh, yes please," Davey played with my nipples. "I fucking love your tits. They're just beyond... but... I also like your ass. Can I take you from behind?"

"Like fuck my pussy, right?"

"Of course, yeah. Just your pussy. That's all," Davey promised, confused.

I didn't want to *have* to clarify, but I didn't want a "wrong hole" scenario like so many of my girlfriends complained about.

I pulled myself to the side, presenting my ass. I watched, mesmerized as he rolled the condom back further and slowly slid himself inside my wet, hungry pussy. It felt even better this way. Davey started slowly at first, gripping my ass and thrusting. With each pump, he gripped me harder, spanking me after a few thrusts. I turned, watching him enjoy how my ass jiggled. Like a kid on Christmas, he did it again, grinning wide.

PART I

BACHELORETTE

AUTHOR'S NOTE

This book is a love letter to where I grew up. Yes, I was a "Region Rat". My childhood experiences in Northwest Indiana informed my characterization of Eva, her family, and her town. I love that I get to bring its lakeshore, beautiful fields, and cute towns into this story.

Eva's experience and family dynamics are rough, but relatable. If I didn't admit it's a story I've lived in some smaller way, I'd be living a lie. That said, please note the following content expectations.

There may be some spoilers, so if that's a concern, don't read on.

Context Expectations

- Accidental pregnancy
- Open-door spice, swearing, dirty talk
- Mention of religious trauma/religious fundamentalist minor characters
- Discussions of bi erasure, but with characters who support the FMC in her identity (that especially includes the MMC)
- A short mention of past sexual trauma in Eva's past

however, were occupied. My mind ticked the faces off as though I'd been keeping a list of who I'd expected to meet. Witch, demon, demon, alchemist. It stunned me how broad my acquaintance list had become since I'd gotten away from Ravenglen.

"Welcome to d'Arcan, Hailon," Vassago greeted me, putting his hand across his chest and bowing.

"Thank you."

"I'm Rylan," the dark-haired brother said, a soft tilt to his mouth as he reached out to take my hand. He gave me a reassuring squeeze before releasing it. "Pleased to meet you."

"The pleasure is mine," I said, nerves kicking in as the lone newcomer to this enthusiastic group. "Thank you for having me."

"I'm Greta," said the woman behind the worktable, raising her gloved hand in a wave after setting down a pair of tongs and a flask with swirling shimmery silver liquid inside.

"Hello."

The gargoyle women traded greetings with everyone, and as I got my pack settled behind the nearest chair, a new woman with the energy of a hurricane flew into the room, arms full, what appeared to be an assistant right behind her.

"Welcome!" She was cheerful as she pumped my arm up and down once she'd set down her baskets. "I'm Grace. I run the kitchen here—"

"And everything else," Rylan grinned.

"If you need anything, you let me know."

"Thank you, Grace." Rylan smiled at her, and I could tell the appreciation between them was genuine.

"If you're hungry, you're in for a treat," Lovette said. "Grace is a gifted cook."

"I've been very fortunate where food is concerned lately," I said, marveling at the selection as the contents of the baskets were set on the long coffee table between the sofa and the lounge chairs.

Rylan scanned the table. He picked up a plate and selected several things, his expression very pleased as he handed it off to Calla, then went back for his own.

"Can you join us, Dragonfly? Or should I bring you something over there?" Vassago asked.

"I'm coming," Greta said, quickly stripping off her gloves and heavy apron. She brought over several small vials of the silver liquid, leaving them next to her cup.

My chest gave a hot thump, the bond reminding me it was still quite displeased with the distance between Seir and I.

"Please, help yourself, Hailon. We don't stand on much formality around here, particularly with family," Rylan said, gesturing widely with one hand. I met his eyes, golden like Seir's, and felt the sincerity. He'd meant to say that, to include me. I wondered how odd it really was for people you just met to embrace you as one of their own. "Grace will be terribly disappointed if you don't eat at least three times as much as you really care to. I'm afraid she's gotten a little too used to preparing enough to feed Magnus, not to mention our students." He must have seen something in my face, as he hastily added, "Classes are not in session just now. It's just us here, for the time being."

Imogen and Lovette had both enthusiastically joined in eating, so I followed their example.

"It is very nice to see you in person, I must say," Vassago said. "That little mirror doesn't do you justice."

"Thank you." My pulse sped up at the mention of the mirror. "Actually, we owe you an apology."

"You do?" He paused, food halfway to his mouth. "Whatever for?"

"The mirror. I'm afraid it's cracked."

He barked a low chuckle. "I knew it. However did he manage it this time?"

"He had it in his pocket. I'm not sure what happened."

Vassago frowned, and Rylan snorted in amusement. "Really?"

"Truly, it was either in his pocket, safely wrapped in one of our packs, or with me. It was fine when he taught me the words, and we spoke to you, obviously. The next time he got it out, it was cracked halfway through."

He shook his head and sighed. "I suppose I'll have to make you both another. He's got the worst luck with them, I swear it."

"We also agreed it would be wise to give you these." I pulled the strongbox out of my pack and opened it, retrieving the little vials and notebooks Dr. Lang had left behind.

Rylan's eyes met mine for a moment as he reviewed the labels, then flipped through the notes. Vassago did the same, both of their wives just as interested.

"I'll keep them somewhere safe," he said, the edge of a growl in his tone. "I'm very sorry for what you went through, Hailon."

"Thank you," I said, unsure what else could be said.

"This doctor ..." Vassago frowned, dropping the notebook he was looking at like it had burned him. "He's dead?"

"Yes." I envisioned Seir's sword piercing Dr. Lang's body.

"Good."

"If you don't mind, could I do some of my own testing on the samples?" Greta asked. "I wouldn't need all of what's here, just a little tiny bit. I want to see if I get the same results they did, if I can figure out what they thought they were collecting." Vassago patted her knee in a loving way. I could tell she was genuinely curious, but unlike them her intentions were not self-motivated.

"Of course."

"Thank you." She smiled and started picking up one vial at a time from the strongbox. Her hand stilled as she flipped over my mother's letter. Her eyes met mine.

"I was actually hoping you could help with that too."

Greta nodded and took out the letter, straightening the worn creases as she scanned the paper with her eyes. Her mouth tightened the further she read, and dread curled in my gut when she glanced at me several times before reading it again.

"It's ... Shall I just read it to you? We can go somewhere private, if you like."

My pulse sounded too loud in my ears. "Is it bad? Or overly personal?"

Greta shook her head. "No, not bad. Not even personal aside from you being the subject of it. There's no great revelations that I can tell, either. I'm sorry."

"It's alright. I don't mind."

She glanced around, Vassago's hand resting on her back in a gesture of support. Rylan dipped his chin at me encouragingly, a gentle lift to his lips. I'd always been independent. I'd never needed anyone else, not even Aunt Sal. But in that moment, I wanted Seir next to me more than anything in the world.

> *My darling Hailon,*
>
> *I hope one day you can forgive us for having to make such an impossible choice. Your life is infinitely more valuable than either of ours, and we cannot selfishly continue to risk the worst by keeping you with us, as much as it kills us both to send you away. Sal has promised to care for you, and I know she'll keep that promise. I know it will be difficult to see it, especially by the time you're able to read this letter, but we love you more than anything else in this world. We'll be back as soon as we can. Do not try to find us. Keep the little horse with you, it will always provide peace.*

Greta looked up. "It's signed with a sigil and a mark that means *snow* in fae. No names."

I nodded, slowly digesting what she'd read. "That last part, it's clever wording."

"Oh?" Rylan asked.

"Yes, this necklace was hidden inside of the horse." I reached into my pack and produced the two broken halves.

Vassago took them from me, both he and his brother curiously looking the little figure over.

"Why would they leave me a letter encoded in fae? I understand it would be meaningless to most if found, but there's nothing in there that had to be so secret."

Greta shook her head, empathy in her eyes. "I'm not sure, I'm sorry."

I reached up and touched the necklace, the hum still present, but not enough to be irritating. To break the heavy silence, Lovette and Imogen helped me explain what we'd discovered with the necklace and dagger, that each was some kind of amplifier for one of the powers.

"Ophelia thought perhaps they needed to be recalibrated to Hailon specifically," Lovette offered.

"Sounds logical." Rylan nodded.

"I have some work to do with the dagger; the grip is not well suited," Imogen said softly.

"And if you take off the necklace?" Vassago leaned forward, long white hair nearly brushing his thighs.

I glanced around nervously, every eye on me. The delicious fruit tart I'd eaten knotted in my stomach.

"Only for a moment," Rylan encouraged.

I lifted the pendant away from my skin, the hum disappearing. As they reached for their magic and found nothing, the group all exchanged glances. Rylan looked at his hands, perplexed. Vassago and Calla just frowned.

"That's a very strange feeling," Rylan muttered. "Thank you." The hum returned as I released the chain and the necklace touched my skin once again. Imogen described how the current inscription had been made and repeated the offer to find someone to make a duplicate. "I'm happy to help with the incantation," he offered. "What is that ring?"

My chest squeezed. "Seir said he's had that since shortly after he fell."

The brothers exchanged a look. "And it's with you because ...?" Rylan plucked it from the box between his thumb and forefinger. In his grasp, it truly did look quite small.

"He snuck it in there before I banished him. He tried to make me choose one when we first bonded. This one drew my attention most from the several he showed me, but I told him rings could wait."

Calla chirped a laugh.

"Sounds about right," Rylan said with a grin. "Have you put it on?"

"No."

"Shall we try?"

I hesitated as he held it out to me. "Is there something special about it?"

"Undoubtedly." His words were cryptic, but his expression told me whatever he thought might happen wasn't dangerous.

The band fit perfectly on my left ring finger and nowhere else. I flushed hot, cheeks burning as I settled it there.

"The hum is gone," I blurted, unable to disguise my relief.

"Hum?" Greta asked.

"The necklace hums when I wear it. It's low, a little annoying unless I'm trying to use my healing magic. Then it's very irritating, like bugs are crawling under my skin."

"May I see the necklace?"

"Take it off? But—"

"Just for a moment," he repeated, truly unbothered that without it I could be causing complete havoc anywhere my magic reached. "I need to see what I'm working with. We can be quick. And the dagger, as well."

I did as he asked, hopeful that whatever was outside this place and within the range of my null ability wasn't too negatively affected.

Imogen went to his side, their combined expertise assembling a plan of attack where the items were concerned. Vassago consulted as well, making suggestions that seemed mostly for aesthetic purposes before getting up to make us new mirrors. Lovette and Calla busied themselves by putting the remains of the food back in the baskets and taking all the dirty dishes down to the dining room.

A consensus reached about how to fix the obsidian items, I was given the necklace for the time being and put it back on as Calla and Lovette returned, talking animatedly. Hands gestured, bright laughs and unconstrained talk filled the room. The demon brothers were exchanging information about mirrors and stones and the best way to adjust an inscription on a polished rock that might be as old as time itself. Greta was examining the vials of her elixir, explaining to Imogen what she was looking for to ensure that it had cured properly.

It was chaos. Organized, beautiful chaos.

In that moment, I understood what Seir had meant about this family. My problems had been assumed as their own and were considered no less important than anything else they were already managing. They'd all considered my feelings at every step, and I knew to my bones would not hesitate to do what needed done, no matter what that might be.

I sat watching them interact around me, more grateful that I could express to have been given such a gift.

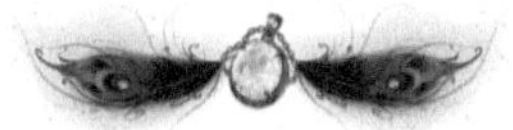

"COME BACK WHENEVER you like," Calla said, pulling me in for a hug as we prepared to leave the school grounds and walk back to Ophelia's hut. "I meant it when I said there's an apartment upstairs, ready for you. Just depends on when or if you'd like to stay here instead of with Ophelia."

I could only nod, the generous offer equal parts tempting and overwhelming.

"We'll coordinate a way to work on your stones so everything is a bit easier for you," Rylan assured me.

"Thank you all, very much." I was still half in disbelief that their immense kindness was genuine. I'd never had more than Merry to occasionally lean on, let alone a whole clan of people who had no ulterior motives behind their helpfulness.

The gargoyles chatted amongst themselves as we strolled, both understanding without a word having been shared that I needed some time to process.

Night in Revalia evoked memories of Ravenglen by scent alone. The smell of cooking onions and spices floated out of apartment windows and hung on the air, florists peddling their wares from carts down the main streets during the rush to get home adding a layer to the scent.

"That's the library," Lovette gestured. "Calla loves to visit. Do you like to read?"

"Yes, well enough. We didn't have many options for books where I'm from, but I always enjoy a good story. I read the few we had in the house cover to cover many times."

Lovette nodded in agreement, curls bouncing. "My medicinal guides get the most use, but there are several storybook compilations that got read so much the bindings gave up between us when we were children."

We curved around the city, very near to what they told me were the magical council buildings, and Lovette tsked as she spotted her father. He was talking to a group of several men.

"Looks like the meeting didn't go very well," Lovette commented, taking in his tense body language.

"I'd be unhappy, too, if I had to go to those boring debriefings." Imogen's face scrunched in distaste. "I'll bet Gaius is thankful to miss them when he's away."

Lovette nodded. "He is. Most things about his post are frustrating, but that's one he takes with great joy." She looked at me, giving a bright smile. "Gaius is my mate."

"Are you all mated? I thought it was a very rare thing, but it seems there are quite a few of you."

"Not all," Lovette said, and between the quirk in her mouth and the tightness of Imogen's, I could tell she was teasing her sister. "Though there does seem to be quite an increase in mated pairs around these parts lately."

I scanned the men standing with Magnus, stopping when I got to the third one. My breath left my lungs as though I'd been punched. The sisters took several steps before they realized I wasn't with them.

"Hailon? Everything okay?" Lovette asked, following my gaze.

"He's the last one," I said, stuck on the thought running through my mind. I honestly couldn't believe he looked so peaceful, just going about his business as though he wasn't living a villainous life.

"Last one?" Imogen's serious, frowning face was shockingly intimidating, especially when she crossed her arms.

I pointed. "The man in the black coat, the one with the mustache. He was part of the group that experimented on me while I was held captive in Olinbourg. He's the last of them to survive."

"Oh." Imogen's surprise melted into something like excitement. "*Oh.* That's Brookes. I've never liked him. Lovette?"

"Yep, leave it to me." Lovette darted off, a smile on her face as she sprinted over and approached the group. She pulled her father to the side, very pointedly not looking our way as she spoke to him. After she'd said her fill, she waved to the group, and the five men eyed her with distaste before going back to their conversation with her father.

She made brief eye contact with Imogen, then disappeared around a corner only to appear in the sky above us, flying in the direction from which we came.

Imogen moved us into the semi-dark of an alleyway. "We must be patient and wait," she said in response to my unspoken question, though she'd pulled a blade from her belt and was twisting the tip on her finger.

Even though I was as tense watching them as I could ever remember being, a sense of relief washed over me. It would be over soon, the wondering if someone was still following, watching. If I was going to be targeted again. There would be nobody left after this.

Then, I heard wings.

CHAPTER 44
SEIR

THE PORTAL DUMPED me out on the grounds of d'Arcan, and my whole body thrummed with relief.

My beautiful mate was nearby, I could feel it.

I sprinted for the doors of the main building, only to have them fly open as I approached.

Immediately my instincts were triggered. "What's wrong?"

Lovette's face was determined but urgent, and my brothers were both in a hurry and armed, their wives lingering in the doorway not far behind.

"Your timing is impeccable, brother," Vassago said, clasping my hand and pulling me in for a hug. "Come, we're meeting up with Magnus. It seems your lovely Hailon has recognized one of the stone kin councilmen."

"We'll be prepared when you get back. Straight to the cellar, if you please," Calla said.

Rylan surged forward and kissed her soundly. "Of course, Little Owl. We wouldn't want to make a mess elsewhere."

My heart jumped in my chest, and I released my wings out of habit. "Oh. I suppose that won't work. Are we running then?"

Rylan smiled and let out his wings. He had feathers on the outside, the same bat-like flesh on the inside as mine. "You've missed a few things since you were gone."

"Oh! Wonderful." I flapped, hovering a bit, then a bit more.

"It's barely dusk," Vassago reasoned, his own feathered wings spread out wide, the white a stark contrast to Rylan's black. "Stay to the rooflines."

Then he was airborne, Rylan just behind, as I scrambled after them. I was going to need a quick catch-up very soon about how this was possible, but I was glad to be in the sky.

I followed my brothers to the council building on the interior of Revalia. We landed a street away and walked the rest, my eyes constantly scanning for the woman I knew had to be right nearby somewhere.

Magnus boomed with a friendly greeting when he saw us, and the man he was talking to spun, clearly nervous from the way his eyes widened, and shifted his stance.

"What's this about then, archmage?" the councilman blustered at Rylan. "What business is it of a mage what the stone kin are doing?"

Rylan tilted his head to the side. "Are we not allies? We've collaborated on several things, Brookes. I'm offended you think so little of our friendship."

"Of course, we're allies. But what's the meaning of this? Why are there so many of you? I feel very—" The man looked up, and his whole demeanor changed. "*You*." A myriad of emotions raced across his smug face, but anger was most prominent.

I turned and found his gaze locked on my lovely mate. My heart beat in rapid time as I drank her in.

"Don't look at her," I growled, dagger point indenting the skin at the man's throat. "Don't you dare."

"What's the meaning of this, Magnus?" he demanded, shifting his attention from Hailon to the large stone kin.

Magnus only chuckled. "Let's go, Brookes. I'm afraid my kin have some questions for you. It's likely to be rather uncomfortable."

"Kin? You're calling the demons *kin*?"

"Indeed." Magus smirked, unmoved by the horror on the councilman's face at such a suggestion.

Brookes yelled and complained, but his voice was drowned out by the heavy sound of wings being deployed and bodies taking flight as they held him firmly between them. Brookes let his own wings out, and there was a struggle as he tried to get away, but Vassago and Rylan had too good of a grip on him, and Magnus was right there with them.

I dashed over to Hailon, sweeping her into my arms before taking flight myself. She yelped, one hand pressing a necklace into the skin below her collarbone. The other locked around my neck, her legs tight around my waist as the city street dropped out from under us. I lifted my tail as well, lashing it around her hips.

"I've wanted to do this with you for ages, Moonflower. This is what I tried to do, that very first night, in fact, when my wings failed me." I smiled, wind rushing over my body as I kissed her like she was the air I needed to survive. Her sweet taste filled my mouth, my hands full of her but still craving more.

I could tell it wasn't just being airborne that left her lightheaded when she finally pulled away. "You're really back?" she asked.

"Yes." I squeezed her closer. "I told you I would come."

"I knew you would, I just worried it would take more time."

"I didn't have any to waste. I hated being away from you." Collegium d'Arcan came into view very quickly, and I braced for impact as we dropped toward the ground. I could see the other members of our group already down, several hands hanging on to the councilman as they led him into the building. "Everything will be fine," I assured her, and we landed with a jolt.

Hailon didn't hesitate to follow everyone into the school. She detoured into Vassago's classroom, then rejoined me in the hall so we could go down the stairs into the cellar.

"What is the meaning of this? Magnus! I'll be filing formal charges against you and this lot of—"

Hailon had pushed her way between my brothers, and with her fancy little blade, shut the councilman up by punching it through the soft place right between his collarbone and shoulder.

"You *bitch*," he snarled, trying to back away from her. Unfortunately for him, the blade was still imbedded, so she stepped right along with him.

"That's unkind," she said softly, twisting the blade, making him scream. "I just wanted to take a *sample*, after all."

My brothers, their wives, and the gargoyles all looked to me, quietly stunned. I shrugged, a wide, proud smile on my mouth.

"A perfect match, then," Vassago muttered. "Well done."

The stout man reached out and snatched at her hair. She cried out, and I pushed forward, stopping him before he could get even a single step away from the cell my brothers had opened for him. I wrapped my tail wrapped around his ankle, and once Hailon had dislodged his fingers from her hair, I gave a tug, and he went face-first into the packed dirt floor with a satisfying *thud*.

"Are you alright?" I asked.

She was rubbing her scalp with the heel of her hand, a scowl powerful enough to melt flesh from bone on her face. "I'm fine." A clump of mixed dark and light strands floated toward the floor when she pulled her hand away.

My fury manifested in a growl, my scalp tingling as my horns burst out through my hair. My teeth grew even sharper in my mouth, and I fought my wings coming forth. There really wasn't space for that down here. I heard my brothers muttering vaguely calming things, but nobody made any attempt to stop either of us.

He pushed himself up on his forearms, turned on his side, then sat up on his knees. He was out of shape and had enjoyed his bureaucratic position and good food for far too many years. "Please," he raised his hands. His begging fueled my rage an unreasonable amount. "Please!"

"*Please?* You *dare* beg for mercy? After you touched her in such a way just now? After all you've done? There's *none of that here.*" He focused on my eyes and reared back, clearly afraid of what he saw in the glowing red there. I flicked my wrist, sending my smallest blade into the man's meaty midsection.

"Seir." Hailon stepped between us as he howled, and I bowed to her authority, forcing my rage to stand down if only for a moment. She turned to the councilman. "What you did to me? That's not where you started being a terrible person. You all were far too comfortable with what you were doing for that to be true. There's a full complement of witnesses here. Perhaps you should confess your misdeeds so you can truly be held accountable."

My chest puffed proudly. I'd never been more in love with her. "You heard the lady." I gripped his collar, pulling him roughly to his feet only to fling him down into the straight-backed chair inside the cell. I yanked out my blade, and Hailon retrieved hers, not a single effort made to ease the pain or flow of blood.

This man wasn't likely to survive the night, and he was going to suffer the entire time as he made his way out. I could see Rylan's electricity around his hands, Calla's green earth magic when she exhaled. Vassago's teeth looked quite a lot like mine, and Magnus looked all too pleased to be a part of the goings-on, as did his daughters. Greta stood off to the side, frowning at the man as though thoroughly disappointed in him.

He would atone for grabbing at Hailon like that, for sitting by while she was abused, after ordering it done. This was her opportunity to make him pay, to make at least one of them die slower, as she'd said she wanted that night. He was going to arm us with everything we could possibly want to know about him, his merry little band of miscreants, and what they hoped to accomplish by taking pieces of my mate to experiment on.

"What do you say we start at the beginning?" Rylan suggested, stepping into the cell with us.

"I don't have to tell you anything." The councilman was putting up a good front, being stoic.

"That's true enough," my brother nodded.

Hailon pulled the little spell book from her pocket. "I suppose I should thank you for this."

The councilman made a grab for it, but she held it out of his reach and gave it to Rylan. "So you're a thief as well as a—"

My fist flew out, a satisfying crunch under my knuckles as his nose gave way. He groaned, hands flying to the new injury.

"Tsk." Vassago shook his head. "That's just foolish."

"Whose was this?" Hailon asked, holding up the obsidian dagger.

"Go to hell," he grumbled.

"Do you really believe that to be a threat in a room with three demons?" I asked. "I was there earlier today."

His eyes snapped up and he glanced between us. I could see the moment he fully understood who he was trapped in a cellar with.

"What were you planning to use a demon for, anyway?" I asked. He only scoffed, but after thinking it over all this time, I thought I'd finally figured it out. I started to laugh. "You thought you were going to summon a demon, and they would just take up the task of making your stolen power potions because you *controlled* them? Perhaps they'd be in charge of handing the vials out after you sold them and took the profit, all while lending you their magic to accomplish it in the first place?" My brothers also snorted at the idea, but the councilman's eyes rounded like I'd guessed correctly. "They would have laughed in your face."

Hailon leaned close, sinking the tip of the obsidian blade into his thigh as he tried to bat her away. "Whose blade was this?"

"Nobody's," he snarled. "It came out of the archives, the same as that useless little book."

"You're a disgrace," Magnus growled. "How was it catalogued?"

"I'm not a fool. It wasn't. The previous owner was unknown."

Hailon seemed disappointed in that answer but removed the blade and stepped back. She seemed to have gone to that faraway place again. It worried me.

Rylan moved in to continue asking questions, and I pulled Hailon off to the side. "You alright, Moonflower?"

"I feel too calm," she said. "I'm so angry, but I can't really muster the energy anymore. He's nothing. He held so much power over me before, but that's done, isn't it?"

I held her face between my hands, looking down into her eyes. "Yes. They won't let him die without finding out every last detail. We can leave. Right now, if you want."

She shook her head. "I want to stay. For now."

We stepped out of the cell, allowing Magnus and Rylan their turn at interrogation. We listened as the councilman began to slowly reveal nearly a century's worth of plots, schemes, and shady deals.

Greta had been quiet as she watched Magnus and Rylan work in tandem, Vassago a quick third when they needed a hand at encouraging the man to keep talking. But suddenly her hand was shaking as she pointed at him.

"Ask him about my mother."

"Little niece?" Magnus turned, a frown on his mouth.

"You're the man in the suit. The one in the woods. She trusted you, and then I never saw her again."

The councilman grunted as Magnus turned his way, fire in his eyes. "You'll never find any of them."

"Any of who?" Hailon asked, interest piqued.

"They were all going against express council orders. I took care of it. All of it. All of *them*. You shouldn't even *exist*." His words were directed at Greta, but Hailon also seemed bothered. Calla, too, stepped forward.

"You're the reason our parents are missing," Calla said coldly, green plumes of smoke billowing around her.

"Someone had to do the hard part. Passing regulations and making rules only goes so far. I told Hugo and Auggie—"

Magnus roared, his hand around the councilman's throat. "Rotten to the core, the entire cursed council! You will tell me what you've done with my sister!" He started making several demands of Brookes, none of which he could comply with given the meaty fist around his neck.

Hailon stepped away from me, boldly walking right up to the councilman, who sneered at her. "Were you going to try to weaponize my healing power? Or was it another ability you wanted to sell?"

"It doesn't matter, does it? You were nothing more than a means to an end. A lucky find from a useless town."

I shook my head at the foolish man. Hailon pulled the obsidian dagger from her belt and approached him. Magnus backed away. Nobody spoke or moved to stop her as she took what she wanted from him.

I recognized the revenge in her strokes. She cut sections of hair, bits of skin, nails. She used the handle to knock out a tooth. When she was finished, she handed the weapon to Imogen.

"I'd like to go now," she said, walking past me and up the stairs to the main floor.

"Third floor, second on the right." Calla pressed a key in my hand, and I dashed after Hailon, leaving the rest of them there to deal with the councilman as they wished.

CHAPTER 45
SEIR

I WAS WOUND TIGHT as I closed the door and locked it behind us, caging her against it.

"Are you alright?" I asked, looking down into her lovely face.

She nodded slowly. "I'm fine. Better now, I think the energy has settled. Don't let the necklace come off my skin though, it's how you can all use your powers near me."

I nodded my understanding, then leaned down, resting my forehead against hers. "You have blood on your face," I said, close enough to smell the iron in it.

"So do you," she countered.

"I was worried about you."

"And I about you."

"You're wearing the ring." My heart thudded rapidly against my ribs as I picked up her hand, admiring how it looked on her finger. I knew what a ring meant in human customs, knew what offering one to her and hiding the one she'd been drawn to in the strongbox implied. I'd lost my breath for a moment when I first saw she was wearing it.

I pulled back, gazing down into her incredible eyes. They were wide and round, her rapid breathing betraying the same lust my body had been pulsing with since she'd begun releasing her rage.

"Yes. It fits. And it helps."

"You've messed up your clothes again," I said low, reaching my hands under her tunic, pulling it up and over her head, tossing it on the floor.

"So have you," she repeated, copying my actions.

"You are a wild creature, Hailon. Suited for violence. A goddess of vengeance. You wield a dagger as well as I do. Better. I love seeing one in your hand, particularly mine. You are my perfect mate. I adore you." Every time I stopped speaking, I kissed a new spot down her neck, along her collarbone. "I've been very, very good, beloved, and I am in awe of your beauty. Is this something you want right now? May I have you?"

"You'd better," she breathed.

I dropped to my knees with a growl, hardly able to focus through the haze that had fallen over me. I tugged at the waist of her trousers, dropping them off her hips and to the floor. She stepped out of them, resting one foot on my shoulder. I traced my hand up her leg, noticing the small trembles her muscles gave, the flush to her cheeks, the gasps she made when I replaced my hand with my tongue.

I buried my face between her thighs, thriving on the way she said my name when I moved my mouth in just the right way. Her eyes never left mine, her gaze fierce as I consumed her. The telltale pulses of her arousal followed quickly on the heels of me pressing two fingers into her wet heat. I suckled the tight bundle of nerves, teasing it gently with my teeth, her hips pushing toward me in response. She moaned, threading her fingers through my hair.

"Horns," she gasped, eyes slipping closed.

I grinned and released them, as she asked. Her hands wrapped solidly around the sensitive appendages once they were out, tingling under her firm grip and sending a throb directly to my cock.

She directed me where she needed me most using them as her guides, her foot simultaneously pushing me away and dragging me closer as her arousal surrounded me. She came roughly and with a shout, pulsing around my fingers, but I kept on. I didn't stop until she begged.

"Seir, *please*. I need you."

I understood. Because I needed her more than I needed my next breath.

She slid limply down the door, and I grabbed her against me, stepping out of my pants as I crossed the room toward the bed. Her eyes were hazy as she looked up at me, her cheeks flushed and the scent of her filling my nose.

"Okay, Moonflower?"

Hailon nodded enthusiastically, reaching for me, but I was still too far back. I leaned over her, pinning her hands above her head with one hand. She arched and wriggled, trying to take what she wanted.

"I love you greedy, Hailon." I pushed forward, filling her up completely. Both of us inhaled at the sensation. I hoped it would always be like this, always feel this way between us. "Fuck, I've missed you."

I leaned down to kiss her as I started to move my hips, her tiny little moans sending shivers down my spine. Her legs tightened around me as I gave in to the instinctual motion, my tail between us stroking her nub, one hand lifting her hip so I could get even deeper.

Her thighs began to tremble, and I sucked air through my nose to try to resist the impending climax chasing down my spine. It was useless though, because those brilliant eyes were fixed on mine again as she gasped and shuddered, and I was powerless not to fall into the abyss with her. Hailon's body clamped down on me, my rhythm stilted as thought became impossible. I plunged in as far as I could go, trying to become one entity with my mate as my release powered through my body.

Panting, I sagged over the top of her and claimed her mouth again, gently winding my tongue around hers, seeking, tasting. I let go of her wrists and slid my hands between her back and the sheet, wrapping my arms around her, making us an inseparable tangle of limbs.

I traced along the tiny raised dots of her scars, sucking lightly along the ridge of her shoulder.

"Are you tired, beloved?"

"No. I'm not tired."

"Good."

I lifted her with me as I stood and took us to the bath. I ran the water extra hot and took my time washing us both, just so I could touch as much of her as possible.

When we finally made it into bed, I tucked myself behind her, my tail wound firmly around her ankle, and her hair tickling my face.

I'd never slept better.

HAILON AND I entered the dining room the next morning to find the round table already well occupied.

"Good morning!" Grace greeted us, her hands full of plates as she crossed from the kitchen to the table. "I'll be right back, okay?"

"Please, don't go to any trouble—" Hailon started, but Grace was faster.

"Coffee is in the big decanter, tea in the pot. I'll be right back with some plates."

"Thank you!"

"It's really quite pointless to argue with her," Rylan smiled. "She's very dedicated and will do what she thinks is right regardless. Pull up some chairs, Seir."

Everyone made space for us, and I pulled over two extra seats.

"We're going to need a bigger family table," Calla said, and I could see the moment her smile went a little extra wide and her eyes started to shimmer. "Isn't that wonderful?"

"I do love seeing everyone's faces," Vassago agreed. "Even that one." He gestured to me with a grin.

"Did we miss anything good after we left?" I asked, Grace dropping a plate under my hands as if by magic.

Hailon was reserved but watchful, sipping at her coffee and politely nodding.

Magnus reached across the table, covering Hailon's hand with his for a brief moment. "We owe you many thanks, Hailon." Her head popped up. "With some encouragement, Brookes told us a great number of truly disturbing things. We may be able to find many lost souls thanks to you."

"I didn't really do anything," she protested.

"That's not true at all." He shook his head. "You helped expose a man who spent nearly a century manipulating his position, exploiting his power. Thank you."

She nodded softly, a blush in her cheeks. I smiled back proudly, meeting my brothers' eyes, silently asking their thoughts on my mate. Both nodded gently.

"We'll get started on your necklace immediately," Rylan told her. "Imogen returned to the conclave last night and said she planned to work on the dagger. I do think it's safest for you under more powerful warding for the time being." He frowned. "Please don't misunderstand, you are more than welcome here, but until we thoroughly vet the members of both councils, I think it's safer for you somewhere your power can't be discovered."

"Wards won't be a problem," I volunteered, glancing up to find Magnus nodding. He had been integral in helping move along my plans, and I was very grateful.

Hailon scooted some of the eggs around her plate. "I can spend time at Ophelia's. Her invitation was open."

Grace returned and took a chair next to Magnus. He dipped down to kiss her temple, and she snuck a sausage off his plate.

Greta set a vial of shimmery silver liquid in front of herself, then handed one each to Grace, Calla, and Hailon.

"What's this?" I asked.

"Elixir of Life," she said in a hushed tone.

"What does it do?" Hailon asked.

"This specific formula will match one's lifespan to that of their mate."

We all quietly absorbed that, my brothers and I looking from one to the other and back to the women we loved.

Grace was the first to speak. "So, if I take it, as a plain old human, what happens to me?"

Greta shrugged. "I'm not sure. Not completely. But I would assume that your human lifespan would be extended by at least several decades, if not centuries. It's calibrated on both demon and stone kin blood, so it should be a significant extension either way. I suspect it will slow your aging, but not make you any less ... fragile ... than your body is naturally. If nothing else, it will give me plenty of time to figure out an alternative if it's not quite what I expect it to be."

"I ..." She looked from the vial to Magnus. "I have to think about this."

Magnus patted her hand, adoration in his gaze. "It's not a small decision. Take your time. I'm not going anywhere."

Meanwhile, Calla had opened hers and, after staring at it a moment, then sniffing it, drank it down. She turned to give Rylan a kiss, a broad smile on both of their faces. Greta eyed Vassago and did as Calla had done—bottoms up, no hesitation.

"One less thing to worry about," Calla said with a smile.

"I know this is all very new, and quite a lot to take in," Greta said to Hailon. "But that's yours. Take it with you. It won't spoil."

"Thank you," Hailon said, one of her hands a claw as it dug into my thigh. My strong, dangerous Moonflower was emotional.

Then breakfast continued as normal—eating, drinking. Talk of torture. Comparing weapons and discussing next steps for righting the wrongs done to our kin.

I loved these people, especially the incredible little creature beside me. And I couldn't wait to start my forever with her.

CHAPTER 46
HAILON

GRETA VERY NEARLY bowled me over when we walked into Vassago's classroom a bit later.

"I found something! In your letter. I knew something about it seemed off."

"Oh? What is it?"

"Watch." She waved the parchment over the flame of a candle, and different ink markings appeared under the letter, like they were somehow between the layers of the parchment.

"What does it say?"

"I think you should sit."

That made me a little nervous, but Seir took me over to the sofa, sitting so close beside me I was almost in his lap.

"I don't know exactly what will happen if I speak it all out loud." Greta frowned. "But this says 'To open your mind,' and I'm afraid that's exactly what it's going to do. Except I don't know what that means."

"Go ahead," I encouraged. "Please, if it helps me control my powers, I want that." Seir squeezed my hand and everyone in the room settled down. I was quickly realizing they all moved as a unit when they were here. I didn't mind it like I thought I would.

Greta listed off three words, watching my face with each one. Seir, too, was staring.

"Keep going." I felt a pressure behind my left eye, like had happened with my right when I got angry with Sal.

"Your other eye is shifting now, too, Moonflower. It's very strange to see."

With every new word, the pressure increased. Frustration rose in my blood, too, and anger. Rage at Sal, that she'd never sought out answers for me, that she'd held onto the letter all these years without being able to read it. That she'd blamed me, instead of trying to find another way. That I'd had tools, a letter from my parents, possibly help to understand myself, but she'd never shared it.

"Now both at the same time. Are you alright?" Seir's tone was stressed.

"Fine. I can't feel it."

By the time Greta got to the seventh word, I felt like my skull was too full, like the light was painfully bright.

"Two more," she said, tone apologetic.

"I'm okay."

Seir's chest rumbled with a concerned growl, and I felt the presence of the others around me.

When Greta said the final word, everything disappeared. My head felt fine again, but I was in that strange nowhere place I went when I was deep in a healing trance.

I could see my healing magic, the cup now a well. The well was deep and wide, only a tiny percentage full. I knew there was more than enough in it to heal Seir again or do a day's worth of work like I had in Olinbourg, without it running out.

My fingers moved, slowly, lifting the necklace away from my chest. The well shrank to a cup again. I truly understood then what Ophelia meant about it being an amplifier. Faint trickles of magic started to flow in. Yellowish orange, blue. Green and gold. I dropped the necklace, realizing I was filling the well from the people around me. Seir, Greta, Calla, and Rylan if I had to guess. The colors disappeared once the stone was settled against my skin.

I wanted to keep that terrible power locked down, to not siphon by accident. I focused on that, visualizing a metal plate over the top of the well. Then I lifted the necklace again. No colors appeared. I mentally cheered, gaining confidence in this new awareness.

Lingering in the nowhere space, I practiced balancing the magic against the need, trying to gain a full understanding as the noise around me increased.

Slowly I came back to myself, Seir's grip on my hand intense as my eyes fluttered open. I frowned, blinking against the bright room.

"There you are." Seir visibly sagged and pressed his forehead to mine before giving me a quick, gentle kiss. "That was terrifying, beloved. Don't do that again."

"Now you know how I felt when you passed out in the ruins." I looked over at Greta, the letter gripped tightly between her hands. "I'm fine. I promise. That did exactly what it was supposed to do. Thank you."

Seir relaxed his grip, and everyone else seemed to take a breath. "Your mind is open? Your eyes are back to normal now."

"Very. I can feel both powers, not just my healing ability."

"Oh good! You're okay?" Greta was clearly very concerned that she'd broken me.

"Fine, I promise. Would you mind keeping that somewhere safe for me? Just in case."

"Of course." She nodded in relief and scurried over to her worktable after giving me a brief one-armed hug.

The pressure in my head was gone, but I could feel a new presence around me. I realized it was magic. *All* magic. From the ambient magic in the earth to the specific types in the people in the room with me. To my relief, I also had the ability to tell my power *no, don't take that*. It was a strange new subconscious negotiation with everything around me that I'd need time to adjust to.

"Can I take the necklace?" Rylan asked. I braced but removed it. Necklace held by the chain in one hand, he summoned his electricity in the other. Relief washed over me. "Well done." He shifted his weight, rubbing his chin with a thoughtful finger. "I've been thinking about your hair, as well, Hailon. I agree with Ophelia's theory, that it was the mate bond waking up." He gestured with his hands. "New magic in the mix inside you. Seir, did you happen to be exposed to her blood during the summons?"

Seir nodded. "Yes. Her original offering and then a bit more when I came back after the circle was broken."

Rylan nodded slowly. "I think perhaps that's the catalyst. It helped you acclimate to her nulling a little bit and pushed the mate bond along. Started to mix the magic between you. Hailon's hair just happened to become the outward evidence of those changes."

I sat there several long moments, staring off into space as I puzzled through that new theory, and what had happened.

"What are you thinking about?" Seir asked.

"When I got angry at Sal, something changed."

"Yes, and it made your eye start shifting."

"I think that was a new side of the healing power. I think that's why she looked older after I grabbed her when I was mad."

"Like anti-healing?" Calla asked. "You were taking her health?"

"Yes, like that."

"That's another way to nullify," Rylan nodded.

"I don't want to use it that way." I frowned. "I don't want to feed off of your magic, or the town."

"You won't." Seir's confidence was far more than I could ever muster. "You won't, Hailon. You can control it."

"And if I can't?" Ravenglen invaded my mind, all the ugly, the hatred.

"You will. You have the necklace and the dagger."

"And us," Calla said, dropping a quick squeeze on my shoulder as she walked by. "We're not afraid of you, Hailon. We've seen far worse. Most of us have *been* far worse."

There was not a single face in the room that disagreed with her. I found myself overwhelmed once again.

Vassago smiled at his sister-in-law and gave a polite little bow, a smile playing on his mouth. "Welcome to the family, Hailon."

I SPENT THE next several days traveling from d'Arcan to Ophelia's hut and back again so I could be safely behind wards while Rylan and Imogen tinkered with my obsidian objects. Luckily, Ophelia seemed to enjoy our time together as much as I did.

Seir always traveled with me, though he didn't stay, and for all the warnings about her, she was hardly scary. Besides, I was pretty sure Ophelia found Seir as amusing as the rest of us did and looked forward to his visits.

Since having my mind opened, I'd been able, though in varying degrees, to manage that side at will. Ophelia was dedicated in helping me hone that skill, and while exhausting, after a few days with her as an instructor, I was pretty confident in my newfound ability.

"Take my shifting power," she ordered.

"What? We've never done specific things like that before, nor have we used you as a subject, Ophelia. I'm not sure—"

"You'll be fine. Take it. I never use it anymore anyway, what's the worst that could happen?"

I could think of plenty of things, honestly, but I didn't argue. I had been told that disobedience was the quickest way to get the ancient gargoyle to anger, so I did as she asked.

Going to the silent place in my mind, I directed it to pull that ability from her, but not to consume it. I'd realized as we practiced that I could be that specific with my powers, which was a pleasant surprise. I could borrow magic and hold it somewhere above the well instead of siphoning it directly into my healing well. I didn't fully understand all the mechanics yet, but I felt like I was getting closer all the time.

"I've taken it," I said.

She closed her eyes and tried to shift. "Good. Now give it back." I requested her power be given back, and her lavender magic obliged.

Ophelia watched me, a playful smirk appearing as she grew half again her normal size, with the same greenish-gray stone skin Lovette had gotten in her other form.

"Nicely done, you," she said after shifting back again. "Shall we celebrate with some tea?"

The woman adored her whiskey, that was for certain.

When Seir came that afternoon to retrieve me, he could tell that we were in a far better mood than we had been in at the beginning of our training.

"I think she's ready, young man." Ophelia raised her teacup to him, as he bit into a slice of her freshly baked bread drizzled with butter and honey.

"Truly?" he asked, and Ophelia nodded. It was like they'd had conversations about me, without me, and were giving me marks while ignoring that I was in the room. "Do you think she can—"

"I'd almost guarantee it."

"Excuse me?" I interrupted. "What are we talking about?"

"Portals." Seir beamed.

"Take the necklace as backup, but I think her control is plenty good enough."

"Portals?"

"Yes, Moonflower. I have something to show you."

Ophelia sent us on our way with an open invitation to return and my gratitude. It felt a bit like a dismissal, but I understood that for a solitary creature, several days in a row of prolonged company visiting was likely far too much and cause for some hibernation.

When we got back to d'Arcan, the classroom was full to bursting, everyone I'd met present at once except Magnus. He'd been taking long shifts at the council building, investigating all the things Brookes had been doing.

"How did it go?" Calla asked.

"She had me steal her shifting ability and then give it back," I reported, still a bit stunned that I'd done such a thing.

"She did?" Imogen asked, barking a laugh.

"Insisted."

Lovette chuckled as well. "Then she was confident you'd be fine."

Rylan came over, necklace dangling from his fingers. "I think you'll find this much more comfortable."

"Thank you." I took off my ring and tested it out, the hum barely noticeable, but the well very easily accessed. "Yes, that's much better, thank you." I took it off again, handing it to Seir. He placed it in the little velvet-lined jewelry box I'd brought with me from Ravenglen.

"This too," Imogen came forward, pride in her eyes as she presented me with a finely worked leather sheath. I removed the clasp to find my knife handle sticking out.

"I thought ..." My words faded as I pulled the obsidian dagger out, not my little herb knife. She'd fitted my knife handle onto the obsidian blade, so I could have the best of both. It was perfectly balanced and felt as natural as breathing in my hand. "Oh, Imogen. Thank you, it's perfect."

She beamed. "You're welcome."

"Well, if we're giving gifts, here are these as well." Vassago gave Seir and I each a small scrying mirror. "Don't—"

"Break it. I know." Seir bowed his head, a blush on his cheeks.

"Why does it feel like we're leaving?" I asked, looking around the room.

"I told you, I have something to show you. We can come right back if it's not to your liking."

"Any time. Always," Rylan said. "Your apartment will remain yours until you tell us otherwise."

"But I think you will. Like it." Seir was practically vibrating with excitement as he tugged me to my feet.

"Alright."

I shared a quick goodbye with everyone, but it felt strange, leaving right that moment. They'd all done such kind things for me, but also seemed to understand and even encourage Seir to take me away. It dawned on me slowly that it was likely the same as with Ophelia, and they knew more than I did about what was happening.

Out on the campus grounds, Seir led me to a stone wall. He spoke a series of words, and a black door appeared. He took my hand.

"It's going to feel strange, Moonflower, but hold on to me and you'll be fine."

"Okay. I trust you."

He smiled, and then I was walking with him into the portal, completely unprepared for what was waiting for me on the other side.

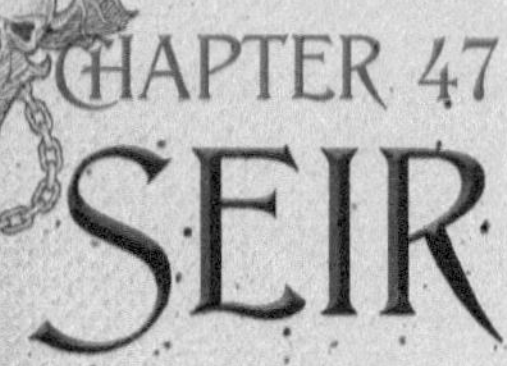

CHAPTER 47
SEIR

"OH, NO," HAILON complained, eyes scrunched shut as she wobbled on her feet. "That's awful. You can't possibly enjoy doing that."

I chuckled. "It's not so bad when you get used to it." I pulled her into my body, resting her cheek against my shoulder while she slowly breathed through her nose.

"Does the sick feeling go away?"

"Was it really that bad?" Concern seeped in, and I lifted her chin with my fingers to look in her eyes.

She smirked. "That was terrible, Seir. I felt like my skin was turning inside out. But if you say it gets better, I believe you."

"Do I need to carry you? I absolutely can. In fact, that's a good idea—" I reached to grab her up, and she jumped away.

"No, thank you," she chuckled. "I can walk just fine."

"You said I'd get to carry you, Moonflower. When you agreed to be my mate, you said that. Asked for it even. When does that start? When do I get to carry you around without you fighting me about it?"

She turned her eyes toward the sky and sighed, then put her arms out.

"Really?"

"Don't make me change my mind."

Without hesitation I scooped her up and walked us away from the ruins, watching her slowly take in where we were, awe on her face.

The stone kin had made tremendous progress in the little time they'd been working. They'd gone for the day, but there were some supplies still scattered not far from the bank of portals.

"I don't ... Are we in the glade?" Her voice went raspy as she looked around. She patted my hand, telling me she wanted to be put down.

"It was the perfect solution, Moonflower," I said, setting her on her feet. "I can help Coltor keep watch on the portals here, so he can take a break from this post, and I can help my brother Tap by moving over some of the active doorways he's in charge of at the crossroads to these ones, maybe even spend some time helping him organize his library of deals. I can visit Hell as often as I need to, then come right back. Most importantly, it's safe here for you. There are heavy wards, no people. You'll be protected. You can skim whatever magic you need without harming anything." I was all but exploding out of my skin with excitement and she was stunned silent, her mouth hanging open. "You can go back to see Ophelia whenever you like. We can visit d'Arcan often. They can come here just as easily."

I took her by the hand and led her beyond the hot springs. There was a perfect spot, just past where the grouping of trees fanned out there across from the pools.

The structure half blended into the greenery, and Hailon stopped walking, eyes shimmery in the afternoon light.

"You did all this ... when? How? It's only been days."

"I had lots of help. So much. I'll owe Magnus and the rest of the stone kin into the next century at least. Though I think you helping expose councilman Brookes may have bought us a little bit of favor."

It was my favorite time of day to look at her, with the glow of early sunset caressing all her features.

"A cabin?" Her voice caught.

My chest squeezed, worry that I'd gotten it all wrong buzzing under my skin. "Please don't be sad, Moonflower."

"I'm not sad." She walked along the path the feet of the stone kin had made by flattening the tall grass, stopping when she got to the little steps that led to the door. She looked at me over her shoulder, tears brimming. "You made me a porch?"

I gestured to the beam along the roofline. "You needed somewhere to hang your wind chimes."

She laughed, the sound a mix between humor and sobbing. I still wasn't sure about her reaction, and my excitement had morphed into anxiety. Her hand reached out to jingle the glass, and her smile reassured me some.

"Open the door, Moonflower."

Hailon did as I asked and stepped into the freshly finished cabin. The smell of new lumber and paint was heavy, but it would fade soon enough.

I'd asked for something slightly bigger than what we'd had in the way-house cabin, and the stone kin had delivered exactly what I wanted. It was their specialty, honestly, as most of the dwellings at the conclave were along the same lines.

The main space was a wide living room with a fireplace in the corner, a cozy sofa, and a plush rug I'd picked out myself. The living room narrowed into the small kitchen and dining area, and the single bedroom and bath were to the right of that.

I stood in the entry, watching her as she took it all in.

"There's no running water yet, but there will be soon enough.

And there's always the springs until then. I didn't pick anything that couldn't be changed easily. I wanted you to be able to go into town somewhere and pick out the linens and dishes you like. Soap. Knives." I fidgeted, her stare making me unreasonably nervous. I couldn't tell if what I was seeing in her face was accusation or excitement. "You were happy in that cabin, I thought. We were both happy, here, that day. I love seeing you dangerous, Moon-flower. But I need you to live happy."

"Seir." She said my name with conviction, her head shaking. My heart pounded, the fear of being rejected riding hard on my nerves. My tail wound and unwound around my own leg anxiously. "It's perfect." She barely breathed the words before the tears finally won. "Thank you." She threw herself into my arms and squeezed. "I'm not sure what I did to deserve any of this. To deserve you."

"Same goes for me, honestly. But I promised to be a good mate to you. I keep my promises."

"I know you do." She nodded, laughter bubbling up.

Hailon took my face between her hands and kissed me, every doubt I had disappearing as she slowly turned the sweet embrace into something incendiary.

I stepped her around the house, never letting her out of my arms.

"Shall I show you the bed you need to buy new linens for then?" She giggled. I melted. "Actually ... not yet. Let's start over here. This is our kitchen. I'll make you hot grain cereal for breakfast, and stew for dinner—"

"Maybe something else. Anything else." Her lighthearted laugh tripped down my spine, sending a bolt of lust straight to my cock.

"Fine, I'll bake you chocolate cakes and fresh bread with honey in that oven. Roast you as many birds as you like. Though I might actually do better with those over the fire." I pushed her up against the counter, lifting her so she was sitting on top of the slab of butcher block. I kissed her thoroughly, tangling my tongue with hers as my hands slid under her tunic and pulled it off. Her legs locked around me, the counter a perfect height for me to nestle my body against hers, my hands on her bare back. I groaned and pulled away.

"Wait," she protested.

I carried her into the living room, kissing her face and neck, one arm locked under her ass. My tail wound around her leg, the tip teasing along the seam of her trousers. "This is our living room. The sofa is secondhand from d'Arcan but guaranteed to be far more comfortable than anything I could have found new." I dropped her onto the cushions, leaning close so I could keep kissing her while my hands worked her trouser ties open, then I tugged the offending garment off her body. I used my hand to tease her through her underthings, finding her hot and wet beneath my fingers.

"Seir."

"We're not done with the tour." I gritted my jaw against the painful throbbing in my own pants and dragged her to her feet, squatting down so she could ride on my back. "This is our bathroom. The stone kin insisted on both the big tub and this strange little rain room, but honestly, I think they're onto something." I slid her off my back and spun, pressing her against the smooth wall under the strange faucet in the ceiling, hiking her leg up over my thigh. Her center pressed against me as I kissed her again, hot even through my pants.

"I'm going to get angry soon," she warned.

"I like you with teeth, beloved."

Still, I took the opportunity to grab her up against me and carried her to the bedroom before setting her on her feet again. Her hands were frantic as they removed my tunic, then my trousers. I allowed her control until I had none remaining. Then I turned her around, her back to my front with her wrists tied up over her ass by my tail. I pressed a hand between her shoulder blades, pushing her down to the mattress.

"*Seir.*" Her exhale was long as she bent over in front of me. I slid my hand along one strong thigh, kicking with one of my feet to make her legs fall wider apart. Her center was fully exposed to me, glistening in the fading afternoon light. "I need you."

"Yes, I can see that." I ground my teeth together as I tried to maintain some calm before guiding myself to her entrance.

She moaned as I pushed inside her, and my body throbbed, her tight, wet heat almost too much in this position. Hailon tilted her hips back against me, and I groaned, grabbing them so I could keep control before I shamed myself. Again.

I started with shallow rocking, and the noises she made and the feel of her around me drove all coherency from my thoughts.

My pace sped in harmony with her, guiding the rhythm, her panting and my shallow breath a perfect match. As the sun slipped below the horizon, her body began to flutter around me, and I dove headfirst into my own release, pounding into her as she moaned into the mattress.

"Mine," I breathed, collapsing against her back, kissing her shoulder, nipping at the sensitive skin by her neck.

"Yours," she replied, turning her head so I could capture her mouth. "Perfect."

Once I could finally bring myself to pull away, I carried my mate out to the springs and bathed us both under the light of the stars.

We floated, dreaming while awake. I pulled my fingers through her hair, which was now almost completely white. My moonflower was in full bloom.

"Are you happy, Hailon?"

"Yes. Are you?"

"I could live here with you and nothing else forever and be perfectly satisfied. Our journey taught me that very early on."

"Should we get you a ring, then?" she asked, making my heart stutter in my chest.

"A ring?"

"To match mine. So I don't have to get murderous when the shop ladies try to impress you. To make an honest man out of you and your untoward intentions."

Her jokes and little smile put a grin on my face. "Definitely, Moonflower. Will you take the elixir Greta gave you?"

"I already did."

She spun and kissed me, the night sky throwing sparkles on the water. I wanted for nothing except to stay in that moment with her, forever. And now I could.

HAILON

LIFE IN THE glade was more lovely than it had any right to be. Seir quickly fell into a smooth pattern with his job, and I even got to meet his brother Tap several times while they got the portals set up to their liking. Coltor was initially grumpy about the changes happening within the castle ruins, but once he realized he could leave for prolonged periods, his mood changed dramatically.

"Sheets, towels, knives, dishes," Seir listed off, then kissed me soundly on the mouth before heading for the door.

"I know."

"You've been unsuccessful at bringing home those things the last several times you went to Revalia. We've been moved in, with running water and a fire in the hearth, for weeks."

"Because I was too busy healing children and the elderly," I reminded him. "Or visiting with your family. Testing my powers. Checking on Ophelia. Besides, all the things we used on our journey are still perfectly functional." And a bit sentimental, if I were being honest. I needed to make a trip to see Widow Callahan soon too.

"Make our house a *home*, Hailon. I beg you. If you don't choose some things soon, you're going to come back from doing all your good deeds to find I've purchased mismatched everything. The couch and rug are just the beginning. It'll be paint and cabinet knobs. Tables and bedding. You might love it, but you might hate it so much you leave me. I'd never survive that. Please, save us both from such a terrible fate by taking this pouch of coins and *spending it*." He shoved a purse overflowing with money into my hands. "Sheets, towels, kniv—"

"Get to work," I teased him, leaning in for one more kiss before he dashed out the door.

I wasn't far behind and took the portal straight to d'Arcan like I had started doing with regularity. My stomach still spun every time I went through the device, but I was beginning to understand why Seir enjoyed them so much.

Today, however, instead of going inside, I met Coltor in the courtyard.

"Greetings to you, Hailon."

"Hello, Coltor. Are you ready?"

"As I'll ever be." We were headed to Ophelia's today, so he could consult with her about a talent he'd started developing. What that was, I wasn't privy to, but I was her most frequent visitor lately, so I was asked to be his escort. He held up my repaired little horse carving. "This is for you."

"Coltor! Thank you *very* much." I stroked the golden hooves before putting it in my pocket. "I've missed him terribly."

The large stone kin shrugged. "I was glad to have a project for a couple of days, nothing of consequence."

He held the gate for me, and we walked out into the city, starting down one of the main roads.

"Are you glad to be away from the ruins?"

He shook his head. "I am, but it's very difficult to be around this many people all at once. Even the conclave is too noisy. I didn't realize how much I'd adapted to the quiet."

"I can understand that. It's incredibly peaceful there. We aren't bothering you, are we?"

"No, no. You're good neighbors." He kept a very small hut right inside the bounds of the ruins themselves, and we rarely saw him.

"Would you like to fly ahead? I'll walk as quickly as I can."

"No, that's alright. I promised to keep an eye on you."

"Oh, you did? Who did you promise?"

"Who *didn't* I promise," he grumbled. "Everyone at d'Arcan reminded me, as did your mate. You even have my father and sisters ensuring your safety."

"I think I feel a bit offended. I can take care of myself just fine."

He snorted. "We all know that, Hailon. Make no mistake."

I forced my steps to move twice what they normally would, taking a route that wound around the outer edge of the city instead of going through the middle.

My magic flowed out around me, touching a child with the sniffles here, a man with sore joints there. I let it soothe their hurts, pulling from what had become an almost endless well thanks to living at the glade.

I'd set up a couple of clinics dedicated to helping those who needed it, but also saw no reason not to sprinkle some aid wherever I went if I could. On the flip side, Magnus had called me into the council once, and I'd been able to incapacitate one of the oldest members while he was interrogated, taking away his ability to shift and holding it over the well. Nobody had been the wiser. Between my dedicated practice and obsidian items, I was settling into confident use of my powers.

Something that never would have been possible had I stayed in Ravenglen.

Soon enough, Coltor and I were crossing out of the east gate of the city, silent as we moved ever closer to the Dread Forest and Ophelia's hut.

The wards pressed in like they always did, Coltor frowning as they hit him.

"Maybe we should have Ophelia come help at the ruins," he suggested. "These hit like a boulder. Mine seem weak in comparison."

"She doesn't leave here. Trust me, I had the same thought."

As we came around the corner, I stopped mid stride. In the side yard of the hut was a horse. A big one, with familiar markings. "Jacks?"

The horse nickered, but didn't stop his ruthless pruning of Ophelia's overgrown grass.

The door of the hut opened, and a smiling Merry stepped outside, along with a laughing Ophelia.

"Hailon!" Merry dashed forward and hugged me.

"Merry? What are you doing here?"

"Ravenglen was no longer the place for me."

"Did something happen? Are you alright?"

She shook her head. "I'm fine, I'm fine. Nothing like that. I just want something more for myself than working at the grocers and cleaning hunting lodges. I remembered what your man said about Revalia. But Jacks decided to have a mind of his own once we got close. Nothing I did would deter him from coming here."

"Hello, nephew," Ophelia said, greeting Coltor.

"Greetings, Ophelia. I brought you some salted licorice." His hand trembled a bit as he handed over the paper sack of candy.

Ophelia smirked. "Appreciated." She looked to me. "Did you need my help today, Hailon?"

"No, I'm doing very well with my control, thank you. I just walked here with Coltor."

She nodded, looking the much larger man up and down. Meanwhile, he was unabashedly staring at Merry. She, on the other hand, was pretending not to notice and looking at me.

"Alright then. Take your friend into town, would you? The horse is fine here."

I nodded, and accepted Merry's arm as she threaded it through mine.

"Be good, Jacks," she warned. "Nice to meet you …"

"Coltor." He dipped his head and awkwardly shoved out a hand for her to shake.

I barely contained my laughter, especially when I met Ophelia's twinkling eye.

"We'll be back later."

Coltor looked bereft, like us walking away was removing his safety net as Ophelia took him inside.

"You can help me do some shopping," I said to Merry, "while you tell me everything."

Today looked promising as the day I brought home linens and kitchenware. We might have another neighbor in the glade soon who'd need use of our handed-down supplies.

I couldn't wait to get home to tell Seir.

What about that special mission
The Boss wanted Seir to do?
Grab the Bonus Scene Here:

https://dl.bookfunnel.com/kfurcuz2ht

What's next?
Book 3 of The Gargoyle Knights Series:
The Gargoyle's Glade — Coltor's story
AND
Book 4 of The Demon Princes Series:
The Demon's Domain – Tap's story

Want to be the first to hear breaking news and
other info from L.? Sign up for her newsletter!

http://bit.ly/ALANewsletter

You can also join her reader group to chat
with her and other readers!

https://bit.ly/LilysReaderLounge

Did you like *The Demon's Delight*?
Leave a review on Amazon, Goodreads or Bookbub
to share your thoughts with other readers!

ACKNOWLEDGEMENTS

I can only hope you love Seir and Hailon half as much as I do. <3 Their story, even more than most, took me on a journey! Nearly a year after starting, I found myself deleting a dozen chapters and taking a whole new direction. In the end, it was the right choice, and I'm so happy with how this story turned out. Thank you for reading!

To my husband, who always reads it first, with the most enthusiasm and best ideas and observations. Love you most.

For my Write or Die friends, Shain & Dannie, I heart you guys even when you send me into full breakdown mode weeks from editing deadlines. Me and my stories would not be who we are without you!

Krista for managing my extraneous use of commas, em dashes and ellipses, and for Jessica & Stephanie for always making the final product gorgeous. I couldn't do it without your help and I mean that.

For Sam who keeps my brain on straight and manages what I simply can't ever get to. XOXO

Beta & ARC readers! Do you even know how vital you are to authors like me? I hope you do. Caroline, Sam, Meri ... there aren't words to express how much I love your real-time reactions because you're kicking your feet to a scene. Seeing any post with my stuff on it is a humbling, thrilling experience. I couldn't do this without you.

I can't wait for you all to see what's coming next! There are more demons to make fall in love, and some stone kin I can't wait to help find their mates.

Note: This world is planned to be seven books, one for each brother PLUS a novella for our stone kin friends in-between. I hope you stick with us!

For sneak peeks, discussion and other fun tidbits, make sure you're signed up for my newsletter, & join my reader group.

ABOUT THE AUTHOR

L. Alexander writes Paranormal and Fantasy romance with sweet & spicy cinnamon roll heroes, fated mates, monsters, magic and more. She guarantees a happily ever after no matter what and has a soft spot for broody anime characters.

www.authorlilyalexander.com

@lilyalexanderwrites on Instagram

Lily Alexander on Facebook, TikTok,
BookBub and Goodreads

L. also writes Contemporary Romance
under the name Lily Alexander.